BREATHLESS

Mariah tried to pull away. Even in the odd-colored light, her palms appeared red and blistered. Her nails were chipped, and her fingers were too sore to open completely. "Please," she whispered, ashamed that the hands she'd once pampered now looked as if they'd passed through the fires of hell.

"They're—" Thorn didn't finish what he was going to say. Instead, he lifted her hands, his head bowed. . . and she felt the soothing softness of his lips upon her burning palms.

She inhaled sharply, frozen while wanting to run. He raised his head once more and looked into her face.

There was sorrow in his pale brown eyes, and a glimmer of something she read as guilt.

"It's all right," she said quietly, pulling one hand away to touch his face. His skin was warm, roughened by the outdoors and by the hint of heavy masculine facial hair, though he was clean-shaven. No matter what he had done in the past, no matter how he castigated himself now because of it, she didn't want him adding her to the many burdens he bore. "I'm fine. This isn't so—"

His mouth stopped hers from finishing. There was nothing gentle in his kiss, despite the tenderness when he'd examined her hands. The kiss robbed her of breath, of wanting to breathe, for she did not want to break the spell.

Other *Love Spell* books by Linda O. Johnston:
THE GLASS SLIPPER
A GLIMPSE OF FOREVER

Point In Time

Linda O. Johnston

LOVE SPELL BOOKS NEW YORK CITY

LOVE SPELL®

January 1998

Published by

Dorchester Publishing Co., Inc.
276 Fifth Avenue
New York, NY 10001

ISBN 0-505-52244-6

Printed in the United States of America.

To Pittsburgh, the home of my childhood and my imagination, and where I met my own true love.

A Special Thank You. . .

...to the library staff at the Senator John Heinz Pittsburgh Regional History Center, for helping me solve the riddle of the many spellings of "Pittsburgh" in the eighteenth century. Thanks also to the people at the Fort Pitt Museum and the Blockhouse Museum for the information they imparted, even when the museums were closed by floods.

...and to Jann Audiss and Barb DeLong, for agreeing and disagreeing.

Point In Time

Chapter One

"You must right a grievous wrong."

The familiar, hoarse voice wavered in Mariah Walker's ears. The final word resounded, the single syllable elongating, its volume intensifying until she nearly screamed.

"What are you talking about?" she whispered. "*What* wrong? Please, explain this time."

She reached out her hand, fumbling in the darkness for a light switch but instead encountering something smooth and hard. She felt cramped, crumpled nearly into a ball, yet somehow erect. Her entire being focused on the voice still reverberating in her head, its residue roaring into one relentless, noisy, growling tone.

"Please," she repeated, choking on the word.

"Miss?" The quiet word broke into her thoughts. "Are you all right?"

Mariah opened her eyes. She blinked, disoriented. In moments, she identified the deafening reverberation, the hard surface she had touched, the source of the sensation of being cramped. She was seated in coach on a commercial jet.

"The cart's nearly here," her seatmate continued. Hers

had been the voice that had awakened Mariah. "Would you like something to drink?"

"Yes. Yes, I would." Mariah aimed a weak smile at the woman in the aisle seat; the center one between them was empty.

The woman, whose white hair was a sparse curled mop, looked over her half-glasses at Mariah, her eyes full of grandmotherly concern. "Tea, I think. I always drink tea when I wake up from a nightmare."

A nightmare? Maybe.

As far as Mariah could recall, she had never before dreamt the voice during the day, even when she napped.

The uniformed flight attendants wheeled their cart beside Mariah's row. One cheerfully requested her order. With unaccustomed obedience, she asked for tea—plus a can of apple juice for energy. She refused a small foil packet of peanuts.

"Feeling better now?" her seatmate asked solicitously.

"Yes, thanks," she replied. But was she?

It had happened again. This time in broad daylight.

The voice in her dreams had issued its incomprehensible command since as far back in her twenty-eight years as she could remember. Her childhood, on top of all the memories she'd wanted to leave behind, was peppered with the voice and its directive.

There was never a visual attached to the rasping vocalization. Only blackness. It always said the same thing: "You must right a grievous wrong."

Strange words. Old-fashioned.

Why did they have the ability to affect her this way? They filled her with a sense of excitement. Anticipation. Destiny.

Dread.

Years earlier, she had forced herself more than once to stay awake all night to avoid hearing the voice. She'd never understood the feelings that resulted from the command. That was what unnerved her—not the voice, but her eager yet fearful reaction to it.

The vocal hallucination was one factor that had drawn her to the entertainment industry, where people often worked all night, slept all day. Gradually, she'd been bothered less by the haunting words.

"How nice that you can nap on a plane," her seatmate said. "I never can. Do you live in Pittsburgh?"

"No," Mariah said, giving no further information. Although the elderly lady seemed pleasant, Mariah did not want to get involved in a conversation. She'd had no business sleeping on the plane. She had work to do.

"I'm going there to visit my grandchildren," the woman continued.

"How nice." Mariah opened the tray for the middle seat and moved everything from hers onto it. She unhooked her seat belt and squeezed forward, reaching beneath the seat before her to pull out her Lemoncake Films tote bag.

Lemoncake. She'd done projects for the small, independent production company for a couple of years, and no one yet had told her the genesis of the name. She suspected it was because svelte Angela Corbin, the company's president, chief producer and a former actress, was a closet cake eater.

On the other hand, it could have been more complicated: when life hands you a lemon of a script, add talented ingredients, throw in some sweetener and, voilà, sell the world a darned good lemoncake of a movie.

"They're six and four," said the woman beside her as Mariah removed a FedEx envelope and stuffed the tote back under the seat.

"Pardon?" Mariah didn't know what she was talking about.

"My grandchildren. Bobby and Missy. I have their pictures right here."

Forcing herself not to be rude, Mariah looked at the proffered photos, making appropriate admiring noises. Then she opened the envelope.

Inside was the letter from Angela that had so startled her that morning. She'd been working with a representative of the Louisiana Film Commission, scouting locations in New Orleans for an earthy romantic comedy that had captured Angela's attention.

The package had arrived at her hotel just as she'd been

about to meet her contact for the day. The letter inside directed her to leave immediately for Pittsburgh to scout locations for the screenplay enclosed.

It was like Angela to send Mariah an order first and explain later. Though Mariah was an independent contractor, she had an excellent relationship with Lemoncake, and when Angela made demands, Mariah always responded. But even so, for Angela to direct her from one location to another so abruptly, and without giving her time to set up local contacts first . . . Mariah had called her from her hotel room.

"Yes, I know it's unusual." Angela sounded impatient. "But it's an unusual situation. The guy overnighted the script, pitched it over the phone before I read it and said it was vital that I respond right away or he'd shop it around. It's an important historical story, set in Pittsburgh after the French and Indian War. From what he says, it has adventure, romance, psychological suspense, lust. . . ."

Mariah had clutched the phone to her ear. "But—"

"No deal yet, but I want you to read the script, then look for suitable locations. Then we'll see."

Mariah was puzzled. No, flabbergasted! Lemoncake had built its excellent reputation on lighthearted contemporary comedy. Why was Angela so interested in a heavy period piece?

And why spend the time and money on scouting locations before anyone had even read the script? The story could be a real lemon, one no amount of sweetening would help.

Something here seemed very strange. Out of character for conservative Angela. Though she was impulsive, her offbeat orders always seemed to make business sense. Until now.

"Oh, and one more thing," Angela had said. Her tone had turned cajoling, and Mariah expected that the other shoe was about to drop.

It was.

"Pierce, the author, will meet you at the airport and show you around town. That was one of his conditions. He'll tell you all about the screenplay, too. Interesting man. Sounds as ancient as the story. Talks almost as though he was there."

Great. Mariah liked to spend a day or so getting a feel for

a new place before meeting local promoters and hearing opinions on where scenes should be shot. Maybe that was a factor of her own, personal quest for a perfect location for herself. A home. Not all unit productions managers scouted locations, but Angela wanted her to. And it worked. She was getting a reputation as one super unit production manager for low-budget films.

That was why Angela hired her over and over for each new project at a sinfully high rate of pay. And Angela was the boss. Swallowing her irritation, Mariah had obediently booked an afternoon flight to Pittsburgh.

Crossing her legs as best she could in the cramped seat, she pulled down her short brown skirt and straightened her beige knit top. Then she took out the inner envelope from the package. It hadn't been opened. That was as strange as the rest of Angela's actions concerning this screenplay; Mariah had never before known her employer not to circulate copies among her staff and proposed crew of a script she liked—and to keep one herself. The return address indicated that the script had been sent to Angela by that Pierce guy, the one who was to meet her at the airport.

She figured she'd better read it now to have something to say to the man.

But the flight attendant returned just then with dinner. Mariah usually skipped airline meals, but she'd left New Orleans in such a hurry that she'd not had time for lunch, and she'd had only her usual cup of coffee for breakfast. She accepted the standard boned chicken that was nearly as stiff as the plastic on which it was served. At least the roll was soft, and there was actually a serving of fresh fruit.

"Have you ever been to Pittsburgh?" her seatmate asked.

Knowing she couldn't concentrate on the screenplay while eating in such cramped quarters, Mariah gave in and chatted with the friendly woman. No, she hadn't been to Pittsburgh before. But she'd been nearly everywhere else.

"My name's Helen, by the way," the woman said, obviously fishing for Mariah's name. She gave it. Then Helen asked, "Do you mind a personal question, Mariah?"

"Go ahead and ask." She didn't have to answer. She

steeled herself in anticipation. Would it be about her job? Her personal life?

What personal life?

"Is that your natural shade of hair?"

Mariah nearly laughed. "Yes, it is."

Helen touched her thin white curls. "I tried for years to get that color. My hair was mousy blond when I was young. I love that rich, honey shade, and those waves . . . very, very pretty."

Soon, thank heavens, dinner was over. The trays were cleared. She'd finished her apple juice and a second cup of tea. Helen, fortunately, became engrossed in a magazine, so Mariah would not have to be rude.

Now, she would read the screenplay. She used her forefinger to tear open the sealed envelope. There was no cover letter, just the script itself, held together at the left side by the customary brads. She lifted it out and read the front sheet, which contained preliminary information. The screenplay was entitled *Point of Destiny*. The author was Josiah Pierce.

Josiah. That was an unusual, old-fashioned name. Suddenly feeling a spurt of irrational bias, Mariah was sure she'd find the screenplay, too, to be outdated. A waste of her time. She should have stayed in New Orleans. She wasn't finished with her scouting there. She'd been terribly rude to the local film representatives, canceling their location tours so abruptly.

But she was under instructions from Angela. And this Josiah Pierce person was meeting her at the airport.

With a put-upon sigh, she turned the page and began to read. "Fade in." The script started with a standard scene-setting description. "Exterior shot, Fort Pitt—1768." Yawning, Mariah scanned the page.

She stopped with a gasp.

The very first line of dialogue read, "You must right a grievous wrong."

Chapter Two

''Is something wrong, dear?'' came the shrill voice from the aisle seat.

Blinking, Mariah turned and looked into Helen's concerned face. ''No.'' The word was a harsh rasp. Gathering her wits, she said again, ''No. Thank you. I'm fine.''

But she wasn't fine. She was hallucinating again. With determination, she picked up the screenplay, which had fallen into her lap. She opened the cover once more and began to read.

''You must right a grievous wrong.''

Biting her bottom lip, Mariah tried to regard the page rationally. The story opened at Fort Pitt. Extras portraying British soldiers at the fort would bustle in the background. In the foreground were a young woman, Matilda, and an elderly man named Porter. Porter would speak those all-too-familiar words.

A coincidence, Mariah thought. People in those times probably made such statements all the time.

Didn't they?

She had to read on. What did the words mean to the Matilda character?

The script showed Matilda's bewilderment. She was a stranger to Pittsburgh, having arrived that very day in the bustling fort town where the Monongahela and Allegheny rivers joined to form the Ohio. She didn't know Porter, yet he had issued to her his strange demand.

What did it mean?

Mariah read further, but nothing sank in. She closed the screenplay and stared at it. Its blue plastic cover was warm where her fingers had clutched it, but the heat seemed fiery, intense. She wanted to hurl away the script.

Get a grip, she ordered herself. It was only a screenplay. She had read hundreds before. Sometimes dialogue in one became indistinguishable from the rest. That was all that had happened here, a repetition of yet another trite line.

But she knew that wasn't true. If she had ever read this one before, she'd have known it.

"You must right a grievous wrong."

This was absurd. Why did that statement send her pulse rate soaring, wreak havoc with the evenness of her breathing?

Because it had haunted her dreams forever. And it had always given her a sense of expectancy—and impending doom.

She tried to recall how old she'd been when she'd had the first bad dream. Impossible, she decided after a few moments. She couldn't recall a time before she'd first heard the words.

Where had she been the first time? She nearly laughed aloud. Who could tell? New York? Boston? London? Trinidad? Somewhere alone with her mother, of course, after one of her father's frequent abandonments. She'd lost count of the places she'd lived as a child, thanks to him.

She lived in Los Angeles now, more or less. At least it was her base. She had always thought, once she was on her own, that she'd settle down in one spot. Never leave it.

But not until she found a place she wanted to call home.

With a sigh, she picked up the screenplay again. She had a job to do, and her nervousness was ridiculous. She would ignore that one line of dialogue and read on. She had to know the screenplay backwards and forwards. How else could she determine tomorrow, when she toured the town, where the script's scenes could be shot?

Her insides suddenly plummeted as the aircraft began to descend. She had to hurry. Pittsburgh must be near.

It was a new town to her, one she'd never before visited. A rarity. But it wouldn't end her quest, not this city that was the butt of so many jokes: dirty, ugly, full of idle steel mills and strong unions that sometimes created havoc for film companies. But, surprisingly, one where a lot of movies were being made these days. Perhaps even the one whose script was in her lap.

If it was ever shot. Which she doubted.

She opened the cover of the screenplay and began reading on page three. The letters on the page blurred. Mariah forced herself to read, word by word.

That didn't work. She tried thumbing through the pages to learn which characters had the most dialogue. It would help, at least, to know who the protagonists were.

Although the young woman Matilda appeared in nearly every scene, from what Mariah could tell, the story wasn't hers. Or Porter's. His name hardly appeared again.

Instead, the script focused on a man. His name was Thorn. Mariah read his description: a robust and moody woodsman, an ex-soldier who had never given up the fight.

"Folks, this is the captain speaking." The words broke into her thoughts. "Due to heavy air traffic, there'll be a delay in landing in Pittsburgh. We'll circle the city once or twice. Meantime—" He described the weather below: warm, sunny, cloudless. A perfect late-summer day.

With a sigh, Mariah looked out her window—and sucked in her breath.

Below her was the most beautiful city she had ever seen.

It sat at the apex of a promontory formed by two rivers. Skyscrapers stretched toward the jet. The tallest was dark and boxy, others were gray or beige. Many were detailed with stepped sides or pointed roofs. One appeared to be a crystal castle, another a steepled cathedral. Among the tall buildings were many much shorter ones along streets that, from above, seemed as spontaneous as the rivers' flow.

Along one river, at the far edge of town, was a steep hillside. On the more level shore, beyond where the two rivers joined to form the third, sat a round stadium. What was it called? Oh, yes—very appropriate. Three Rivers, if Mariah recalled correctly, though she wasn't much of a sports fan.

But what really captured her attention was the park at the point of the triangle. In its center geometric forms, oddly star-shaped, bisected its green surface. Walkways lined with trees spanned the riverbanks, and at the point where the rivers met stood a fountain, its plume of water reaching toward the sky.

The rivers appeared to flow lazily. A few small boats meandered down them; she could barely make them out but saw their trailing wakes. There were a few larger craft, too.

Mariah looked forward to seeing the rivers more closely. Perhaps taking a boat ride.

Visiting that intriguing park.

"Nice town, isn't it?" Helen asked. Despite knowing she was being rude, Mariah ignored her. She wanted more than anything to soak in all she saw by herself.

She realized she'd been holding her breath, and with a silent laugh at herself drew in some air, then let it out again. How ridiculous could she be! She practically had her nose pressed against the coolness of the plane's small window, the proverbial child at the candy shop entry aching to be inside.

She, instead, yearned to be on the ground. In the park.

The plane continued its circle. She sighed, eager to be down, to explore this town. An ugly city? Not from this angle. Dirty? No; it sparkled in the sun beneath the cloud-free sky. How had it ever been tainted with such criticism? Maybe in time gone by it had been a hellhole. But today it was wonderful.

Mariah felt herself smiling. No, glowing. She was filled with a delightful sense of anticipation.

Could this be it? Might her quest be at an end?

Perhaps, after all this time, she had found the place she would want to call home.

The plane circled Pittsburgh twice. Finally, the engine's growl lowered and the plane began its descent. A flight attendant gave the normal litany about seat belts and tray tables. How many times had Mariah heard that? Too many. She had taken more flights than she could possibly remember to cities all over the world.

This one was bound to be, on closer inspection, as disappointing as the rest. How could Pittsburgh, Pennsylvania, be more appealing to her than Paris? London? San Francisco? Washington, D.C.?

The plane landed. When it reached the gate and a tone bonged, people scrambled for their belongings.

"Enjoy your stay," Helen said, her kind eyes dubious.

"I intend to." Mariah crammed the screenplay that had so unnerved her into the heavy Lemoncake tote bag that also held her camera and small purse. She let Helen get ahead of her before she joined the stream of people getting off the plane.

A surge of warm, humid air hit her as she moved from the plane onto the departure ramp. Late summer in the east. Mariah had it categorized in her mind: uncomfortably hot and damp. Visiting other similar towns, she'd been eager to return to her base in Southern California, where at least the heat usually remained dry.

The airport's waiting area was no different from others: impersonal, noisy, lined with rows of seats. Air conditioning fended off the humidity. Hordes of people stared at deplaning passengers with anticipation brightening their faces.

Sometimes Mariah wished someone waited for her with such eagerness.

Hiking the straps of her tote bag up her arm, she slowly shook her head. What had gotten into her today? She usually reserved her imagination for production planning and location scouting. Besides, there *was* someone waiting for her. Maybe even eagerly, if he thought she was the key to his making a fortune on his screenplay.

But how would she identify Josiah Pierce?

She spotted him immediately. He looked as she imagined he might with a name like that: small, thin-boned, with a sharp-featured face and a receding hairline. He was dressed in a white shirt and dark trousers.

And he was staring right at her.

As the wave of people pushed her forward, he approached her without hesitation. "Miss Walker?" he called.

"Yes." She stepped from the surging crowd and waited. Although she was of only moderate height, she found herself looking down on him. "You must be Mr. Pierce."

He nodded. She offered her hand and he took it, holding it at an odd angle in his papery, cool fingers, as though unsure what to do with it. He raised it toward his lips.

Instinctively, Mariah began to draw it back. His grip grew stronger, and he shook her hand in a curt, businesslike manner. Then he smiled, revealing a mouth full of large, yellowing teeth. "Please, come this way," he said, his voice as nasal as if he'd used his gnarled fingers to pinch his pointed equine nose.

"I appreciate your meeting me," she lied, walking beside him. She realized he was taller than he'd first appeared, but he bent forward at the shoulders as though in pain. "Angela said you spoke with her last evening about your screenplay."

"Yes. You and I will talk about it over coffee before we go downtown. An early supper as well, if you wish. I have been told that airline food is not especially palatable."

Told? That indicated to Mariah that this stooped scarecrow of a man had never been on a plane himself, adding to his seeming strangeness.

He took a large white handkerchief from his pocket and blew his nose. "I beg your pardon," he apologized. "I believe I am catching the ague—I mean, a cold."

Despite the stuffy quality of his voice, there was something about it that appealed to Mariah. She was used to hearing actors try out new accents and tried to place Josiah Pierce's faint lilt. A touch of Irish? More British, perhaps. In any event, his choice of words and their syntax was charming, nearly old world.

Mariah was pleasantly surprised by the remainder of the airport. Once they had passed the gate area, it was filled with shops and boutiques. They took a mechanized shuttle from the gate area to baggage claim, where Josiah Pierce insisted on lifting her suitcase from the carousel. It wasn't heavy, or she'd have worried about injuring the stooped man. With all the time she spent on the road, she made sure her luggage was convenient, on wheels. After she pulled a handle from her suitcase, Pierce insisted on towing it behind him.

"If you would please follow me," he said. He led her to the parking lot and stopped beside an aged Mercedes. Mariah stifled a grin at her surprise that this old-fashioned man actually drove, though the stately old car fit him.

She wrinkled her nose as she sat down inside. The old leather reeked of cigar smoke.

As they drove from the airport, Josiah Pierce asked, "What kind of fare would you like this evening? I believe I can locate Italian, a steak house, a family restaurant or just coffee."

"Room service," Mariah said firmly. "I'm sorry to be a party pooper, but I just received your screenplay this morning and didn't finish reading it on the plane. I want to check into my hotel room and read."

He parted his lips as though to protest but said with a frown, "As you wish."

Mariah watched out the car windows as Pierce drove along the route he called a parkway. It was a four-lane freeway, surrounded by office parks, shopping centers and rolling green hills. It did not give her the same sense of welcome that circling Pittsburgh in the plane had, and she felt disappointed.

"We shall meet for breakfast," Pierce told her, "after you have completed your review of the screenplay. At that time I will explain to you anything you wish, and we will look together for filming sites."

Mariah was accustomed to giving most of the orders when planning a production. But, concerned the strange little man would withdraw the screenplay from Lemoncake, she bit back her irritation. "Sure," she said.

Soon, they drove down a long hill. "Downtown is on the far side of the Fort Pitt Tunnel," Pierce said as they drove into a hole through the mountain.

As they emerged at the other end, Mariah gasped. As though someone had raised a curtain, there was the city she had seen from above. But she was part of it now, swiftly approaching over a bridge, the tall buildings shimmering in the summer sun and reflecting on the surface of the joining rivers.

"A beautiful sight, is it not?" Pierce asked.

Mariah did not want to tarnish the moment by speaking. She only vaguely noted Pierce's weaving among lanes of merging traffic on the bridge as she stared at the enthralling city with its skyscrapers interspersed with older, more historic buildings.

In moments they were off the bridge and stopping. "This is the Hilton Hotel," Pierce said. "A room has been reserved here for you."

"Thank you," she whispered. Then, clearing her throat, she said, "I appreciate your driving me here. When shall we meet in the morning?"

They established eight o'clock as the time for Pierce to come for her. He helped her into the elegant lobby with her bags. And then he was gone.

A bellhop showed her to her room on the twelfth floor. The first thing she noticed was the view. It was gorgeous! It looked over the park. *Her* park. The open space was grassy, triangular, traversed by walking paths and surrounded on two sides by the rivers. At the far end was the fountain she had seen from the plane, at the rivers' confluence to form the Ohio.

She unpacked quickly, though she'd learned from experience to carry only clothing that wrinkled minimally. She washed her face, then got a glass of water after retrieving ice from the machine down the hall.

Finally, with a contented sigh, she moved the room's single upholstered chair so she could sit in it and glance out the window. Her magnetic park was still there. A few people, looking tiny from her hotel aerie, meandered along its paths.

Mariah turned on a lamp in the corner. She wasn't sure if she'd be able to concentrate on the script, but she wanted to be by the window as she tried.

Two hours later, she stood with a gasp. "No!" she exclaimed.

Her mind reeled. Angela had been right to jump right on this screenplay. It was wonderful! The characters had come alive, practically strolling into her hotel room to tell their stories.

But the ending . . .

Mariah rushed toward the nightstand beside the bed and lifted the telephone receiver. The room was dark except for the lamp she had lighted earlier. She punched in the numbers for her credit card call, then switched on the bed lamps. The brightness in the room was startling. For a short while, Mariah had been in an era where the nights were illuminated only dimly by candles, oil lamps and moonlight.

She sat on the edge of the firm bed, her short fingernails tapping on the nightstand while the phone rang once, twice. "Be home, Angela," Mariah demanded.

As though she'd heard, Angela answered on the third ring. "You're there?" she asked Mariah without ceremony.

"Of course. Look, Angela, I've read the script."

"What do you think?"

"It's outstanding! Strong dialogue, action, adventure. And the characters—they're utterly memorable. If it's cast right, the whole thing's Academy Award material." She paused. "Except for one thing."

"The end? Yes, Pierce warned me about that."

Mariah shook her head, willing Angela to see it her way. "We *can't* kill Thorn. I mean, the whole story is about his reacclimation to society. And just as he finally adjusts, he dies."

"In a fair fight, Pierce said. One that the entire story builds to."

"I'm not sure how fair it was. The whole thing was a setup. I'll bet the fight was rigged."

Angela laughed. "You sound as if the hero is real, like

you actually met him. Fell in love with him.''

Mariah rose abruptly from the bed, the receiver still clasped against her face. Protests formed inside her head, ready to spill from her lips. But she stopped. And laughed weakly. ''Maybe I did, just a little.''

In the script, Thorn had been an outcast from his society. The scene after the one that first unnerved Mariah with its directive about righting wrongs was a flashback to the past. In it, Thorn had shirked his duty. As a consequence, a boy from the town near Fort Pitt was kidnapped by Indians, and the youth's mother subsequently killed herself. Stripped of uniform and self-respect, Thorn fled into the wilderness to atone.

Later scenes occurred after civilization overtook him, turning the small cabin he built into a stopping place for settlers going west. Befriended by an outcast Frenchman and the Matilda character, he braved wild animals, renegade warriors and more while fighting his own internal battles. Never running from any challenge, the character had grown, matured, until he was ready to resume his place in Pittsburgh society.

But then he had been called out by a relative of the missing child. In a duel fought at the tip of the land forming Pittsburgh, Thorn died.

That could be fixed. It had to be. The script required major revision anyway; it never even revealed the wrong Matilda was to right, let alone having her fix it.

She certainly hadn't saved Thorn.

''Look, Angela,'' Mariah reasoned, ''let's keep my emotions out of this. Bottom line, we want to do a great film. Draw a substantial audience through word of mouth as well as promotion. We fix the story, cast it right, and Lemoncake can make big bucks here.''

''Maybe we should hire you as the female lead.'' Angela's voice was teasing.

''Yeah, right.'' Mariah snorted. ''Then you can kiss those big bucks good-bye.'' But she raised her eyebrows thoughtfully. Though she thought little of her acting ability, she did identify with the Matilda role. After the strange demand about righting wrongs issued by the character named Porter,

Matilda bought downriver passage from some ruffians who later attempted to assault her. She swam ashore, only to be followed. In a scene Mariah could envision enticingly well, Thorn appeared silently from the woods. He chased off the villains with a hard stare—and his well-aimed rifle.

He was a strong, heroic man. Mariah pictured him as tall, broad-shouldered in buckskins, with eyes that reflected his inner pain. She couldn't even imagine what actor could play the role. Alec Baldwin? Mel Gibson?

Unsurprisingly, Matilda and Thorn fell in love. Though Thorn remained anguished by his faults, he was always there when Matilda needed him. Steadfast.

Reliable.

Oh, yes. Mariah realized that this fantasy character displayed the traits of the only kind of man who would appeal to her.

One who existed, of course, only in the movies.

Mariah had learned her lesson well over the years: not to rely on men. First and foremost, there had been her father. And then, just after graduating from college, she'd fancied herself in love with a handsome young doctor.

Doctors were surely reliable, she'd imagined, when she'd become engaged to him. But she'd caught hers being relied upon for more than medicine by a female patient.

"Well," said Angela, interrupting her thoughts, "we'll consider letting your hero survive, though we may have to fight with our writer to allow it. Meantime, stop drooling and get some sleep. Keep an eye out for wonderful shooting spots tomorrow. Think about schedules, budgets, the works. If this is as good as you say it is, we'll want to snap up the screenplay and get into production as soon as possible."

"As soon as possible" in the film industry still meant months. Maybe years. But this was a project that Mariah wanted to be associated with as much as she wanted to eat, to breathe . . . to find a home.

"Good night, Angela," Mariah said. "And thanks."

She felt less like thanking her boss the next morning when Pierce knocked on her hotel-room door at seven thirty.

"Just a minute," Mariah called, dragging herself from the bathroom and pulling on a blue silk shirt and charcoal slacks. The guy was half an hour earlier than scheduled. He obviously wasn't closely associated with the entertainment industry, where most people awake at this ungodly hour were either those who had never gotten to bed or those on an early morning shoot.

Mariah was neither.

But she had been awake nonetheless, because she hadn't slept well. While in the shower she had been thinking about the story, about the coincidence of the voice in her head and Porter's statement to Matilda in the script.

About the strength, the appeal of the Thorn character.

He could be as memorable as Rhett Butler. As sensual and magnetic as the Sheik.

But he couldn't die at the end. That kind of a climax had irritated audiences a few years back in a post–Civil War story called *Sommersby,* where the charlatan protagonist turned heroic and let himself be hanged for the good of others.

That couldn't happen in *Point of Destiny.* Not to Thorn.

When she was dressed, Mariah opened the door—and looked down at the stooped man who leaned against the wall. Pierce didn't look dressed for walking; he wore a suit and shiny, wing-tipped shoes. The heavy odor of cigar smoke wafted from him.

"Good morning, Miss Walker," he said. "Are you ready for breakfast?"

She'd begged off dinner the night before and hadn't the heart to tell the man who'd written such a phenomenal screenplay that she usually didn't eat breakfast. "Give me a minute," she said, heading back to the bathroom.

She skipped putting on her regular makeup; she didn't need to impress Pierce with her outstanding good looks. Smiling at her pale mirror image ruefully, she combed her blond waves back behind her ears. She needed a trim, she thought; her hair hung just below her shoulders. Her green eyes looked washed out, tired. Yet they shone a bit with excitement. She was about to explore this city that had so unexpectedly intrigued her. To work on production ideas and to scout locations for a film whose script had touched her like no other ever had.

She rubbed lotion onto her smooth, youthful hands, her one vanity. She kept her nails short and unpolished but perfectly shaped. When she returned to the bedroom Pierce was staring out the window toward the Point and the view that had enchanted her.

"That's a wonderful sight," she said, cramming her camera into her handbag. "A marvelous town."

"Yes," he said. "It is."

Mariah quizzed him over toast and juice at the hotel coffee shop. He was self-effacing, though his eyes, set in folds of wrinkles, regarded her with an unwavering stare, as though testing her. She kept herself from squirming uncomfortably in her chair, unsure of the yardstick he was using or how she measured up. She only knew she had to make a good enough impression so Pierce would let Lemoncake Films shoot his screenplay.

They briefly discussed a few of the scenes. "I'll show you where most can be filmed," he said. Mariah stopped herself from contradicting him, though she would be the one to contact the local film office for suggestions and make recommendations to Angela, not him. Plus, even though the story took place here, it did not necessarily have to be filmed in this town. It probably wouldn't be.

The most important site, Pierce said, was across the street from the hotel. He would take her there first thing. In his nasal, sniffly voice, he thanked her profusely for her compliments about the script as he dug into a hearty, fat-laden breakfast of ham and eggs. His nose was long and as pointed as the chin that dipped with determination as he chewed. "No, I'm not originally from Pittsburgh," he said after they'd conversed for a while, "but I am a student of history. The script is based on a true story."

Ah-hah! This was the reason for Thorn's death. But history could be rewritten for fiction. "I loved everything about the story except the end," she began.

He held up a knobby hand. "It cannot be changed. Not by me or anyone else—for now."

"But—"

"Are you finished? Good. Then let me show you around."

Mariah decided not to confront him further about the ending until they'd developed a better rapport. Maybe she'd leave it to Angela, whose tact far surpassed Mariah's when it needed to.

They walked out of the hotel and across the street. Mariah immediately missed the air conditioning. The morning was humid and already uncomfortably warm, although a moisture-laden breeze was blowing. Her blouse had short sleeves, but she wished she'd worn something cooler than silk—cotton, maybe, despite the ease with which it wrinkled. Breathing was uncomfortable as the heavy, moist air blew into her face, smelling faintly of car exhaust.

"This is Point State Park," Pierce said. "It's where four forts used to be, not counting the temporary garrison when Fort Pitt was being built. The earliest, begun by Virginians, was overrun by the French, who turned it into Fort Duquesne. When the English took over, they built Fort Pitt. After it was demolished, a fourth fort, Fort Fayette, was built before the end of the eighteenth century as protection against a final Indian uprising."

Mariah appreciated the history lesson. She wished she'd learned more before coming to town to scout locations for this film so rooted in its past.

But then, she hadn't known of the script's rich historical background.

The park's entrance was festooned with a bed of riotous red and yellow flowering bushes flanked, at both sides, by wide paved paths. At the far side of the river Pierce identified as the Monongahela towered the tall hill known as Mount Washington, capped by houses and apartment buildings.

"I'm not sure how much actual location shooting we'll be able to do here," Mariah commented, trying not to let her disappointment show as she dutifully snapped pictures. This was the park that had so attracted her from the air and her hotel room. But there was too much civilization around to allow an easy shoot of a historical film.

She was talking now as though this movie would be made.

Premature, of course—but she would fight for it.

Especially if the ending was changed.

Mariah saw no other pedestrians as they walked down the path on the left, though cars poured downtown from the roads surrounding the park. They reached a concrete wall with a weathered metal plaque embedded atop a pillar. Mariah stopped. A strange, prickly feeling tiptoed up her back.

The wall opened onto a flight of steps. At its base was a cleared area surrounded by a symmetrical brick wall built into a low hillside. A sign on the plaque proclaimed that she was viewing the remnants of original rampart walls from one of the five bastions of Fort Pitt. A drawbridge had been located here.

Mariah could not, from the abbreviated wall, imagine how Fort Pitt must have looked. Still, something seemed unnervingly familiar about this place. Why did she have a sense that this location was of immense importance to her?

"Shall we go on?" Pierce touched her elbow, and she blinked at him. For a moment, she'd forgotten him.

"Of course." Metallic clangs assaulted her ears as he led her between two tall flagstaffs, where ropes anchoring the flags slammed the poles in the growing breeze. The giant flags of the United States and the Commonwealth of Pennsylvania snapped sharply, adding to the din.

Mariah found the dual bridges they reached next fascinating: Pierce and she passed beneath one long, rounded bridge over which automobiles rumbled, and at the same time crossed a paved bridge under it that spanned a small pond.

Though a couple of buildings to the left appealed to Mariah, Pierce led her to the right instead. They walked along the path closest to the Allegheny River, passing a broad lawn lined by a stand of trees. The breeze grew even stronger, whipping Mariah's hair into her eyes. She turned into it to blow her hair back from her face.

"This area would make a good site for filming the picture." Pierce's stern tone left no room for contradiction, but Mariah was dubious. It didn't have the atmosphere of an old fort.

They seemed to be the only visitors to the park that morning. Strange, to see a site so empty that must once have been the busiest locale in the area. Wouldn't these waterways have been vital to the first settlers for transportation of goods and people?

Mariah chuckled to herself. Maybe she had a sense of history after all.

In a few minutes, they reached the point where the rivers met, a cobbled and concreted point of land. The fountain Mariah had noted before rose from a round pool, billowing spray all about in the heavy breeze. It was beautiful. But Mariah felt unbidden tears well in her eyes. This was the spot where Thorn, in the screenplay, had fought his duel. And had died.

"I don't suppose this area looked half so lovely in the era of Fort Pitt," she asserted, more to make conversation than because she cared. She cleared her throat, as though the raspiness in her voice was from stuffed sinuses and not emotion.

"Not at all," Pierce agreed. "The riverbanks were uneven and muddy, though a few ferry boat landings extended out a ways. The King's Garden was pretty at certain times of the year, though."

He must have spent a lot of time researching the history of this place, Mariah thought, to sound so definite.

They walked back along the other river, where modern concrete defined the bank. Mariah took hold of her emotions. Silly, for her to have felt so upset where the historic duel might not even really have been fought. Pierce might have placed it there for atmosphere.

She'd ask him someday.

Small pleasure boats zipped up and down the Monongahela, and a paddlewheeler plied its way upstream beneath the nearest bridge.

Bypassing an even older-looking, freestanding structure in the shape of a pentagon, Pierce led her to a brick building stuffed like a bunker beneath a roadway. "I'd like to see that," Mariah protested, pointing toward the more antique-looking building.

"In time," Pierce said. A strange, wise smile appeared on his narrow face, revealing his yellowed teeth.

A sign above the door identified the place as the Fort Pitt Museum. Another sign explained that the pointed brick structure was a reconstruction of the fort's Monongahela Bastion. Pierce opened the door for Mariah. "You will see, in here, how people lived back when this was the fort." He insisted on paying the nominal entrance fee for both of them, then stopped at the large relief model in the center of the floor.

Mariah stared at the depiction of the way Fort Pitt had once been laid out. She wanted to recall as much as she could so she could pick out the remaining landmarks when they went back outside.

She found the museum fascinating. It even contained a fully furnished log cabin, complete with mannequins of a trader conducting business with an Indian, plus a life-size model of a garrison inside the fort. This would be a wonderful resource for researching costumes and props. She pulled a small pad of paper and a pen from her purse and made a few notes.

"Come," Pierce said finally. "There is more I wish to show you of Pittsborough."

" 'Pittsborough'?"

"Pittsburgh," he corrected himself.

He led her out of the museum and toward the small five-sided building beside it. The bottom part of the structure was built of dark stone, the upper of brick. The roof was pointed. The wrought-iron fence that surrounded it prevented anyone from getting close to any part but the fence-lined entry. Brick pillars surrounded the gate.

"This," Pierce said, "was the Blockhouse, built for extra protection outside the walls of the fort. It is the only building of the original Fort Pitt that remains standing."

They walked up the path toward its entry. The small wooden door was locked, but Mariah tried peering inside through a barred opening. Too dark to see anything. She'd have to find someone to open it; the place had an atmosphere of age. It might even be a good shooting location.

"Come," Pierce said again. He took her hand. Mariah tried to pull away, but he didn't let go.

"Hey," she protested.

"Please feel this stone, Miss Walker," he said, placing her hand against the cold rock beside the wooden door.

Her imagination immediately became rampant once more. She thought of the thousands of hands that must, over the centuries, have rested right there. Of the hands that had diligently constructed the fort and the blockhouse.

"That's right. Do not resist." Pierce's voice murmured soothingly into her ear. He sounded far away. She heard a pounding in her head. Was it her own heartbeat? It sounded rather like the sounds of tramping feet.

Her eyes stared at the stone, but they began to close.

She felt sleepy. So sleepy.

The last words she heard before she fell unconscious were Pierce's. His voice had lost its nasality. Its tone was familiar.

"You must right a grievous wrong, my daughter," he said.

Chapter Three

Harsh musical notes pealed in the distance, as though from the hunting horn in a comedy Lemoncake had recently filmed.

In response, Mariah heard a soft, miserable groan. She tried to open her eyes to determine its source, for it sounded as though someone needed help.

Her eyelids were too heavy to budge.

Heat suffused her body, as though she were covered with a wool blanket under the hot sun, yet she could not move to throw it off.

Instead, she let herself fall limp. She needed to sleep some more.

"Miss!" A sharp voice penetrated her lethargy. "Are you injured?"

There was another groan, and Mariah realized it came from her. With an effort, she blinked.

A terrible bright glare stung her vision, and she gasped, shutting her eyes once more.

"What ails you, miss?" came the voice again, now tinged with impatience.

"Come along, Milson." This was a new voice, higher but still masculine. "We are wanted inside the fort at the parade ground for drilling. Did you not hear the call to arms?"

"Of course I did hear it, but the sergeant can wait."

"Aye. No sense seeming too eager to listen to His Highness's commands, eh?"

"That is your opinion, Jacko, not mine. But this lady looks to be hurt."

A dubious snort erupted from the man called Jacko. "Lady, is it? Besotted wench be more like it."

Mariah felt a rough tug on her arm, pulling her to her feet. She stumbled but made her seemingly boneless body stiffen.

She forced her eyes open again, squinting at the glare. Two men stood before her. They wore faded red coats, trimmed with frayed piping, from which high white shirt collars emerged. Their trousers were beige and short, ending just below their knees. Dark stockings hugged their legs before disappearing into boot tops. One sported a black three-cornered hat pushed back from his face, and both had long hair tied back at their necks with leather thongs. Each held a long-barreled gun.

"Please." Her voice sounded muzzy even to her own ears. "I'm afraid I lost track. What movie are we shooting?"

The two men looked at each other. "What is this 'movie'?" asked Jacko. "Be it some new game to shoot in this pestilent backwater?"

"A game?" Mariah was puzzled. But a little came back to her. She was outside the Blockhouse in Pittsburgh. Wasn't she? She looked at the building beside her. It seemed lighter in color and less weathered than she recalled, but, yes, it was the Blockhouse.

"Hush!" said Milson to Jacko, peering around as though making certain they had not been heard. "The sergeant would run you through should he hear you complaining thus."

Jacko snorted again. "The sergeant can go and be hanged." At a nervous movement from his companion, he glared at Mariah. "My compatriot and I would deny all, miss, should you carry tales to our commander."

These men, probably only extras, had certainly gotten into character, Mariah thought. They were costumed like the British soldier mannequins in the museum, even down to their Pennsylvania rifles, and their accents even sounded British.

"Do not worry, good sir," she said with a self-conscious laugh. "I would not do such a thing." She might as well play along, pretend to be one of the characters at old Fort Pitt.

But . . . Angela had just hired her for the project. Mariah had read the script only last night, started scouting locations today. She hadn't even thought about the rest of the production planning.

How could Lemoncake have begun filming so quickly?

It was impossible. They hadn't even acquired the rights to the screenplay yet. Hundreds, maybe thousands of things had to be done between the time a suitable property was acquired and commencement of filming: budgeting, securing funding, assembling a production staff, casting, contracts . . . the list seemed endless.

Yet here they were. Dressed extras already milled about. How could this have happened?

A frightening explanation crossed Mariah's mind. Maybe she'd suffered some kind of memory loss.

She lifted her hand to her head. It hurt. Did it ever! Had she had some kind of mini-stroke? Oh, lord, no! That couldn't be. She was never sick.

"Miss, are you ill?" Milson, the taller of the two men, echoed her thoughts. He had a broad nose and myopic-looking eyes.

Jacko, who had an underslung jaw, laughed mirthlessly. "More likely, Milson, my friend, the wench has spent too much time at the tavern."

"Sssh, Jacko! Such disrespect for a lady!" Milson seemed scandalized.

"Ladies," intoned Jacko, "do not pass out against the redoubt wall. They have their vapors in more auspicious locations. If this is a *lady*—"

"Hey, cut it out." Mariah didn't want to interrupt their

concentration on their roles, but the one called Jacko was downright insulting.

Besides, she needed to pause and understand what had happened.

She placed her hand against the uneven stone wall of the Blockhouse for support. It felt cool, easing the unbearable heat she had felt. Looking around, she noticed that the wrought-iron fence was gone.

She closed her eyes and took a deep breath. Well, of course it was gone. It had been removed for the filming.

Opening her eyes again, she looked around to see what other changes had been made.

That was when she noticed her own clothing: a long gown of a wrinkled cotton material, in the pink shade of cherry blossoms.

No wonder she felt warm; she was covered from head to toe in clothing despite the blazing summer heat.

How had she changed clothes?

An uneasy tingling began at the nape of her neck. Something was terribly wrong. Time had passed that she could not recall.

What was the last thing she could remember?

Pierce's voice.

There had been no nasality to it then. It had sounded like the voice in her dreams, hoarse, sure and demanding. "You must right a grievous wrong . . . my daughter."

His *daughter?* Where had that come from? Where had *any* of that haunting command come from?

More notes sounded from a bugle in the distance. That had been what had awakened Mariah.

"Come along," said Milson to his cohort. "No more dallying here. The sergeant's displeasure with you needs no more call to increase."

"And my displeasure with our esteemed sergeant as well." But Jacko turned to go.

Milson, touching the brim of his hat, cast a worried look toward Mariah. "I have heard that a physician is passing through Pittsborough, miss," he said over his shoulder as he followed his friend. "Perhaps you should call on him."

Pittsborough? That was how Pierce had mispronounced the name.

Mariah looked about her and let out an involuntary gasp. Perhaps, she thought, I should have my head examined.

Where the Fort Pitt Museum should have been, there was a ditch, and beyond that, a jutting earthen embankment in the shape of the pointed museum walls. All the bridges had disappeared, and she couldn't see the tops of the tall skyscrapers. Across the river, the hills to which apartments and other structures had clung were covered with trees. A few log buildings huddled in the foreground.

Her light-headedness returning, Mariah forced herself to inhale and exhale slowly. The air smelled sweeter, fresher, with no evidence of car fumes.

She noticed the noise, then—or the lack of it. No vehicles thundered on roadways into and out of town. Instead, she heard a breeze rustling through the trees, and the songs of several birds. Dimly, she was aware of raised voices in the distance and the clumping of feet marching in unison.

She must be on location somewhere in a spot designed to resemble the Pittsburgh of long ago.

A lovely spot. A countrylike haven, full of classic charm. Welcoming, if she ignored the actors she'd encountered.

But a place whose appearance was more than enigmatic.

She looked around for her purse. It wasn't there. She *always* had her purse with her, with pen and paper for jotting down production notes. And where was her camera? Had she been robbed on top of everything else?

She took a few steps on the unpaved ground and nearly tripped in the coarse, laced boots she wore. The building constructed to represent the Blockhouse was certainly authentic-looking. Stumbling a little, her head spinning, she walked along the top of the ditch in the direction in which the men had gone. The trench was, she presumed, the moat she'd read about on the rampart plaque, but it was dry. Strange that Angela hadn't had it filled for authenticity. But maybe she'd do that only when it was time to film the scenes across from the fort.

Soon, near the river, Mariah came to an earthen barrier.

From it extended a bridge over the ditch. Mariah considered entering the fort. Maybe she'd find Angela and some of the crew there, cameras rolling while the extras she had met, and their counterparts, drilled on the parade grounds. She climbed the wood stairs, then stepped out on the span, the low heels of her unfamiliar boots clacking on the wooden planks. The sound hurt her aching head.

At the end of the bridge was the tall, grassy bank that constituted the fort's ramparts.

Amazing, how authentic this set looked, Mariah thought—just like the replica in the museum. Though her head hurt, her mind, used to juggling production details, began to estimate a budget. This must have cost a fortune! That was one reason Angela usually stayed away from period pieces. She could shoot a great current comedy for peanuts by using actual locations. But Mariah had to agree this screenplay had been special.

Why couldn't she remember all that had happened to get the production to this point?

At the fort end of the bridge, a uniformed man with a Pennsylvania rifle at his side stared at her with keen interest. But not recognition. Odd. The cast should know who she was. Unless Angela had fired her. Surely she'd at least recall if *that* had happened.

"State your business, miss," the man said in a coarse British accent, sounding as bored as though he'd repeated the line dozens of times.

Annoyance engulfed Mariah. Actors! They didn't have to keep up the pretense off camera.

"Miss?" The actor-soldier had taken a step forward. He was young and quite homely, with pockmarked skin and tiny eyes beneath his tricornered hat. The skin blotches were a wonderful makeup detail, Mariah thought. He blocked her entrance to the compound, and she raised one hand in a conciliatory gesture.

"Peace," she stated. "Is Angela Corbin here today?"

"I know no Angela Corbin, miss."

"She's only the producer of this film," Mariah snapped. "I'm Mariah Walker, her UPM."

The man repeated the sounds suspiciously as though they were a foreign word instead of an abbreviation. "Eeoopee-em?"

Mariah spoke slowly, unclenching her jaw. "Unit Production Manager. Angela will be wondering what's happened to me." *I'm* wondering what happened to me, she thought.

"What is this 'unit production manager'?" the man persisted, peering at her as though she'd lost her mind.

"Tell you what," she said a bit too sweetly. "Why don't you just let me go on in and look for Angela?" She took a step toward the man and got a whiff of unwashed uniform and old horse. She wrinkled her nose. These people were certainly taking this character thing too far!

"There's no women inside the fort this morning," he insisted, still using a thick accent. "The sergeant wants no interruptions to the drills, either. Why don't you look in town for your friend, miss?"

She opened her mouth to protest, then stopped. Why not visit the town set? she thought. She didn't want to argue with this strange young actor, and she could always come back if no one there gave her the answers she sought. Besides, her head still hurt, and it already pounded in time with the footfalls of the drilling soldier extras inside the fort. She had no desire, for now, to get any closer to the source.

Going back the way she'd come, she stopped outside the fort near the Blockhouse. There was a river to her left and another beyond the town to her right, both angled to meet a third straight ahead. They seemed similar to the Monongahela and Allegheny as they met to form the Ohio at Point State Park. Whoever had done the location scouting had done a magnificent job. This place was just like Pittsburgh must have been soon after civilization had arrived.

Where could anyone have found a spot as perfect as this? It had to have been undeveloped before the sets were built. Was it in some foreign country?

And why couldn't she recall participating in the selection process—or even getting here?

Her breathing quickened as fear burst through the muzziness in her head. She forced herself back to calmness. There was an explanation.

There had to be.

Her progress was slow, thanks to her headache and a touch of vertigo. Plus, the area that, in modern Pittsburgh, had been flat and covered with paving or grass was uneven, rutted dirt here.

The temperature seemed warmer than when she'd awakened, and the heat added to her discomfort. She glanced at her wrist and wasn't surprised to learn she'd lost her watch. Looking at the sky, she saw the sun nearly straight overhead, and she assumed the time to be nearly noon. The high humidity added to the discomfort of her aching head.

She wished she could at least bare part of her arms, but, unhooking the buttons of her heavy dress at the wrists, found the material too bulky to stay rolled.

Eventually, she reached the set resembling a town. It was just a conglomeration of maybe a dozen buildings, plunked down on what appeared to be an embryonic layout of a city, with dirt streets somewhat parallel. All structures were of wood, most of natural, unplaned logs daubed in between with mud, though a few actually used sawed boards. Most were tiny. One of the larger ones had a sign at the door: Allen Traders. A signpost outside another, from which raucous laughter and the smell of ripe liquor emanated, proclaimed it the Pittsburgh Tavern.

She peered around the buildings. They were whole structures, not the facades common to movie sets. She sniffed at Angela's extravagance. This film had better be a box-office hit to earn back its expenses.

With the screenplay she'd read, that kind of success was a real possibility. Especially with the development of the Thorn character.

What actor had Angela gotten to portray him? Mariah was dying to know.

A man exited the building marked "Traders." He wore a wrinkled and dirty white shirt over equally filthy pants. He touched his hair as though to doff a cap. "Morning, miss." He regarded her curiously.

Yet another actor into his role. Mariah smiled grimly and nodded as she walked by.

A woman approached. Her dress was gray, ragged and dirty. It covered her from chin to ankle, as Mariah's did. She looked Mariah up and down, not particularly cordially. Mariah halted her by saying, "I wonder if you could help me."

The woman looked older than Mariah had at first thought, with pleats at her sad and distrustful dark eyes. "What do you want?"

Mariah suspected that this remote woman wouldn't tell her what was going on even if she knew. "I'm looking for Angela Corbin. Do you know if she's somewhere around town for the film shoot?"

A fearful look crossed the woman's face. "I know no Angela Corbin. But have you heard shooting? Is it another Indian uprising? We must enter the fort for protection."

Mariah held her temper in check. Why wouldn't someone just stop the pretense long enough to help her out? "Maybe the Cleveland Indians are on their way to attack the Pittsburgh Pirates," she said sarcastically, then regretted it, for the woman gasped and ran off as though terrified.

Mariah sighed, touching her aching temple with her fingertips. She was getting tired of all this. If she could simply find Angela, she'd borrow some money and tell her she was catching the next flight back to L.A. She didn't appear needed on this project, and she was beginning to detest it.

Despite its captivating screenplay.

She'd reached the end of the row of log buildings. Where could she go now to look for someone familiar? And why hadn't she seen anyone here, where there was no filming going on, out of character and in a pair of blue jeans?

The ache in her head turned into a sharp, painful pounding. Something was dreadfully wrong. There was too much that seemed authentic. Too many actors taking their roles much too seriously. Sets that seemed very real. Rivers resembling the ones that formed Pittsburgh, but without the skyscrapers and traffic.

She suddenly felt certain that she wasn't on a movie set. But if not, where was she?

It was as though she'd stumbled onto Pittsburgh the way it had actually been over two hundred years ago.

Her vision blurred, and not just from the tears that filled her eyes. Her dizziness nearly overwhelming, she swayed against a building. Could she be dreaming? But dreams didn't last this long. Unless . . .

She'd already worried whether a mini-stroke might have affected her memory. Maybe that was it. Or maybe she'd hit her head when she'd fallen near the Blockhouse and was lying in a hospital somewhere unconscious.

Did people in comas have such authentic, chilling dreams?

"Miss Walker?" A high male voice sounded in her ear.

Someone here knew her!

With a grin of relief, Mariah turned—and felt her smile freeze. Here was yet another man in costume. A stranger.

This guy wore the cleanest, neatest period clothes she'd seen yet: a brocade vest over a white woven shirt, knee britches with buckles, dark stockings and buckled shoes. He even wore a white wig pulled back into a pony tail at the nape of his neck. Very dressy, very presentable—and still very disturbing to Mariah. She hadn't any idea who he was.

She swallowed hard at her disappointment. "I'm Mariah Walker," she said. "I'm afraid I don't remember you . . ."

"My name is John Brant," he said. He was only slightly taller than she, and his accent was cultured British. He seemed barely out of his teens, and he had a ready smile. "Pierce sent me."

Pierce! "Where is he?" Mariah demanded. He'd have an explanation, she was sure of it.

"Some distance from here," he said. "He asked my partner and me to take you to him."

"Sure," Mariah said, hope pulsing through her. She'd find out soon what was going on. "Let's go."

Mariah was less enthusiastic when she learned that reaching Pierce would involve a boat trip down the Ohio River.

John's partner Samuel, though rather stout, was dressed just as smartly, with an even more intricately brocaded vest. He waited for them near the water.

John handed her from the muddy riverbank onto the flat-bottomed wooden boat they'd called a bateau. Then John and Samuel began loading barrels of several sizes from the shore. Samuel, surprisingly agile for his girth, arranged the goods to one side of Mariah.

"Gunpowder," Samuel explained when she asked about the barrels' contents. "And lead and flints, some dried corn and beans and a bit of rum. For trading."

She brimmed with more questions but was afraid of sounding insane if she asked any of them. She merely watched, feeling the bateau lurch each time the men hoisted a new keg on board.

After a while, out of breath, Samuel told her, "Here are your bags." His grin turned his flushed, fleshy face into a round jack o' lantern. He had a lower tooth missing.

"My bags?" Mariah looked at the two bulky cloth satchels he'd caught from John and loaded onto the bateau beside her.

"Aren't they? Mr. Pierce told us you recently arrived from the east with them."

Pierce again. "Yes, of course. They're mine." She hesitated, wondering what he had put in the bags. Was her purse there? Her watch? Her camera? She'd check as soon as she could. "Where did Mr. Pierce tell you he'd meet me?" The elusive Pierce seemed to be directing not a film but her life. Or the dream she was living. In any event, she needed to know what he'd planned.

"At a new trading post down the Ohio, Miss Walker," Samuel said. "Harrigan's place. We were heading there anyway to conduct some business."

Harrigan's name meant nothing to her. "How long will it take to get there?" she asked.

"Not long. A few hours."

It sounded like an eternity to Mariah, who craved answers. But she vowed to be patient.

John and Samuel finally settled themselves on the flat boat, then poled off. There had to be an art to keeping the craft straight, Mariah thought as they glided off down the Ohio, the men using oars as rudders.

The breeze, dampened further by the river, blew into her face. She could imagine how wild her hair must look. She tried to find a comfortable position on the narrow wooden logs that comprised the bateau's base, finally settling on crossing her legs beneath the voluminous folds of her skirt—not particularly ladylike in pioneer times, she suspected, unless one happened to be a Native American.

Pioneer times. The fear had begun to niggle in her mind that the only one acting was she. Was it possible she had traveled back in time?

Of course not.

If she hadn't, though, someone was playing an elaborate trick on her. Pierce?

If he *had* sent her back in time, that would have been the most terrible trick of all.

Ridiculous. No one could travel in time, let alone engineer such a trip for someone else.

She found it easier to believe that she was lying somewhere in a coma. She had to pull herself out of it. Soon.

She saw no sign of cities or other people as they made their way downriver. Both banks were heavily forested, sometimes with evergreens but mostly with deciduous trees in a variety of shades of green. Her head began to clear as she inhaled air that smelled fresh and verdant.

Water lapped noisily at the sides of the bateau. Ducks bobbed in the river here and there, and other birds flew about the tops of the trees, calling raucously. Sometimes, a hawk or other bird of prey swooped and glided overhead in the wind, large wings outstretched. Forests as thick as those must also shelter other kinds of wildlife, Mariah imagined. How lovely this untamed area seemed.

Maybe she should sink into a coma more often!

She untied the bag nearest her and pulled its cloth edges apart, but all she could see were some unfamiliar clothes. She'd need more room to explore them thoroughly. That would have to wait until later.

She retied the string and relaxed, lulled by the boat's soothing motion. Neither John nor Samuel said much except to direct one another how to maneuver the boat.

"Left here, fool!" Samuel shouted eventually from the front. "Do you not see that sandbar?"

Mariah was startled from her nearly somnolent state. Till then, Samuel and John had been unfailingly polite, not only to her but also to each other.

But there was something more. Samuel's words had been familiar.

Mariah had read them in Josiah Pierce's screenplay.

"I see nothing from back here," John grumbled. "Let me take the lead."

They switched places, rocking the boat so violently that Mariah was afraid they'd capsize. But her fear resulted from more than a concern about being dunked.

She'd recalled a scene in the script. In it, the Matilda character had arrived in Fort Pitt-era Pittsburgh from the east and had to go down the Ohio River to meet a relative who waited for her. She'd met Porter, who'd spoken those terrifying words to her—words Mariah had heard from Pierce: "You must right a grievous wrong."

But Pierce had added the strange twist of "my daughter," and Porter hadn't. Matilda had bought passage from a couple of men heading downriver. But the men had turned out to be ruffians, and they had attacked her.

Mariah's situation was, of course, different. Matilda's men had been described as common, trappers, perhaps. Rough-looking. Nevertheless, foolishly, she'd hired them.

John and Samuel, well dressed, seemingly cultured men, had claimed to have been asked by Pierce to take her to him. She hadn't remembered Matilda's predicament in the screenplay when she'd agreed to go with them, and even if she had, she wouldn't have equated Matilda's coarse attackers with these men.

But they no longer appeared so genteel. Their neat clothing was rumpled and sweat-stained. They'd stopped acting polite.

Were they about to attack her, just as Matilda had been set upon in the script?

Mariah wasn't sure why. If her purse was in the bags, John and Samuel could have stolen it before Mariah even knew the men existed. The script hadn't indicated that Matilda had had anything worth stealing, either. Perhaps the men's plotting was because women were rare here in the wilderness, except, maybe, for those who sold their favors.

Whatever their reasons, she suspected their game, thanks to the script.

She glanced at John, at the front of the bateau. They'd navigated around the sandbar, and now he turned to stare at her. The eyes that had seemed youthful and friendly before were now cold, hard pebbles.

She smiled nervously. "Will our journey be much longer? I already feel as though I was born on this bateau." She started so violently that the boat rocked. Her fingertips leapt to her throat. Her own words had seemed familiar, too. She'd read them in the script.

She bit her bottom lip nervously as tears welled in her eyes. What was happening here? She had somehow been cast involuntarily in the role of Matilda, even getting into the role herself. But no one else around her appeared to be acting.

Feeling as though she were Alice fallen down the rabbit hole, she only heard dimly when Samuel, behind her, replied with the dialogue she'd read, "This river gets into your blood, miss. Everyone who sees her feels he's lived here forever."

The screenplay was unfolding around her. She would be attacked, just like Matilda. She was certain of it. But at least, unlike Matilda, she expected it and could plan ahead.

She craned her neck, watching the riverbanks and waiting. She glanced now and then at Samuel, behind her. The portly man usually stared back, and she didn't like the predatory nature of his jack o' lantern grin.

Then there was John, who turned often, as though to make sure she was still there. Somewhere along the way he'd dropped the pretense of being pleasant.

Nervously, Mariah continued her surveillance. Could she be wrong? She doubted it. She had to act.

She waited until she saw a small wooden pier jutting into the water from the bank at the left, like the one mentioned in the screenplay.

Luckily, the bateau had drifted so it was not too far from the left shore. She glanced at Samuel and John. For the moment, neither was looking at her.

She had a fleeting thought about the bags she'd been told were hers. Well, she'd no choice. She'd leave them.

She was a good swimmer, thank heavens. With no further thought, she jumped into the water.

She hadn't considered the effects of water on her long, heavy dress. Matilda had not jumped into the water; she had fallen in as she fought off the men. The script hadn't mentioned her struggles in the river. Though Mariah was strong enough to strike out for the bank, the waterlogged material weighed her down, slowing her.

"Hey!" called one of the men behind her. "Grab her." That was not dialogue from the screenplay. "She's getting away!" She heard the splashing as they must have worked to slow the bateau's progress downstream and come back for her. She did the crawl the way she always had, letting the even kicks of her legs propel her forward, though they tangled in the cumbersome material of her dress. The long, even motions of her arms helped. She turned her head every few strokes for a breath.

She felt exhausted almost immediately. When she hesitated, she felt herself begin to sink.

An arm grabbed her before she went under—from the boat. "No!" she screamed. Wrenching free, she kicked hard, plunging below the surface.

The water was clear and blue. The sun lit the sparkling surface, but she stayed below, kicking and holding her breath.

"Catch her!" shouted a loud voice somewhere above her.

"Can't! Damned bateau's drifting too far away again."

Had the men in the script spoken those lines? She could not recall.

She heard the splashing of the oars, but she couldn't tell their distance or direction. Her lungs stung. She longed to head up for a breath, but she forced herself to stay underwater and out of easy reach, fighting to keep herself from sinking further.

Her arms continued their sluggish stroking ahead of her. After what seemed like hours, her hand struck something solid. The pier!

She pulled her head from the water and sucked in a deep, welcome breath, practically gagging in relief. Wheezing to catch her breath, she looked around. The men in the bateau were still a distance offshore. "Hey!" one called. "She's on the bank."

At least she was better off than Matilda; the screenplay's heroine had been followed right behind by the ruffians.

Gasping for air, she dragged herself from the water. Her heavy, dripping skirt still weighed her down, keeping her from running as the men also reached the shore, not very far downstream.

No, she was *not* better off than Matilda.

Terrified, her heart hammering, she tried to think what to do. How could she hurry in her waterlogged clothes? Yet she didn't dare take the time to remove them. She had to run. But where? Along the shore? Into the woods?

And then she remembered.

This was the time in the screenplay that Thorn had come to Matilda's rescue, tall and broad-shouldered, aiming at the marauders with his Pennsylvania rifle.

There was hope.

"Help!" Mariah cried. Although there had been differences, much of what had, so far happened followed the screenplay—even if it had all occurred in her unconscious mind. Thorn would come. He had to.

Seeing the two men approaching, she sped into the thick of the great green forest ahead. Dead leaves carpeted the ground, and only a little light trickled in among the thick branches. She barely noticed the odor of moldering leaves, still fighting for breath as she tried to find a place to run, to hide.

"Help!" she cried again, her voice a mere whisper. "Please, Thorn."

And then, as if he'd heard her call him, there he was, standing directly before her in the forest. He was every bit as tall and wide-shouldered as she'd imagined him. His hair was straight and uneven and seemed the color of some rich, polished wood. His jaw was thick and broad, and his neck had the heavy contours of a weightlifter's. He wore a fringed buckskin jacket and brown pants that reached to the tops of his moccasins, and in his arms he cradled a long-barreled Pennsylvania rifle.

Behind her, she heard the loud footfalls of the men.

"You might as well halt, Miss Walker," taunted John. "We will catch you."

"We're traders." Samuel's voice held a frightening laugh. "There's an Indian we've dealt with. He likes women with light hair; you'll bring a lot of pelts."

Mariah winced. "Please," she said to the man she thought of as Thorn. "I need your help."

In the shadows, she couldn't make out the color of his eyes, but she could see them staring at her piercingly. His narrow lips were a tight, angry slash across his face. He didn't move.

Recalling in desperation the words in the screenplay that Matilda had used to galvanize the Thorn character into action, she cried in desperation, "I'm relying on you!"

"No one," said the man in a deep, gravelly voice, "should rely on me." He turned away and began to walk back into the forest.

Chapter Four

"Wait!"

Despite himself, Thorn hesitated at the terrified voice behind him, but just for a moment. He took a few more determined strides into the great expanse of woodlands that formed his refuge, his home. This woman's problems were not his.

But with a sigh more like a groan, he gritted his teeth, clutched his rifle more tightly in his right hand, and, against his better judgment, pivoted back toward her just as the woman reached his side.

Grabbing his arm with surprising strength, she looked up at him with eyes the soft, clear green of the topside of a silver maple's leaves. Her fear radiated from them as though they spoke to him.

The top of her head rose just above his shoulder. She was a pretty woman despite being wet and unkempt, with a small, straight nose and a smooth complexion. Her lips, pale in her anxiety, were slightly parted. Her hair, strangely short and uncovered, hung in wet waves about her face. It seemed light in color. He wondered what shade it would be when dry.

Her wet pink gown clung to her every curve. She was thin but shapely, and he felt a stirring deep inside him that seemed nearly unfamiliar. It had been a long time since he had allowed himself to become attracted to any woman.

He was not about to change that now.

From behind her came an angry, crude voice. "Wait up, bitch. You're worth too much for us to let you get away." The footsteps crashed through the woods. To Thorn's acute senses, they sounded only a few hundred feet away, though the men remained invisible in the thick copse.

"Please help me," she begged in a low, frantic voice. Her pleading touched him. How could he leave her here to face what those men wanted of her?

How could he not? Was not every time he attempted to help someone doomed to disastrous failure?

Stonily, he looked away, stepped around her, and took a stride in the direction in which he had been heading.

"Please," she repeated from just behind him. "You have to help me. You're Thorn, aren't you?"

"Yes," he said, without slowing his pace, though he wondered how she knew him. "I'm Thorn." His voice sounded mocking even to him. And why not? The man known as Thorn was not one who could speak his name with pride. Maybe someone at the fort had mentioned him scornfully to her.

The woman pushed herself in front of him, again staring up at him. She must not have liked what she saw on his face, for her expression fell. "I should have known better," she whispered. "It was too good to be true."

She took him by surprise as she wrenched his rifle from his grasp and took several steps away from him.

"What are you doing?" he growled, going after her.

"I'm helping myself. Like always." She stared at the long, heavy weapon in her hands, as though studying it. She started to swing it awkwardly up to her shoulder, her finger on the trigger. As it moved, it pointed at him.

He ducked, grabbing it from her. "That's not how you use it."

"Then show me. Please!"

The men were nearly upon them. Thorn had his rifle back. He could leave her here, and . . .

No, he couldn't. Despite all reason, he could not ignore her plight. He was about to aim the rifle at the men when the woman, unaware of his intentions, said in obvious desperation, "I'll pay you."

"How much?" He was curious, although it made no difference.

"Whatever you want."

"Hey!" The two men burst through the last trees sheltering Thorn and Mariah from their sight. They stopped for a moment, staring at him in surprise.

He, too, was surprised. They were bedraggled and nearly as drenched as the woman, but both were well dressed, apparently gentlemen.

But he knew far better than to be deceived by appearances. He swung up the rifle, pointing it in their direction and supporting its barrel with his left hand.

"Keep out of this, mister," said the older, larger of the two. He looked even more furious than his youthful companion.

"Certainly," Thorn said, aiming at the speaker. "I have no quarrel with you. If the lady wishes to accompany you, then you may all three be on your way."

"I've no intention of going with them," the woman said, defiant despite the frightened quaver in her voice. He glanced down over the side of the rifle barrel. She stared at him as though unsure whether he would cede her to these ruffians, her green eyes fearful, her moist lips parted in what looked like supplication.

Her look stirred something else long dormant deep inside him: a sense of protectiveness. Of caring what happened to another human being.

Foolhardy. He knew it. But he had made his decision. He sighted toward the men.

"Now, look, mister," the younger one whined. "This woman made an agreement with us for her passage. She was to come along with us to a trading post downriver, where she was to meet someone who would pay her way. Isn't that right, Miss Walker?''

The woman hesitated. Thorn suspected there was a grain of truth in what the man said.

But he had heard what the men had called as they'd followed her. They intended to sell her to an Indian.

''Bring Pierce to me, then.'' She made her demand bravely despite her obvious fear. ''He can pay my fare here, and his own to join me.''

''That wasn't the arrangement,'' said the heavy man. His round face was set in a scowl. ''Come along, Miss Walker.''

''No!'' She glanced at Thorn, her eyes again pleading.

He allowed the heavy rifle to sag just a little. ''Since Miss Walker chooses to stay here, gentlemen, you'd best be on your way.''

The heavy man's hand moved, and a flintlock pistol appeared in it. It was pointed toward Thorn. ''It seems we have a deadlock, mister. There's no sense in your getting hurt for a contrary woman.''

''Maybe not,'' said Thorn, steadying his firearm once more and preparing it to shoot. ''But I might say the same to you.''

Sensitive to the tiniest movement his adversary might make, Thorn anticipated the man's firing the pistol. He pulled the trigger of his rifle before sparks from the pistol's firing mechanism could ignite the priming powder. As intended, his bullet struck the man in the upper arm, making his shot go wild.

''Hey,'' cried the younger man. His right arm moved, and in moments he, too, was aiming a pistol at Thorn. Thorn, unfortunately, did not have another rifle. He grabbed the woman, pulling her with him behind the thick trunk of the nearest oak, just as the pistol went off. A piece of shattered bark whizzed past his head.

The pungent odor of burned gunpowder hung in the air. Thorn carefully looked around the tree, praying that neither man had more than one firearm. No. The young man was reloading. His larger companion leaned against a thin sycamore that barely sustained his weight, holding his bloody upper arm and moaning.

Ducking back behind his shelter, Thorn quickly pulled the strap of his powderhorn from around his neck and poured the coarse propellant powder into the muzzle. Then he shoved the horn at the woman. "Hold this," he demanded. He pulled from a pouch a small bullet he had wrapped carefully in buckskin soaked in tallow and slid it into the barrel, pushing it down with the narrow hickory ramrod slid from the base of the barrel. He primed with fine powder, snapped the pan cover shut and cocked.

In moments, his prized possession, the Pennsylvania rifle he had won in a card game with a passing settler, had been readied. He had practiced rapid reloading many a time. He felt certain he was faster than anyone else.

Right now, his life might depend on it.

Cautiously, he peered once more around the tree. Sure enough, the younger man was still struggling to reload his pistol.

Thorn sprang from behind the tree. "Best get back on your way, gentlemen," he spat through gritted teeth.

The young man glared at him defiantly, then glanced uneasily at the pointed rifle. "All right," he said after a long moment. "Guess she's yours . . . for now." Supporting his companion with obvious difficulty, he headed back toward the river.

Never willing to trust anyone, Thorn followed. He kept his rifle ready to shoot.

When they reached the bateau tied to the small dock, the young man unceremoniously shoved the larger man onto it, causing it to rock violently. Thorn wondered if the flat craft would tip sideways, but they managed somehow to steady it and pole off without losing any cargo into the water. The heavier man still clutched his bleeding arm.

"Good riddance," whispered a voice from beside him. Thorn turned to find the woman at his side, glaring at the men who had been her tormentors.

A glimmer of admiration shot through him. He'd have expected the woman to have run off by now, or at least to remain cowering where he'd left her. She was a brave young thing. He'd come to respect courage. These days, he'd little enough himself.

Before they got far into the river, the younger man pulled a cloth satchel from one of the piles and tossed it into the water. He hurled a look toward shore that might have been defiance. He did the same with another bag as the craft caught the current and floated downstream.

"Your belongings, I presume," Thorn asked the woman.

"I-I believe so."

Her uncertainty seemed strange, but perhaps she had been unsure because of the distance. No matter. Still, he could not help goading, "I suppose now that you will say you cannot pay me, with your bags beneath the waters of the Ohio."

The glance she tossed to him from those intriguing green eyes appeared startled. "I suppose that's true." Her words were slow, contemplative. "But if I remember correctly . . ."

She tilted her head in apparent bewilderment that he could not understand. Her brow furrowed into shallow wrinkles. An urge to smooth them away, to touch her pale cheeks, rocked him, and he nearly gave in to it. Even more, he wanted to pull her into his arms, to wipe away her confusion, to reassure her that all was well. That he would take care of her.

No! He fought the inclination with even more vehemence than he had used to rout those scoundrels. These were feelings he could never indulge again—not if he wanted to save himself, and certainly not if he wished to help this woman.

For his sanity and her safety, he had to send her on her way.

She stopped looking confused. To his surprise, she straightened her shoulders beneath her bedraggled pink gown and planted herself before him.

He opened his mouth to order her off, but her next words shook him more than anything else she had yet said. "I'm here for a job, anyway. Mr. Thorn, please hire me to work at your inn."

* * *

Ignoring the throbbing at her temples, Mariah held her breath as the man stared down at her. She could see now that his eyes were a light shade of brown, the color of dry, solid earth—or of turbulent rivers.

A few moments before, they had been soft, almost caring. The sweet and troubled eyes of the Thorn of the screenplay. She had wanted to take his hand, to tell him that all that had hurt him had not been his fault.

But then, quite suddenly, those eyes had grown chilly. Perhaps she had imagined their earlier warmth.

And now, he stared at her with apparent incredulity, with his thick, dark brows creating formidable arches.

She wanted to shout at him, "Why do you seem so surprised? I'm supposed to work for you. It was in the screenplay." Instead, she remained silent, watchful, ambivalent.

When he turned away without saying anything, though, she hurriedly said, "I've nowhere to go. I haven't even a change of clothes. You can't leave me stranded here in the woods."

But she didn't believe her words. He could abandon her.

The last thing she wanted was to stay around this travesty of the man she'd come to know from the screenplay. *That* Thorn had been kind, heroic. *This* one, though he'd come through in the end, had nearly been forced into it by her actions, and then he'd done so ungraciously.

But what choice did she have? Even if Pierce had sent for her from somewhere downstream, she'd no way of getting there, no way of finding him even if she could scrounge up transportation.

Where *was* Pierce, that ancient son-of-a-gun? He'd have answers to give about what had happened to her. Was she really, incredibly, in the past, or was her telltale headache a sign that she was lying somewhere injured, dreaming this entire episode?

If that were so, her dreams should follow the screenplay, shouldn't they? But things were unfolding so differently here.

She looked around. The two still stood on the packed-dirt riverbank. The air smelled damp, and the water gurgled beside her. A few feet beyond was the beginning of the woods, where the spreading branches of dark-barked black oaks were interspersed with tall, lighter ashes and shaggy hickories. The growth was dense and dismal, though breeze-disturbed leaves shimmered in the sun at the forest's edge. She'd had no time to consider how uninviting the forest appeared when she'd been forced to flee into it, but now . . .

Bracing herself for further argument, she stared up at Thorn's rigid back. His buckskin jacket stretched across his broad shoulders. The fringe hanging at the level of his shoulder blades was motionless, as though he had turned into a statue.

She thought she heard something then. Was it just the rustle of wind through the trees, or had Thorn muttered?

She said, "I'm sorry. Did you say something?"

His head turned, causing the ends of his dark hair to skim the top of his jacket. He glared at her over his shoulder, then said irritably, "Come along." Looking ahead again, he strode into the forest, his rifle, pointed at the ground, clenched in his hand.

Chomping down on her bottom lip, Mariah followed. She felt relieved that he had relented, yet apprehensive of what was to come. "I'm Mariah Walker," she called to him. "Thanks for helping me."

He didn't stop but shrugged in acknowledgment. "The name's Thorn," he said, loud enough for her to hear. "But you know that." There was a deep, gravelly quality to his voice, and an accent that seemed the cultured British she'd heard affected in some historical films.

Was Thorn his first name or last? she found herself wondering, for the script hadn't said, one way or the other.

She had to struggle to keep up as he weaved between trees along ground thickly carpeted with fallen twigs and leaves. The crunching of her footsteps was much more frequent than that caused by his longer stride. She was glad she wore boots, for she kept her balance easily—even though they still squished when she walked from the water she'd gotten into them. Plus, there was no telling what might lurk beneath the underbrush. She'd not have been surprised to see snakes.

Her clothing was uncomfortable. Her long skirt almost dragged on the ground, and the dress's snugness about her chest made her want to gasp for breath.

The gloom was nearly unbroken, but now and then a bit of light broke through the canopy of branches overhead, casting a sudden glow on the forest floor. Birds chattered and sang all about them.

They skirted wide trunks of fallen trees. Though Thorn's pace seemed certain, his movements sure, Mariah couldn't imagine how he found his way through growth that looked the same to her no matter which way they veered. The forest smelled dank and moist, mostly pleasant but spoiled occasionally by the odor of something rotten.

And then they broke through into a clearing. Sunshine illuminated a compound of several buildings as rustic as the ones Mariah had seen in the area that had appeared to be early Pittsburgh. An unfinished fence of upright logs, each carved to a point like a huge pencil, spanned about a third of the clearing. She counted three main structures: a small, square one of dark stone and two others of the log-and-daub construction she'd seen before, one much larger than the other. The ground around them was bare earth, scattered here and there with dead leaves. A rail Mariah assumed was for tying horses stretched before the front of one of the log buildings.

What a perfect setting for a historical film, she thought.

Thorn stopped so abruptly she nearly ran into him. She walked around to his side. "Nice," she said conversationally. "Is the largest building the inn? Or do people stay in all the structures? I particularly like the looks of that stone building."

He stared down at her as though he'd just recalled her presence. "The stone house is mine," he said coldly. "There is no room for you there."

"Of course." Her irritation burst through in her tone. The last thing she wanted was to be anywhere near this man, let alone intrude on his private domicile. "Now, tell me what my duties will be, and I'll get right to work."

She swallowed so hard she nearly gagged. Those words

were dialogue from the script, the statement Matilda had made so pertly when her Thorn had brought her to his inn. She hadn't intentionally said them; they'd just burst out.

The screenplay's Thorn had been impressed that Matilda was eager to assume her role as serving wench. Would this Thorn react similarly? She hoped so. At least it would be a sign of human kindness from this difficult, remote man.

Sure enough, the look he turned on her seemed surprised, one dark brow raised higher than the other. "If you intend to repay me by work, I'll have to find you something to do, won't I, Miss Walker?" There was irony to his tone, though for once he didn't sound angry.

Perhaps she had misjudged him. He had saved her life, after all. And he hadn't abandoned her there on the riverbank. Now, he was simply holding her to the bargain they'd struck.

She was going to be a servant. A servant! With all her education. Her hard-won managerial expertise.

She gritted her teeth. "Whenever you're ready," she said, determinedly pleasant. After all, she wouldn't know the first thing about digging in to work at a primitive inn in the wilds of pre-Revolutionary Pennsylvania. If that was where she really was. Surely all this detail couldn't be a dream.

But to accept the alternative . . .

"Could you show me where I will stay?" she continued. "I haven't any other clothes, of course, but maybe I could freshen up a little anyway." Perhaps she could even find something resembling a bathroom, if any such thing existed. If not, then what? Outhouses? Chamber pots?

He pointed to the smaller of the two log structures. "You'll stay there. In the stable."

Picturing a bed of straw beneath a horse's hoofs, Mariah was horrified. "But—"

"You wished for me to hire you, did you not?"

She nodded slowly. Her insides roiled and churned as though caught in an electric blender. No, not electric. Not here.

"That is where servants stay." With that, he abruptly

walked off. He paused outside the stone house to look back at her.

She refused to give him the satisfaction of acting as miserable as she felt. Instead, she saluted jauntily.

His scowl seemed angry. No, furious. Despite the distance now between them, she felt like flinching, but she didn't. She hadn't intended to provoke him but had succeeded all the same.

She recalled, belatedly, the story of the screenplay Thorn and his unfortunate experience at Fort Pitt. If this Thorn's background was similar, the emotional wounds of his military history were still too raw to be trifled with. He would hardly welcome a satiric salute. Her lack of tact, though this time unintentional, had shone through.

He entered the stone house, slamming the door behind him.

With a devastated sigh, Mariah looked around. How was she to survive this? She couldn't quite believe it, yet she seemed to be caught in what appeared to be a primitive past. Her sole company was this ill-tempered man whose only resemblance to the troubled but heroic Thorn she'd admired from the screenplay was his gorgeous appearance.

There had been times in her childhood when she'd lived in virtual hovels, but at least they'd been modern hovels, with electricity and running water, which she apparently wouldn't find here. And she'd made sure every place she lived was spotlessly clean, despite . . .

No, she'd put all that behind her long ago, had built a wonderful life for herself.

Until now.

Now, she had nowhere to go—except the quarters Thorn had designated. With slow, weary steps, she trudged toward the stables. Her head still ached, and the adrenaline she'd felt since her adventure had begun seemed to drain out of her all at once, leaving her limp and exhausted.

As she expected, the inside of the stable was dark and gloomy. The few windows had no glass but, instead, some kind of paper plastered over them, letting in scant light. There were stalls on both sides, with hay strewn on the wooden floor. Only three of the dozen were occupied by horses that stamped and made snorting noises as her steps resounded behind them. The place smelled . . . well, like a stable.

Mariah wanted to sink to the floor and cry. But what good would that do? Instead, she decided to find the most desirable corner of this horrible building and stake it out for herself.

At the end of the stalls was an archway. She went through it and found herself in a hall lined with four wooden doors. The one on her right was locked, but the others were open. The three rooms were small, and only one was fully furnished. It contained a bed covered with a handmade quilt, a commode on which stood a basin with a pitcher beside it, and a wooden clothes tree. It was clearly a bedroom. Maybe even *her* bedroom, a servant's quarters in the stable.

Not exactly a suite at the Hilton, but it was better than sleeping in a pile of soiled straw. Even better, in some respects, than a twentieth-century hovel. And at least here, things seemed quiet. Peaceful.

She'd manage. No matter what, she'd manage.

If only she understood what had happened to her.

"Mademoiselle!"

Startled, Mariah sat up, blinking in the soft light. Where was she? Oh, yes—at Thorn's inn. In the room in back of the stable.

Sometime, if she could believe her senses, in the past.

"Mademoiselle?" The raspy masculine voice that had awakened her spoke again, and she stared at the form in the doorway. She couldn't make out his features, but the man seemed shorter, more squat than Thorn. And Thorn had not spoken French to her.

"Yes?" she replied warily, still groggy and light-headed.

"You are resting in the wrong place, mademoiselle."

Her heart sank. Maybe she was, in fact, to sleep with the horses. "I—I'm sorry. I—" She rose quickly, realizing in dismay that, on top of everything else that had occurred in the past hours, she had been tired enough to collapse onto the bed still wearing her snug, damp dress. At least, she noted in relief, it had almost dried. There was a damp spot on the wool blanket on which she'd slept, though. She hoped she hadn't ruined the bed beneath. Quickly, she pulled the blanket off and began folding it. The area beneath it seemed dry, thank heavens.

"I am René," the man continued, helping her fold the blanket. "I help out here. Come, I will take you to the guest house."

She still couldn't make out his face in the dimness, but he seemed small and burly, and he spoke with a growl.

"And you'll show me what I'm supposed to do there?" Her confusion grew. She had thought he would show her where she was really to sleep.

"Do?" The man sounded confused. Perhaps his English was not good.

"Put me to work. *Le travail.*" One good thing about her scattered childhood was that she had learned a smattering of different languages. One bad thing was that she'd acquired no fluency in any of them.

"Work?" His tone was horrified. "You do not work here."

"I do now." Mariah sighed despite herself. "Mr. Thorn hired me."

"But—" That was all he said, and then he was gone. Mariah heard his heavy footfalls echo through the stable. Slowly, she followed. She was still tired, but she had a bargain to keep.

Assuming all this was real.

When she reached the cleared area outside the stable, she noted that daylight was waning. She wondered how long she'd been in the past, how long she'd slept. As a busy film executive, she'd been a slave to time. Her wrist had invariably been shackled by the bonds of a watch.

But now she could only guess at the hour, and minutes seemed irrelevant.

She didn't want to just stand there. Since she couldn't go to Thorn's house, she first visited the small structure that was clearly an outhouse. Then she headed toward the largest log building, which she assumed was the guest house.

Before she reached it, footsteps thudded behind her. She turned. The short man had come back. In the sunlight, his looks startled her. He had odd, toadlike features, with a wide mouth and large, protruding eyes beneath jutting brows. Mariah did not recall a similar character from the screenplay. "Thorn says that you indeed work here now." He did not sound pleased. "Come with me, *Anglaise.*" He practically spat the last word.

Mariah hesitated at his apparent venom. "Oh, I'm not English," she said as pleasantly as she could muster. "I'm American."

"Of course you are, now that the French have ceded this territory to *Les Anglais.*" He walked toward the guest house, and she hurried to catch up with him. He wasn't much taller than she and his legs were short, so she had no trouble matching his strides.

"No," she replied, "I mean I was born in the United States."

He stopped again and stared at her, incredulity bulging his eyes even further. "Pardon?"

She lowered her eyes for a moment as she thought fast. If she was when and where she suspected she was, there were no states, and there was nothing united about the colonies. "The colonies, I mean. I was born in . . . in Maryland," she fabricated. "I consider myself a native, no matter what my family's heritage."

"Commendable," he said, although he did not sound convinced. "In any event, Thorn says you must stay, and so you must. You were asleep in the right room. And soon I will give you some duties." There was a gleam in his strange eyes, as though he were contemplating the worst chores to hand to her.

No doubt at the direction of his boss, Thorn.

René took her through a wooden door in the back of the guest house. "Here is the kitchen," he said. It was like no kitchen she had ever seen except in films. There were no familiar appliances, no cheerful tilework or vinyl. Instead, the large room was drab and dark, constructed of the same mostly natural materials she had seen before. One wall was covered by a huge brick-and-stone fireplace adorned with a variety of alcoves and metal shelves and hooks. Heavy wooden tables were scattered throughout, and pots, pans and strings of dried food hung from thick ceiling beams. The plastered walls were stained and greasy. A waxy paper hung in the few open windows, dimming the sunlight, and open shutters hung on the wall beside them.

Mariah looked at the wood plank floor, trying not to show how heartsick she felt. Though she'd moved around a lot, she had taught herself to be a good cook—with food processor, gas range, double oven and microwave. She hadn't the slightest idea how to put together a meal here.

Maybe she could get René to relegate her to upstairs maid.

As though he read her mind, he said, "Come. I will show you the rest first." He led her from the kitchen.

The remainder of the inn's first floor consisted of a huge common room that smelled of old beer and burnt wood. Mariah had to squint in the darkness to make out its contents. Though the glass-free windows were not covered with coated paper, the waning light of day hardly lit the place. The walls were the bare insides of the mud-daubed logs. One contained a smaller fireplace than the kitchen's. Primitive tables and chairs were scattered throughout, made of scraps of logs nailed together haphazardly, with patches of bark still remaining. Her footsteps and René's pounded on the floor's rough planking. On the floor were a couple of brass spittoons.

The most amazing thing to Mariah was that, in the middle of all this rusticity, a surprisingly civilized-looking bar ran along one wall. Its surface was smooth and polished, of a dark, shining wood that looked like mahogany. No stools squatted before it; apparently Thorn's bar patrons were expected to stand. Behind it were rows of antique, thick blown-glass bottles.

No, Mariah amended—here they would be new bottles.

"Follow, please," René continued. Mariah complied, and he led her up the wooden stairs along one wall. The second floor consisted of two large rooms, both strewn with beds no larger than cots. In the corners of each were piles of neatly folded blankets.

Mariah felt shocked. "Travelers have no private quarters?"

René laughed. "If they expect luxury in the wilderness, mademoiselle, they should not be in the wilderness!"

Mariah realized then that Thorn had done her a favor by relegating her to the stable. There, she had her own room.

She had, indeed, misjudged him.

Turning to head back downstairs, she found Thorn standing behind her. She started; she hadn't heard him arrive. Glancing down, she noticed again his hand-sewn leather moccasins. She'd heard that Indians could move silently in such footwear. Obviously Thorn could, too.

She'd have to watch her back around him.

"Has René given you your chores yet?" he asked as the Frenchman preceded them down the stairs. Thorn's rich, throaty voice sounded less cold, more friendly.

"Not yet." She smiled. Though he didn't return the gesture, his brown eyes, too, seemed warmer than they had earlier. Maybe, Mariah thought, he wasn't so far from the Thorn of the story. That Thorn had become friends with Matilda almost immediately.

And Mariah sorely needed a friend here, wherever and whenever she was.

"I do not yet know how many we will be for supper," René said as he led her into the kitchen. "I began a stew hours ago over a small fire so it could simmer nicely, but the fire has gone out. Me, I left someone else in charge of tending it while I went to pick mushrooms—" He glared at Thorn, who had followed them into the kitchen. Thorn merely regarded him mildly, but Mariah imagined what he was thinking. If he'd been here minding the fire instead of saving her, the fire would not have gone out. "Perhaps mademoiselle could start the fire again," René continued.

"Fine," agreed Thorn.

"Sure," Mariah said, nervously pushing her hair back from her face. Her heart sank. She stared at the men's retreating backs as they left her alone in the large, intimidating room.

Oh, she'd been a Girl Scout once, for a short while, in one of the many places she'd lived as a child. Had it been Albany? Alabama? She couldn't remember. But it was one of the happier memories of her childhood.

Now and then, as an adult, she'd stayed in resorts where she had lit fires in her room. But many of them had been equipped with gas jets. Had matches even been invented in this time? What would she do if they hadn't?

She gamely approached the huge fireplace. Sure enough, a huge cauldron hung from a system of ornate metal bars right over a pile of ashes and half-burned wood. Interestingly, the support bar seemed hinged. Using a metal tool that looked designed for such things, Mariah pulled out the bar till it was perpendicular to its original position. The pot dangled from another bar hanging from the first, and heat radiated from it. The fire must not have been out for too long. Maybe there were some embers she could encourage to burn again. . . . But when Mariah prodded the ashes and wood with a poker, she saw not even the slightest glow.

She looked around. From a rack beside the stonework, she picked up first a couple of large pieces, then some smaller ones. Maneuvering around the hot wood still lying there, she laid a fire in the best manner she could remember.

Working in her long skirt was awkward at first, as she stooped, rose, then stooped again, but she soon forgot about it. She took her time and was finally pleased with the careful pyramid of wood. But now what?

Near the wood pile was a small metal box. Might it contain matches? No, just a piece of what appeared to be steel and a rock. She put it down again and, feeling frustrated, turned to hunt again for a way to light the fire.

She nearly bumped into Thorn's solid, muscular frame. "Oh!" she exclaimed, retreating a step, but not before she had taken a pleasing whiff of soft leather and wood smoke. She realized that was the closest she had been to Thorn since meeting him.

He'd crept up on her silently yet again, damn him! Any

warmth she'd seen in his brown eyes had been replaced with scorn, and he crossed his arms impatiently. "I gather, Miss Walker," he said, "that you are more used to depending on servants than on being one."

She opened her mouth to protest. She was as self-reliant as anyone, not the pampered fool his gruff tone implied. But she stopped herself. In a way he was correct, though the servants on which she'd relied had been mechanical devices. "If you'll show me what to do," she said curtly, "I'll know the next time."

Without another word, he picked up some straw from a pile Mariah hadn't noticed, in a corner behind the fireplace. He scattered shafts throughout the wood Mariah had arranged so carefully, then made a neat pile on top of some small kindling pieces.

Next, he picked up the metal container. "This," he said, as though speaking to a not-very-bright child, "is a tinderbox." He lifted out the metal piece and struck it against the stone, creating sparks. Then he handed it to Mariah. "Here."

Smoothing her bedraggled pink skirt beneath her knees, she knelt back down on the hearth. She glanced up at him just once, wishing she could capture and use the sparks flying from her eyes. Instead, she turned back to the small pile of hay he had laid and went to work.

The minuscule beads of fire she created did not immediately ignite the straw. In fact, it took forever before she got the tiniest thread of smoke. She blew carefully on it—and it went out. Frustrated, she tried again. And again.

She heard Thorn thump from the room. The noise had to be intentional, since he was so prone to sneaking. She turned to stick out her tongue at his retreating back, then returned to her work.

Eventually, her efforts paid off. The small heap of straw ignited, setting the kindling wood on fire and then, finally, thanks to her gentle blowing and prodding with a stick, the larger pieces.

Mariah rocked back onto her heels with a self-satisfied smile, ignoring her stiffness. Success!

"Congratulations," said a deep, masculine voice from behind her.

She rose swiftly. He'd done it again! Thorn had crept, unnoticed, into the room.

She didn't react, only continued to smile smugly. "It's a fine fire, isn't it?"

He had removed his fringed jacket and now wore a plain woven shirt above his breeches. Its looseness did nothing to hide the fact that the man beneath was brawny, for it hung from wide shoulders, bulged at his thick chest, and flowed toward the narrowing at the waistband of his pants. "Yes," he agreed, "a fine fire. Now, come. I will show you another of your responsibilities."

She wanted to ignore him. He didn't own her!

But, in a way, he did. If she was truly in the time she suspected, servants were practically chattels of their masters.

With a sigh, she followed.

His stride was quick and sure as he led her through a door in the kitchen and outside toward the stable. She bet he was going to have her muck the stalls.

Instead, he took her to a tiny stone building she had not noticed before. "This," he said, "is where I cure meat." He opened the door—and a gust of heat hit Mariah in the face. She peered in, and the perfectly delicious, salty aroma of the cured meat hanging from the ceiling and stretched out on rows of metal racks reminded her she was hungry.

A small wooden barrel of what appeared to be salt sat in one corner. Mariah immediately noticed a small fire burning in a pit in the center of the room. "This fire," Thorn said, "never goes out. We all keep an eye on it. You will see to it, too. And you can always bring a faggot from here to light other fires at the compound, should they die."

Mariah's fists balled in frustration. Damn the man! Why hadn't he shown her this in the first place? It would have saved her an hour of back-straining labor, playing with that fool tinderbox and straw.

She opened her mouth to complain—and noticed the twinkle in those enigmatic brown eyes. "Have you a problem, Miss Walker?"

"No." She had, after all, learned a valuable survival tool if she were truly in pioneer times—how to start a fire.

She'd learned something else, too. Despite his normally remote demeanor, Thorn had a sense of humor—warped though it might be.

She smiled again, though this time perhaps a bit grimly. "Thank you for everything today, Mr. Thorn."

"You are welcome, Miss Walker." Raising his broad chin almost pugnaciously, he opened his mouth as if he had something to add but quickly closed it again.

He turned, and Mariah found herself alone in the smokehouse.

Chapter Five

René Lafont leaned his elbows on the wooden supper table. It was fortunate, he thought, that the inn had but one guest that evening.

Not that the woman his employer had brought home with him was unwilling to work, but she was amazingly inept.

Thorn seemed not to notice, or at least not to care. At his usual place across from René, the large man listened quietly to their talkative guest, occasionally taking a bite of rabbit stew.

René had taken much effort to make Thorn join his guests for meals, a gesture any inn's host should make. Thorn, he preferred his solitude. Why, he had asked, should he ruin the appetites of the persons who paid for meals by sitting with them?

Yet René had proven himself right. More guests returned now that Thorn supped with them—though he mostly remained silent. Perhaps it was the curiosity of being with a host whose sad story still resounded in this area, who could tell? René kept conversations going, except when something captured Thorn's interest enough to make him join in.

Now, the golden-haired woman named Mariah Walker entered from the kitchen with a tray, shuffling across the wooden floor with her dark boots. She was like no woman René had seen before, perhaps shameless, perhaps ignorant of what was proper. Her blond hair hung in loose waves at her shoulders, and she wore no cap. She was still dressed in the crumpled pink gown she had worn earlier that day. It clung as though it had shrunken when wet.

Ah, perhaps she intended to serve more than food! But that was not Thorn's purpose. Though René's employer had not intended at first to run an inn, now that he did, it would remain respectable. Thorn would allow nothing less.

Still, this Mademoiselle Walker was pretty, with her smooth, clear features, a petite, perfect nose, a rosy mouth to entice the most celibate of men—though such were seldom found here on the frontier. At least not by choice, though often, alas, by the lack of women. If only this one did not frown so much when she thought no one watched. Like now, when Thorn seemed attentive to the gabbing of their guest. But René saw him look beneath his lowered eyelids toward the woman. René knew Thorn well, but even he could not always interpret his thoughts.

"The settler problem must be solved," their guest insisted. He was a scout from the army, sent to find an area downriver where a new settlement was said to have been begun secretly.

This was good. Thorn was interested in visitors who spoke of the issues of the day. Sometimes, he even responded.

"Do they not know," continued the man, "that it is illegal to take lands farther west? Stupid as well. The Indians have been told there will be no more settlements, and they will enforce that edict even if we do not. It was for the safety of those in legal settlement areas that the law was enacted."

The woman said, "Then there is a law against moving west?"

The scout, whose weathered skin and squinty eyes bespoke a life outdoors, turned to her in surprise. "Do you mean, living out here, you have not heard of the Proclamation Line? The government established it near five years ago."

The woman turned nearly as pink as her dress. "I—I only

recently moved here.'' She busied herself straightening the food on her tray.

The scout went on. ''Only Indians are to be allowed to settle west of the line, miss, to maintain the peace.'' He hesitated. ''The actual line is not being maintained, but no settlement is allowed west of *this* area.''

She seemed not to care for the wilderness, nor to know how to dwell within it. René wondered why she was here. Perhaps he would get her to talk. He himself liked to talk, and sometimes to listen.

With Thorn, he usually had only the opportunity to speak, for his employer kept his own counsel.

The man looked at Thorn. ''I saw you are constructing a palisade wall. Have you Indian troubles?''

Thorn did, at least, respond to direct questions—usually. René relaxed now as his employer replied, ''Not lately.''

''Were you affected by Pontiac's uprising those five years back?'' The man was persistent, and René feared Thorn would leave the table.

But, no. ''I was burned out then,'' he said, the catch in his voice showing his irritation with the guest's prying.

The woman stared in what looked like surprise. Did she not know?

''I rebuilt everything quickly,'' Thorn continued, ''except that I am just now getting to the palisade.''

René was amazed by the length of this speech to the stranger. Thorn seldom kept conversation going so long.

''I'd of thought it should come first,'' the guest said.

Thorn drew in his breath audibly, causing René to cringe. ''Perhaps,'' he agreeed, his teeth gritted. ''But though its appearance makes guests feel more secure, one did not prevent the fire last time.'' He paused, apparently deciding upon a distraction, which he quickly found. René watched him look from the guest's empty plate to the woman, who stood watching.

She grew red, whether from embarrassment or anger René could not tell. ''May I serve you gentlemen any more?'' Her voice was clear and soft. The words were correct. But there was a muted defiance in her tone, as though she chafed at being a servant.

René did not think, either, that she was a suitable servant. She was too skinny, though her strength had not yet faltered. Worse, she seemed not to know the first thing about . . . well, anything.

René had peered into the doorway earlier to see the woman's strange inability to light a fire. Later, although she did not seem surprised that water had to be drawn from the nearby stream, she had stared at René when he'd bade her fetch some as though *he* should have been the one to go. She had fumbled with the cooking utensils about the fire and acted as though she had never set foot in a kitchen before. An upper-class *Anglaise,* René thought with distaste. One he would never have thought Thorn would wish to have around except to take money from as a paying guest.

On the other hand, perhaps this was a form of Thorn's revenge—allowing one like those who had ill used him to become his servant.

René had yet to hear the story of her hiring from Thorn.

He knew he might never hear it, at least not from his employer.

But there was a look in Thorn's eye when he glanced at this woman that René had never seen before. He was not certain yet whether this was good or bad.

But he would not let this woman hurt his friend Thorn. Thorn had been hurt enough.

Carrying a candle, Mariah dragged herself back to her room in the stable that night, weariness causing her steps to falter.

Despite the darkness illuminated only by the tiny flame she nurtured, she found the betty lamp where René had said it would be, on the edge of the small table that also held an earthenware pitcher and a washbasin. Careful not to spill any oil, she hooked the lamp by its strap to a nail protruding from the wall. Then, with her candle, she lit the edge of the rag wick that hung over the side of the lamp's irregular-shaped metal pan, the way René had shown her. The room brightened immediately—though far from the way a single electric lightbulb would have illuminated it. The burning oil smelled foul! Probably the grease of some deceased animal she didn't even want to think about.

She blew out the candle to conserve it. Then she sat on the edge of the bed. It made a crunching sound, and there was no give to it, as though the mattress was packed with unyielding straw. She hadn't noticed much about it before, when she'd collapsed in exhaustion upon it.

Now, she placed one elbow on her knee and rested her chin in her hand. She felt stiff and uncomfortable in her clothing, hardly able to breathe. She wished she had something fresh to change into for bed. Instead, she'd have to strip down to her underwear—or whatever you called it in this time. The light in the outhouse had been too dim for her to tell for sure what she wore beneath her dress.

This time. She'd all but given up imagining she was lying somewhere in a coma, dreaming all this. Her headache had at last disappeared, for one thing. More telling was the fact that there was simply too much detail, and not even the smallest incongruity.

She was in eighteenth-century Pennsylvania, just like Matilda in the screenplay.

"With Thorn," she said aloud, then stopped, listening. Had anyone heard her?

She had learned that René's room was across the hall, but she'd left him still talking to Thorn and their guest. As far as she knew, she was the only one in the stable. Except for the horses, of course. "Didn't mean to slight you guys," she called out. But she didn't even hear them stamping in return.

She thought again of Thorn. Matilda's Thorn had been a brave, romantic hero who had leapt from the forest to save her from the scoundrels who'd kidnapped her. Scoundrels who had looked like the ruffians they were, even when Matilda had been foolish enough to hire them.

Mariah's scoundrels, though, had resembled gentlemen. They claimed to have been hired by Pierce, curse his nasty heart, and probably had been. How else had they known his name and hers?

Pierce had put her here. She wasn't certain how, but she

knew that he had orchestrated this entire mess. But he'd fouled it up. In the screenplay, Thorn had been a willing hero.

But not the real Thorn.

He had, of course, come through in the end. But only after she'd tried to help herself—and had offered to pay him.

Matilda had intended to come to Thorn's inn to work. Mariah had no choice, not if she wanted to pay her Thorn for saving her.

Her Thorn? Hardly! Sure, he was as gorgeous a specimen of manhood as she had ever seen, with those flashing brown eyes, that physique that strained his clothes, screaming of the muscles that must be hidden beneath.

And now and then he'd even acted human. Sympathetic. Kind.

But mostly he turned his back on her whenever she needed help. Teased her in her neediness.

Refused to let her even think about relying on him.

No, he wasn't *her* anything. The only kind of man she could ever be attracted to would be one she could count on—if there were such a male creature.

Which she doubted. She'd tried once to forgive the male species for including her father among them. She'd gone so far as to get engaged to a man she'd thought broke the mold, and look where that had led: more hurt, more distrust, more certainty that men were undependable.

Well, just in case there *were* a reliable man somewhere, sometime, he certainly wasn't this Thorn.

What next? she wondered. So far, her life here had paralleled the screenplay, though it hadn't followed exactly. In the screenplay, there'd been Indians and settlers and—

That was it! She had to get organized. If she'd been in her time, she'd have grabbed her laptop computer and begun a new file. Now she needed a piece of paper and a pencil.

Had pencils even been invented yet? A pen, then; she'd seen pictures of colonials wielding quills.

She rose, lit the candle again, doused the betty lamp and hurried from her room.

* * *

Thorn had just doused the light in the kitchen when he heard a noise outside, much too loud to be Indians or any other man or beast trying to raid his inn. René had gone upstairs to see to their guest's comfort and had doubtless become involved in a protracted conversation.

It had to be the woman. Miss Walker.

Mariah.

He should not think of her by her first name. He should not think of her at all. Had she not proven she was some pampered female from the east who had no business on the frontier?

There had been that other pampered woman from the east who had needed his help. And look what he had done to her. . . .

The wooden door banged open. In walked Mariah, light from her candle flickering softly on her lovely, pale face. Her hand was cupped about the flame, as though it were something to be protected, fragile.

Like her.

He laughed aloud. No, whatever this woman was, she had shown her bravery against those men who had come after her. She might need protection, but she was not fragile.

"Oh!" The woman gasped at his laugh. She started—and the flame of her candle went out. "Now look what you've done." Her voice sounded irritated.

"You know where to get more fire." He stood unmoving in the dark. "Or to start your own." He knew his tone was belligerent, inviting her to argue. Or to complain about the way he'd teased her earlier.

Instead, she laughed. "Yes, I suppose I do, though I wish I could see where I was going now. Is this a test?"

He said nothing, though in a way he supposed it was. So far, she had passed it admirably. Instead of shouting with the outrage of the spoiled rich woman he knew she was, she had laughed at herself. And when she edged past him, apparently following a faint glow from beneath the door into the common room, he held his breath. She probably did not know how closely she had drawn near him.

Or perhaps she did.

The light in the kitchen increased slightly as she opened the common room door. In a minute, she returned to the kitchen with her candle lit once more. She carried a second one as well.

She handed the extra candle to him. "For you," she said. "Unless you prefer the darkness."

He had, he thought. Before.

He took the candle from her and placed it in a holder on a worktable. He sat on a bench, swinging his leg over it easily. "I thought you had retired, Miss Walker," he said. "What brings you back to the kitchen? Have we not given you enough chores to allow you to sleep easily? I am certain we can think of more."

"I appreciate your concern." Her tone was dry. "No matter how tired I am, I doubt I'll fall asleep easily tonight. But that's fine," she added hastily. "It's just that a lot has happened, and I'm afraid there's more to come." She took a place on another bench. Her face seemed shadowed by more than candlelight.

"Would you care to discuss it?" He didn't want to know. Not really. He had ample troubles of his own without asking to hear another's.

Still, he felt disappointed when she said, "Thanks, but no. I've a lot to think about, but I need to sort it through myself. It would help, though, if I could borrow paper and a pen."

"Then you are literate?" He heard the surprise in his own voice. Many women in this new land knew nothing of reading or writing but were instructed only in female pursuits—the very things of which Mariah Walker seemed ignorant. In addition to the fire-laying episode earlier, Thorn had heard from René of all the lessons he had had to impart to her in the art of setting a simple meal on the table.

She responded with indignation. "More than you, you—" He heard her catch herself, saw her shake her head.

She thought *him* illiterate. He nearly laughed aloud. The many scholarly tutors from his youth would not, however, have been amused.

"I'm sorry," she continued. "That won't help, will it? Yes, I am literate, Mr. Thorn. I read and write quite well.

I'm also skilled in accounting, scheduling, staffing, screenplay evaluation, location scouting and other aspects of film production management, though I realize you don't understand half of what I'm saying. Never mind. Just remember that if you need help in any of the three *r*'s—reading, 'riting and 'rithmetic—I am sure I can be of assistance.'' By the time she had finished speaking, she sounded quite fatigued. Or was she dispirited?

He did not like the idea of her sorrow—but he disliked his own confusion at her words even more. ''What is this 'film production'?'' he demanded. ''And some kind of play evaluation? Location scouting I understand, although I did not follow what you meant by it. Did you travel west to scout a new location for settlement?''

''Not exactly.'' She sighed, running one hand through wavy hair that appeared golden in the faint light. It hung just below her shoulders, shorter than he had ever seen the unbound hair of a woman, and he wondered if she had been ill. He had yet to see her cover it with a cap, but of course she had, for now, no clothing but that on her back. It was unusual hair, but it became her, framing her face. That beautiful face.

She interrupted his thoughts. ''Please, just forget everything I said. I know it didn't make sense. It doesn't even make sense to me right now. But could I borrow that pen and paper, please?''

''You do not ask for much,'' he said, not hiding his sarcasm. Beautiful she might be, but spoiled. ''A woman of wealth from the city may think nothing of such things, but they are precious here. And scarce.''

She looked abashed. ''I'm sorry. I didn't think . . . I'll pay you for them, if you have any. Just add them to what I owe you.''

''Fine.'' Not that he would ever charge her for them. But the woman seemed to lack sense, and that annoyed him. ''I will return with them shortly.''

He had to go to his house to get them. The night was clear and cooler than the day had been. He found the evening air quite pleasant. He could have taken his time sauntering through the compound, obtaining the items Mariah wanted to borrow and returning to the kitchen.

Instead, he found he wanted to hurry back to her company.

When he returned, she was still sitting where he had left her, on the bench by the worktable. She stared, apparently unseeing, toward a dark wall. In the flickering candlelight, he saw a small tear at the corner of her eye. As he watched, it rolled slowly down her face.

He stopped breathing for an instant, then made himself exhale in a snort of disgust. He didn't care, he told himself. He had no interest in finding out what made this pretty, spoiled woman unhappy. Decisively, onto the table before her, he placed the pen, the bottle of ink he kept mixed for his own use and the blank piece of paper he had torn from the inn's ledger journal. "Here, Miss Walker," he said sternly.

"Thank you, Mr. Thorn." Her voice sounded distant. Moist. Lost.

Taking no time to think, he suddenly found himself moving as though someone else had control of his body. Bending to kneel beside her, he said, "Miss Walker—Mariah—tell me what bothers you. Please." He touched her hand as it lay on her lap. It was warm and very soft. A lady's hand.

"You wouldn't believe it. *I* don't even believe it." She stood abruptly, pulling away. "Thanks again, Mr. Thorn." She moved as though to scoop up the items he had placed on the table. "Have a good night." Her voice was thick, as though she were swallowing cotton, and as she turned away he could see that she was hiding yet more tears.

Before he could consider what he was doing, he had taken Mariah Walker into his arms.

"Hey." Her voice was still uneven, but she pushed against his chest. Good. Perhaps he was making her angry enough to forget her sorrow.

She was much stronger than she appeared. Her thinness was deceptive.

Very deceptive, he learned, as he found he did not wish to let her go. Instead, he pulled her tightly to him. Her breasts were full and firm, and the feel of them against his chest caused his breathing to tighten.

As did his trousers.

She had been traveling unchaperoned, and yet she had behaved as though she were a lady, with all apparent morality. He expected her to continue to struggle, to shove him away. But as he lowered his head toward hers, she grew very still.

"Oh, Thorn," she murmured. And he was lost.

His kiss was gentle at first, testing how receptive she was. How receptive *he* was. He could not recall the last time he had kissed a woman.

It no longer mattered.

His lips moved against hers, ever so softly rubbing her smooth lower lip with his own. He let his tongue caress her ever so gently, taste her. She was salty from her tears, yet sweet, very sweet, and the small sip made him yearn for more. The smoky scent of the fire she had tended clung to her dress and was somehow intoxicating—or was it her own sweet and wholly feminine scent that so affected him?

He was unsure who moved first to deepen the kiss, for she was far from shy, pressing her own mouth against him, letting her tongue search out his. He teased it back inside her mouth so his could follow it, playing small, darting, erotic games with it until he felt himself throb below.

More tightly he pressed against her until he was certain she, too, could feel the growing tautness of him. His hands strayed along her back, finding the sweet curve of her buttocks. He molded them in his fingers, pressing her ever closer until the pressure at his groin made him shudder. She moaned against his mouth, and he felt his knees weaken.

"Come," he whispered against her. Somehow, despite the craving that yearned for instant slaking, he would have to make it to his cabin. With her. His Mariah.

He grew suddenly still. *His?* She was not his. No woman could be, not ever.

He meant to pull away from her gently, but instead she was the one to draw quickly back. "What are you doing?"

she whispered. Her voice sounded scandalized, and he was unsure if she spoke to him or herself.

"I am giving you another test," he said, knowing how cruel his words sounded. She had done him no harm. But the pain from the past that welled up once more inside him required venting, no matter who else was injured. "This time, I am not so certain how you are succeeding. We have yet to find that out, do we not?"

"Not with me, you don't!"

Grabbing her candle, Mariah Walker threw open the kitchen door and ran outside.

Though Mariah knew she'd run in the wrong direction for the stable, she didn't veer off when she reached the forest.

She had to get away from this place, this horrible, backwoods inn in the middle of nowhere. In 1760s Pennsylvania. In the middle of a nightmare.

She had to get away from Thorn.

For the smallest moment, when he'd held her tightly against his hard, substantial body, had kissed her, she'd allowed herself to feel cared for. Protected and wanted by the man who had seemed so caring—in the screenplay.

But that wasn't the real Thorn.

This Thorn had played games with her mind, turning away from her when she most needed help.

And now he had played games with her body.

She heard dead leaves crunch beneath her feet. Somewhere, she realized, her candle had gone out, but the moon's light sprinkled through the trees, illuminating a frightening path through thick, grasping branches.

"Why?" she moaned aloud. She heard an echoing *whooo* from an owl. Frightened, she missed her next step and crashed to the forest floor, landing on her knees.

The undergrowth here was thick, but not thick enough. Pain shot through her knees. When she tried to rise, it wasn't physical pain that stopped her, but anguish. She was breathing too hard, fighting to keep from crying.

She turned to sit, to catch her breath, to calm herself. She brushed twigs and leaves from her wrinkled skirt, keeping her legs straight while the ache in her knees subsided. She clasped her hands together.

Somehow, impossibly, she was trapped in the past.

But why?

Oh, yes. How could she have forgotten, even for a moment, those awful words that had haunted her forever? The words Pierce had thrown at her as he'd bewitched her and sent her back to the past. "You must right a grievous wrong."

What did it mean? She still didn't know.

Pierce had added two more words that made the command even more unnerving: "my daughter." Was she related to that horrible man who'd put her into this predicament?

And if he'd done this on purpose, why hadn't he written the screenplay so it would follow real life here?

Why was this Thorn so different?

She took a deep breath to calm herself, though she heard the quiver as she exhaled. The cool evening air smelled clean, fresh. Her chest muscles remained so taut that she kept shuddering. But she knew she'd do herself no good if she gave in to hysterics. She'd force herself somehow to be patient, to see what happened. To manage her life here as best she could. It shouldn't be too difficult, if she recalled the episodes in the screenplay.

Of course, even if her memory were perfect—which it wasn't—she had learned already that things here didn't follow the script exactly. Plus, the screenplay, as all screenplays, had been a series of connected scenes, not a moment-by-moment replica of its characters' lives. A lot went on here that wasn't contemplated by the sketchy writing.

Still, since some things happened as written, whatever she recalled would help her survive. Maybe she'd even discover a way to leave this primitive time and return to her own.

She'd left the paper, pen and ink in the kitchen, darn it! Well, she'd caught her breath. She was calmer now—at least a little. She'd get those objects, then go back to her room and jot down all she could recall.

Except, after she rose and started back in the direction in

which she believed the inn to be, she realized almost immediately that nothing looked familiar.

She nearly cried aloud in frustration. On top of everything else, she was lost.

She recalled then an episode in the screenplay in which Matilda, too, had become lost in the forest at night. She'd been terrified, particularly when she'd begun to hear all the frightening sounds of an unfamiliar woodlands.

Sounds like those now surrounding Mariah. More owls. The cries of other creatures she could not identify. Moanings. Rustlings.

Oh, dear heavens! The memory of what had happened to Matilda suddenly filled her mind. The screenplay heroine had been set upon by wolves.

That was when Mariah heard the first howl. . . .

Chapter Six

Wolves!

The night was too dark, despite the leaf-spattered moonlight, for Mariah to see their approach, but she knew they were coming. Swiftly. Inexorably.

She heard their footfalls in the underbrush, their ugly, harsh growling as they approached. And then another howl, taken up by two of the beasts. Three. How many?

Mariah quaked as she hugged the rough bark of a tree trunk for support. Surely they wouldn't hurt her. Weren't wolves just like overgrown dogs?

Yes, but dogs that had not been tamed. Dogs in which the instinct for domination had not been subdued.

Hungry, brutal dogs.

They couldn't be after her . . . could they? She recalled then her clumsiness in clearing the table. She'd spilled a little stew on her dress, then rinsed it off with water. She no longer smelled it, but maybe she smelled like food to the animals' keen sense of smell. Once they saw she was a human and not small game, they'd leave her alone.

She hoped.

Or had they another reason to come after her? Not that the reason mattered. Maybe their attack was somehow preordained from the screenplay.

What had Matilda done?

Waited for her Thorn, of course. He had come, for she could rely on him. He had beaten the brutes off, had saved her.

But this was an episode from the screenplay that would turn out differently in actuality. The real Thorn would not even know she was here. And even if he did, he would not come after her.

She had to save herself.

She looked around. She needed something to use as a weapon, something to fend them off.

There. A huge tree had fallen to the ground near her. She could make out its black outline in the gray light. Its trunk was a large, moldering shaft; most of its branches had rotted away. But there was one limb, a large one, leaning from the main hulk. It was attached now by the merest connection of torn wood.

Mariah ran toward it. She grabbed the branch. She tugged.

Its anchor to the trunk was stronger than it looked. "Please," she whispered, as though the inanimate object could respond.

She heard the wolves' heavy panting.

Mariah pulled again. Her hands gripped the roughness of the wood. Sharp edges of bark pierced her fingers and she nearly cried out, not only from the pain but because of what she was doing to her hands. But if she didn't get a weapon, more than her hands would be hurt.

No luck. In desperation, she stood on the log and bent the limb from one side to the other, pulling on it. Tugging. Almost crying in frustration.

There! With a snap, the large branch became hers.

Just in time, for there they were, three running animals, their eyes nearly glowing in their eagerness to reach her, their thin muzzles open and slavering, their tongues hanging out.

"Get away!" She whipped the branch toward them. It was heavy and irregular. She could barely hold it as it pulled her off balance. She twirled with the momentum, then pivoted back to face the beasts, afraid she'd left herself vulnerable for a vital instant.

They stopped, staring in uncertainty. Good! She'd show them who was master.

But as though they had anticipated her reaction, they began to fan out. "No!" Mariah shouted. More carefully, she swung her weapon toward one, then another, trying to herd them back together. To control them.

They would not be mastered so easily.

"Okay, fellows." Mariah's voice was shaky and shrill. "Go eat something your own size." Using her branch, she poked at the nearest wolf, a large, malevolent-looking creature. It growled, and Mariah reflexively drew back the stick.

Another circled behind her. She spun around. The third, too, was stalking her. She smelled their ugly, fetid breath. "Go away!" she cried. She was tiring. She could not hold them off like this all night.

Would they even leave her alone by the light of day?

Seeing a movement from the corner of her eye, she whirled, just as a wolf sprang at her. Holding the stick out as though it could protect her, she screamed.

The sound was joined by a loud blast from nearby.

The leaping wolf slumped, lifeless. The others scattered.

Gasping in relief, Mariah looked around. The tall, shadowed form of Thorn emerged from the trees, his long rifle cradled against his body.

She ran toward him, ready to throw herself into his arms in gratitude. But even with her eyes blurred from shock she saw him stiffen in the faint moonlight.

She stopped herself before she reached him. "Thank you." Her voice shook.

"I hunt a lot at night." His chin was raised, as though he dared her to contradict him. He hadn't, of course, come out here looking for her. He stared into the distance. "You should not come into the forest after dark, Miss Walker." His tone was wooden. "You can't rely on me to save you."

"Of course not," she said snappishly, anger overpowering her fear. "I'll be more careful next time."

He turned. She followed him silently, on wobbly legs, back toward the inn.

Exhausted, Mariah peeled off her wrinkled dress. Now, finally, she could make out what had been hidden in the outhouse's dimness. No wonder she'd felt so stiff and warm; she wore a corset contraption with stays beneath it, plus a chemise and petticoats. All were trimmed in lace.

She'd examine her outfit further tomorrow. Maybe even borrow some of René's clothes; Thorn's would be too large.

Would they be scandalized by her donning men's clothing? That wasn't done, she was sure, in this archaic time. Too bad. She couldn't wear that pink dress forever, and she'd no idea where to find more feminine attire.

Hearing footsteps outside, she started. A door was closed, and she realized she'd heard René going to bed. With her emotions still overwrought, she felt vulnerable dressed in only her undergarments. Tiptoeing barefoot, she tried her door. It was closed tightly but had no lock. Still, though René didn't seem to like her much, he was unlikely to molest her. Besides, despite Thorn's protestations of unreliability, she doubted he'd tolerate anyone bothering her at his inn.

She blew out her candle and lay down, her eyes wide in the darkness. Despite her fatigue, she couldn't sleep. Her head no longer hurt, but her thoughts battered her brain like a loop of endless film clips: Pierce. Pittsburgh. The Blockhouse and fort. The river rapscallions. Hiring on as a servant in Matilda's place.

And Thorn. His miserable, unanticipated attitude. His searing, startling kiss.

He was so different from the story version.

He was still gorgeous.

Something about him drew her. Something else repelled her.

He was unreliable.

The straw that managed to stick through the blanket scratched at her skin beneath her flimsy shift, and she moved around as her mind swirled till she found a tolerable position.

Her eyes finally closed.

* * *

A knock on her door awakened her. Startled, she sat up. She must have slept for a long while, for the sun streamed in through the room's small window. "Just a minute," she called. Dear heavens! Thorn would be furious that she'd overslept. Weren't servants supposed to rise at dawn to tend fires, cook breakfast, clean and do whatever else servants do?

Never mind that she often slept till ten or later in her own time—after staying up into the wee hours to work.

She didn't seem to be in her own time. And her work was to be done during the day.

Ignoring the corset, she threw her pink dress back on and was buttoning it over her chemise when she pulled open the door.

Thorn stood there. She didn't mean to smile at him, but no matter; her grin disappeared as his thick brows knotted and he frowned down at her. His dark, uneven hair hung against his face and shoulders in wet clumps; did people in these days take baths on awakening? His broad jaw looked set, as though he had locked it to keep from yelling at her, and she cringed despite herself at the thought.

"Sorry I overslept." She tried to sound nonchalant. "My only excuse is that yesterday was a big day. A lot happened. I'll just get ready and see what René wants me to do." She began to sling the heavy wood door shut in his face.

He blocked it with the toe of his moccasin, and she stopped pushing, not intending to hurt him. "Here." He lifted two sopping cloth bags from the floor and handed them to her.

"Th-thank you," she stammered. They appeared to be the bags that the vagabonds claimed had been left for her by Pierce. The bags those men had dumped into the river.

"You're welcome." He watched her with those cool brown eyes that so unnerved her.

Stopping herself from biting her lip, she asked levelly, "Is there anything else you want?"

Was that a twinkle in his eyes? Surely not. But a corner of his mouth seemed to lift as he said, "The kitchen fire needs tending.'' He turned and strode away, leaving her staring.

As Mariah freshened up, she thought of the previous night. Thank heavens her sleep had been untroubled. No voice had demanded that she right a grievous wrong.

With everything else, that would have been all she'd needed.

When she was ready, she carried the heavy, dripping bags with her outside. She set them on the ground outside the kitchen door and opened it. René had already hung a large kettle over a roaring fire. The entire kitchen was filled with a heavenly aroma of something hot and meaty cooking. Since it was too late to cook breakfast, Mariah assumed René was working on lunch.

''Sorry I'm late,'' she said.

René, kneading dough on one of the tables, looked at her with his large toad's eyes. He wore a wrinkled gray shirt with a stand-up collar. ''So am I, mademoiselle.'' His voice was stern. ''Perhaps you would like me to wait on you in your room.''

''Of course I would.'' She grinned at his glare. ''But instead, let me take over while you sit down. Put your feet up. Get used to giving me orders.''

His stare gave way to a smile. ''Ah, you are in a fine mood today, are you not, *Anglaise?*'' He called her that once more, although this time there was not the anger in the word she had heard before.

''Certainly, *Français.*'' Though she wasn't sure she'd gotten the form of the word correct, his smile widened. But he was right. She *was* in a good mood, without knowing why. Maybe because she was alive. Thanks to Thorn.

But despite his having saved her twice, she understood she could not rely on him.

She began kneading the soft, sticky bread dough. She'd made bread before in one of her early incarnations, and at least this part was familiar to her—a reminder of the too few pleasant memories of her youth. How they'd cook it without a gas oven, though . . .

"René, may I ask you a favor?"

At the hearth, he was stirring the kettle's contents with a long wooden spoon. The expression on his ugly round face grew suspicious. "What is that?"

"Mr. Thorn found my belongings. They'd been dumped into the river, and now everything needs to be washed."

She grimaced at his expression as he straightened. "And you wish me to wash your clothes, mademoiselle?"

"No, René," she said with a sigh. "Like everything else around here, I don't know how to do laundry. I want you to tell me how to do it. Maybe even show me on one garment. Then I'll know, and I'll do the rest myself. In my spare time—if you'll be so kind as to let me find some."

He seemed to relax. "Of course." He hesitated. "By the way, mademoiselle, Thorn said you left these here last night." He lifted the paper, quill pen and ink that Mariah had forgotten when she'd run from the kitchen.

"Yes," she said. "Thanks. I'll take them to my room later." She watched as he set them on a corner of a table. She certainly would remember them next time.

She'd wrack her brain all day as she performed mindless chores. By evening, surely she'd recall most of the episodes from the screenplay, which she could then jot down—and be prepared for. Without Thorn's help.

She worked hard for the rest of the morning, doing servant things. Amazing! She took orders instead of issuing them. More than once, she swallowed a sharp retort. René would never understand if she protested.

No, she was here as Matilda. And Matilda never complained.

Matilda! While forming the dough into loaflike shapes, Mariah thought once more about Matilda. Many other characters in the screenplay existed here. Did she? If so, where was the *real* Matilda, into whose life Mariah had so blithely slipped? Would she show up one day and oust the imposter? If so, what would happen to Mariah?

Yet another point of confusion now swirled about in Mariah's already overloaded mind as she prepared to place the bread dough in the stone oven.

* * *

The day was broken up by the serving of lunch. There were half a dozen guests for dinner, as René called the ample midday meal: a trader and two British officers with three of their men. René let Mariah serve them. "Pah!" he said as he helped her fill plates with the game stew she had smelled before. "It is not good for Thorn's business if I am in contact with the English; I run them off."

"Why?" Mariah asked, arranging filled plates on the tray that rested on one of the tables.

"Because they are English," he said, as though it explained everything.

"Wasn't the French and Indian War over a few years ago?" What year was it supposed to be here now? The screenplay took place in the mid-1760s, as she recalled.

"If that is what you call our war, yes, mademoiselle." He waved a wooden spoon in the air in irritation.

"Please call me Mariah," she insisted. "After most wars don't the hostilities cease?"

"The fighting, yes, Mariah," he agreed. "But not the ill feelings. I had many a comrade butchered by the English."

"And I'd imagine your group did some butchering of its own."

He turned a furious expression on her that slowly melted as he considered her words. "There are two sides to everything, are there not?" he replied. "But even though you are right, I do not forgive easily. My country had a right to expand here, to have trade routes, too. Now we are only in the north."

"If you feel that badly about it, why don't you go up north to . . ." She hesitated. Was the area called Canada now? "Or just go home to France?" She hefted the tray onto her shoulder and wiggled a bit to arrange its weight. Acting as a serving wench required strong muscles, she decided.

At least the work hadn't hurt her hands. Not yet, at least. And they'd seemed fine this morning, despite last night's grabbing of sharp tree bark.

"This is my home now," he said. "Remaining is my form of still waging war." He put up his stubby fingers at the look she tossed at him; she realized she must look horrified. "I kill no English, now, Mariah—unless they expire from my ill will."

She laughed and went to serve the guests.

Thorn was seated at the table with them, wearing a loose-sleeved ecru shirt. He acted the lord of the manor, waiting for her to serve him, too.

She considered dumping the food in his lap, then decided it wouldn't be politically expedient. She needed this job.

More important, she probably needed to be here to learn what Pierce wanted of her—and how she could return to her own time.

"Who is this?" asked one of the officers, still wearing a bright red coat, though his tricornered hat was hung on a nail on the wall right behind him. "New help, Thorn?"

He nodded curtly, taking a sip of his soup.

"We must be giving you too much business, if you can afford to hire more servants," the man continued.

"She doesn't cost much," Thorn replied.

Mariah nearly made an indignant retort before she realized she still didn't know how cheaply she worked; they hadn't yet discussed her wages. But of course they were considerably less than she'd brought in as a highly regarded unit production manager. And she didn't know yet how much she owed Thorn for saving her life.

"Does she know what kind of man she works for?" the officer went on.

Mariah was aghast at the officer's incivility. "Yes," she snapped, "I do. He's—"

"An innkeeper," Thorn interrupted, his voice tight. "That is all." He stood and stalked from the room, followed by loud laughter from the soldiers.

As soon as Mariah had served everyone, she returned to the kitchen, fuming. "Did you hear all that?" she asked René. "I don't know what those men were after, but they were terribly rude to Thorn."

"Yes." René helped her remove from the tray the dirty dishes she'd taken from the other room. "And he allows it because he believes it."

"Believes what?" Mariah began scraping the dishes the way René had shown her.

"I will tell you later, when we work on the laundry. That way, no one should interrupt us."

A stream ran in the woods behind the compound, a lovely, clear rivulet gurgling over smooth rocks that must have begun in the pine-covered mountains just beyond. René had shown it to Mariah the day before. On her shoulders was a sleek wooden contraption shaped like half a peanut shell. It helped her balance a bucket at both ends.

In the distance, she heard the clatter of horses' hoofs and shouts of "good-bye." The lunch guests were on their way, and not a moment too soon.

Mariah lugged the heavy buckets back to the kitchen and put them down. There, using rags as potholders, she gingerly removed one steaming cauldron of water from the fire and dumped some of the contents into a small basin near where the dishes were stacked. She then poured more of the water she'd hauled into the cauldron and put it back on the fire.

Not bad, she thought, for a woman whose idea of domestic pursuits had previously consisted of making her bed. Usually. When she wasn't staying in a hotel.

Oh, how she missed air conditioning, though. This room, with its blazing fire and few windows, was unbearably close in the summer heat and humidity. She'd even have given a lot for an electric fan to keep the air moving—if there'd been electricity.

She washed the wooden lunch dishes in the basin. As she began to dry them with soft, ragged towels René came in and started to help. They worked together for some time in a silence that seemed almost companionable to Mariah. Except that she was eager to hear what René had to say about Thorn's past. Why couldn't he begin now?

She understood the delay a short while later when Thorn entered the kitchen. She wrinkled her nose when she noticed the dead rabbit dangling from his hand.

"*Bon!*" cried René, beside her. "But I heard no shot. How did you catch it?"

"On the run," Thorn replied. "I tossed my knife at it."

"Well done," René said. He looked at Mariah as though she, too, should congratulate Thorn.

"Show off," she muttered, then allowed, "I guess that's more sporting than shooting it." She assumed that, after the rudeness of their lunch guests, he'd have preferred throwing his knife at targets on horseback.

"Then you are not impressed by skills in casting knives?" Thorn sounded tense, as though she'd insulted him.

"I'm sure it's a good thing to know," she replied as brightly as she could. She hadn't intended to offend Thorn. But poor bunny . . .

Poor me! she thought a moment later when Thorn tried to hand the rabbit to her. She put her hands behind her back, trying not to wrinkle her nose in distaste. "What am I supposed to do with it?"

She had to look up to make out the expression in his stony brown eyes. Speaking of distaste! This man, with his lips a straight, unyielding line, clearly wasn't pleased with her.

Well, she wasn't very pleased with him, either. And the sudden pang of sorrow she felt had nothing to do with his low opinion of her. She just felt sad for the rabbit.

She took a few steps back, turned toward a table and began busying herself with drying the tankards she'd just washed.

She'd never been a vegetarian at home, but the only meat she'd eaten had been from animals raised to be eaten. That way she could maintain that she was a wildlife lover—though she'd chosen not to listen to animal-rights activists describe how cruelly the animals that became her dinner had been raised.

Here, there was undoubtedly an abundance of game in this primeval forest. However irritable and unpredictable Thorn might be, she felt sure he wouldn't let the animals he killed suffer. They were creatures who would have lived wonderful, free lives, and were part of the human food chain.

She could justify eating meat here. Maybe even more than she could at home. As long as—

Her worst fears were confirmed when Thorn interrupted her thoughts. "You, Miss Walker, are to skin and clean this rabbit."

He was testing her again. She knew it.

And this time she would fail. Well, she'd never planned on being a servant. Let him fire her. "I don't know how." She let her tone show that she didn't want to learn.

"All right." He placed the rabbit on the table. She watched warily as he went to a cabinet and pulled out a sharp knife, which he began stropping on a large stone beside the fireplace. He returned to the rabbit, placing the knife blade against its soft, brown fur.

Mariah turned away.

"Oh, no, Miss Walker." His voice was stern. "For now, you may watch. Next time—"

She ran from the kitchen.

Mariah only dared to return to the kitchen after Thorn had brought what was clearly meat from the poor rabbit to the smokehouse. Then, she hurried back to be instructed in her next chores by René. Nothing could be worse than skinning a rabbit.

But she'd not imagined how hard washing clothes might be.

"*Je suis heureux*—I am happy," the Frenchman told her, "that I made plenty of soap the last time. If we had to do that, too, the chore would take several days instead of one afternoon."

As it was, Mariah had to haul water to the largest kettle, get it boiling, then carry the hot container outside, using rags on the handle, to dump the contents into a large washtub right in the center of the half-fenced compound. Her shoulders still ached from carrying water from the stream.

When the tub was full, she knelt in front of it as René had shown her, arranging her long skirt about her legs. She couldn't help thinking of the last film for which she'd been a unit production manager for Angela: a romantic comedy that had involved a couple who had met at a laundromat.

A laundromat! Automatic washers that filled, then did the washing, all by themselves. Heaven!

But here and now were her current reality. "Okay," she told René. His earlier promise had never left her mind. "I'm ready to hear about Thorn." She wondered if the story she was about to hear would follow what she'd gleaned about the screenplay Thorn—how he had let down his guard, resulting in a child being kidnapped by Indians. More likely, the real Thorn's background was as skewed as the other episodes she'd encountered here so far.

First, René handed her a dress from her bags and demonstrated what to do. Taking it from him, she began to scrub the material vigorously against the ridges of the wooden washboard.

Her hands immediately stung from the hot water and strong brown soap that smelled of lye, and tears pricked her eyelids.

Well, so what if her hands were ruined, she told herself. She should know better than to have such pride in anything.

Especially here.

At least, she thought, she had a wardrobe, thanks to Thorn. He'd apparently dived to the bottom of the river, though near the shore, to retrieve the bags. That was quite a kindness to perform for a woman who'd barged into his life and insisted that he hire her. Especially from an aloof man like Thorn. If she asked how he'd rescued her clothing, he'd probably just say he'd been fishing. He'd never admit to having gone to any trouble for her benefit.

Now she had three additional cotton dresses, some undergarments, a nightgown, a robe, stockings and several caps—though she didn't intend to wear the latter, no matter what the fashion in this time, any more than she'd wear the corset. They were all filthy, covered with river slime and starting to smell.

What she wouldn't have given for a T-shirt and blue jeans.

René hunkered down on his haunches on the ground beside her. "What I am about to say, Mademoiselle Mariah, you must keep to yourself," he began. "I do not tell you to make the gossip, but only so you will understand why the soldiers who come here are so—how do you say . . ."

"Insulting."

He nodded. "Insulting—and why Thorn does not call them out because of it."

"I'll be quiet," she affirmed, slightly out of breath already from exertion and holding her breath against the smell of lye.

"I will make my tale brief. Thorn, he came from England. There was a reason why he left, something about the death of his older brother, but *moi,* I do not know that story. Here in the new land he became a soldier guarding the town of Pittsborough just after my people and his had ended in this area the battles you English call the French and Indian War."

" 'Pittsborough'? I saw a sign in the town that said *Pittsburgh* Tavern."

René looked surprised. "*Oui,* that is its spelling, but the end is pronounced *borough.* Yet another oddity of *Les Anglais,* like their Scottish people call the town spelled Edinburgh as *Edinborough.*"

"I see," Mariah said.

"*Alors,*" René continued. "One day, visitors came to the new Fort Pitt." He took from her the dress she had been scrubbing. It was still crumpled into a wet ball, and he unrolled it. "Ah, *non.*" He pointed to a remaining spot of slime from the river. Silently, she took it back and began scouring it against the washboard once more.

"The visitors were settlers," René continued. "A mother traveling with her boy, who had the age of about twelve, and several other families who spoke of beginning a new life in the Pittsborough area. There was not yet much of Pittsborough, you understand."

Mariah nodded. Of course, in her opinion there *still* wasn't much of Pittsburgh—Pittsborough—in this time.

So far, René's tale tracked the script. He remained kneeling on the ground as he took the dress from her and plied the bar of strong soap over the offending stain. Then he wrung out the garment, examined it and rose to hang it over the rail of the nearby hitching post.

Mariah glanced sorrowfully at her crimson, stinging hands.

Keeping her sigh to herself, she grabbed another dress and began rubbing it vigorously against the washboard in the steaming water.

"Anyway, Mademoiselle Mariah," René continued, "I cannot tell you the details, for Thorn does not talk of this incident or any other. I learned what I know from his good friend, another soldier called Ainsley. Have you met Ainsley?"

Mariah shook her head.

"All I heard," René continued, "is that some of the mothers and children went into nearby woods one day to pick blackberries. Thorn was assigned to guard them, for always there was the threat of Indian attack. Among the party was a pretty, unmarried girl. While Thorn flirted with her, the boy disappeared."

The script hadn't implied that Thorn had been flirting. That didn't seem in character, Mariah thought.

René moved to sit cross-legged on the ground beside Mariah. He watched her efforts at washing intently, as though ready to criticize if she did anything wrong. "The mother was distraught," he continued.

"Naturally," Mariah huffed as she scrubbed.

The Frenchman nodded. "A search party was formed. Tracks indicated that the boy was taken by Indians, but local friendly savages said they heard of no tribe seizing the boy. The mother nevertheless insisted on searching." He sighed. "She met with a terrible accident, and Thorn blamed himself for this, too."

Mariah stopped scrubbing for a moment. "She died, didn't she?"

"Yes. She drowned in a river—although Ainsley said the bank was dry and she had seemed sure-footed enough." He hesitated. "Ainsley hinted of suspicions that she killed herself in despair."

A wave of pity for Thorn gripped Mariah. Bad enough that the boy was stolen on his watch and that the boy's mother died accidentally while looking for him. But for her to have killed herself . . . "What did Thorn think?"

"He says nothing, but his thoughts are obvious. He blames himself either way. So do others. That is why he left his career as an officer with the terrible army of *Les Anglais* and came here. He saved my life, at this inn, when some English soldiers decided the war continued against this one remaining Frenchman. Now I, who hate the English, can be his friend."

There was a warning implicit in his words. His friend was not to be hurt any further by this story or anything else, if René could help it.

Well, Mariah had no intention of hurting Thorn.

If only she, herself, could avoid being hurt, too.

She stared ruefully at her burning hands—the hands of a servant in the eighteenth century, in the turbulent times of Indian wars, of outhouses, of fires that needed tending and game that had to be hunted for food. A time when the suspicion of dishonor could ruin a man's whole life.

Could she really be here?

Of course not. But if not, why couldn't she just wake up, go home and film the screenplay?

But now she'd have lots of editing to do.

Mariah finished scrubbing her last garment, an undershift, and hung it to dry from a tree limb behind some leaves. Not that she'd be embarrassed to have it seen. Not really. But it might offend the tender sensibilities of the hopelessly macho men of this time.

This time. Pierce, you creep! she thought. He'd been on her mind a lot while she'd worked on the washing. Why didn't he show up here? He undoubtedly knew where she was, but she was in no position to hunt him down. Not without transportation and a guide in this difficult, backward time.

How had he haunted her dreams forever with his incomprehensible order to right a grievous wrong? He had to tell her this, and more.

She wanted to scream at him. To beg him to fix things. Send her home. How could he expect her to fill meek, proficient Matilda's role here—especially when no one else followed the script?

Where Thorn was so different. So unpredictable.

At least now her clothes were clean. Her hands, though ugly and raw-looking, were long past stinging. She'd simply have to get over feeling sorry for herself for their appearance. Better to dwell on how good she felt at having developed one small skill here—this laundry business.

René had gone off to do other chores. She decided to ask whether he had any garments he wanted washed.

She found him in the stable cleaning out a stall. Great! He hadn't foisted that nasty chore on her.

Not yet, at least.

At her question, his eyes bugged in surprise. "*Merci,* Mariah. Yes, I do have things I would like to have washed."

He brought from his room a bulging shirt, its sleeves tied together over a bunch of clothing inside. As he handed the bundle to her, his look was quizzical. "Perhaps you would like to be relieved of tending the fire for supper?"

She shook her head. "That's not why I offered to wash. If my chores are supposed to include keeping the fire going all day, I'll do that, too."

He nodded thoughtfully. Then his small smile brightened his entire ugly face. "There is more to you than I thought, Mademoiselle Mariah. Someday soon I will show you how I cook my famous *potage de caille.*"

Mariah translated in her mind: quail soup. Maybe that was the equivalent of chicken soup in the wilderness. In any event, she felt a tiny thread of pride wriggle through her. She was meeting with the approval of this formerly unfriendly Frenchman.

Now, if only Thorn would come to like her.

Not the way the screenplay Thorn liked Matilda, she told herself sternly, hurrying from the stable with her arms filled with dirty clothes. But if she was going to be around for a while to accomplish whatever Pierce had sent her to do, she'd need to feel she could trust the real Thorn.

To have another friend here, in the middle of nowhere.

Impulsively, she stopped in front of Thorn's stone house. Shifting the lump of clothes under one arm, she knocked on the door.

She heard a muffled noise from inside. Had Thorn called to her to enter? She carefully placed René's laundry on the dusty ground beside the door, then touched the weathered iron knob, warmed by the sun.

The door swung open easily, as if it had been left ajar. "Thorn," Mariah called. She heard only a skittering noise. Maybe he was busy and hadn't heard her. She stepped inside.

The place smelled of old smoke, overlain with the fresh scent of outdoors. The single room was lighter than the others Mariah had been in. The windows were larger, though they were covered with the ubiquitous coated paper. The indoor shutters were open, and light passing through them bathed the room in a dim golden glow.

"Thorn?" Mariah again heard a noise without discovering its source.

But as her eyes became accustomed to the yellow light, she saw a creature scrabbling in the far corner beyond a large, cluttered table.

"Oh!" Her involuntary cry must have startled the animal, for it stopped moving and stared suspiciously at her.

It was a small, gray squirrel. Something was clasped in its tiny paws.

"Uh-oh," Mariah said. "Are you scavenging in here? Not a good idea."

She didn't think squirrels hurt people, but she had heard of rabid ones. Even some whose fleas carried bubonic plague—not something she wanted to think about in these days before antibiotics.

She approached the little animal carefully. "Okay, fellow. Why don't you just scoot out of here?"

As though it understood, the squirrel gave an angry chatter, climbed the wall and maneuvered behind the paper covering one window. The last thing Mariah saw of it was its fluffy, waving tail.

She laughed aloud, then looked around. She realized uneasily that Thorn wasn't there, and that she undoubtedly wasn't welcome. Still, she was curious about the man's home. She hoped she'd scared off the squirrel before it had chewed anything he valued. She should leave it to Thorn to find out, she told herself, as she crossed the room to look.

The rustic furnishings were sparse. On the large table stood a variety of items she didn't recognize and some she did: a pitcher and washbasin, long rods that resembled thick nutcrackers, lumps of metal, pieces of leather and an assortment of wrapped bullets like the one she'd helped Thorn load into the rifle to scare off her river rats. The single wooden bench had been slid beneath the table. Then there was the bed, of sturdy, straight tree branches lashed together with leather thongs. Its mattress was covered in blankets of dark wool, similar to those in Mariah's room.

And of course there was a fireplace. On its stone mantel was an assortment of lethal-looking hunting knives.

But Mariah's gaze stopped at the wall opposite the fireplace. She drew in her breath. "Oh, my," she whispered, feeling pain grip her heart.

Hanging on the wall, like a tapestry splayed for decoration, was a British army uniform, even more ornate than the ones Mariah had seen at Fort Pitt. An officer's, maybe. It obviously had been made for a large man.

Thorn.

He kept it here, hanging on the wall, as though to remind himself of what had happened. To feed his guilt. Mariah shook her head. Aloud, almost involuntarily, she asked, "Why?"

"Why what, Miss Walker?"

Mariah jumped. The fury in the unexpected deep voice sounded barely in check.

"Why are you in here?" Thorn continued. "That's the 'why' I'd like to know. I made it quite clear that I wanted no intruders in my private quarters."

She turned to face him. Thorn filled the doorway with his large, menacing frame. Though he was backlighted, she could discern the anger that slitted his eyes and tightened his lips into a cruel scowl.

"You just said there was nowhere for me to stay in here," Mariah protested weakly. "You didn't say I was forbidden to see the place."

"I'm saying so now." His tone was level but allowed for no contradiction.

"Fine." She was in the wrong, and she knew it. But she didn't want to admit it to him. She walked slowly toward him, for his body barred the only exit she saw. Nervously, she tossed her head so her hair swayed away from her face. "I only came to ask if you had any clothes you wanted me to launder."

"That was no reason to enter uninvited."

"I thought you invited me," she found herself arguing, then amended, "I mean, I heard a sound that I assumed was you, so I opened the door. There was a squirrel in here. You'd better check to make sure he didn't chew on something you care about."

"He only chews the nuts and grains I leave him." Thorn's voice had softened almost imperceptibly. Mariah felt her eyes widen in amazement. This hard, unyielding man apparently kept a pet squirrel.

"Then he belongs here," she said. "And I chased him away. I'm sorry."

"He'll be back when he's hungry."

Nearly at the entry, Mariah stopped. Thorn hadn't budged. His body still loomed ominously in the doorway. Was he going to punish her for violating his privacy? He'd seemed calmer when talking about the squirrel. Had his mood shifted again? "If you'll excuse me . . ." she managed.

He stalked into the room, closing the door behind him. His boots thumped on the wooden floor. He drew even closer. "I thought you washed my dirty clothes."

Mariah felt trapped as he stopped a scant foot away from her. She could smell his aroma of smoke and leather. All she wanted now was to get out of there. "Sure," she said brightly. "You can bring them to me outside. I've been doing washing in front of the inn." She pointed in the general direction in which she'd been working, wincing a little at the pain as she moved her fingers.

Before she realized what he was doing, he'd reached down and lifted her hands in his. He used them to tow her closer to the window. He tugged her hands into the golden light and examined them, turning them over, then back again.

Mariah tried to pull away. Even in the odd-colored light, her palms appeared red and blistered. Her nails were chipped, and her fingers were too sore to open completely. "Please," she whispered, ashamed that the hands she'd once pampered now looked as if they'd passed through the fires of hell.

"They're—" He didn't finish what he was going to say. Instead, he lifted her hands. His head bowed . . . and she felt the soothing softness of his lips upon her burning palms.

She inhaled sharply, frozen while wanting to run. He raised his head once more and looked into her face.

There was sorrow in his pale brown eyes, and a glimmer of something she read as guilt.

"It's all right," she said quietly, pulling one hand away to touch his face. His skin was warm, roughened by the outdoors and by the hint of heavy masculine facial hair, though he was clean-shaven. No matter what he had done in the past, no matter how he castigated himself now because of it, she didn't want him adding her to the many burdens he bore. "I'm fine. This isn't so—"

His mouth stopped hers from finishing. There was nothing gentle in his kiss, despite his tenderness when he'd examined her hands. The kiss robbed her of breath, of wanting to breathe, for she did not want to break the spell.

There was a kind of desperation in the way his lips ravaged hers. He tasted of something she had sampled only once before, fierce masculinity in this new, old land. His tongue plunged into her mouth, and she welcomed it with her own.

He pulled her tightly to him, and she felt the hard ruggedness as she had once before. His fingers were motionless on her back, holding her against him, but she couldn't still her own. The soreness of her hands was forgotten as she touched his broad, strong neck and the prominent muscles of his shoulders, stroked the taut planes of his back, moved lower yet. . . .

With a growl, he pulled away. Gripping her upper arms, he stared down at her.

Aware of the tingling of her abandoned lips, she nearly cried aloud. Her attempt at forgiveness must have hurt rather than helped him; his anguish was etched even deeper in the lowering of his brow, the pain in his eyes, the set of his narrowed lips.

"Your chores still await you, Miss Walker. Go." He was not gentle as he pulled her to the door and thrust her outside.

But she turned and stepped in front of him before he could disappear into the house. Ignoring his angry scowl, she ventured, "Your laundry . . . ?"

She nearly smiled at the show of emotions that eased his fury for just a moment: amazement, maybe even a glimmer of admiration. "I'll bring it, Miss Walker." He hesitated. "Thank you."

Chapter Seven

One hand on the smooth wooden doorframe, Thorn watched as Mariah bent her slender form to pick up a bundle of garments near the entry, then stood and walked from his house along the leaf-strewn ground.

There was a soft sway to her hips despite the almost masculine determination in her stride. She was his employee, yet there was nothing mincing or subservient about her.

Or compliant. She had participated fully in that ill-conceived, impulsive kiss. The kiss he still felt on his lips—and elsewhere.

She still remained clad in that soiled and wrinkled pink dress, but he had noticed, while returning to his house, that her laundry hung about the clearing: a small assortment of dresses, skirts, blouses, aprons . . . and a few white undergarments.

The latter articles were hung behind some branches with surprising modesty, considering the woman's bold ways. He had barely glanced at them; she deserved her privacy. Yet he had not been able to keep from wondering what the shapeless items would look like filled out by the curves hidden beneath that familiar pink dress.

The thought had made him wipe his brow from a heat that had little to do with the beating sun.

When he'd noticed the laundry, he had been returning from one of his quick, frequent sojourns into the woods to scout for persons who did not belong in the vicinity—mostly Indians. Immediately, he had realized someone had invaded his domain, for the door to his home was open.

He had run silently toward it, prepared to wage war with any marauder, whether beast or man.

It had been neither. Mariah Walker had been inside.

Perhaps her invasion had been the most intrusive of all, for she did not merely enter to steal or destroy. She had trespassed upon his soul.

He had seen her stare at the uniform he had fastened upon the wall as a reminder of who he was and why he could not be trusted in civilization.

And when she had noticed him, after the first look of shock and fear had passed, there had been a glimmer of pity.

She wanted his laundry? He would get it for her!

Pivoting on his heel, he went back inside the house.

He needed pity from no one. Nor did he wish to pity anyone else.

But he glanced now at the spot where she had stood when he had looked at her hands. "Blast!" he swore aloud.

He had noticed before, when she had so diligently yet inefficiently worked at starting the fire, how soft and pretty were her hands. The hands of a pampered woman who had never toiled in her life.

And now they were the blistered, reddened hands of a servant.

"A servant?" he heard himself mutter. He knew how a servant should act. He'd had servants aplenty until the disaster that had forced him to the colonies. Mariah Walker did not act like a servant. She had not denied that she was a rich woman from the east, either, and yet something did not quite fit: her sweet voice had an accent he could not place. She was more forward in many ways than any woman he had ever met, more wise and yet more naive.

He stomped farther into the house. There, beneath a bench in the corner, he had crammed his shirts from the last week. He had intended to request their washing from René soon. Thorn spent his days in hunting. In patrolling the area on foot and on horseback to watch for intruders. In building the palisade and doing all necessary to care for his inn, his domain. He had no time to do laundry. Fortunately, his employee and friend René did not seem bothered by such mindless chores.

Mariah Walker would mind them, he was certain. But she was stalwart. Feisty. She hadn't complained. Not yet, at least.

And she had let him kiss her.

He had not intended that kiss any more than he had the first the night before. He had determined then never to touch her again. Women meant naught but pain, and lusting after his employee could lead only to trouble. But she had vanquished his defenses with her burned hands, her pitying looks, her lack of complaints despite what he was putting her through.

"What *I* am putting *her* through?" he demanded aloud. She had come to his territory and demanded his help. Then she had insisted upon a job.

She deserved those kisses, and more. He wanted to take that tempting body of hers and show her what could happen to a woman alone in the wilderness.

He sensed, though, that Mariah Walker was not one to allow anyone to take advantage of her.

And she was not alone in the wilderness, damn it. He was with her.

But he would stay far away from her now, no matter how her slim, graceful body tempted him. No matter how she amused and amazed him by her unmistakable determination to overcome her ignorant, pampered upbringing.

He would not, could not, care for this woman.

And woe to her, should she ever believe she could rely on him.

* * *

So the mighty Thorn had deigned to thank her. Hurrying away from him, her arms again filled with laundry, Mariah figured she should have been grateful for Thorn's small showing of gratitude.

Instead, it made her angry.

That and his pity. How dare he stare at her hands!

Those poor, burned, shriveling hands.

Flexing them slightly beneath their load of laundry, she nearly sobbed aloud at the pain. Had it been only yesterday she'd been proud of her hands?

Of course, she'd been in her own time then. Now she was living a dream.

A nightmare.

One where she thought she knew what was to occur, only to have it come out different. Skewed. Worse.

Thorn had kissed her again. She still felt the erotic pressure on her mouth. Her knees weakened at the very thought.

She had to remind herself that he was not Matilda's Thorn, and she, unfortunately, was not Matilda.

What would it have been like to be loved by a reliable Thorn?

Well, she would never know, and she refused to feel sorry for herself. She dropped the load of René's shirts on the ground beside the washtub, careful to avoid the mud she'd made earlier by sloshing water over the sides. She knelt and tested the water. It was, of course, tepid.

She grabbed one of the wooden buckets she'd used to fill the tub and dipped out more than half, carrying each load around the half-built palisade to the seam of land where the clearing met the forest. She emptied the bucket at the edge of the encroaching trees and brush. Then, after filling several buckets from the nearby stream, she began the tedious task of heating the fresh water over the kitchen fire.

Eventually, the washtub was again filled with hot water. Mariah knelt on the ground, gathering her skirt close to avoid the mud, and began to scour René's shirts against the washboard. She gritted her teeth against the renewed stinging of her tender hands. But that was all right. Physical pain was better than thinking about Thorn. His kisses. Kisses that seemed so incompatible with his aloofness.

Why was she letting that changeable, frustrating man affect her this way?

A slight movement in the corner of her eye made her glance sideways.

A pair of moccasined feet stood beside her. Legs in trousers rose from them to tower over her. She drew in her breath. Once again, Thorn had crept up on her. She found herself smiling.

Raising her eyes, she gasped and rose quickly to her feet. It wasn't Thorn, but an Indian.

He wasn't much taller than she, and he wore a buckskin shirt, breechcloth and leggings. His head was shaved except for a swathe of black hair that ran from the center of his scalp into a long braid. He smelled of something she couldn't identify—an animal odor.

"H-hello," she stammered. Being a child of the twentieth century, she abhorred the way Native Americans had been treated during the history of her country. Nevertheless, this man was a product of his own era and might not take the time to learn her opinions before treating her the way he would any invading European of the eighteenth century.

But Mariah recalled a similar incident in the script. She relaxed—but only for a moment. The Indian, though he had crept up on Matilda, had been Thorn's ally.

But other things in the screenplay hadn't been completely correct.

"You scared me," Mariah said with a nervous laugh. The man said nothing, but his dark eyes flashed a look that she could only interpret as venomous.

Could this really be a friend of Thorn's?

"Do you speak English?" she asked.

The man's frown deepened.

"Le Français?"

Still no positive response.

"Look," Mariah said uneasily, reverting to English. "I don't really understand what's going on here. Maybe I should go find Thorn or René." She began to edge away. "I'm sure one of them—"

Darting toward her suddenly, the man grabbed her by the hair and pulled. Pain hurtled through her, and she screamed.

A large hunting knife in his hand, his pulse racing like the Ohio in a spring thaw, Thorn leaped from the shadows beside his house and approached Nahtana. His long gun was tucked beneath his other arm.

He had been watching the encounter between Mariah and the Iroquois chief. The woman was either incredibly stupid or incredibly courageous.

Perhaps a bit of both.

Then again, she did not know Nahtana. Perhaps the Indians of her acquaintance were not the marauding murderers of his.

"Stop!" Thorn called.

The Indian did stop, but Thorn was certain it was not because he had told him to. Instead, with a growl of words that Thorn did not understand, the Indian glanced about, as if weighing his options. Beneath his hands, Mariah appeared to go slack, as though wishing to slide away from the Indian, but Nahtana tightened his grip. Mariah cried out.

An answering pain pierced Thorn's mind, but he forbore from wincing, from making any sign that he was affected by the woman's suffering. To do anything else would give Nahtana an additional weapon against both of them. She'd be dead, too, if he tried to point his gun.

He knew why the Indian was there—to wage his personal battle against Thorn and his inn. The Iroquois conquered other Indians. They wished to claim this area as their own.

Nahtana had made it clear that Thorn's inn was an unwelcome intrusion, a toehold that, if permitted to remain, would give the encroaching British settlers confidence that they might find new homes in Indian territories.

Dragging Mariah by the hair, Nahtana edged toward the woods. He brandished a large hunting knife in his free hand.

A knife that, in the blink of an eye, he could plunge into Mariah Walker's chest. Or use to slit her throat.

Thorn did not let his internal quaking show. He demanded, "Let her go, Nahtana." This woman, no matter how foolish, no matter how brave, meant nothing to him, of course. Still, he needed no further acts of cowardice on his conscience.

There were already far too many.

Thorn looked at her, at the loose, wavy hair that only reached her shoulders wound in Nahtana's fist. Those eyes, green as the forest, stared at him beseechingly.

Damn those eyes! She was depending upon his help yet again. He had no help to give.

Foolish woman, he thought, for relying on him.

The pain wracking her scalp was unbearable. Mariah couldn't ease it by staying still. She couldn't even do so by following along with the Indian toward the woods—not that she wanted to do that.

But she had little choice, not with his hand wrapped in her hair.

Not with that knife he waved in her face. A knife with a long, long blade. A blade that appeared sharper than a razor.

Trying to still the small, terrified noises she heard issuing from her own throat, she dared a glance at Thorn, her only chance at salvation. His face was impassive. She prayed that was simply his way of dealing with the terrible situation. If he showed emotion, might things go worse for her?

And staring at the knife being brandished menacingly in front of her face, she was sure they could.

Was her recollection of the screenplay correct? Was this man supposed to be Thorn's ally?

If so, this was a heck of a way to treat a friend's employee.

Tears spilling from her eyes, she dragged her feet as much as she dared as the Indian led her by the hair toward the shadowed darkness of the forest. "Please." Her voice sounded squeaky, but she tried to keep it calm. "Don't hurt me. Just let me go."

"No!" the Indian shrieked, giving her hair a sharp yank that stabbed a new agony through her head. She cried out. Maybe he understood some English, for all the good that did her.

If she went with him, she would be dead. Or perhaps better off dead. Didn't Indians in this time keep woman captives as slaves? Some married them, she thought, but would that be any better than slavery?

It was one thing to feel compassion for abused Native Americans in the abstract. It was something else altogether to be here in the past with this angry, threatening man who was hurting her.

Much too soon, they were at the edge of the woods. Every muscle in her body tensed and trembled. Her head hurt unbearably, reminding her of her earlier headache. The one that had made her wonder if she were lying somewhere in a coma, dreaming this entire escapade.

She knew better now. This was reality. Somehow, thanks to Pierce, she had wound up in the past, living a grotesque parody of the wonderful screenplay she had read.

One that put her, far too often, into danger.

Where was Thorn?

She recalled only too well his words when she'd been chased by those two boat characters. No one should rely on him.

Where was René?

Better yet, how could she help herself?

Quite suddenly, the tug on her hair ceased, and the Indian screamed something unintelligible. As she was released, her resistance to the pulling bounced her onto the ground with a thud that left her behind aching. She glanced up.

The Indian was clutching the bloody wrist of his right hand, the one that had been waving the knife.

The knife was on the ground beside Mariah. No, two knives, the second as long-bladed and lethal-looking as the first. She grabbed for them both as the Indian disappeared into the forest.

"Where did this come from?" Drawing herself slowly to her feet, she waved the second knife as Thorn approached, his gun aimed in the direction in which the Indian had gone. He'd saved her again, and in her relief she wanted more than anything to throw herself into his strong arms, be held against his hard chest, be comforted by his embrace.

But he was the real Thorn, not the screenplay version. He would resent the contact, reject her touch. And so, shuddering, on rubbery legs, she remained standing where she was.

"You see, Miss Walker," Thorn said calmly, lowering his rifle, "there is value after all in learning how to fell a rabbit with a knife."

Still trembling inside, Mariah forced herself to get back to work. Kneeling on the hard ground, she scrubbed René's shirts in hot, hot water that hurt her stinging hands. She barely watched what she did, glancing around frequently. Would that Indian return?

Surely not. His hand must hurt, and he undoubtedly feared Thorn and his rifle.

But wouldn't he want revenge? She bit her lip uneasily.

Her hair hung in damp, sweaty coils beside her face. At least she still had it—along with a renewal of her headache. But at least now she was sure of its source.

There was no use dwelling on what she couldn't help. But if she'd had any residual doubts that she was in the past, they'd vanished with that Indian's yank on her hair.

Pierce had sent her here. "To right a grievous wrong," he'd said. It had been his voice haunting her dreams all those years.

But why?

And what was the wrong she was to right? It had to have something to do with the screenplay.

She'd hated the ending before: Thorn's death. Now that she'd met him, the duel seemed even more of a travesty. Even if he wasn't the Thorn of the screenplay, she couldn't bear the thought of seeing his life cut short in such a needless way.

Was she here to prevent it?

Beginning to shake her head, she saw a pair of moccasins beneath the legs of leather trousers. Gasping, she rose to her feet.

She relaxed immediately. It was Thorn. "You're jumpy, Miss Walker," he said. He carried a roll of cloth beneath one arm.

She managed a smile. "I've a right to be."

He nodded. He didn't return her smile, but his brown eyes sparkled beneath their thick, strong brows. Small lines radiated from their corners in his tanned face. His firm, smooth lips were not set in their usual grim line, either.

"Thanks for helping me." She paused. "I think I've said that before."

The anger returned to his gaze. "Do not bother." His voice was as hard as the ground on which he stood. "I helped because it would harm my business if word spread that I let an employee be captured by Indians."

"I understand." She felt like stomping on his moccasined toes. Throwing hot water on him where it would hurt.

Anything to get him to show real emotion.

She'd just met the man. Heaven help her if she was to stay with him for a while to right Pierce's wrong.

"Here." He thrust the wad of cloth toward her. "My dirty garments for you to wash."

Not a "please" to get her to take them, or any sign of gratitude when she did. She inhaled sharply, tamping down her irritation. "Sure," she said sweetly. "Heavy on the starch, I'd imagine. And no creases."

"What?"

"An inside joke." No use trying to explain to him the dry cleaners of her time and the instructions customers gave.

What *would* he think if she told him she was from more than two hundred years in the future? He'd believe her crazy—and she didn't want that to happen. She'd no idea what people did with the insane in this era.

"I'll return your clothes to you as soon as possible," she told him. She wasn't sure whether she wanted him to keep her company or to leave. He took the decision out of her hands; he began walking away.

But after just a couple of steps, he turned back toward her. "Thank you, Miss Walker."

She felt a flush of pleasure well up in her face, probably turning it as pink as her hands. Irritated at her disproportionate reaction to such minuscule encouragement, she corrected grumpily, "Mariah."

"Mariah," he repeated, the word as soft as a caress from his lips. She was glad that, this time, he did not turn back as he strode away.

Sighing, she returned to her work.

She still couldn't keep her thoughts from returning to the Indian attack.

She didn't belong in this time. Muggings and carjackings and drive-by shootings—those were dangers she understood.

But Indian abductions?

She finished washing René's shirts, keeping her eyes resolutely turned away from the stack of Thorn's washing on the ground beside her. She'd get to his stuff when she got to it, and not a moment before.

But as soon as she'd wrung out the last of René's shirts and hung it, dripping, from a tree limb, she dipped out some of the now-tepid water, retrieved more from the fire, on which she'd set fresh water to boil, then knelt again by the washbasin.

Her knees were rough and sore, and her joints ached with the unaccustomed bending and kneeling, but she was determined to finish the task. After all, hadn't she asked Thorn for his dirty laundry?

The stack consisted of four long pullover shirts: two ecru, one white and one a faded brown. The shirts were larger than René's, sewn of sturdy, woven cotton or flax, some material as natural and outdoorsy as Thorn. They appeared rugged, able to bear up under hard use, and they smelled of leather and smoke and the masculine scent she'd noticed before that was Thorn's own.

Mariah got to work on them. Her poor, sore fingers tingled, but this time it wasn't only from the heat of the water. Instead, she was affected by the intimacy of handling Thorn's clothing.

She hadn't had the same sense with René's shirts and was certain that laundry employees of her time didn't have such feelings.

She hurried, eager to complete the task, to rid her hands of Thorn's soft but substantial garments, to rid her mind of her absurd thoughts. These weren't the screenplay Thorn's clothes but the garments of the very real Thorn.

He'd saved her from that Indian, but he'd had an ulterior motive—the health of his business. A motive that might not apply in her next predicament.

She, of all people, knew what it was to rely on someone undependable. To expend emotions on such a person.

To want him to care, to come through when it really mattered.

She'd grown up with that futile longing. But her father had disappointed her over and over. Each time, he would seduce her gullible mother with talk of yet another fine, new job. Move the family to another exotic locale. For a while, they would live together. Mariah would bask in her father's presence, acting as perfectly as she could, hoping to win his love. But the good times never lasted. He lost every job. Blamed everyone but himself. Abandoned his family, leaving them lonely and penniless until the next impractical opportunity arose.

Her mother had died the last time he left. Mariah had used the opportunity to leave *him.* She had seen him rarely since.

She had experimented with caring for someone again just once as an adult. Her fiancé had also proven unreliable.

She would never make that mistake again.

Still, Mariah had a sense of regret when she'd hung the last of Thorn's shirts on a limb. This small, tenuous contact with him had ended.

"Idiot," she told herself aloud. As long as she remained here, there would always be more laundry to do.

And she was an utter fool if she let herself think that touching his clothing brought her closer to that remote, uncaring man.

That evening there were no guests, so Thorn, René and she sat and dined peacefully, as though members of a family.

Not that Mariah felt like part of Thorn's family. Not when he sat there so quietly, making no conversation but glowering when he deigned to look at her at all.

Did he resent her presence or the fact that he'd had to save her from that Indian?

Shuddering to think where she might have ended up this day, she shot a smile at him. There was no answering softening of his glare, and Mariah felt her features set into a stony mask.

How would this scene play if Angela filmed her script? Probably with sweet, brave Matilda staring boldly at her Thorn, sharing smoldering looks that told the audience to expect an R-rated scene.

This man, gorgeous as he was, hurled only glacial glances at her that would freeze a firestorm.

She turned to René. "So tell me. What kind of meat is this?" She had been eating the salt-tangy meat by hand as the men did.

"Smoked venison," he replied.

Of course. She should have guessed. But for a moment she felt ill. "I've resorted to eating Bambi," she whispered to herself.

"What was that, mademoiselle?" René's look was puzzled.

"Nothing." Mariah took a swig of ale from a tankard.

She was glad when supper ended. She helped René clean the wood plates and wondered about the lead content of the pewter cups. No matter. People in these times were likely to die far more quickly from violence or contagious disease than from lead poisoning.

Would she die here? Or would she ever be permitted to return to her own time? She missed comfortable clothing, makeup and sanitary bathroom facilities.

And people, too. There was Angela, and . . . Who else? She couldn't think of anyone, but she would.

Though not, of course, her father.

"Show me where these things go, will you, René?" She had stacked the plates on a table in the vast kitchen. Yesterday evening, her first in this era, the Frenchman had put away all the supper paraphernalia. But since she was still here, Mariah figured she'd need to know everything a servant would.

"*Comme ça*, mademoiselle."

"Mariah," she corrected.

"Mariah." The broad grin lit his toadlike face, and Mariah smiled back. "Like this." He showed her how to arrange the plates and tankards along wooden rails of various sizes nailed to the wall. As she worked, she noted the paper, ink bottle and quill she had forgotten in the kitchen the previous night.

That was what she would work on when she returned to the privacy of her room later. But this early in the evening it was lighter in here, with the larger windows, so she decided to practice here first. She waited until René left, then sat on a bench at the long utility table. She carefully wiggled the stiff cork out of the ink bottle without spilling any, then dipped the end of the quill into it.

Her first touch of point to paper turned into a big, black blotch.

She tried again. Another big, ugly inkspot. "Damn!" she said aloud. At this rate, she'd be able to give excellent Rorschach psychology tests to the people of this time, but she'd never be able to keep notes for herself.

"Do you have a problem, Mariah?"

She started in her seat. Her right hand, on the table, nearly upset the ink bottle, but Thorn caught it.

"I have no problems." She knew she sounded petulant, particularly since she'd kept her jaw clenched as she spoke. He'd crept up on her yet again.

"We have already established that you are literate." He sat beside her. "Why is it you do not know how to write?"

She felt heat emanating from his hip as it nearly touched hers, and she scooted quickly down the bench.

He reached out to take the quill from her, deftly dipped its end into the ink, then began to write in a bold, swirly hand, "Thorn Inn, West Pennsylvania."

There was a question pending, and she was not certain how to respond. "I—I learned with different writing tools. A . . . pencil would help." Were there pencils now? She doubted they'd be the neat graphite sticks of her era, jacketed in wood of yellow or some more decorative design. And with handy erasers, too.

"I have no pencil. You will need to use this or nothing at all. Here."

He thrust the quill into her hand. She took it, feeling the ends of the feather tickle her fingers. She gripped the thing as she'd seen him hold it. Dipping it carefully into the ink bottle, she let the excess ink drip off, then scraped its tip at the edge of the bottle.

And then she put the tip to the paper.

A huge blot of ink smeared the page.

"Damn!" Mariah cried. She had to learn how to do this. Without Dictaphone, computer, even good old ballpoint pen, it was the only way to record her recollections of the screenplay.

She looked beseechingly at Thorn to find him staring at her, his head slightly cocked. "Most ladies of my former acquaintance do not speak such words so easily," he said. He didn't sound condemning. If anything, he seemed amused.

"I am not most ladies of your acquaintance, former or otherwise. Now, show me again what to do."

"Like this."

He stood and walked behind her. Once more, he placed her fingers on the quill, but this time he manipulated them with his own until he was apparently satisfied with her grip. And then his hand closed over hers. It was warm and rough, large enough to span hers and hold it steady as he drew it toward the ink bottle.

Mariah found it difficult to breathe. He was leaning over her, and their contact was not limited to the grasp of his hand. His firm chest was against her back, and she felt his breath stirring her hair.

Once again, she was aware of this man. Oh, how very aware, for she had not learned her lesson before. She had a sudden need to touch more of him. To have him touch more of her.

He twisted his hand to show her how to make the quill retain only the smallest amount of ink. She inhaled his masculine scent once more, but now it seemed to surround her, intoxicating her, making her feel as though she could do anything as long as he held her.

A long-forgotten warmth flowed through her. How odd, she thought, that she should be so sensually stirred by a man she didn't really trust.

His arm spanned the length of hers from shoulder to wrist, as though they were joined, and she could feel the bulging strength of his substantial muscles along her own, trembling arm.

No. She didn't dare tremble, or she would blot once more.

And yet, as she tried to still herself, she realized that all of the shaking did not come from her. Did she make him as nervous as he made her?

Unlikely. Nothing seemed to disturb Thorn.

"Now, we will write." His mouth was close to her ear, and his soft words in his deep, buckskin-soft voice with its British intonations nearly made her jump. What he had said wasn't sexy in the least. Why did it make the stirring she had been feeling turn to a full-fledged yearning?

She watched, fascinated, as his hand guided hers along the page. Together, they wrote, "Mariah Walker." The handwriting was his, not hers, and the swirls intertwined with those of his name, where he'd written it before as part of the name of the inn. The intertwining seemed intimate, like a joining of the two of them, and Mariah felt her mouth go dry.

She didn't want to stop when the final *r* was written. "Let's try *Pennsylvania,*" she whispered, her words barely audible even to her.

They did, their arms now as closely entwined as the letters in their names.

"Now," she said, when the words were complete, "let's—"

She didn't get to finish. His hand dropped from hers. She barely noticed when the quill fell to the table as Thorn pulled her to her feet, knocking over the bench. He took her into his arms.

She wanted that kiss. As his mouth closed over hers, she threw her arms about his neck, drawing him nearer still.

There was something feral about the way he nipped at her lips, taunting her with his questing tongue. She twisted her head as though trying to get away, but her motions were involuntary, a reaction to his erotic onslaught that served only to tease him and not to free her.

Not that she wanted to be free. He held her tightly to him, seeming to anticipate her movements so that her mouth could not escape his, and she reveled in the sensual imprisonment. She ached to be closer still, to feel the hard planes of his body against her without the barriers of their constricting clothing.

She felt his hand writhe up between them, inhaling sharply as he reached her breast, teasing it with his fingertips till her nipple hardened, then clasping it firmly. His breathing grew ragged, but still he tantalized her mouth, then caught it in a hard, firm, passionate kiss.

She was melting, as surely as if she were leaning over a fire; her bones lost substance and her body moistened. "Thorn," she murmured against the pressure of his lips, reaching up to feel the thick column of his neck, the silkiness of his hair.

He answered, but she couldn't understand his words, didn't need to. She felt his free hand move yet again, descending the front of her layers of obstructive clothing till his fingers lay only centimeters above, yet miles away from, her sensitive core. She was consumed with a longing she'd never before experienced with such intensity. Without volition, she pressed herself toward that questing hand and—

The sound of voices cut into her thoughts. With a small gasp, she pulled away from Thorn, just as René entered the room from the outside door, followed by a short stranger carrying a cloth satchel. "We have a guest tonight after all," the Frenchman said.

Mariah saw his low brow raise as he looked first at Thorn, then at her.

She ventured a glance at Thorn, who now stood beside her next to the table. His tall form was straight and taut, and he looked toward the intruding men. "Welcome," he said to the stranger.

Amazing, Mariah thought, that he could seem so cool after the passion he'd evinced just moments before.

But there was a slight swollenness of his unsmiling lips that doubtless matched her own.

And, looking very hard, she thought she detected a bemused look in the depths of his brown eyes.

Chapter Eight

Embarrassed at having nearly been caught kissing Thorn, Mariah picked up ink, paper and quill. "I forgot these again," she told René, shrugging as nonchalantly as she could. She greeted their guest with forced pleasantness, trying to ignore the speculative gleam in the mouselike man's beady eyes. She shifted the things she held to lift her still-glowing candle and hurried out the back door.

The air was chilly—or maybe her shivering was from her recollection of that torrid, nerve-tingling kiss with Thorn. Why had he done it again? To demonstrate her vulnerability to him?

"Think again, mister," she whispered aloud. The kiss had been fun but was as meaningless to her as to him. Just as the last couple had been.

There'd be no more. She didn't dare allow it. She had to stay objective. Unentangled. Ready to act when she found out what that infernal Pierce wanted, then go home to her own time. There was no future but frustration in kissing that man.

She hurried along the hard earth of the compound, her way

illuminated by the small light of her candle and the greater brightness of the moon. In all her travels, no matter how far from a city she'd been, she'd never seen as many stars in the night sky of her own time.

Amazingly, she loved it.

Still, the edge of the forest loomed before her, and she shuddered. There were Indians out there—maybe even that Nahtana, lurking and watching for his next chance to . . . what? She didn't want to know. She recalled, too, her foray into the woods the previous night—and her encounter with the wolves. The rustling of leaves in the slight breeze and the night birds' calls did nothing to dispell the eeriness. She picked up her pace.

There was an extra horse in the stable, a pretty white mare that must belong to the mousy guest who'd just arrived.

In her room, Mariah put down her writing utensils and lit her betty lamp, hanging it on the wall. When she closed the inside wooden shutters at the windows the room filled with the unpleasant odor of burning lamp grease. She moved the small table close to the bed, avoiding the clothes tree where her laundry now hung. She sat on the edge of the rustling mattress, uncorked the ink bottle and lifted the quill pen.

For a moment, she stared at her right hand, recalling the feel of Thorn's fingers surrounding hers. Something as warm and slow-moving as heated maple syrup moved through her, and she closed her eyes. Thorn was getting under her skin, and she didn't like it. Not one bit. It was one thing for the screenplay Matilda to fall for her Thorn, but for Mariah to feel anything for the real thing was absurd. Not when his moods were as changeable as the surface of a river.

"It's just lust, dummy," she told herself. The softly spoken words had the chilling effect she wanted. Matilda and her experiences notwithstanding, Mariah would stay far away from Thorn.

She stared at the ink-spotted paper, thinking. For self-preservation, she needed to anticipate everything that might happen here, all the screenplay's episodes.

Writing small, wrapping her words around the blots, she

jotted down what had already transpired: the river rapscallions; the wolves; the Indian.

What was next?

Amazingly, her own life had become even more exciting than Matilda's. Matilda hadn't had so many adventures. Her story had been told in one hundred twenty short, exciting pages, the standard for a two-hour film.

Mariah's life, though—there might be no limit.

Damn Pierce anyway! After years of misery, she'd finally taken control of her life, started a career based on her skills, gained self-confidence—only to find herself here with no power at all. She slammed her fist against the small table, making it wobble. As she stood to stabilize it, her quick motion caused the flame on the betty lamp wick to flicker and almost go out.

"Cool it!" she commanded herself, sitting down again. Her fingers still clenched, she made herself take one calming breath, then another. Making notes would give her back some small sense of control.

What could she remember from the script? If only her memory were photographic. If only she'd known her life might depend on memorizing the screenplay. As it was, she had perfect recollection of some parts of the story, but only dim recall of others.

There had been something about a group of settlers, though she had skimmed over that part. Now Mariah understood why an army troop followed the homesteaders, though she hadn't while reading the script. She jotted down all the detail she could remember, listening to the scratching of the quill on the paper, pleased she didn't make even one blot.

Thanks to Thorn.

No. None of that. She set her mind back on her task.

There was an Indian uprising in the screenplay, and Matilda's capture. Mariah shivered at that recollection. After her brief ordeal with Nahtana, she prayed that this was one incident in which the script would be way off base. What she'd gone through had been scary, but it was minor compared to the incident in the screenplay. If that took place, she wouldn't want to be in Matilda's boots.

Especially since Matilda had had to rely on Thorn to free her.

The same strange thought she'd had before struck Mariah: Where was Matilda now? Had Pierce done something to a real woman so Mariah could take her place?

The idea unnerved Mariah further, and she bit her lower lip. Somehow, she'd have to learn what had happened to the woman whose life she now lived. She only hoped her counterpart was all right.

She recalled another frightening incident from the script: a siege of the inn by raiders. Why had the men attacked the inn and its inhabitants? She racked her brain in frustration, but all she remembered was that the outcome had been violent, the norm for scripts of adventure movies.

She wished she could at least recall the order in which the script's events had unfolded.

The only other incident she remembered well was the duel. A young soldier had called Thorn out. What was his name? She couldn't recall. "Damn it!" she said aloud, stamping her boot on the floor. Pressing down on the paper, she nearly broke off the nib of the quill in frustration before she calmed herself. Fortunately, only a tiny inkblot appeared on the page.

That duel at the end was the most important part of the screenplay, and she could only remember a few details about it.

Thorn would die in it.

A spasm of something icy plunged through Mariah. That couldn't happen. Not here. Not for real.

If that was the wrong she was to right . . . not that Thorn meant anything to her. But in his way he'd been good to her, sheltering her, saving her more than once, however grudgingly.

She owed him. She wouldn't let him die.

Not if she could anticipate and prevent it.

That was enough for tonight. With a sigh, she recorked the ink bottle and placed the paper and other materials under her bed. She'd find a better place to hide them in the morning.

Among the clothing she'd washed was a pretty white

nightgown with a touch of lace at the throat and sleeves. She put it on and lay down.

She couldn't sleep. Her experiences in the past weren't what preyed on her mind. Nor was her frustration at being unable to remember the details of Pierce's screenplay.

Nor, for a change, was it her nightmare of that cursed Pierce's voice commanding her, "You must right a grievous wrong."

Instead, she kept reliving the kisses she'd shared with Thorn. His caresses, his heated, arousing touches.

If only he were more like Matilda's Thorn. If only . . . She drifted, finally, to sleep.

"Mademoiselle! Mariah!"

Groggily, Mariah sat up in bed. "Yes?" she croaked.

"It is morning. Get up, please." The sound of hurrying footsteps on the wooden floor outside her room receded quickly.

At least René had been polite, she thought as she pulled herself from bed. He'd said *please.*

She didn't feel polite herself.

She wondered if Thorn was awake, or if he let his servants get breakfast ready before he deigned to arise.

Somehow, she doubted that. He was probably already out in the forest flicking knives at poor, defenseless bunnies.

She could only guess that it was dawn. With the shutters closed the light coming in was faint.

She was a servant, after all. She'd been coddled the previous morning by being allowed to sleep in, but that had to be an aberration. She was expected to work.

And she'd once considered dawn the time of day when only others awoke.

If she were home, she'd drag herself to the microwave and put in some instant flavored coffee. Then, she'd go down the hall to the bathroom, use its facilities, shower and put on her makeup. She'd . . . But she wasn't home. She was here. And now.

She wouldn't get coffee; they had tea. She'd have to make

it herself after stoking the fire, drawing water from the stream.

Then, if she wanted breakfast—which she rarely did at home—there would be mush. Or porridge, as they called it here.

As to facilities, she'd made the acquaintance of the outhouse and had gotten used to holding her breath upon entering.

The one thing she hadn't found a substitute for yet was a shower. She'd made good use of the washbasin. But maybe she could bathe in the stream sometime when she went for water.

Not now, though. After her experience with the Indian the day before, she couldn't imagine going to the stream alone again. She most certainly didn't want René as an audience. Or Thorn.

Definitely not Thorn.

Although she wondered what he would look like—

Ridiculous. Turning her thoughts in a less dangerous direction, she smiled as she realized that she didn't have to wear that same pink dress that day. She took the clean brown one from the clothes tree and put it on. It fit perfectly.

Why wasn't she surprised? That interfering twit Pierce had thought of everything.

But how had he known her size?

And where was he? If the river rats hadn't lied, Pierce was somewhere here, in the past. If she ever met up with him again, she'd have the truth from him about why she was here. She'd wring his ancient, scrawny neck to get it, if she had to.

She put on an apron and glanced down. She even looked like a serving wench. Mariah checked her notes from the night before, placed everything carefully beneath the mattress, stuffed a handkerchief into her pocket and left the room.

One good thing about being here, she thought as she hurried past the stabled horses a short while later, was that she didn't have to worry about makeup. Even if she had some, she probably wouldn't dare put it on. Weren't the only women who painted their faces in these days prostitutes?

"Good morning," she said cheerfully to René as she raced into the kitchen.

"Ah, so you did rise." A broad smile lit his toad face. "Then I have won the bet with Thorn."

Mariah scowled. So Thorn didn't think she would get up, did he? Well, she'd show him how wonderful a servant she could be.

It was simply acting a role. She'd watched actors get into character. She could do that, too.

René had already gotten the fire roaring. "I have served the porridge already," he said. "Thorn, he is with our guest, who wishes to leave early, once breakfast is over. This was another visitor who has much to say—the easiest kind for me to convince Thorn to keep company." He sighed, then looked embarrassed, as though he had said too much.

"I'm sure Thorn can be quite hospitable." Mariah hoped she did not sound sarcastic, but Thorn hadn't struck her as particularly friendly to anyone.

Although those kisses of his hadn't exactly been antagonistic, they'd lacked follow-through.

And caring.

René seemed not to consider her comment offensive. "Both of us, we wish to learn what others know about the settlers, the Indians, the traders, the political situation—whatever each visitor can impart." He leaned toward her conspiratorially as she stood beside the hearth. "Do you know, there are—how you call rumors that some people in this land wish to gain independence from England?" He looked delighted.

"Really? So soon? I assumed this was around 1765." Mariah cringed at René's puzzled frown.

"It is 1768, Mariah." He hesitated. "Were you perhaps ill before you came here?"

"No . . . just taught the wrong things." Careful, she admonished herself. The last thing she wanted was for anyone here to think her crazy.

No—the last thing might be for them to think of her as a future-predicting witch. Though this was long after the Salem witch trials, superstition still had to be rampant. They might not burn what they didn't understand, but she didn't want to find out what they *would* do.

To change the subject, she said with a rueful smile, "I blew it again, didn't I? I got up too late to help you with breakfast."

"Blew?" The short Frenchman glanced toward the fire and the unlit candles on the wooden mantel shelf.

She was really making a mess of things this morning! "I—I mean, I made another mistake."

René shrugged his massive shoulders and gave his broad, toadlike grin. "It is nothing, mademoiselle. I am used to making the breakfast. But if you wish, you may redeem yourself. I saw yesterday there were gooseberries ripening near the stream. Come, you can gather them while I fish."

That sounded like fun—particularly since René would be there. She'd no interest in wandering into the woods on her own.

As they walked across the compound, René carried a rope net tied to a wooden frame and a bucket. Mariah held a couple of empty buckets for the fruit. She stepped into the dark confines of the forest and began picking her way along the well-beaten path, over the undergrowth and between trees. There was no breeze that morning. The air was fresh and verdant, and she inhaled deeply, loving the smell. Surprisingly, loving this place.

If only she didn't feel so nervous about its dangers, she might believe she'd found somewhere she could call home.

She gave a quick, amazed shake of her head. Where had that thought come from? Give her someplace cosmopolitan in her own time, not this primitive, perilous backwood, despite its beauty.

She followed René, who made no effort to be silent in his tromping through the underbrush. When she heard a rustling off to one side, she stopped to listen, but the sound soon ceased without revealing the forest creature who'd made it.

Several birds began to warble, and Mariah found herself smiling at the cheerful songs. Surely there could be nothing dangerous lurking on a day when the birds sounded so unconcerned.

Then why, suddenly, did she have a sense of foreboding?

Foolishness, she told herself. Still, her breathing was shallow as she hurried to catch up with her companion.

They reached the stream. It meandered off through the woods, gurgling and pulsing over its shallow, rocky bed. She spotted a small fish darting between rocks, and then another.

"*Ici.*" René handed her his bucket. "Here." He stepped a few paces into the woods, and Mariah saw a bush with deep green leaves from which clusters of lime-colored berries hung.

"I've never eaten gooseberries before," she said, trying one. Its tangy taste resembled a plum's. "Wonderful!" She began picking them and putting them into a bucket.

"I am going to catch the bigger fish for supper," René said, heading again for the stream. Mariah followed. "There is a deep spot in the water close by." He began to walk upstream, then turned back. "I will not go far. You must call if you have a need for me."

She nodded, then watched with dismay as he disappeared around a curve. She had a need for him to stay near, but she said nothing. Women of this time weren't sissies, even if they'd recently been in danger.

Where was Thorn? She didn't see him trying to keep her out of trouble.

Then again, why should he?

She'd call René if anything, however small, bothered her.

Anything but the uneasiness that sent pulsing jitters through her chest. Had something happened in the screenplay that foreshadowed something now? She couldn't remember. Still . . .

What about that Indian? Where was he?

Her throat had gone dry. Staring apprehensively in the direction in which René had gone, she knelt and cupped her hands in the stream. It was cold! It soothed her poor hands, though, still sore after yesterday's laundry ordeal.

She refused to think of Thorn's caress. The way he had guided her, taught her to use the quill pen. Kissed her . . .

She had to turn her thoughts in other directions.

She walked beneath the trees to gather more gooseberries . . . and then she heard it.

She froze, nearly dropping her bucket. Surely she'd been mistaken. The sound had seemed so low, after all, that the noise of the rushing stream almost hid it.

But then she heard it again. A low, painful cry.

It sounded like a human moan.

Couldn't be. She looked wildly around. Weren't there animal cries nearly indistinguishable from human?

She heard it a third time. It seemed to come from downstream, from the opposite direction from the way René had gone, from somewhere in the darkly ominous forest.

The noise could be a trap, luring her away from the stream. But why? If anyone were after her, it would be easy enough to snatch her. Of course, she'd scream for René.

Why wait? "René," she yelled.

"Mademoiselle!" She saw him run around the stream's bend; he must have been just out of sight. "Is something not right?"

"Yes. I heard strange sounds." She pointed. "That way."

René caught up with her, then stomped off in the direction she'd indicated.

Slowly, carefully, her breathing so slow that she felt lightheaded, she picked her way after him.

René practically stumbled over the noise's source. "*Mon dieu!*" he cried, then knelt.

A woman lay on the leaf-strewn ground. She was battered and bloody.

"Oh, no!" Mariah cried as she fell to the twig-prickly ground beside René, then shot her hand over her mouth. What if the woman's attackers were still around?

"Are you all right?" she whispered to the unconscious figure. Stupid question. The woman didn't move. As René touched her head, Mariah felt her neck for a pulse, as she'd seen countless times in the movies.

She was alive.

At home, Mariah would have run to the nearest house and dialed 911. An ambulance would have been dispatched quickly to take this poor woman to the nearest hospital.

There were no hospitals in this wilderness. Mariah doubted that even Pittsburgh had one at this time, although there would probably be medical help for the soldiers. Hadn't someone mentioned a visiting doctor when she was there?

No, as with everything else in this time, she had to put up with primitive conditions. "Let's get her to the inn," she said.

"*Oui,*" René agreed.

Though the lady didn't seem taller than Mariah, she was built more fully. Still, after Mariah helped him lift the dead weight of the unconscious woman, the Frenchman effortlessly carried her in his arms back toward the compound.

"What should we do with her?" Mariah asked, following quickly behind.

"Thorn, he will know," said René.

"Take her back," Thorn commanded.

Mariah rose from where she'd been kneeling beside the woman who lay on her bed. She stared in indignation toward the large man filling the doorway. "Okay, Mr. Lord-of-the-Inn Thorn, I'll just toss her back into the woods so the wolves can get her. Or Indians. They could have done this to her, but we won't know till she wakes up."

He scowled. He must have been interrupted from something active, for a sheen glistened on his brow, and sweat formed patches on his white linen shirt.

Mariah decided to make her intentions clear. "Look, Thorn, I don't know what your problem is, but this poor woman is going to stay right here till she's better. Understood?"

"It is understood, Miss Walker." His clipped British voice was colder than the stream had been that morning. "But you will be responsible for her; do not look to me."

"Fine." Mariah spoke through clenched teeth. What was wrong with this unfeeling man? "I thought people took care of strangers in these days. Let them stay overnight in their homes, because there weren't a lot of inns. Took care of injured strangers, because there weren't many cities with doctors, let alone hospitals."

The anger on his face segued into confusion. "That is how I began my inn, Miss Walker. I came here to be alone, but strangers came to my door begging shelter. I decided to provide it to them—for a price. But that was not long ago. You speak as though you discuss a time far past."

Mariah dropped her gaze. Oops. "I—I misspoke. It's just that I come from . . . the east, where there are more towns that already have established inns and doctors' practices."

She turned back toward the woman. She didn't remember a similar character from the screenplay. Was her arrival an event that was unforeshadowed?

"If you despise the frontier so," Thorn spat, his anger apparently overcoming confusion, "then go back to your comfortable existence in the east. Where servants cater to you so your hands stay pretty and soft."

To Mariah's dismay, tears flooded her eyes. She blinked them away, angry with herself.

Her hands. She glanced at them. Their redness was less dramatic now than the day before, but their skin was beginning to flake. She couldn't help thinking again of his tenderness when he had touched them. . . .

Angrily, she thrust them behind her back. "My hands have nothing to do with anything. I'm here because I have to be, but that doesn't mean I'll let someone treat me badly. Or anyone else for that matter. Why does this woman's staying bother you?"

She watched as Thorn hesitated. When he spoke, it was slowly, with a deep emotion that Mariah did not understand. "Because she's helpless. And because—"

The rest of what he said was interrupted by a moan. Mariah turned to see the woman struggling to rise. Rushing to her side, Mariah gently pushed her back to the bed.

"There," she said triumphantly. "She's waking. She'll be better soon, I'm sure." But when Mariah turned back toward the door, Thorn was gone.

Only then did she realize that his last, interrupted words had sounded a lot like, "I'll fail *her,* too."

* * *

Mariah sent René back toward the stream for her buckets. She certainly didn't want to go back there alone, not until she knew what had happened to the injured woman.

While he was gone, Mariah unbuttoned the woman's dress and loosened the uncomfortable-looking stays she found beneath. The woman was bruised all over. There were what appeared to be rope burns about her wrists and ankles. Mariah hadn't any idea how to check for internal injuries, but at least the woman had no fever.

When René returned, he brought a pail of water. Using a clean rag, Mariah bathed the blood off the woman's swollen, filthy face.

"*Pauvre petite.*" René touched the woman's limp hand.

Petite? To Mariah the woman looked somewhat buxom. She certainly was pitiable in her current condition, with her wheat-blond hair streaked with mud, one eye blackened and her wrists and ankles raw. She seemed younger than Mariah—mid-twenties, perhaps.

Mariah liked the idea that René was concerned about her. Maybe he'd help Mariah stand up to Thorn.

Had she really heard him say something about letting her down?

"Please . . ." came a soft whisper from the bed.

"You're awake!" Mariah exclaimed.

The woman's eyes were open. They blinked in confusion. Her lashes were so light in color they were almost invisible near her unbruised eye but contrasted severely with the blackened one.

"Please," she repeated. "I don't . . ."

Apparently the effort was too much for her. Her eyes closed and her breathing deepened.

"She's unconscious again," Mariah told René.

He nodded. "But not for long, I think. Mademoiselle Mariah, she will need something soon to eat. What—?"

"Chicken soup," interrupted Mariah with a laugh. At home, she'd just open a can and throw the filled bowl into the microwave. Or maybe she'd send out to the local deli that delivered.

Here, if they even had chickens, they'd probably have to start with killing and cleaning one. And they might be as precious as pen and paper. Quail soup, maybe?

René's toad eyes narrowed in concentration. "Turkey," he said finally.

"Sure." Did they have wild turkeys wandering around like wolves? Maybe they'd domesticated some, though she hadn't noticed any.

"I will see what I can do," the Frenchman said.

Their injured guest didn't regain full consciousness that day, though they were able now and then to get her to sip water. But that evening, Mariah was just coming into her bedroom to spell René, who'd taken turns keeping an eye on the woman, when she heard raised voices—a male and a female.

She threw open her door to find René glaring at the woman in the bed, who glared right back at him. Her wheat-light hair was pulled away from her face and she sat up, blankets propping her back. She looked like a Jack Russell terrier, with a pronounced overbite and the bruise ringing her eye. "The French are as savage as the Indians who fought with 'em," the woman spat at René. She seemed to have little strength to hold up her body, but her voice wasn't weak. She'd a strong accent Mariah couldn't quite place, though it sounded more or less British.

"*Anglaise,*" growled René, as though it were the most vile swear word he could imagine.

Maybe, to him, it was.

"Hey, break it up," Mariah commanded.

They both turned their glares on her.

"Glad to see you're awake." Mariah approached her charge and held out her hand.

The woman leaned forward. Her grip was weak but not flaccid. "If you're Mariah, Reenee here—" She pronounced René's name oddly, and Mariah wondered if it was on purpose. "—says I have you to thank for my rescue."

"No need to thank me," Mariah said. "And you're . . . ?"

"My name's Holly. Holly Smith." The introduction

sapped her of her remaining strength, for she blanched and sagged, her face nearly as pale as her hair. Her eyelids fluttered and closed.

"Take it easy, Holly," Mariah said in alarm. Before she could reach the injured woman, René was straightening her.

Holly's eyes opened just a little, and a faint smile played at the corners of her ashen lips. "Thanks, Frenchy," she murmured. She nestled back, her breathing becoming even as she slept once more.

"Bah!" René scowled and backed away. "Foolish *Anglaise.* She needs her rest, but she is arguing like she's hale as a French farmwoman. I have work to do; I cannot be bothered with her." But Mariah noted with interest that he stopped and looked at Holly one final time before he scuttled out the door.

He returned to spell Mariah awhile later, carrying a small wooden bowl that contained broth and a pewter spoon. "We had the smoked turkey," he explained. "I boiled it for this consommé."

Mariah took a sip. Its smoky, salty flavor was wonderful. "Delicious!" she pronounced. "I'll feed it to her while you—"

He waved his free hand. "Ah, no, Mariah. You have tended this foolish woman enough. And Thorn, he wishes you to serve supper. There are guests this evening, and I have prepared for cooking the squirrels he brought from today's hunting."

Thank heavens, Mariah thought. She couldn't slice and gut a poor, dead squirrel any more easily than a bunny rabbit. And how could Thorn kill squirrels, when he kept one as a pet?

René put the soup bowl down on the table and sat on the edge of the bed. He gently shook Holly, who stirred. Her moan sounded irritable rather than pained. "Time to eat, *Anglaise.*" René seemed to take pleasure in disturbing her. "If you do not, you will have no energy to torment the French any longer."

Holly's eyes opened, and she glared at the Frenchman. "Bring me some food, then," she whispered.

"Here." He dipped a small amount of soup onto the spoon. As he brought it to Holly's mouth, Mariah left her room.

As she walked through the stable and across the compound toward the inn, she noticed no strange horses. If their guests had arrived, they must have come by water.

She heard loud clumping and soft mutterings as she opened the kitchen door. To remove loaves of bread, Thorn was shoving the long-handled paddle into the recess in the fireplace used for baking. He shook his head in apparent irritation as he worked, causing the ends of his long hair to sway at his collar. The full sleeves of his white shirt slid along his arms while he carried the bread on its wood paddle and set it down on a table.

"Hi," she said cheerfully.

"You have work to do, Miss Walker," he growled.

"What did you ever do without me?" As she took the paddle from him, their hands brushed. Startled at the contact with warm, hair-sprinkled skin, Mariah glanced at Thorn. The heat in his gaze was speculative, suggestive, as though he had ideas of what he would like to do with her.

Ideas she shared and found more than a little appealing.

Ideas she dared not have, not here, in this time, with this man.

She moved with deliberate calmness to pick up a loaf and set it down beside the others. "How many guests are here?" she asked. Her matter-of-fact tone was perfect, not letting on in the least that she'd been unnerved.

"Three," he said. "A family. And to answer your earlier question, what I did without you, before you arrived here, was to rely on René. He had no distractions like sick intruders to take him from his work."

Instead of throttling him, Mariah put down the paddle and pulled a tankard from its shelf along the wall. "Maybe when Holly is feeling better," she snapped, thumping the cup down on the table, "she can apologize for having been attacked."

"Holly? She's awakened enough to tell you her name?"

Mariah nodded as she continued gathering wood and pewterware to serve the meal. Then she approached the hearth. A series of meat slices were on a rack ready to place over the fire. "Should I cook these now?"

"Yes. In fact—"

He stopped as a woman slowly walked through the kitchen door and peered around hesitantly. She was an Indian, with plaited black hair, cheekbones Mariah would have killed for and shy ebony eyes. She wore a fringed doeskin dress that hung loosely on her slight form. "Excuse me, but I would like to help," she said in perfect English, though with a slight coarseness to her accent.

Mariah glanced at Thorn, who was sharpening a knife on a whetting stone at the hearth. The scraping sound grated on Mariah's nerves, and so did the pretty woman's presence. Thorn had hardly glanced at her, but his avoidance seemed deliberate. Who was she? Thorn's lady friend?

The thought caused a lump the size of the whetting stone to harden in Mariah's stomach.

"Nice of you to offer, Mrs. Rafferty," he replied. His tone was a growl, as though it pained him to be polite. "Mariah, here, can tell you what to do."

Mariah eyed the woman doubtfully. "Well, let's see—" Using rags to protect her hands, she placed the meat-laden metal rack over the fire and looked around. René had begun a side dish that looked like hominy, though its aroma was sweet. It hung in a small pot from one of the iron bars over the fire. The meat would take little time to broil; the fire was hot. Mariah lifted the pot. "Mrs. Rafferty, maybe you can put this into a serving bowl." She rested the pot on the hearth and went to get a wooden bowl and pewter ladle.

Two men burst through the kitchen door as Mrs. Rafferty spooned the mixture into its container. "What's the holdup, Thorn?" barked the older one. He had a scruffy beard and looked as though he'd never bathed in his life. "Me and my boy's hungry. Ain't Elkie here helpin' out? When's supper?"

"Soon, Rafferty," Thorn retorted. "Sooner yet if we just let the women finish."

Rafferty? This was the Indian woman's husband? He looked a half century older, and Mariah couldn't imagine the lovely lady letting someone like him anywhere near her. Or the other man, for that matter. Boy, rather. He seemed to be in his late teens. His scrawny black beard was as unkempt as the older man's, and he appeared equally unwashed.

Was this a family as Thorn had said—husband, wife and son? Mrs. Rafferty, though she could be older than she appeared, looked as though she belonged with the others as much as a kitten belonged in a lion's den.

It dawned on Mariah that Mrs. Rafferty was working here as though she, too, were a servant. With a smile at the woman, who quickly looked away, Mariah approached Thorn. He was honing another knife. She said sweetly, "Mr. Thorn, shouldn't our guests relax in the other room while we finish up in here?"

"That's right nice of you, ma'am." Rafferty drew closer to her. She did her darnedest not to gag at his smell.

"We want to treat our guests right," she said with a bright smile. "Now, why don't you and your family pick a table in the other room, and Mr. Thorn and I will bring the food in a minute."

"Yes, ma'am," Rafferty said. "Come on, Zeb." He gave a curt nod at the boy, and the two of them headed for the door.

"Mrs. Rafferty, you go, too." Mariah said. "Thanks for your help."

All three men stopped what they were doing and looked at her. Mrs. Rafferty seemed unusually absorbed in the chore of scraping the bottom of the pot she'd emptied.

"She's our guest, too." Mariah glared at Thorn for support.

He tilted his head, as though trying to figure her out. "She's right," he finally grumbled. "Mrs. Rafferty, we're here to serve all our guests."

Mariah noted the wideness of Mrs. Rafferty's luminous black eyes as she allowed herself to be shooed away to a seat in the other room. During the meal, Mariah made a point of serving the woman first, smiling at her each time their gazes met and ignoring her husband's and son's scowls as they waited for food.

After a while, Mrs. Rafferty seemed to relax and enjoy being served. Mariah guessed this might be a first.

Thorn joined the family for the meal, while Mariah, trying to accept humility, waited on them all. In the course of the conversation, she learned that Rafferty was a trader who traveled from post to post, bartering goods. Given the names he dropped and the stories he told of who'd found what goods or been attacked where, she suspected he also exchanged gossip. And thanks to his wife, who was the daughter of an Ottawa chief, he was also welcome to trade in the camps of several Indian nations.

That explained why he had married her. More questionable was why she had married him.

Her name, Mariah learned, translated to Little Elk. The coarse Rafferty had nicknamed her Elkie. Mariah wasn't sure whether she was being treated like a second-class citizen because she was Indian or because she was a woman.

Either way, Mariah didn't like it.

Rafferty mentioned that their son was seventeen. Youthful Little Elk must have been little more than his age when she'd borne him.

"We'll be off first thing in the morning," Rafferty was saying. He spit crumbs of bread from between his teeth as he talked, but that didn't stop him from either stuffing more bread in his mouth or from talking. "Next post downriver ain't too far off, a new one named Harrigan's. We'll hit it, then go on a bit. No fine inns like this where we're heading."

Harrigan's. Why did the name sound familiar to Mariah? She knew nothing about any trading posts in this time. Her hands were full of dirty dishes, but she hesitated at the common room door to eavesdrop further.

"You been to Harrigan's yet?" the younger Rafferty asked Thorn. Mariah hadn't heard him say much, but his voice, though higher, was as gruff as his father's. His table manners weren't much better, either.

"Several times." Thorn seemed oblivious to his guests' foul habits, though he, too, ate as though he'd been hungry. "It's farther down the Ohio than Pittsborough is upstream, but I've found it worth the trip."

"The tradin's fair, then?" Rafferty leaned his head toward Thorn conspiratorially. "I heard tell that Harrigan had a stingy heart you couldn't pierce with an arrow."

Pierce. Harrigan. That was it! The river rats had told Mariah they were taking her to Harrigan's to meet the old schemer who'd somehow brought her here.

Mariah did not recall the Raffertys from the screenplay, but maybe they had a role to play here anyway.

She rushed over toward the awful-looking Rafferty as though he'd suddenly offered her a ticket home. Maybe he had. She avoided looking at Thorn as she planted herself at Rafferty's side and tried not to wrinkle her nose as she gently touched his shoulder. With a small smile at Little Elk, who regarded her quizzically, she said, "Please, Mr. Rafferty, take me along."

Chapter Nine

"No!"

Thorn's response surprised him as much as it did the others, judging by their stares. Still, he clutched at the sharpened knife he'd been using to cut the squirrel meat. He raised it as though preparing to skewer Mariah Walker with it.

She couldn't leave. They had unfinished business between them. Hadn't she insisted that he hire her?

The fact that her leaf-green eyes besotted him, that her body drove him mad with its lithe, sensual grace, that she'd the courage to stand up to him, to work hard despite her obviously coddled upbringing—they had nothing to do with his demand that she stay.

He had half risen from his seat at her words. She stood across from the table beside Rafferty's chair, still holding the supper plates she'd been carrying into the kitchen. She looked every bit the serving wench she was, in her brown dress beneath an apron, yet the spirit within her remained untamed.

Now, there was surprise in those spellbinding eyes as she

watched him. A question or two. And maybe a bit of relief as well?

Not likely. If she wanted to leave, he should let her. He'd be better off with her gone. Things at his inn would return to the way they'd always been.

He felt the eyes of their "guests" on him as well. That's what she'd called them. To him, they were just the fools who handed over silver or goods to hire a roof for the night. On a clear night with no storms, they could just as easily have made camp anywhere in the forest, cooked their own suppers and saved their wealth.

That way, too, they would not have had to waste their time in the presence of the cowardly Thorn.

"I—" Mariah seemed at a loss for words, unusual for the woman who'd burst into his life making demands. "Mr. Thorn, if you're concerned about my repaying what I owe, I've been working for you the last few days. Whatever I haven't earned, I'll send to you, if you'll tell me what it is."

His laugh was not particularly pleasant. She expected him to trust her. He knew better than to trust anyone.

People had trusted him once, and look where it had gotten them. Even his own kin.

"I am certain you would, Miss Walker," he lied. "I am more concerned about that woman you took in. Who would look after her if you left? René would certainly have no time."

She looked stricken. Ah, the kindhearted Miss Walker had somehow forgotten about her charge.

"Maybe," she said tentatively, looking down beseechingly at her unlikely rescuer, Rafferty, "we could take her along?"

"Forgit it!" Rafferty pushed back his chair so it scraped along the wooden floor. His wide grin revealed he'd more missing teeth than remaining ones. "No room, Miss Walker," he said. "We're too loaded down on our boat to carry even one more person. I've hidden the craft well in the weeds by the river along with our goods, but it's small. Besides, we'd have to charge passage, and I figger you're already in debt. Ain't that right?"

"I guess, but—"

"It's settled, then."

Thorn watched the sympathy in Little Elk's coal-dark eyes as Mariah's sought them, but then the Indian woman looked away, her dark braids catching on her shoulders. For a moment, Mariah appeared defeated. He had an urge to rise, to touch her sweet, determined chin and use it to raise her lowered head. Instead, he pursed his lips. Nonsensical, that he should feel sorry for her.

Especially when he also felt a ludicrous sense of relief. She wasn't leaving.

She raised her own head then, and circled the table. Putting the plates down once more, she knelt at Little Elk's side. "May I ask you a favor?"

The woman glanced first at her husband, as though asking his opinion. Rafferty's eyes narrowed suspiciously, and he gave a curt shake of his head.

But then Little Elk raised her own chin, though not as high as Mariah's. "If I can," she said, not meeting her husband's irritated gaze.

Mariah had clearly caught the exchange, for she said, "It's a simple request, really. And it costs nothing. Just, if you happen to meet a man named Pierce at Harrigan's, please tell him that Mariah is eager to see him. You can mention you saw me at Thorn's Inn, but I'm sure he knows I'm here."

"I will do that, Miss Walker," the woman said in her soft voice. "Or if I meet this Pierce somewhere else on our journeys."

Thorn tightened his grip on his knife, although he had no target in mind. At least none that was present. Who was this man Pierce whom Mariah wanted to join?

And why did the idea of her wanting to meet up with any man turn his blood as cold as a mountain stream in winter?

Mariah took Little Elk's hand and grasped it. "Thank you," she said.

For a quickly discarded instant, Thorn wished that she would regard him with such warmth.

''Miss Walker, me and the boy would have a whiskey.''

Mariah had just returned to the common room after clearing the supper dishes to find Mr. Rafferty and his son Zeb leaning against the polished bar. Surprisingly, Thorn had helped her, and he was still in the kitchen. She didn't know what his policy on serving drinks was, nor whether Zeb was legally old enough for hard liquor in this time, so she said, ''I'll find Mr. Thorn. He'll take care of you.''

Zeb swaggered toward her. His shirt was spotted with food he'd aimed toward his mouth that night, and his trousers were damp from where he'd spilled half a tankard of ale—which he apparently was permitted to drink. ''I'd like you to take care of me, Miss Walker. Maybe you'd like a whiskey, too. We could go outside and drink in private.''

His father guffawed. Mariah didn't look at his mother, who still sat at the table where they'd eaten dinner. She was sure she'd see mortification on the poor woman's face, and she didn't want to add to her pain.

''Thanks, but I only drink with people old enough to keep their pants dry.'' With that, Mariah flounced from the room.

The older Rafferty's laugh followed her. He didn't care at whose expense he gained amusement, even his own family's.

How could his poor wife stand him?

She heard quick footsteps behind her. Obviously Zeb didn't take well to being insulted. She cringed a little and hurried into the kitchen.

Thorn was there scraping plates. He turned, and for a moment her heart leapt, for he seemed glad to see her. But then his expression hardened, and Mariah deflated. Yet again. A while earlier, when he'd objected to her leaving, she'd also felt a glimmering of pleasure—till he'd expressed his ulterior motive. He didn't want her to saddle him with poor Holly. Otherwise he didn't care whether she stayed or left.

His wishes shouldn't matter in the least. Maybe she was relating to him as a kidnap victim might with her captor;

reliance on even that kind of person sometimes resulted in gratitude and false caring.

That was the explanation she'd decided on long ago for her mother.

But she wouldn't let it be true of herself. Even though she was alone and needy in a strange time, she'd not make the mistake of relying on Thorn. Of caring for him.

Just as she was about to say something scathing, she realized his current icy stare was for Zeb, behind her.

"Something I can do for you?" he asked, taking a menacing step toward them. Only then did Mariah realize that Zeb, reaching forward, had almost grasped her arm.

"Nah," the young man mumbled, quickly retracting his hand. "My pa and me's just waiting for some whiskey, that's all."

"I will get it for them," said a voice from the doorway. René stood there, his squat body just inside the room.

"How is Holly?" Mariah dashed toward the Frenchman, stopping just before him.

The small man snorted derisively. "Ah, that *Anglaise*. She is awake, and such a nasty tongue on her. She wishes to be left alone now, and so I leave her alone."

Making sure Zeb wasn't following her, Mariah ran to check on her charge. Sure enough, Holly was sitting up in bed, looking utterly bored. At Mariah's entrance, she straightened. "Mariah! It's glad to see a friendly face, I am, after that Reenee's frowning, ugly puss." The bruises on her own face were not exactly glamorous. Her accent sounded British to Mariah, though she doubted it was the King's English, even in this era.

Mariah couldn't help smiling. "Glad you're awake. Are you well enough to tell me what happened to you?"

The young, tow-haired woman seemed to grow even more pale. "Indians," she whispered.

Mariah sat on the edge of the bed. "Do you want to talk about it?"

Holly's head shook so vehemently that Mariah was afraid she'd pass out again from dizziness. "Someday, but not now."

Mariah changed the subject. "I hear you've been giving René a hard time."

"Silly Frenchie wants to convince me that the English are what's wrong with this wilderness. We know, though, that it's the French who's egging on them Indians." She crossed her arms in front of her chest, and Mariah noticed she was now in a man's long-sleeved shirt that made her appear almost elfin, despite her buxom figure.

She wondered if it was René's shirt, and whether he had helped her into it.

Mariah saw to Holly's comfort, then said she'd bring her more to eat. But when she returned to the inn, the Raffertys were preparing for bed.

"Need to get up before sunrise," old Rafferty said, rubbing his scruffy beard. His words were slurred; he must have belted down quite a bit of whiskey in the short time Mariah had been gone.

Thorn and René showed the men to their room, while Mariah took Little Elk to hers. She prepared the bed in which the Indian woman was to sleep. "I am not used to being idle," Little Elk told her.

"Enjoy the moment," Mariah said with a smile.

As Mariah finished, Little Elk said, "We will leave in the morning before breaking our fast. I wish to thank you, Miss Walker. For everything."

"No big deal," Mariah responded.

"To me, it was a 'big deal.' " The Indian woman savored the last two words, as though using them for the first time. "A very big deal. I will try to deliver your message to that Mr. Pierce. And I will never forget you."

Mariah hadn't considered where she would sleep that night, but when she returned to the stable with her candle, Holly was still in her bed, sound asleep. She didn't want to bother Little Elk, but instead decided to find a spot in one of the other rooms in the stable.

She heard a noise in the first one as she touched its doorknob. Oh, great! Was Thorn's tame squirrel camped out there—or something worse?

She shoved open the door, hoping to scare away any critter that didn't belong. Instead, she found Thorn standing inside—and she knew he didn't scare easily.

His shoulders flexing beneath his loose shirt, he was placing a straw mattress on the rope-strapped wooden bed frame that Mariah had seen in there before.

"Oh," she said stupidly. Maybe he was sleeping here that night for some reason. "Excuse me." She turned to leave.

"Where are you going?" he demanded.

She shrugged. "I—"

"Since you've given up your own bed, you weren't about to do something else foolish like sleeping outside tonight, were you?" He straightened his tall, broad torso.

Why did he often make her feel like an irresponsible child instead of a grown woman who could take care of herself?

Maybe because this grown woman didn't know how to take care of herself. Not here. Not now.

But she wouldn't admit that to him. Again she shrugged. "I can sleep in the common room in a chair. I've slept sitting up before." The last time was on a jet, in a comfortable, reclining seat. But she wasn't about to tell him that.

Nor was she too keen on being somewhere Zeb could find her alone.

"No need. This is for you." He pointed toward the bed he'd just fixed.

"Really? Thanks." She felt a shimmering of pleasure that she quickly tamped down. The man had no interest in her comfort. He simply didn't want her to be in his way at the inn.

"You're welcome," he replied.

The silence grew disquietingly long. He watched her with brown eyes as unfathomable as the depths of the Ohio, and she found herself unable—unwilling—to look away.

Why was it she felt so uncomfortable around him at the same time she yearned to throw herself into his arms, to beg him to be her friend in this strange place?

He'd kissed her more than once, had shown an undeniable, intriguing physical interest in her, but he'd not made the tiniest overture about becoming her friend.

And yet, there were times when he was so caring, so sensitive. Like now, when he'd anticipated her need of someplace to stay for the night.

Finally, unable to stand the silence any longer, she began, "I wanted—" at the same time as he said, "One day soon—" They both stopped.

"You first," she said. She tossed her head nervously to get the hair out of her eyes.

"No, you." There was a hint of amusement in the softening of his strong features, the barest quirk upward at the edges of his well-defined lips.

"Now that Holly is feeling better, I could ask again if the Raffertys could take me tomorrow, so I won't be in your way."

"You still can't go," he stated, his expression hardening. She felt herself brighten. Did he actually want her to stay? But then he continued, "They already told you they haven't room."

"Oh. That's right." What a dummy she was, she told herself, for imagining he'd care whether she stayed or left. She looked down toward the planks of the wooden floor. This room was dustier than the one next door; she'd have to give it a good cleaning soon. If she were given time out from her chores for business of her own.

At least, with Holly improving, René and she both could work at the same time.

She remembered then. "What were you going to say before?" she asked Thorn.

"Just that, one of these days soon, I'll have need for some trade goods. If I go to Harrigan's, you may come along."

"Thanks," she said, her voice low. He would hate the idea that she was relying on him yet again.

He had to pass her to reach the door to the room. As his arm brushed hers, he stopped.

The point of contact tingled, spreading a current of heated awareness through her.

She recalled the times they'd touched before. The kisses he had plied her with so passionately. She closed her eyes, afraid he'd try it again.

Afraid he wouldn't.

But he moved again, toward the door. ''Good night, Mariah,'' he said. His voice was hoarse and low, and she wondered if he, too, was affected by their nearness. If he recalled their kisses.

''Good night, Thorn.''

Before she went to sleep that night, Mariah took her candle and sneaked into Holly's room. She wasn't as concerned about the quill pen and ink, though she'd learned her lesson well from Thorn and now realized they were precious commodities. But more important was the retrieval of her notes of what had happened in the screenplay. She wanted no one else to see them.

She still had no idea how Pierce had maneuvered her back here into Matilda's life, why he'd written this place and time, these people, into a movie script. Whether she'd correctly guessed the grievous wrong she was to right.

But here she was nonetheless, with no idea of Matilda's whereabouts.

She tried to be quiet as she slid her hand between the straw mattress and its wooden supports but couldn't help the slight crackle that resulted. She stood still as Holly turned over but, fortunately, didn't awaken.

With her fingertips, Mariah found the important piece of paper and carefully slid it out, returning to her room next door. She glanced at it in the candlelight.

Things had happened here in the past that hadn't even been suggested by the screenplay: Holly's rescue, the appearance of the Raffertys at the inn.

Maybe neither event had been significant enough to warrant Pierce's throwing them into the movie scenario, though Mariah had certainly thought them worthy. She believed she'd saved Holly's life, for the young woman would have died out there in the woods, alone and without help.

But that wasn't part of Thorn's story, and, after all, the screenplay had been about him.

And then there was Mariah's meeting with Little Elk. Again, it wasn't important to Thorn. Maybe not to Mariah either, or even to Little Elk. But Mariah was proud she'd been able to show the woman that she was worthy of men treating her well in this chauvinistic time.

She only hoped the woman remembered it, and tried to train those horrible men in her life accordingly. If she could.

Then there was Thorn and his story. Not even that followed the screenplay. Not exactly.

She needed to learn a lot.

And to understand why a man so admittedly unreliable set her blood pumping, contrary to every ounce of sense she possessed.

''You *shall* write a grievous wrong, my daughter.''

Mariah sat up with a start, gasping in the dark, unfamiliar surroundings.

She'd been dreaming—or had she?

Now, she recognized Pierce's voice issuing its order. But it had changed considerably from the directive that had haunted her dreams forever.

His daughter. He'd called her that before she'd slipped into unconsciousness at the Blockhouse. No wonder that had been added to the too-familiar directive. But it was no longer a command. It didn't tell her that she *must* right the wrong, but that she would.

And no longer did it sound so portentous, so ominous. Instead, there was a gleeful note to it.

''Don't be so sure, Pierce,'' she said into the darkness. ''Tell me for certain what it is and how to right it, and then we'll see.''

''Time to rise, Mariah.'' This time it was René knocking on her door.

She drew herself from bed. With all the physical labor she'd been doing lately, muscles she'd never become acquainted with before were now introducing themselves with soreness in some of the oddest places.

''Be with you in a minute,'' she called. She poured water from the pitcher into the basin and splashed her face—a far cry from her more time-consuming morning ablutions at home. She donned a cream-colored blouse and dark blue skirt, ran the wooden comb from her satchel of belongings through her hair and wondered what she looked like. Mirrors probably existed in these times, though perhaps they were luxuries that hadn't yet hit the wilderness.

Preparing to hurry to the kitchen, she peeked into the room next door—and found her charge out of bed, peering out the window.

"Holly!" Her exclamation erupted at her delight at seeing the woman conscious and moving. "How are you feeling?"

Holly turned. There was color in her cheeks now that wasn't just caused by bruising. Her pale hair, nearly clean, framed her round face, and her close-set hazel eyes were wide open and smiling. She still wore the man's shirt she'd slept in. "I'm fine, Miss Mariah. Feeling quite fit, in fact, and ready to pay back them who's helped me."

"Pay . . . ?" Mariah hesitated, not wanting to embarrass Holly.

Holly laughed. "No, I haven't got a bit o' coin or tradin' goods with me. But Frenchie told me this here's an inn. I did a bit of serving back east before . . . before, and I can help out till I'm on my way again."

"But you need to get your strength back," Mariah protested.

"Oh, I'll not be doing any more than I can stand." She hesitated for a moment. "Only problem is that I can't find my clothes."

"They were pretty well destroyed." Mariah surveyed the woman. She was shorter but much curvier. "I'm not sure anything I have will fit you. Let's see."

She pulled her sparse wardrobe from the neat pile she'd made in one corner.

"Oh, this is your room?" Holly sounded upset. "You didn't need to put yourself out on my account."

"No problem at all," Mariah said. "I just slept next door last night."

"Well, we'll switch, then, tonight."

"Sure." But Mariah wondered whether Thorn would put Holly up for another night. He had to; he couldn't turn her out if she had no place to go.

But he was so unpredictable: acting kind one moment, shouting about how unreliable he was the next.

As if she'd called him, he appeared in the doorway, filling it and the room with his domineering presence. "You are lucky, Mariah, that our guests chose to leave before eating this morning." Though his brown eyes were expressionless, there was no doubt from the thin set of his lips that he was displeased.

"Why is that?" She could no more keep herself from baiting him when he acted so arrogant than she could give up breathing. He wore a fringed leather shirt that morning with lines that emphasized the breadth of his chest. The soft, suede appearance of the shirt tempted her to touch it. To touch Thorn. To feel his arms about her again—

She'd do herself a favor, she thought, if she'd stop thinking of those kisses from this difficult man. She was not Matilda from the screenplay who dared to let loose her hormones around her fictional reliable Thorn.

"René said he awakened you fifteen minutes ago. You should have begun working on the fire and food by now."

"It's my fault, sir," piped up Holly, placing herself in front of Mariah as if to protect her from Thorn. "I kept her from getting to her work, but I can help out now, too. Once I have some clothes to wear, that is."

Mariah noted the way Thorn scanned her in the clothing she *was* wearing—the shirt that bulged out around her ample bosom and stopped at her knees, a length that was probably quite scandalous and suggestive in this time. Irritation with Holly flooded Mariah, and she opened her mouth to tell the woman to stop flaunting herself.

But she immediately recalled the situation: how ill Holly had been the day before, how her own clothing was shredded. And she realized the real source of her irritation; she was jealous that Thorn was eyeing the young woman with something more than relief that she was feeling better.

He had finished his ogling; in fact, he looked embarrassed, his eyes focused on the window beyond Holly as though he could see through its coated paper.

Mariah felt like laughing at his discomfort—and at her own reaction to it. Why should she care if Thorn found a dozen nude women to entice his libido?

"Miss Walker," he said, "can you perhaps help Miss—?"

"Smith," the woman supplied.

"—Miss Smith find something suitable to wear?"

"I'll try, Mr. Thorn." Mariah, enjoying his discomfort, couldn't quite keep the laugh from her voice. When Thorn shot an angry glare at her, she raised her eyebrows in an expression of innocence. He didn't look at her again as he stalked from the room.

"Handsome fellow, that," Holly Smith said, her wide, pale eyes still focused on the now-empty doorway. "But looks like he's got the temper of a stuck bull."

Mariah laughed. "An apt description," she agreed. She pulled the pink dress in which she'd arrived from the pile. It had cleaned up well, and she felt its color would suit the soft coloration of Holly Smith. But, glancing again at Holly, she remembered that the material had shrunk. No way would that dress fit Holly's ample bustline.

Instead, she pulled her remaining dress, a gray one, from the stack. She hadn't tried it on yet, but it had to be looser than the pink.

Sure enough, it fit Holly, though it was a bit snug on top. "Thank you, Mariah." Holly's tone was fervent as she whirled, dipped and tugged here and there at the drape of the dress. "Now, if we can just find a bit of material here, and a needle and thread, I'll have me a new dress in no time. You, too. I'm a good seamstress. How about you?" She stopped her restless movements and looked expectantly at Mariah.

Mariah shrugged. "I'm not much good at any of the skills necessary to survive around here." She attempted a smile but failed.

"Where you from?" Holly's head was cocked as she studied Mariah, as though trying to guess from her appearance.

"The east," Mariah said vaguely.

"Me, I'm from Yorkshire. Came here as a bond servant

to pay my passage, along with my brother Mack.'' Her soft, close-set eyes grew troubled.

''Where's Mack now?'' Mariah asked gently.

Holly didn't answer. ''Let's go fix some food for that dour woodsman and his French friend.''

Holly seemed to have recuperated completely from her mishap, except for an occasional wince when she bumped one of her bruises. She was a dynamo for the rest of the day, demonstrating to Mariah a multitude of the skills helpful to survival on the frontier: starting a fire quickly with just a tinder box; preparing simple recipes from few ingredients; cleaning clothing between washdays; sewing. And, yes, René did have needle and thread.

Holly turned out to be quite garrulous—about everything except herself. Nevertheless, Mariah learned, in bits and pieces, that Holly was older than the teenager she appeared. Her service as a bondsperson had finally terminated two months earlier, and so had her brother's. The two of them had joined up with a band of other former servants to head west for settlement.

But their band had been attacked by Indians. The men, including Holly's brother, had been killed, and the women taken captive.

Holly, who'd been treated badly, had managed to escape, and that was when Mariah had found her.

''And here I am, safe and sound here, at the inn of your friend Thorn.''

''He's not my friend,'' Mariah said immediately.

''Then why are you here?''

''It's a long story.'' Though Mariah sensed a potential comrade in this woman who told her horrible tale so briefly and in such an offhand manner, she wasn't ready to tell hers to anyone. Not yet. Maybe never.

Holly Smith had an instinct about people.

She thought about that fact as she and Mariah Walker finished scrubbing the wood floor of the kitchen and common room in the inn in the wilderness owned by the man Thorn.

Holly had known just by looking at him that the New

Jersey farmer who'd bought her bond off the boat was a fair chap; he'd smiled at her so exceedingly at the auction, his big teeth sticking out of his face.

Her belief had come true as soon as she'd thought it; Mr. Rice had agreed right off to buy Mack's bond, too, so she had not been separated from her brother for the seven years of her indenture. He had even paid them a small wage, which they'd saved, so they'd been ready to start a new life together on the frontier, where land was free for the taking but other goods were dear.

There'd been other times she'd known about people just by looking at them. Mr. Rice's neighbor, Hank Burrows, had wanted to pay off her bond and marry her, but she'd refused. There was something not quite right about his eyes.

Sure enough, he'd married Dora, another bond servant, and the poor woman had lost more than one baby thanks to the beatings Burrows had given her.

And she'd known right away when Mack and she and the group of other freed indentured servants had run into the band of Indians. The chief marauder had stared at her so evilly. . . .

No need to think about that now. Or about what had happened to Mack.

She was with Mariah Walker now, and her instincts told her that, though dark secrets swirled around this quiet lady, she was someone who could be trusted.

Lifting her sopping rag from the final corner she'd been cleaning, she put her dry hand at the small of her back and straightened, though she remained on her knees in her borrowed gray dress. Slowly, stiff from bending over, she stood, and found Mariah doing the same. They looked at each other and laughed.

Ah, yes, her instincts had not misled her this time.

"I haven't shown you upstairs yet," Mariah said. "Would you like to see?"

"Only if we can leave cleaning the floors there till another day."

Again Mariah shared with her a most gratifying laugh. But Holly wasn't fooled. Not she. From the look of Mariah earlier, she lacked merriness in her life. Perhaps, thought Holly, this was the first laugh for her compatriot in many a day.

And Holly was not one to just wonder why. She would see what could be done to help her new friend.

They climbed the steps at the edge of the common room. "These are the guests' quarters," Mariah told her. There was pride in her voice, as though she had an interest in how the inn ran. Holly knew she was just a servant, as she'd once been, but that kind of pride showed she was treated well.

Holly had earned her keep for that day, she had. Maybe there'd be an extra position here for her, till she could get her bearings, decide what to do now.

Now that Mack was gone.

No glumness now, Holly, she told herself. Time enough for that. She looked at the rooms pointed out by Mariah. "Nice!" she couldn't help exclaiming. They were, too. The two rooms were spacious and airy, with beds and blankets aplenty.

Mack and she, and the other servants of Mr. Rice, though well treated, had all been crammed into a hut half the size of one of these rooms. Not that they'd spent much time there; there hadn't been much time for sleeping on Mr. Rice's farm.

"Nice job, ladies."

Holly turned to see René, the Frenchman, coming up the stairs behind them.

"Pardon?" Mariah seemed unsure what he was talking about, but Holly knew. The floor downstairs was so clean he could serve bread on it.

Now, he was one her instincts warned her about. An arrogant blighter, was he. Hated all things English, including her.

That bothered her. He'd treated her kindly. She'd been aware of him hovering about while she slipped into wakefulness and out. But as soon as she could talk, he took to insulting her.

"Me, I've never seen the inn so clean downstairs," Frenchie said in that accent of his. Surprising, for such a nasty man, that he was so free with his thanks.

Of course they were directed more toward Mariah than her.

He was one she'd have to watch out for.

"Thank Holly," Mariah said. Nice lady, she was, though too free with her compliments. Her own contribution had to be recognized, too.

"But Mariah was the one who—"

The Frenchman waved his hand with a smile that brightened a face that was otherwise ugly. "Both of you," he said.

"Then there's a job for Holly." Sweet Mariah, pushing so to help her, Holly thought. She'd told her as they'd worked that she needed a position till she decided what to do.

Holly had felt the sympathy pour from Mariah as she'd told her tale of loss, and it had been all she could do not to cry about it. She'd been strong so far, but kindness might do her in.

"Ah, that is Thorn's decision," said Frenchie.

As the three of them returned downstairs, that very Thorn came through the door. He was a big one, he was, tall and straight. And talk of arrogance!

Now, with him her instincts said trouble. He was the one she'd need to impress to be allowed to stay, but he was not one to notice hard work. Not he. Kept his distance, he did.

And yet . . . there was something in the way he and Mariah did not look at each other, except sideways, when each thought the other wasn't looking.

Ah, Holly thought. Here was the trouble. Poor Mariah. She was attracted to the devil, she was.

But the dear, sweet lady wouldn't let Holly fight her own battle. "Thorn, did you notice how clean the kitchen and common room are?"

He nodded. "You're earning your keep after all, Miss Walker."

"It wasn't just me," she insisted. "Holly did a lot of the work. She needs a job, too." Kind thing, worrying about a stranger so.

The man put down on the table all he'd been carrying: a long rifle, the kind they used out here, and two dead rabbits.

He had a wide neck and a grim mouth. Here was another one who needed to laugh. "You've been here a few days, Miss Walker. You see that my inn has few guests. I've myself and René to feed, and now you. How can I afford yet another person?"

She approached him, though her head came only to that nose of his that would have looked as well on an aristocrat. "You've plenty to eat. There's lots of food in that smokehouse." She looked at him as though they shared some nasty secret about the smokehouse, arousing Holly's curiosity. She'd have to ask Mariah about that, she would. "And you keep bringing in more all the time." She looked pointedly toward the rabbits on the table.

"For security," he said. "We never know how many will come for supper or stay the night."

Her smile was secretive—again tickling Holly's interest. "No, I don't suppose you have an 800-number reservation system." Holly felt as puzzled as Thorn appeared. What did that mean?

"I will strike a bargain with you," Thorn said. There was a slight but nasty curve to those stern lips of his that Holly did not trust. "If you clean these rabbits, I will hire your friend for a week. Then we will see."

Mariah turned as white as the clouds in the summer sky. Poor thing must be a squeamish one. But with no hesitation she said, "All right."

Cruel man, Holly thought. She would help Mariah, for such things bothered her not in the least.

She noticed from the corner of her eye that Frenchie, too, took a step forward. She turned her head to look at him in surprise. He had a heart after all, that nasty one.

But Thorn did not leave Mariah's side. Instead, he handed her a sharp knife and motioned toward the table where the animal carcasses lay.

Mariah, bless her, did not hesitate but took the knife and approached the table. She drew in her lips and straightened her arms as though to distance herself from her own hands.

"No, Mariah," Holly said. "If you find this so distasteful, it is not fair that—"

But her words were interrupted by a noise outside. Frenchie hurried out the door, to return in moments. ''Guests,'' he said. ''A lot of them, come to spend the night.''

With a wry twist of his mouth, Thorn took the knife from Mariah. In a minute, he was done cleaning the rabbits. ''You and your friend had better hurry and cook them for supper,'' he said to her. ''It sounds as though our supply of food will be put to the test tonight.''

Chapter Ten

Thorn worked in the kitchen while the others went to greet the new guests.

This was *his* inn. He had carved it out of the wilderness from his own shame and despair. His home in England had been lost to him by his own misdeeds, and then his commission at the fort. Now he was master of his own domain. *He* made the rules.

He never took in strays. Yet here he was, burdened with two new servants he'd had no intention of hiring.

He reluctantly admitted to himself that he'd not yet regretted Mariah's presence, despite the trouble she had caused him. Contrary woman. Beautiful, brave, appealing woman. She'd pricked through the thick skin he had grown about himself, yet the irritation somehow was welcome. It made him recall, for the first time in years, that he was alive.

Today, he had been impressed by her fortitude—though unsurprised. She had surprised him enough already in their brief acquaintance so that nothing more she could do would catch him off guard. To help her new friend, she had been willing to swallow her pride, face her fear and skin those rabbits.

He finished cleaning the butchering table, then rinsed out the piece of cloth in a pan of water he poured from the bucket.

Not that her fear was rational. He had done her a favor by issuing the challenge. If she were to survive, learning to dress game was a vital skill.

What was she doing here?

The lovely but spoiled young lady had plainly been born into wealth in the east.

And yet she was smarter, spunkier, sassier than any rich girl he had ever met—and long ago he had known many.

Still, to survive, Mariah Walker would need to face further challenges and to soil those hands even more.

Her hands. He recalled how soft they had been when she had first arrived, how red and abused they had become when she had spent the day washing clothing, some of it his.

He had taken her hands into his own in regret, used them to pull her closer, and . . .

"Here they are!" René burst through the kitchen door, followed by Mariah, Holly and a dozen people in plain but serviceable clothing. Eight were men, the rest women and all chattered excitedly.

They had a look he recognized: anticipation, hope, and yet, a touch of dread.

They were settlers.

"Welcome." At a nod from René to remind him of his duty, he moved forward. He extended his hand to the closest man, not meaning his greeting in the least. Settlers were fools. Worse, they could bring trouble to his inn.

For tonight, though, with this many guests, the help of the extra servants, Mariah and Holly, would be most welcome.

"I'm Francis Kerr," said a tenor voice. Its owner shook Thorn's hand heartily. "This is my sister Ann, my friend Edgar and his wife. . . ."

Thorn stopped listening. He did not wish to know the names of these people. Better that he not know, for the entire group was unlikely to survive.

But Mariah Walker offered to each, in greeting, one of those small, work-roughened hands. She repeated each name in turn.

As she welcomed the others, Francis Kerr prattled on about their brief business at the inn. "The opportunities farther west are like a magnet, drawing us here and beyond until we find a home."

When Mariah proffered her hand to Kerr, he held on to it much too long. Thorn felt his spine stiffen, as though he had backed against a stone wall. Kerr was not a tall man, nor did he appear of great breadth or strength. His hair was a bright orange shade that would be too conspicuous in a forest, would attract Indians. Fool, for undertaking such a venture!

But Thorn himself was more the dunce, he told himself, for minding in the slightest the visitor's attention to Mariah.

"I'll bet you're hungry." She showed them to seats about the tables in the common room as though she were the mistress of the inn.

"What have you to pay for your meal?" Thorn did not like Mariah's fleeting irritated expression. But he had an inn to run, and no one without means to pay was welcome.

The settlers had English shillings, a most suitable medium of exchange here on the frontier.

Mariah and Holly, who, except for the bruising on her face, seemed to have recuperated, swept to and from the kitchen serving the travelers. It mattered not at all to Thorn that Holly flirted shamelessly with the men in the party, even sitting on one's knee when invited.

Thorn noted, though, that René, who served the men ale from a cask behind the bar, glowered when that occurred. Might his friend be attracted to the pale-haired woman whom Mariah had inserted so unexpectedly into their lives?

Perhaps, however, no more unexpectedly than Mariah herself.

Thorn, as René always insisted, joined his guests at their meal. He made certain to sit at the table with Kerr to keep an eye on him. Thorn liked not at all that the ever-present sorrow and watchfulness on Mariah's face was swept away by the tide of frivolity issuing from Kerr's lips. The man's expression was light as he spoke of the tribulations he would face, as if they were the greatest of adventures, and Mariah seemed to hang on his every word.

"Of course there will be Indians," the man said. "But we will treat them as the men they are, and in time they will respect us as well."

"And if they wish their land returned?" Thorn did not conceal his ill humor.

"You managed to keep this area, though I understand not all natives here are welcoming." The man raised his pointed chin and cast a wink at Mariah, who instead of responding with equal lightheartedness, turned away. It was obvious to Thorn that she was thinking of the incident with Nahtana.

He did not deign to explain the manner in which he had bargained with those who would have claimed this property as their own, or the continuous struggles he'd endured to maintain it. His once-burned inn and half-completed palisade told that tale. Not to mention his continued distasteful negotiations with the soldiers from Fort Pitt.

Kerr apologized to Mariah, though he could not have understood her reaction, for she did not explain. He kept up his damned teasing, however, and she eventually responded. As she passed in and out of the common room with her arms laden with food and soiled plates, she beamed and blossomed and traded witticisms with the blasted man as though they had known each other for years.

Happen they did. Perhaps she was here for some unknown purpose that involved this Kerr.

Thorn would find that out. He would trust Mariah Walker no more than she dared trust him.

As Mariah finished clearing the plates before Kerr, she bent over slightly, and Thorn noticed that the man stared brazenly at her bosom. Fortunately, her blouse was modest, buttoned to her lovely throat. But Thorn had seen enough of the man's effrontery. He rose from his chair and approached them as Mariah straightened, her arms filled.

Breathing deeply to quell the urge to grab the man by his neck and drag him outside, he instead took the dirty plates and cups from Mariah. "It is time," he said through gritted teeth, "for you to allow the master of this inn to care for his guests. You may retire."

She stared as though he had sprouted ears like the rabbits she treasured so. "But I thought—"

His other new and uninvited servant had come into the room to clear the tables. He nodded to Mariah. "Perhaps you and Miss Smith can finish cleaning in the kitchen while I entertain."

Mariah's eyes flashed, and he had a sudden urge to grab her and kiss those sweet lips that immediately formed a protest. The impulse reminded him of the kisses he had already stolen, how delightfully she tasted, how her warmth and softness pressed against him had caused his body to throb, how—

"I'll help, too, Miss Mariah," the dratted man Kerr said, standing and interrupting the moment. "I'm a wonder at cleaning dishes; we'll finish in no time."

"Thank you, Mr. Kerr," Mariah said. Her tone was as syrupy as the maple sap that ran in spring, and Thorn knew she taunted him.

Well, let her spend the evening with her Mr. Kerr. And the night, too. And perhaps she would wish to join the useless rake and his troop as they forged their way westward into danger.

Thorn would be better off, he knew, if she did.

But the idea made him wish to drive an ax into the nearest oak and chop it until naught but wood chips remained.

Mariah washed dishes in one basin, ignoring the way the hot water stung her hands. Holly rinsed in a second basin, then handed the dishes to Francis Kerr for drying.

Mariah had nearly forgotten what it was to laugh. She basked in Francis's flirtatiousness, appreciating the break from the deep emotions that always seemed rampant in Thorn's presence.

Appreciating, too, the recollection of the dark looks thrown at Francis by Thorn. Not that Francis modified his behavior in response. Flirting seemed as integral to his personality as his eagerness to forget his years of servitude and become a landowner.

Francis was kind-looking, with a nose too large for the rest of his face. He was short and lanky, with pale eyes hardly darker than mushrooms, and his bright red hair was closer cropped than the style of the day. Even if she made a fool of herself over Francis, Thorn wouldn't care. Mariah didn't understand his peevishness. Maybe she was comparing the lightness of Francis's demeanor with the heaviness of her employer's.

"So, Miss Walker, what brings you to the wilderness?" Francis stood near her as he briskly toweled a wooden plate.

"Fate," she said. And a nasty, conniving little man called Pierce, she thought.

"Myself as well. I am fated to become my own man. Own a farm. Build a house, take a wife, raise a family. Enjoy life."

As he'd said *take a wife,* he'd tried to catch her gaze, but she didn't meet it. She didn't need another complication in this time. She would not even hint of leading this sweet man on.

Besides, he'd need someone with all the day's skills. Holly would make him a better wife. Their backgrounds were even similar. Mariah nodded toward the woman working diligently beside her. "Holly came out here as a settler, too."

"Really?" Francis's attention turned to the other woman, who was clad in Mariah's gray dress and one of the caps she refused to wear. He questioned her about her travels westward. As she spoke of the ill-fated expedition that had led to her brother's death and her own capture by Indians, tears came into her eyes—just as René entered the room.

The squat, beefy man stared angrily at Francis, then strode forward. "Do not upset yourself, Miss Smith."

Oh-ho. So that was the way things were. Mariah had suspected as much. Despite René's outward hostility toward the woman he called *Anglaise,* he was attracted to her.

Mariah allowed the tiniest of grins to raise the corners of her lips as René put away the dishware. She wouldn't worry about Holly, who trained her hazel eyes first on the surprisingly graceful form of the ugly Frenchman, and then on the eager, smiling face of the red-headed Kerr. The young woman would have some choices as to the next path her life would follow.

Unlike Mariah, whose lot was to be governed by a screenplay, of all things.

The screenplay! How could she have forgotten it, even for a moment?

In it, a band of settlers had come to Thorn's inn, followed by a troop of soldiers bent on arresting them for breaking the laws against homesteading. A fight broke out. Settlers were injured, maybe even killed.

Francis's group could be the one in the story. Were enforcers after them?

How could she mention the subject without revealing that she knew what the future held—if, this time, the screenplay was accurate.

She didn't dare ignore it. Some characters had turned up here, though they had been different from the way they'd been depicted in the script. Some plot points, too, resembled things that had happened.

She hesitated, then said, "You know, a couple of days ago a fellow passed through. He was hired by the government to locate a new settlement rumored to have sprung up west of here. He was supposed to enforce the law against homesteading."

Francis shrugged. "I am aware of the law, but it is absurd, with all the empty, bounteous land just ripe for the taking."

"Is it really empty?" Mariah protested. "The Indians—"

"This is not the traditional homeland of any tribe remaining here."

"That doesn't stop them from warring over it." Thorn filled the doorway, his arms folded. Mariah wondered how long he had been listening. As usual, she hadn't heard him approach. "Some tribes displaced from other areas of European colonization wish to adopt this as their new home. In any event, they do not want to encourage further usurping of what they regard as their birthright."

"Farms mean the cutting down of woodlands," René

added, gently taking another plate from Holly. ''Woodlands that provide ample game as food for the Indians.''

''But farms mean food, too.'' Francis used his drying rag vigorously on a plate. ''We'd sell crops to the natives as much as to anyone else.''

Thorn snorted. ''But you would charge them for produce grown on land that once supplied them plentiful food for free.''

Mariah stayed out of the argument. She knew how inevitable the displacement of the Indians really was, and how cruel.

There was, however, one more thing she had to say. ''I don't think Indians are the only danger. What if the soldiers get too zealous about enforcing the law? They could do more than just arrest you.''

''Like what?'' Francis asked. ''Declare war on us?'' He laughed, handing Mariah several knives she had not yet washed.

''Well . . . maybe.'' Mariah turned back to the basin, searching for a convincing lie about why she believed them to be in danger.

''Although they must enforce that absurd law, they are charged with protecting us. We'll be fine, but thank you, Miss Walker, for your concern.'' His voice was soft in her ear, and Mariah turned, startled. He stood beside her, his gaze warm. She sighed, concerned that he had misinterpreted her warning.

She glanced around him at Thorn. Judging by his cold expression, he might have thought the same thing.

Damn them both! They were too busy acting like strutting roosters to listen to her. She glared at Francis, irritation turning her careless. ''You don't understand. Tomorrow, soldiers will come through here to stop you. There will be fights. People will be hurt. You have to go back.''

Francis looked dumbfounded. Before he responded, though, she heard the clumping of footsteps on the wooden floor behind Thorn, who moved aside. He stared at her, looking as surprised as if she had suddenly slaughtered a whole roomful of rabbits. She felt herself redden as she glared back defiantly. The others settlers entered the kitchen. "We need an early start," a dark-haired man in a blue-striped shirt told Francis.

He nodded. "If you would be so kind as to show us to our beds . . ." He looked at her.

"I need to finish here, but maybe Holly . . ."

"Come along," Holly said, and Mariah was relieved when Francis dutifully followed with the rest.

After the settlers were shown to their beds, Holly came downstairs. "Nice folk, aren't they?" She seemed wistful.

"Very." Mariah wondered if Holly wanted to leave with them.

The rustic kitchen was clean, every dish put away. It was empty of people as well. No René. Or Thorn. A wistfulness crept through Mariah, too. She'd have liked to have said good night to her employer, to have him say good night to her.

But why would he bother with a servant?

"Time for bed," she told Holly.

"Not without banking that." The younger woman pointed a slender finger toward the still-blazing fire.

"Of course," Mariah agreed, with an inward sigh. She'd no idea how. Since she'd arrived here, René or Thorn must have dealt with that fire.

In fact, since she'd arrived here, she'd done nothing till someone told her what to do and showed her how.

She scrunched her mouth in misery as she considered her incompetence. She was used to taking care of details, relying only on herself. Being so efficient that others relied on her to organize entire multimillion-dollar movies.

Here, she felt helpless.

As she had early in her life. It was a feeling she detested.

Fortunately, Holly knew the skills necessary for survival and was generous in sharing her knowledge, including how to bank the fire by piling ashes over it. She tactfully avoided questions about why Mariah was so inept.

Soon, they walked together toward the stable. "Now we

will rearrange things so you are back in your own room,'' Holly said.

There wasn't much to rearrange, though the most important item, Mariah's precious paper with her screenplay predictions, was hard to move surreptitiously with Holly hovering about. She managed to hide it in the folds of her skirt and to slide it under the straw pallet atop the leather straps of her bed.

By the time they were finished, Holly looked exhausted.

''I'm sorry,'' Mariah said. ''You were so energetic today, I nearly forgot all you've been through. Sleep as long as you want tomorrow, and I'll take care of . . .'' She hesitated. ''Unless, of course, you intend to leave with the settlers.''

The expression that crossed Holly's face looked longing yet full of pain. ''No,'' she said quietly. ''I need to make some decisions about what to do now that I am alone. I still wish to make a new life at the frontier, but after . . .'' She tapered off.

''Make the decision when you're ready. Thorn won't toss you out.'' She made herself sound more certain than she felt. ''He's more likely to send me on my way now that he has someone who knows what she's doing.''

''You learn quickly, Mariah,'' Holly protested. ''And I do not think Thorn will send you away. The way he looks at you, with such yearning . . .'' She smiled. ''I believe you have made a conquest of this quiet warrior.''

Fat chance, Mariah thought.

Not that she wanted to make such a conquest.

But Holly's words sent a small, incongruous shiver of pleasure through her.

She said good night and returned to her room. A short while later, lying on her bed in her white nightgown, she realized she couldn't sleep. She hadn't closed the wooden shutters, and moonlight through the paper at the window cast a faint mustard luminescence about the room. She donned the robe that had been in her belongings, slipped her boots on over her bare feet and left the room.

She heard the stamping and nickers of the horses in their stalls as she picked her way carefully through the dark stable.

The closed room smelled of horse droppings and sweat.

When she shut the stable door, she inhaled the sweet, smog-free fragrance of the cool wilderness night as she glanced nervously about the compound. All seemed still in the darkness. She hurried toward the inn.

A large shadow suddenly loomed beside her, and she gasped, then managed, "Who is it?"

"What are you doing out here?" asked a familiar, iron-hard voice.

"L-looking for a drink of water," she stammered. She should have known. Who but Thorn would creep up on her so silently?

Except, perhaps, an Indian.

"What are you doing?" she asked in return.

"Making sure my guests are safe," he retorted, standing so near her that she could feel his body heat in the cool night air. His large form blocked the moonlight. "My foolish employees, too. Did you not learn that it is perilous to be abroad at night?"

"Yes." She didn't like being called a fool, but she felt like one. "I'm sorry. I'll go back." She turned toward the stable, but a firm hand grasped her upper arm, jolting her with its gentle strength.

He said nothing for a long moment, though she was sure something was on his mind. Finally, he said, "You do not seem the type to fit in at the frontier. Why did you come?"

She considered carefully what to say. "Because I had to. I was drawn here."

A snort escaped from him. "By what? A love of danger? Of building fires and washing clothes? Of being far from the family that pampered you?"

"Pampered?" She hadn't intended to raise her voice, but his scornful tone infuriated her.

She'd been forced here by a total stranger who'd stolen control of her life by means she couldn't begin to comprehend.

She'd been given glimpses of the existence she'd fallen into, Matilda's, but she remained off balance, since nothing was as she anticipated.

She'd been kidnapped, manhandled, and made to feel totally inadequate, despite all her years of education and business experience, because she didn't know how to light a fire.

And her hands, her lovely hands, had been ruined.

She flexed them now, allowing the pain to stoke her fury. On top of everything else, this man had dared to call her pampered. By *her* family.

"Do you consider being abandoned time after time by a father addicted to get-rich-quick schemes pampered? Or how about being the parent to a hopeless dreamer of a mother? A mother who was always surprised, after the family was uprooted and moved to yet another godforsaken outpost, that this wasn't the end of the rainbow. A mother who always fell apart when her husband astonished her and left yet again."

She noticed then that Thorn still held her arms. She wrenched away from him, ready to return to her room. Her breathing was ragged, and she had an urge to cry.

But she wouldn't. She absolutely wouldn't.

She found her way blocked by his body. With a sound of irritation, she sidestepped, trying to get around him. But as large as he was, he had the grace of a cat and moved to block her once more.

His voice erupted with emotion she did not understand. "Perhaps it is better to walk away from a family in which you are disappointed than to disappoint and shame a worthy family."

"What do you mean?" Mariah stood still, her anger fizzling out. She waited for him to go on. Was he about to tell her about his childhood, too? No longer did she want to cry; instead, she was ready to listen.

René had mentioned an incident in England, the reason Thorn had left. René knew no details. Was Thorn about to tell her?

Though he said nothing for a long while, when he finally spoke again his tone was composed yet gentle. "You said you were thirsty. We will find you a drink."

She realized suddenly how parched her throat felt, as though all the moisture inside her had risen to her eyes. "Just water,'' she found herself agreeing. Idiot! she told herself. Why not insist he tell her more?

Because he wouldn't.

This impossible man had caused her to lose her temper. To reveal things she never, ever spoke about.

He'd hinted at matters of great importance to him, but she was certain he'd not disclose more.

''This way, then.'' He took her arm once more.

''Where are we going?'' He was surprising her yet again; he was leading her away from the inn.

He was much too close, and as she felt him match his stride to hers, she stumbled on the uneven ground. He pulled her closer, his grip tightening to keep her upright. ''There was no clean water left in the buckets this evening, so we must go to the stream.''

She stopped, ignoring the tug on her arm, the warmth of his body so near hers. She glimpsed his face in the moonlight, the soft shining of his eyes as their gazes met. ''That's too dangerous.'' And not just because of wolves and Indians, she thought. She didn't want to be alone with herself . . . with him.

''There is little danger if we stay alert.'' There was a tautness in his voice, as though she had hurt his feelings.

His vulnerability touched her, yet how odd! He was the one who'd so often made it clear that she didn't dare rely on him.

Didn't he realize how raw he'd made her own feelings?

She should forget about the drink, return to her room. And not just for peace of mind. Who knew what jeopardy might confront her here in the darkness, with only Thorn to protect her?

Yet a tiny smile niggled at the corner of her mouth. For the first time he'd hinted that he would take care of her.

They entered the woods along the path that was so familiar during the day. At night, the multitextured blackness from undergrowth and leaves, tree trunks and the spaces between them, seemed menacing. Mariah heard the hoot of an owl and the rustlings that could mean a breeze, small forest creatures—or the wolves she feared. Or, worse, Indians. Nahtana.

But she was with Thorn, who held her arm tightly against him. Somehow, his closeness left her feeling more defenseless than any peril she imagined. She continued forward, though her heart raced.

The water's gurgling soon became louder than the rustling. As she stepped from behind a tree, Mariah saw the meandering stream's reflection shimmer in the moonlight.

"There," Thorn said. "Take your drink."

She stooped and, cupping her hands, lifted cool water to her lips. It felt refreshing as she swallowed. She *had* been thirsty.

Scooping more water into her hands, she started as Thorn knelt beside her. "I want some, too," he said.

She expected him to drink from his own hands. Instead, he touched her forearm with his broad fingers, guiding her hands toward his mouth. He drank from the cup she had made, and the feel of his lips on the sides of her fingers caused a shiver of desire to rocket through her.

"Oh," she moaned as his tongue snaked out and licked her palm. She reached to touch his cheek, roughened by the day's growth of beard, then let her fingertips move toward his mouth, where they, too, felt the soft caress of his tongue. She closed her eyes, swallowing hard. Her upper body bent toward him as though it had a will of its own, until her cheek rested on the rough linen of his shirt. She put her arms about him, taking crawling steps on her knees to draw closer to him.

She could feel the hammering of his heart, smell his leather-and-smoke aroma. She waited for him to cast his arms about her, to kiss her as he had before. She wanted it, more than anything else. Here, in the wilderness, with the night and the moon and the trees as witnesses, she wanted to lose control with Thorn. To make love with this aloof but vulnerable man so different from, yet similar to, the man in the screenplay.

But he didn't move. She heard his breath come in painful gasps, as if he fought for control.

Despite all rational thought, she didn't want control. She moved her hands along his back, kneading the muscles of his shoulders, moving down the length of his long, rigid back, touching his tight buttocks and moving—

He sprang to his feet and backed away. "No!" he whispered hoarsely.

He stopped within a shaft of moonlight. If the feel of his body hadn't affected Mariah, the anguish etching deep, pained lines at his eyes and beside his sorrowful mouth would have drawn her to him. But she obeyed and stayed still.

"I am sorry, Mariah." There was a roughness to his voice that told her he, too, had been affected by their closeness. "You do not understand. I wish . . ." He hesitated, then, almost to himself, continued, "We must all learn to accept what cannot be."

She wanted to cry out to him, to take him back into her arms. To comfort him. But he was right. For reasons he could never comprehend, their closeness was impossible.

His unreliability made it so.

As did her coming here from the future for a purpose she'd yet to fulfill. If she had in fact figured it out.

And then?

Then, who knew where she'd be?

"You're right," she said, standing and turning her back toward him. "Please take me back to the inn."

Shaking inside with emotion, she was even more aware of Thorn's presence as she followed him back through the woods, this time without touching. In the dim light, she watched his graceful stride, wondering with regret what it would have been like if they'd gone on. Glad, though, since she had to work with him. How awkward it would be for them to serve inn guests together if they'd made love tonight and regretted it in the morning.

Yet Mariah was sorry, so sorry, they had stopped.

Chapter Eleven

"Mademoiselle!" René stared at Mariah in disbelief as she entered the kitchen, fully clad in the pink gown she had washed hurriedly the day before. The sun had barely risen. He had not intended to rouse her for a while yet.

Or Mademoiselle Holly either—though he had opened the door and peeked into her room when he awakened. To make certain she was still alive, he had told himself. Who knew what difficulties the injuries she had suffered might cause? She had been breathing softly, her gossamer hair, the color of cornsilk, spread across her sheet to frame her pretty face, and he had gently closed the door. He would allow her to awaken in her own good time, he had decided. She would need her sleep.

And if she slept through their guests' departure for the wilderness . . . well, he would not mind that in the least.

Mariah looked as though she had not slept last night, *pauvre petite,* the circles beneath her eyes as dark as the soot-stained three-legged pot in which he was about to cook the breakfast porridge. "Is something the matter?" he asked her.

She shook her head wearily. "No, René. I just . . ."

Her soft voice grew fainter still until it simply faded away. But then she looked at him and smiled, and he found himself beaming back. This mademoiselle, she was a good-natured lady despite being so ignorant of the simplest skills. Perhaps she was, as Thorn said, a *fleur,* a pretty but useless flower from the east who had never had to lift a finger to serve herself, let alone anyone else. And yet, she had not complained.

René found himself liking her. He suspected that, despite his growling like a flea-bitten bear, Thorn liked her, too.

That was not good.

"So, what would you like me to do this morning?" She hesitated. "Are the guests awake?"

"I have heard them stir, and Francis Kerr settled their bill, but they are not yet ready to depart. We will have food waiting for them, eh?"

"Sure. Tell me what to do."

"Fetch some water from the stream, if you please."

A strange expression clouded the mademoiselle's face, as though fetching water from the stream was the last thing she wished to do. "Have you fear the Indian lurks about?" he asked. Although there had been no sign that their unwelcome visitor remained, he would not force Mariah to go alone.

Yet again uncomplaining, she took up the pair of buckets and placed them on the wood harness across her shoulders. "I'm sure he's gone. I'll be right back."

René had barely poured cornmeal for porridge from the metal canister and readied the salt pork for frying when Mariah returned. "Here we are." She set down the pails near a table, then turned toward the fireplace. "Is the fire ready?" She prodded it with a shovel, as though tending it were a skill she had perfected long ago. He smiled as Thorn entered the kitchen.

He greeted René, then nodded at Mariah, who looked up from the fire. A light brightened in her eyes, then dimmed as though she had doused it. René watched in curiosity. He had guessed she was *enchanté* by Thorn but suspected the feelings ran far too deep for such short acquaintance—and for such an impossible relationship. Poor mademoiselle.

René handed Mariah the cornmeal and pot and explained how to mix it with water and cook it over the fire. He glanced up while arranging the salt pork in the pan. Thorn watched Mariah as she mixed the porridge. He must not have known René observed him, for there was a yearning in his expression that amazed René.

Thorn was attracted, too. This would not do. He could withstand no further anguish from a woman. This Mariah, however much René liked her, would never stay in this wilderness inn. René cleared his throat. "Are you going with the settlers this morning, Mariah? That Francis Kerr said he hoped you would change your mind."

She tossed a guilty glance at Thorn. Good! Perhaps she was considering leaving.

But she said sadly, "I'd go if it would save them from being hurt by the soldiers, but I doubt I'd be any help."

Thorn snorted. "Oh, yes. That tale of yours about the soldiers. It was fascinating, and this group might in fact be tracked by those attempting to enforce the law. But to insist that they will be attacked and injured—"

"Absurd, I know," she interrupted. "But though my knowledge isn't exact, I know things before . . ." She stopped, looking at Thorn and then at René in horror, as though expecting them to accuse her of witchery.

René wondered what she had been intending to reveal. *Was* she a witch? It did not matter to him, but it might to others. He had never spoken to Thorn about his beliefs about such beings but suspected that his friend and employer, who had put so much of civilization behind him, cared not whether someone was a blasphemer or a sorcerer.

But so long as Mariah did not hurt Thorn, René wished her no ill. He only hoped she would bite her tongue, not suggest to others that she might have powers beyond those given to man by God.

They remained silent for a while, the sole sound in the room the sizzling of the fragrant salt pork and the scraping as Mariah, kneeling on the hearth, stirred the simmering porridge.

Noise sounded from the common room. The settlers were

coming down the wooden steps. "Please ladle the porridge, Mariah," René directed. "We have guests to serve."

Mariah took up the long-handled ladle and spooned white porridge, the consistency of paste, into a long wooden trencher.

The stuff had hardly any aroma and was as insipid as it smelled. Nevertheless, despite not being a breakfast person, she'd begun eating porridge in the morning, since it was available. The days here were long and arduous, and she couldn't start out without eating something. The travelers would probably feel the same way. Or maybe they liked the goop.

But they did not immediately sit at the tables. Instead, they congregated in the kitchen. Francis's young sister Ann, in a brown-checked gown and with a bonnet in her hand, approached Mariah. Her wide-set gray eyes were troubled. "Miss Walker, Francis said you believe soldiers will follow us closely, perhaps even stop us before we find a place to settle."

Mariah took a deep breath, trying to find a way to explain her concern without sounding nuts. She looked into the trencher of porridge as though it held an answer.

Before she spoke, Thorn broke in. He stood near the hearth beside her, clad in a fringed leather shirt. "All the soldiers have done thus far is to tear down settlements that did not belong. They have not harmed settlers, and to think they will—"

"Is prudent," interrupted Mariah. She again looked at the young woman and the others hovering uneasily in the doorway. "I hope I'm wrong, but just in case, it wouldn't hurt to wait here for a few days." But would that be a solution, or would the soldiers go after them whenever they left? Damn that screenplay for giving hints without details—or reliability!

And damn Pierce all the more for putting her in this untenable position.

She heard a noise at her side and turned to find Thorn with his jaw clenched. "If you wish their company so badly, Miss

Walker, perhaps you should accompany them after all."

Mariah ignored the pang of hurt that shot through her. Even after last night—especially after last night—he wanted her gone. "I'm just trying to—"

"Hey, Thorn!" A man's shout came from the common room. Mariah counted the settlers who'd dined last night. All were there in the kitchen. Thorn and René, too. Had another guest arrived for breakfast? It seemed early, but maybe someone had camped close by.

"Innkeeper!" came another shout, followed by laughter more derisive than merry. The settlers scrambled from the door to make room for a group of red-coated soldiers. The large kitchen seemed suddenly tiny as the would-be homesteaders took positions at one end, staring suspiciously. At a nod from the soldiers' apparent leader, the other ten roamed about, tricornered hats in their hands. Their demeanor was decisively nonchalant as they tossed snide smiles at the settlers.

Thorn remained motionless in the center of the room, his stony expression unwavering, his arms calmly at his sides. "What brings you here, Corporal Maitland?" he addressed the thin, arrogant soldier who appeared to be in charge.

"Orders, Captain Thorn. Oh, that's right. *Mister* Thorn." He spoke the word *mister* as though it were the ugliest epithet in the English language, and Mariah noticed Thorn's fingers curl ever so slightly, as though he prepared to make a fist.

"And what orders might those be?" Thorn's voice tightened almost imperceptibly, and Mariah admired him for his outward calm. "Finding a new pet for Captain Edmonstone? I smell skunk around here. Perhaps that would be fitting for Fort Pitt's commanding officer."

Maitland took an angry step toward Thorn, then stopped. "You have nearly guessed our mission. There have been threats by angry Indians, and to prevent another uprising like Pontiac's we are to rid the wilderness of a certain species of skunk that smells of breaking the Indian treaties." He glared in the direction of the settlers, then abruptly strode toward them, planting himself in front of Ann. "You, madam. What is your purpose being here?"

The poor creature blanched as she stammered, "I—we—"

"They're on holiday." Mariah placed herself between Maitland and the girl. "They'd heard wonderful things about Thorn's inn and decided to try it." She smiled from one soldier to another. "Breakfast is ready, gentlemen, and there's plenty. Would you like some?"

Maitland had sharp features and cold, dark eyes. The expression he turned on Mariah was contemptuous, and she had to keep herself from flinching. "What would this group be doing on holiday? We have been sent to follow them. They are former bondspersons who—"

"Who intend to begin farming south of here, and east of the Proclamation Line." Thorn was suddenly beside Mariah, and though his arm barely touched hers, it lent her support. She could have kissed him. Almost. "But they wished to see this area before settling down. Is that not correct?" He directed his comment to Francis, who appeared ready to say something else until the young woman raised her hand pleadingly.

"That is correct," Francis snarled. It was the first time Mariah had seen him anything but cheerful. "We will stay one more day, then be off to our new homes. South of here, and east."

Maitland snorted. "Perhaps, then, we shall join you in this holiday. We shall begin by partaking of breakfast. Let us take seats in the other room, men."

Men? From what Mariah could see, half the soldiers were no older than Ann. One appeared particularly youthful, although he sported a small, dark mustache and goatee, as though attempting to look older. The kid had stared at Thorn the whole time with narrowed pale green eyes, his hand hovering about the hilt of his sword, as though ready to run Thorn through at a sign from the officer.

Strangely, the kid looked a bit familiar to Mariah. Maybe she'd seen him at Fort Pitt when she'd arrived in this time.

The men took seats all over the room, leaving no table

free for the settlers. Their arrogance was not lost on Francis, who stood in the doorway, breathing deeply, as though to maintain his temper.

"If you want," Mariah whispered, "we can serve your group in the kitchen or even outside."

"I wish not to give them the satisfaction," Francis said through gritted teeth. With a final resigned look at one another, his people ventured into the common room and scattered among the soldiers.

"What is happening here?" Mariah turned to see Holly peering over her shoulder. She was clad in the same dress she had worn yesterday, and Mariah realized they would have to acquire more clothing between them soon or wear out the few things Pierce had provided for her. "Are them the soldiers you said was coming? What're they doing with our guests?"

"Just harassing them for now," Mariah said grimly. "I only hope the settlers keep their cool."

"Their cool what?" Holly questioned.

"Heads," Mariah replied, wondering how many other expressions from her day might be incomprehensible to people now. She'd have to be more careful.

Holly and she bustled between the common room and the kitchen, setting spoons and trenchers on each table. On one trip Maitland grabbed her arm. She smelled a rank odor, as though he had been sweating profusely beneath his red wool uniform jacket. No wonder Thorn had spoken of skunk.

"We want real service here," the soldier said. "We started downriver from the fort before the day broke, and we are hungry. Tell Thorn he is to serve us and to refill our trenchers as we empty them."

"Right," said Mariah sarcastically. "Do you want him to eat for you, too?"

The young soldier who'd been staring at Thorn was at Maitland's table. "Yes," he hissed, "but only after we have tossed the food onto the floor for the other dogs."

His words brought a laugh from the nearby soldiers. The settlers at the table kept eating, as though ignoring the situation, but their solemn expressions told Mariah how much of a strain this meal was on them. She realized by now that it was the custom of the day not to serve people individually, but for them to be eating from the same trenchers as the soldiers must turn their stomachs.

She turned to go back to the kitchen, only to find Thorn standing there. Had he heard that last exchange? She felt herself redden, as though she had contributed to the insult. She wished she could apologize for their rudeness, to remove the hurt their comments must cause.

If he'd heard, he chose to ignore it. "So, Maitland," he said, "why did Ainsley not accompany you on this expedition?"

"Your friend Sergeant Ainsley was planning to come," Maitland replied, "but I volunteered to allow him to remain at the fort to handle more important matters."

"Then you consider your mission unimportant?" Mariah could have bitten her tongue for taunting him, but she couldn't call the words back.

"Only the objects of it, those who intentionally flaunt the law of this land, are unimportant. Beneath our contempt."

A chair scraped on the wooden floor, and Mariah saw that Francis had risen to his feet, anger written on his formerly mild features. "Only the absurd laws are contemptible," he shouted. "We have been treated with scorn long enough. It is our turn to be respected."

"Then behave in a manner worthy of respect," Maitland said. With a rumble of chairs and feet, he and his soldiers also rose, each with a hand poised over the hilt of his sword. "Do not break the laws, even if you find them as contemptible as we find you."

"Ah, gentlemen." Holly entered the room with two metal pots she gripped by rags about the handles. She was followed by squat René, who balanced a tray covered with an assortment of mugs and earthenware cups. "Tea. I'm sure, I am, that you'll all wish some." She put down the pots on two tables, one of them Maitland's, then took cups from René's tray. With Mariah's and René's help, she put cups at all the places, whirling between people as though cutting the strings between them that had caused them all to remain standing.

Dear Holly! Mariah thought. She had succeeded in defusing the situation, for the soldiers began to sit down again, and so did the settlers. The room was soon filled with the aroma of spices.

"What kind of tea is that?" Mariah asked.

"Sassafras," Holly replied. "My own receipt. I'll teach it to you if you wish."

Receipt? Recipe, Mariah translated in her mind. "I do wish." And I wish I'd come up with a diversion like that, she thought.

Even Thorn seemed mollified. He helped serve the guests—even Maitland's table, ignoring the smug smiles on Maitland's and the irritating boy's faces. Mariah wanted to tell him to sit down, that she'd serve him as the innkeeper should be served, that he shouldn't cater to these clowns in uniform, but she kept quiet, not wanting to embarrass him further.

In a while, the meal was over. The soldiers stood and walked into the courtyard—all but Maitland.

"More tea, *Mr.* Thorn," he demanded.

Mariah caught the look of anger and disgust that crossed the innkeeper's face and suspected Maitland did, too. But he again looked impassive as he poured more tea—letting some spill onto the corporal's lap. Maitland rose, sputtering.

"My deepest apologies." Thorn sounded not in the least repentant. "But should you wish a more cordial welcome next time you visit my inn, bring Sergeant Ainsley."

The sharp-featured corporal gave a nasty smile. "Do you admit you did not treat us with your best manners, Mr. Thorn?"

"Bring Ainsley and you will see." Though Thorn's tone was mild, he abruptly left the room.

So did Mariah, hiding her grin. Good for Thorn! She'd had enough of Maitland and his miserable attitude but hadn't had the guts to retaliate.

The settlers followed her to the kitchen. "Thank you for all, Miss Walker," Francis said.

"Where will you go now?" Mariah asked. "They'll chase you if you go west." And attack them, perhaps. The screenplay had been right about the soldiers following the settlers. And the rest . . . ?

"Then we will head east toward Pittsborough to enjoy the remainder of our 'holiday.' And when they forget to watch us—"

He was interrupted by Maitland's appearance in the kitchen. He held a linen napkin against the front of his trousers. "Are you people—" he said the word as contemptuously as he'd used any other that day, "—going somewhere?"

Francis had apparently regained his sense of humor. "Of course we are going somewhere, since we cannot partake of the hospitality of Thorn's inn forever."

"Then where—"

Francis interrupted the soldier. "I was just telling Miss Walker that we will conclude our holiday by making our way back to Pittsborough. Perhaps you would enjoy some intelligent company on your way back to Fort Pitt. I had the impression that your men had but a single brain between them—is it yours?"

Maitland glared at Francis. "Perhaps we will travel with you back to the fort, to make certain that is your intention."

"We will welcome such illustrious company." Francis almost managed to keep his words from sounding sarcastic. "Farewell, Miss Mariah. And thank you for your hospitality—and warning. We shall heed all you said."

The inn was quiet that afternoon, as Thorn sat at the table in his room. He preferred it that way. On days after a normal crowd's departure, he always wished that he had not turned his home into an inn.

And the day's horde had been far from normal.

But civilization had encroached upon his refuge, making him yield to the practicality of collecting fees from those who would eat his food and sleep in his shelter.

He would have left all hosting to René if he could. After an ordeal like that just past, the idea seemed even more appealing.

Ordeals. Never before had so many arisen in so short a

time. River rats, wolves, Indians and now damnable soldiers after damned settlers.

Were they all due to the arrival of Mariah Walker?

She had certainly upended his ordered existence. Because of her, he'd found himself thinking of all he had turned from so long ago: career, camaraderie, family . . . a future.

He had not thought of what was to come for a long while. Now, he suddenly pondered how bleak, how lonely, would be the time that stretched ahead after the departure of the sweetly belligerent Mariah Walker. For leave she would.

She did not belong here. But she had nevertheless managed to insert herself into his inn. Made her presence known. Goaded him into reacting. Into wishing once more that he could command the respect of others . . . of her.

Of himself.

Solemnly, he cracked nuts and dropped them for the squirrel that scampered from one treat to the next, making skittering sounds on the wooden floor.

Even his own home had not been sacrosanct. Mariah had invaded it, scaring off the amiable squirrel so it had not reappeared for an entire day.

How had she known that soldiers would be so close behind this group of squatters? Others had visited his inn—it was one of the last such at the edge of the unsettled western wilderness—but none had been so hounded by authorities set on preventing their homesteading.

Was she working with the soldiers? He could not believe that—not when she seemed so inclined to support the settlers' efforts.

Unless that was a ruse to encourage their trust. But for what reason?

And where was the trouble-attracting woman now?

As though she were privy to his thoughts, he heard a tentative knock on the door. It could only be she. A warm surge of unwanted anticipation made him smile, but only for a moment.

He rose and strode toward the door, then stood for a few seconds composing himself. He straightened his shoulders and made certain his face would not appear welcoming. She had no business intruding at the inn, after all, and most certainly not at his home.

He pulled open the door—and stood looking down at the woman on his stoop.

It was the other one, that Holly Smith, with her pale hair gathered up under a cap and narrow-set eyes that peered up at him craftily, as though she, too, knew his thoughts. Her bruises were fading.

"What is it, Miss Smith?" He knew he sounded angry, though the situation merited no such emotion. Still, he felt disappointed. He had been expecting, somehow, Mariah Walker.

"René wishes you to come to see what was done," she said.

René, was it? Not Mr. Lafont, or even Mr. René. Was this woman merely forward, or was there something brewing between her and the Frenchman? Was she thinking she would remain here, now that she seemed to have recuperated?

He followed her through the blazing sun in the compound's clearing and into the shelter of the pleasantly cool forest.

At the side of the gurgling stream that sparkled in the sunlight stood René and Mariah. Both had stooped, gathering something, but rose as Thorn said, "What has happened?"

He saw then that they were scooping salt into wooden bowls, but the amount was hardly worth the bother. On the ground near the stream lay the small barrel that had held the commodity so precious for the preservation of food, its side bashed in. "Who did this?"

"I'll give you three guesses."

He did not care for Mariah's sarcasm but understood it; only one of their visitors in the past day was likely to have stooped so low: Maitland.

"Why does he dislike you so much?" Her voice was quiet, and as sorrowful as if she had taken his troubles upon her own shoulders.

Thorn could have provided her with an earful of reasons: disgust, anger, disdain, hatred. All emotions he had felt against himself. But he chose not to respond. "I believe," he said as mildly as he could, "that I must make a venture to a trading post for replacement."

"Will you go upriver to Pittsborough?" asked Holly. She sounded eager, as if anticipating an invitation to join him, her method of escaping this place.

Thorn observed the wave of pain that crossed René's countenance. "I could go to the new post, Harrigan's, downriver, but I expect salt will be less dear in the larger town by the fort."

"I think you should try Harrigan's first." Mariah sounded upset, and he recalled that she had hoped someone going downriver would deliver a message for her to a man named—Parks, was it? No, Pierce. The idea of her wishing so fervently for contact with another man caused his throat to tighten. All the more reason for him to forbear from heading in that direction.

"Then perhaps," Holly said, "you can pick up some supplies for us." She looked toward Mariah, who nodded.

"That's right," she said. "If you'll advance me the part of my wages that isn't going toward repayment of my debt to you, I'll come along to buy extra dresses."

Her voice trailed off as Thorn glared at her. "I would have thought you used to having seamstresses at your beck and call to create the latest of fashions." He was angry that she appeared to be mocking the scarcity of goods here in his wilderness. "Ready made clothing seems unlike your style."

She had the grace to appear abashed as she turned to Holly. "I made another boo-boo, didn't I? Mistake," she hurriedly responded to the question in the other woman's eyes. Mariah looked toward Thorn, who also wondered at the strange word she had used. "Why don't we all go with you to Pittsborough so I can see what's available?"

She seemed too eager to go along. Why? To further conspire with the soldiers against the settlers? Unlikely. At least she was not harping on his venturing downriver instead. But why not? This woman was full of contradictions that he could not understand. Better that she stay here out of trouble.

"Who will tend the inn if you all accompany me, Miss Walker?" Thorn did not keep the irritation from his voice.

"Me and René." Holly approached him, picking her way over the uneven bank of the stream. She was not a tall woman, and she seemed to gather courage as she walked. "We'll both stay. But first you'll need to hire me, you will. I've decided to stay till I make some decisions about my future. But I'll need a position. May I work for you?"

Thorn glanced toward René, who stood at the edge of the stream, the sparsely filled bowl of salt in his hands. There was a pleading in the Frenchman's glance that Thorn could not discount. Still, René said scornfully, "We do not need another *Anglaise* here, one who will wish to be waited upon and be paid a wage."

Holly trod toward him. The angry stiffness of her gait nearly made her trip on the rocky ground. "I've been helping for no wages, *monsieur.*" Thorn's French was skilled enough to understand the English-accented butchery she had made of the word, and he was certain it was deliberate. "Or have you been sleeping too deeply to notice?"

"I have noticed that you do a little here, a little there—"

"And I will do a little more to show you what a no-good—"

"Enough!" Thorn shouted. "René, with all the guests we have had recently, and my other new servant's lack of skills, we need more help. I will hire Miss Smith for a period of two weeks. If she proves satisfactory, then we will decide whether to keep her on."

Relief stole across René's ugly features, nearly making Thorn laugh aloud. But a small voice beside him said, "I suppose you don't really need me." He looked down to see Mariah Walker staring unblinkingly, yet there was a moistness in her eyes. With the others arguing, he had not thought of her reaction. He wished now to pull her into his arms, to reassure her that he needed her in a way he could need no other woman, to—

But how foolish. That was not what she had meant at all. Nor what he intended.

Mariah Walker meant nothing to him. She never could, for if she did, he would destroy her.

"You still have a debt to work off, Miss Walker." He let

the icy feeling of self-loathing show in his voice, acting as though he directed it toward her. ''If you wish to quit my employ, you must find another means to repay me.''

''Of course.'' She, too, looked relieved, though she said, ''But I want to sit down with you one day and determine how much you think I owe you.''

''You owe me for your life, Miss Walker. And not just once. How much is that worth to you?''

''A lot,'' she said slowly. ''But there are others' whose lives are worth more.'' Her forest-green eyes, magnified by their moistness, seemed to penetrate his very skin, yet he did not understand her intensity.

''Those settlers'? How did you really know, Miss Walker, that the soldiers would follow them so closely?'' He finally had voiced the question that had haunted him since that morning.

She sighed, and her shoulders slumped. ''Just another of those things that didn't quite work out the way I anticipated.'' She brightened then. ''But all for the better. No one was hurt—at least not this time.''

He did not appreciate her riddles but knew she would not explain. He said in irritation, ''I will go to Pittsborough tomorrow, Miss Walker. If you wish to accompany me, be ready at daybreak.''

''Thank you,'' she murmured, with a fervency that surprised him. ''Maybe I can make sure that another thing I anticipate—'' She seemed to catch herself, and turned bright scarlet. ''I'm talking out of turn. But I'll be delighted to go with you bright and early.''

Chapter Twelve

The journey upriver was quite different from the one Mariah had taken to Thorn's inn.

First, she wasn't in fear for her life. Far from it. She felt utterly at peacc, lulled by the restful sounds of the wind over softly rushing water. She recalled her tension on that first trip, how she had watched for the pier that gave her the courage to leap into the water, believing from the screenplay that help would arrive.

And it had, though not exactly as expected—the real, and not fictional, Thorn.

Now, she felt a surprising serenity just being with him on the water. His boat was a hollowed-log canoe that he called a pirogue. He had taught her, before pushing off from the shore near the inn, how to sit on one of the crosswise slats to keep the craft balanced. She felt like a pampered creature instead of an overworked servant as she sat doing nothing while he knelt in the pointed prow, watching ahead of them and rowing. She considered asking him to teach her how to row, too, but for now she just appreciated the restfulness—and the scenery.

Though her hair blew into her face, she had a wonderful view of Thorn without his being able to observe her in return. Kneeling in the base of the canoe, he was nearly as tall as she, seated on a slat. His chestnut-brown hair ruffled in an early morning breeze that seemed intensified by the speed at which he propelled the craft forward. The same breeze that carried away her words the few times she tried to speak.

He used a single paddle, dipping it into the water on first one side of the boat, then the other. His motions were graceful and regular, and she could see his muscles work beneath the loose beige shirt made of a coarse woolen fabric that she knew now, thanks to Holly, was called linsey-woolsey. Dampness appeared behind his broad neck and beneath his arms. The scenery along the river was outstanding: mountains covered by thick, rustling forests, from which now and then a family of deer or elk appeared to drink at the riverbank. But Mariah found herself staring mostly at Thorn's wide shoulders and strong back, telling herself that she didn't really want to touch him, to feel those straining muscles beneath her fingertips.

After a while, they rounded one more bend, and in the distance Mariah could make out the promontory between the two lesser rivers joining to form the mighty Ohio, with the first signs of civilization she noted on the trip: the earthen embankment rising above the town outside Fort Pitt.

And the Point. The spot where the fictional Thorn had lost his life.

Mariah hadn't realized she'd gasped aloud until Thorn turned around to stare at her. "Are you well, Mariah?" he called.

"Sure," she said, the word catching in her throat. Fortunately, he wouldn't be called out in a duel here today. Too many things described in the screenplay hadn't yet happened.

Looking at the shoreline ahead, she recalled her reaction on first seeing the Pittsburgh of the twentieth century from the plane. She'd felt so attracted to the place, as though it were her long-sought home, her destiny.

Especially the Point.

Surely she could not feel such an affinity for the location if she were going to watch Thorn die there.

She had to stop the duel.

Where was Pierce? If he were here, in the past, why hadn't he joined her? Guided her? He wanted her, after all, to right his damned "grievous wrong." Why didn't he help?

Except . . . he had helped, some. He had written the dratted screenplay in the first place.

A name came to her then, one she had read in the script. Not that the story was necessarily accurate, but the man who'd called Thorn out for the duel had been named Billy.

Billy! She could ask that day if anyone knew of a Billy in Pittsburgh.

And if so, she might be able to save Thorn.

She took in her surroundings with new interest—tinged with watchfulness, anticipation and fear for Thorn. There was river traffic around here; nothing like the motorized pleasure craft she'd seen in the Pittsburgh she'd left, but more canoes, bateaux and other man-powered boats. Thorn easily sleeked the pirogue among them, reaching the shore at a landing area at the opposite end of the Point from the small dock from which Mariah had left with the ruffians—had it been just a week earlier?

A substantial thump told Mariah that the canoe had reached the shore. "Come along." Thorn helped her from the boat, though she had to wade in her boots through shallow water. Once she was standing on the dry bank, Thorn easily lifted the canoe and dragged it farther along the sloping shore, where it rested among several other dugouts strewn about.

They were on the Monongahela side of the Point. Ahead was the small town of Pittsburgh—Pittsborough, as it was now pronounced—and Fort Pitt loomed to their right. Thorn did not spare a glance across the dry moat to the tall earthen barrier that hid the rest of the fort, but headed instead toward the enclave of small wooden buildings of the town. Mariah followed, scurrying to keep up with his long, swift strides along the well-worn dirt path from the shore. She nearly tripped once, and he stopped to take her elbow.

She looked up to find him staring at her in bemusement. The heat and strength of his grip felt somehow comforting, as though she weren't alone in this foreign time and place. She recalled watching his back in the boat, and a molasses-thick warmth spread through her as their eyes caught, swirling about her in the most intimate of places. "Thanks," she whispered. He bent his head down, as though he, too, felt the sensual urges pumping through her, as if he wanted to touch her lips, as they spoke, with his own. She felt a tiny shiver of anticipation start inside. But instead, he glanced around, apparently recalling where they were. He dropped her arm and continued forward.

Ridiculous, that she would feel so magnetized by the man, especially in such inappropriate circumstances.

With a sigh, she went after him. She glanced back toward the fort and the spot where she had first left her time and entered this old world. To her right, the tiny Blockhouse crouched defensively outside the walls of the fort, the only remnant in the future of the great bastion that now spread so ominously along the peninsula at the forks of the rivers.

Mariah recalled the confusion she'd felt on awakening, her severe headache and vertigo, the rudeness of the two soldiers.

She looked toward Thorn. He'd stopped ahead, waiting for her. She hurried to catch up.

"Where are we going first?" She was slightly out of breath, her hair dangling in her face. He, on the other hand, seemed not at all winded even after rowing them all the way upriver.

He glanced down at her. Was that a glimmer of amusement in his cool brown eyes? "I, Miss Walker, am going to the largest trading post in town, Allen's. You may come there, too."

"Oh, thank you, kind sir."

His hand raised toward her face. Was he angry about her sarcasm? But, no. He pulled a lock of her hair away from her cheek and tucked it tenderly behind her ear.

"Thanks," she managed.

"You're welcome, Mariah." His voice, with its delightful British accent and gravelly tone, was as gentle as the breeze had become, and she wanted to take his hand, to hold it against her cheek. Instead, she smiled into his eyes until he said, "Let us continue."

They quickly reached the town, so different from the entrancing Pittsburgh she'd flown over in a plane. But the tiny borough of this day somehow held even more appeal, with its small and sparse log buildings along dirt roads, fresh, sweet air, and nearby stalwart fort.

Mariah had noticed Allen Traders along the main street when she'd been there before. It was a log cabin, as were most of the structures, but larger. It had glass in the windows, a nicety she'd ignored before, assuming all windows had glass. The glass's quality, though, left much to be desired; it was thick, with numerous bubbles marring its smooth texture.

She followed Thorn through an open wood door. Inside, the single room was crammed full of goods. A bear skin, with head intact, hung on one wall. Other furs formed a tall stack in the corner. Pots of many sizes hung from the rafters, and barrels scattered between tables were laden with everything from rifles to food. Two walls held narrow shelves filled with more goods.

The place didn't smell particularly appealing, and Mariah tried to identify the conglomeration of odors that caused her to hold her breath: mustiness, spoiled food, gunpowder, rancid tallow, tobacco?

Patrons fingered goods from the tables or lifted the lids of barrels to peek inside. Not exactly the sanitary packaging of her day, Mariah thought, but customers could see just what they were getting—bugs, perhaps, and all.

Thorn's moccasins made no noise on the wooden floor, but Mariah's boots clumped as she walked toward the first table. People murmured, and Mariah heard the rapid footsteps of the portly man who approached them. He wore an apron. "Mr. Thorn, I have not seen you in many a day. Welcome."

Thorn, touching a long-barreled rifle among several on a table, glared as though waiting for the man to admit he wanted this particular uninvited customer to leave, but the small, round man looked sincere to Mariah. His cheeks were as big as a frugal squirrel's.

"Who is this lovely lady?" the man asked.

"That is Miss Mariah Walker," said a familiar tenor voice from behind her. Mariah turned to see Francis Kerr rush toward her from a doorway. "I thought that was you coming from the river, Miss Walker. I am so pleased to see you again."

He took her hands in his warm, moist ones and squeezed. His orange hair was ruffled about his head, and his mushroom-colored eyes glowed with apparent happiness.

"How are you, Francis? Is everything all right here?"

His smile was grim as he turned toward the door. Another of his band of settlers had entered the shop, and behind him stood the glowering young man in Maitland's troop. A second uniformed soldier squeezed inside the door.

"Everything is fine," he said, "for those of us who enjoy caretakers. We can enter privies on our own, but little else."

"But why?"

"I must echo the question," Thorn said softly. He now stood beside Mariah, glaring down at her hands as they were still gripped by Francis's. Flushing, Mariah pulled hers gently away. Thorn continued, "I have not heard before of such interest being paid to a single group of homesteaders."

"Unhappily, we are to be the examples." Francis's scowl and jutting jaw showed how much he detested the idea. "We were informed so by Maitland. Many more indentured servants land upon these shores every day, and as they arrive others who have completed the time of their servitude depart to find homes. If the soldiers allow us to settle west of the Proclamation Line, others will believe they can as well."

"Isn't there anyplace else to go?" Mariah asked.

"South," Francis admitted, "but opportunities abound westward."

"And so do Indian fights," Thorn said.

Francis took a step toward him. He was shorter and leaner than Thorn but raised his head belligerently and looked him straight in the eye. "Would you run from such adversity if you thought you were in the right?"

Thorn gave a humorless laugh and shook his head. "When I first occupied the land on which my inn stands, I was not exactly welcomed, either by Indians or by the soldiers at the fort." He seemed to hesitate, then continued, so low that he seemed to speak almost to himself. "But there were reasons other than my scoffing at the law for the latter to be less than pleased."

The wince of pain that crossed his face was replaced immediately by his usual cool expression. Mariah knew, from the screenplay and René, a bit of what had caused him such grief. Being here, so close to the fort, must have triggered some of his worst memories. She reached toward him, almost touching his arm in comfort, but stopped herself. He'd not welcome any such gesture, particularly here, with others around.

Others. Would someone in this crowded store be the one to challenge Thorn to a duel? Not Francis, surely, or roly-poly Allen, but what about those two burly men in fur hats who looked like trappers? Francis's companions? The soldiers . . . the soldier. One of the two wasn't there any longer—the nasty-looking young man who'd been with Maitland.

She turned to Francis, asking in a low voice, "Have you met anyone here named Billy?"

He looked at her quizzically. "No, but I shall ask around to see if any of my fellows knows of a Billy. Is it important?"

"Sort of." She didn't want to admit how vital it could be, so she changed the subject. "But more important, I've come here for some cloth for Holly and me."

"Please allow me to show you where to find it," Francis said. Mariah looked at him in surprise. "I have hired my services to the proprietor temporarily," he explained with a wry grin. Taking her arm, he led her toward a corner of the store. "The soldiers," he whispered conspiratorially, "might be led to believe we are sincere about remaining in this town. But once they let down their guard . . ."

He did not have to finish. Mariah knew from the faraway look in his eyes that the lure of the west was too strong to keep Francis here, despite all the dangers he might encounter.

With Francis's assistance, Mariah selected a large panel of lightweight material in a pretty shade of pale blue, figuring Holly might want a dress from it, too. She also chose a dove gray linsey-woolsey for another dress, a delicate plaid for a skirt, white for undergarments, plus a more vibrant green fabric for Holly. She also bought thread and a paper with several needles hooked into it.

She stopped then and looked at Francis. "Am I spending a small fortune here?" After all, she needed to clothe Holly from scratch.

"We shall make you a deal," he assured her. He brought over the proprietor. "Mr. Allen, Miss Walker wishes all of these, but she is but a newly hired servant. What is the best price we can make for her?"

"You are working for Thorn?" The small, chunky man clasped his fat hands in front of his soiled apron.

She nodded.

"There are many reasons we wish to encourage Thorn's business here," Allen began. "Though he comes here little, we know how prosperous is his inn; it is a natural stopping place for those entering the wilderness to hunt or trade with the Indians . . . not to settle." Allen looked sidelong at Francis. "There are other trading posts not far away: Croghan's, for example, and the home of the Indian, Queen Aliquippa. But their accommodations—and politics—are not always as inviting as Thorn's inn."

"What do you mean?" Mariah asked.

"Some traders get too involved with Indian matters. They sometimes wish to know the business of their patrons for their own purposes. Thorn cares not why people venture to and past his inn. He asks few questions—though he listens carefully to those who wish to speak."

Mariah had the impression that this little, round man would want to talk Thorn's—and everyone else's—ear off.

"So, Miss Walker, since I know the excellent reputation of Thorn's inn, I wish to maintain a good relationship with him so he will come here to trade. I will charge you, therefore, less than anyone else would." He named a price that consisted of a few shillings. At Francis's beaming, she assumed it was a reasonable amount, but she would need to check with Thorn.

With a sigh, she thought of the big bucks she'd once earned from Lemoncake Films for work that had seemed tough—till she had her chores here to compare it to.

She turned to look for Thorn, only to find him standing at the next table, his back to her.

He must have heard every word the proprietor said, Mariah realized, and nearly laughed aloud. The little man had achieved more than just good customer relations with her; he might also have gotten Thorn's attention.

Mariah touched his shoulder. "Mr. Thorn, could you advance my salary so that—"

"I believe you could do better elsewhere." His voice was calm, but she noted the gleam in his brown eyes. He was baiting Mr. Allen.

"Not at all, Mr. Thorn!" The proprietor's voice was indignant. "I provide the best bargains west of Philadelphia; you know that."

"What I know is—"

"Thorn!" A boisterous male voice erupted from the front of the store. Mariah turned to see a thin man in an unbuttoned British uniform coat maneuvering his way through the tables and piles of goods.

"Ainsley!" Mariah couldn't remember having seen Thorn smile so broadly before. In seconds he, too, was picking out a path through the crowded store toward the other man.

Ainsley. Mariah had heard the name before. . . . Oh, yes; Thorn's friend whom René had told her about. The one who'd explained to René all the horrors of the time when the boy had been lost and his mother killed herself—and Thorn blamed himself.

The two men met between a keg of whiskey and a table laden with knives and miscellaneous goods. They embraced; then Ainsley stepped back. "Life as a tradesman agrees with you, brother," he said.

"And life as a soldier, how does it treat you?" Thorn's voice was low and tinged with an emotion Mariah guessed was jealousy. Uncertainly, she drew closer. She didn't want Thorn to run off with Ainsley without paying for her purchases.

"Quite well. In fact, you must come to the fort this afternoon. The men will be conducting special parade drills for which they have been practicing, and you must watch."

Mariah watched as Thorn's neck stiffened. "Some other time, perhaps."

Ainsley drew up beside Thorn and slipped his arm around Thorn's proud shoulders. "You have been running for too long," he said in a low voice. Mariah suspected she was the only one beside Thorn who heard it. "You must show that none of what happened matters any longer," he continued. "Only then will you regain the respect of your former fellows at the fort."

"Of course." His words were clipped, his pride speaking, but Mariah heard what he didn't say, that what had happened before *did* still matter. "Let us go."

"Wait!" Mariah touched Thorn's back. "I thought you'd advance my wages so I can buy that fabric."

At first, when Thorn turned to look at her, there was no recognition in his eyes, as though she'd just appeared for the first time. She flinched but didn't look away. She realized Ainsley's words had probably taken him back to his past, when he was a soldier in disgrace and she hadn't been there.

His blankness wounded her nevertheless. In an instant, though, his expression thawed. In fact, if she hadn't known better, she'd have thought he looked relieved to see her. Happy, even.

But, no. He'd simply put his memories behind him. It had nothing to do with her.

"Of course, Miss Walker," he said. "Have Mr. Allen tally your bill."

"Who is this?" Ainsley looked at Mariah for the first time. His narrow lips, stretched forward by teeth too prominent, curved in a boyish grin. His small, nearly black eyes were set deeply beneath sketchy dark brows. Holding his tricornered hat in his hands, he regarded her expectantly.

"This is Miss Mariah Walker," said Thorn. "She is a new servant at the inn."

"Welcome." He bowed with a flourish, then reached for her hand and kissed its reddened back. Mariah found herself blushing, and she reveled inside at Thorn's obvious irritation. He might treat her like the servant she was, but he couldn't expect everyone to do so.

She noticed that Francis, who'd gone to wait on another customer, was scowling at Ainsley. That was a situation she'd have to diffuse quickly, particularly if it had anything to do with her. She knew Francis had developed a crush on her. The last thing she wanted was to trigger a confrontation if it could lead to the screenplay's story coming true—the part where the soldiers attacked the settlers.

"Thorn has needed more help at the inn for some time," Ainsley continued. "I am delighted he found someone as charming as you."

"Thank you." But Mariah found herself left behind as Thorn paid Allen and the two men walked from the trading post, leaving her to carry her own purchases. By the time Allen had tucked the thread and needles in a fold and bundled the fabrics together with string, Mariah couldn't see where Thorn had gone.

Great! she thought. What was she to do if she lost him?

She tried to hurry out the door, but Allen stopped her. "One thing I must say, Miss Walker. I tried to warn Thorn whilst you were looking at goods, but he did not wish to hear. There are rumors hereabouts of a new Indian uprising. It has been five years since Pontiac's War, and with settlers even now not stopped from heading into the West, the savages grow upset."

Mariah felt alarmed. "Do you think they'll attack Fort Pitt?"

"More likely they'll set at undefended places like Thorn's inn," he said, a troubled expression on his fleshy brow. "Best be on your guard, Miss Walker. And try to convince Thorn as well."

"I will, Mr. Allen. Thanks." An Indian uprising. That had been in the screenplay, along with— "Mr. Allen, do you know of someone around here named Billy?"

He scratched his ear pensively. "I cannot say that I do."

Mariah finally hurried from the store, then stood on the edge of the dirt street, looking around.

"They headed toward the fort," said Francis, who had followed her outside. "I kept an eye on them while Mr. Allen finished up with you."

"Thanks." She looked toward the fort. Spotting a couple of figures who could be Thorn and Ainsley, she took a few steps in that direction, then turned back. "Oh, and Francis, good luck with . . . well, you know."

"I will let you know what happens, Mariah, for you are always welcome. . . ." He let his voice drift off.

Impulsively, she touched his cheek, then, after rearranging the package in her arms, hurried after Thorn.

The last time she'd tried to cross the drawbridge over the moat to the fort, the guard hadn't let her pass. Now, as she skirted the edge of the dry moat, she again heard the rhythmic footfalls of marching soldiers. This time, she knew someone she could ask for—Ainsley. Still, her heart thudded uncomfortably as she recalled the way her head had ached the last time, how confused she'd felt, and how afraid.

She reached the jutting dirt parapet to the drawbridge. The grass on the tall bank hiding the fort looked dry.

The fort end of the bridge was guarded by a uniformed man she didn't recognize, though he held one of the long-barreled rifles so common in this time.

"State your business, miss." He sounded as bored as his predecessor had.

"I was to come here with—" She fumbled for Ainsley's rank. That would, she was certain, be important. "Captain Ainsley," she tried.

The grizzled guard, in a buttoned blue uniform coat, who looked rather old to be a soldier, seemed to try hard not to sneer. "Sergeant Ainsley, you mean, miss?"

"Yes," she agreed. "He just came through here with—with my employer."

The guard's eyes narrowed. "You work for Thorn, miss?"

She nodded. "More's the pity," he continued. He leaned toward her, as though ready to commiserate.

Mariah didn't want to debate Thorn's character with the old fellow, but she hated the idea that this man apparently thought badly of him. She said brightly, "Mr. Thorn has been very kind to me so far. And understanding. And brave. Now, if I may see Sergeant Ainsley . . ." The bundle of cloth wasn't heavy, but it was growing awkward in her arms.

"Of course, miss," said the guard, snapping back to attention.

At the guard's nod, she walked slowly between the high earthen sides of the embankments, where some of the grass was yellow and patches of sod were peeling away. Then, studying everything with the trained eye of the production specialist she'd been in her own time, she passed by the tall and sturdy brick bastion walls and into the fort area.

The inner structures of the fort seemed in no better condition than the patchy embankments. Some of the long wooden buildings appeared to have portions rotting away. They even smelled rank.

Mariah followed the sound of the rhythmic footfalls till she reached the parade grounds. Men marched in several long lines, Pennsylvania rifles slung over their shoulders. The uniforms were far from uniform; though most men wore red coats, a few wore blue or green; others were in shirttails or buckskin. The clothing blended well with the dismal, ill-maintained feel of the fort; most was ragged and faded. They kicked up dust with their dirty black boots, and Mariah tasted the grittiness on her lips. She felt sorry for them, in their heavy uniforms and bulky hats in the sweltering, humid summer heat.

She wondered if any of them was named Billy.

An officer shouted orders at them from a raised wooden platform at one end of the field: Ainsley. Beside him stood Thorn, his chin raised proudly, his eyes chilly but alert, as he watched the soldiers drill.

Mariah stood on the edge of the field observing until the group wheeled and came marching right toward her. With an uneasy whoop, she hurried toward the platform and climbed up the stairs at its side.

The iciness of Thorn's gaze seemed to thaw for just a moment. "What brings you here, Miss Walker?" he asked, his raised voice barely audible above the rhythmic footfalls.

"You do, of course," she said. "I'm your servant, after all." She carefully put down her bundle at the edge of the platform.

A ghost of a grin teased the edges of his mouth. "I shan't forget that, Miss Walker. Shall you?"

She snorted and looked away, only to find Ainsley regarding her speculatively. "Perhaps next time I visit Thorn's inn you will tend to me; you seem like a fine serving wench."

She dipped her head in acknowledgement, looking sidelong at Thorn to see if he reacted at all to Ainsley's request that Mariah tend to him.

Sure enough, there was a very gratifying scowl on Thorn's face. "I've another serving girl besides Miss Walker, plus René is still with me," he told Ainsley. "When you come for a visit, there will be plenty to tend to you, never fear." He took Mariah's elbow, and the strength of his grip sent a pleasant warmth cascading through her. "We must leave soon so as to be back before nightfall," he said.

"Wait!" Ainsley's statement was issued like a command. Mariah stared at him. Even Thorn appeared slightly taken aback. "You may not leave until I have provided to you the hospitality of the fort."

"Unnecessary, Randolph," Thorn said. His eyes had narrowed, and he watched the still-parading men uneasily.

"Of course it's necessary, Charles," boomed Ainsley.

Though she had wondered when she had first met him, this was the first time Mariah had heard Thorn's first name: Charles.

To her, he seemed more like a Thorn.

"Parade, halt!" Randolph Ainsley called. Immediately, the lines of soldiers stopped, continuing to stand at attention. "Michaels, come here!" Ainsley waved to one of the soldiers at the end of the parade line. The young man hurried over, appearing every bit as much at attention as he stood in front of Ainsley as if he'd remained with his immobile cronies.

"Take two men and bring refreshments to my guests."

"Yes, sir," the young man said. He saluted, touching the side of his tricorner hat, and Mariah noted the beads of sweat pouring down a face that was as red as his coat.

In minutes, three soldiers, including Michaels, hurried back with a wooden table and chairs, which they placed on the ground in the shade of the raised platform. Then they brought tea and fresh bread.

"Corporal Maitland!" Ainsley called. The sharp-faced soldier took one step out from the ranks of the men. "Take charge," Ainsley commanded. "Continue the drill."

"Yes, sir," Maitland acknowledged, saluting without drawing closer, then turned back. "Attention!" he ordered. In moments, the men were again marching on the sun-drenched parade ground.

Ainsley pulled out a chair for Mariah and she sat. She felt uncomfortable as she tried to sip tea and eat bread. Both were tasty enough, but as the soldiers approached before turning and marching in the opposite direction, Mariah felt their resentment pouring out. Not toward Thorn, she hoped. She looked at him. He appeared discomfited, too, but he said not a word.

How could the men survive marching in this heat? How insensitive of Ainsley. But he was Thorn's friend. And maybe this was normal in life at a frontier fort.

Mariah was delighted when the small meal was finished. "We must leave now," Thorn said.

This time, Ainsley did not disagree. "Company, halt!" he called at last. "At ease, men."

"One more thing," Mariah said to Ainsley before they left. "I almost forgot. As I left Allen's store, a woman asked me to give a message to Billy, here at the fort. Do you know him?"

Ainsley shook his head. "I know no Billy," he said, but he looked at her strangely. "Tell me about this woman."

"Never mind," Mariah said, taking up her bundle of cloth. "Time to go back to the inn."

"That it is," said Maitland, reporting to Ainsley as the drill ended. He had marched with his soldiers, and sweat slithered down his fox-sharp features and onto the dirt-streaked shirt collar that stood above his red coat. He looked pointedly at Thorn. "Running an inn—that's as good a place to play at being brave as I've heard of for those who neglect their duty."

Mariah was about to make a suitably nasty retort when she saw Ainsley place a restraining hand on Thorn's arm. No, she'd better stay out of it.

But she understood from Thorn's silence as they walked quickly toward the riverbank, and from the stiff set of his shoulders, how the words had hurt.

"What Maitland thinks isn't important," she finally blurted out as they reached the pirogue. "Or anyone else."

But her words failed to soothe him. "I do not need your foolish chatter, Miss Walker," he snapped. "There is truth in a widespread opinion, and this is one I, too, must share."

Although he didn't meet her eye, she was struck by the agony she saw in his. But there was nothing she could do.

Not if he refused to help himself, darn the man!

What would Matilda, in the screenplay, have done? The right thing, Mariah was sure, for her Thorn loved her.

As he handed her onto the boat, one of the lines suddenly came to her, and she spoke it without thinking. "If two people care enough, the notions of the rest of the world about either of them make no matter at all."

She felt him freeze beside her. His hand clasped hers more tightly. And then he gave her a small shove onto the boat and let her go.

"Do not let yourself believe you care for me, Miss Walker. As Maitland said, I live a sham of a life. And I care for no one. Do not forget that. No one."

Chapter Thirteen

Holly Smith, scrubbing down the seat and walls of the outhouse with lye soap and coarse rags, was happy. No, rapturous—as if she'd died and gone to heaven.

Not that serving at the inn wasn't hard work. But compared to farm life, it wasn't any too taxing, even with Mariah gone for the day and all the chores falling onto her. She was still a little weak from her prior misfortune, but she wasn't one to lie around and mope. She had to be doing things, she did.

Though she wasn't pleased with the smell of her current chore, it wasn't much worse than mucking out a stable or chickenhouse. Plus, there weren't all them animals to tend: cows to milk, eggs to collect from peevish hens, pigs to slop. Nor was there the backaching job of dealing with crops: plowing, planting, watering or picking.

Not that this place didn't have a little garden. Too little. She'd see to expanding it, if she was here long enough.

Depending, of course, on that Thorn. He was a strange bird, he was. Though Holly took pride in the way she could read people, that one was a mystery. Nasty at times, and proud of it. But he'd not kicked Holly out on her behind yet, thanks to the way Mariah handled him. And from what Holly gathered, Mariah hadn't been serving here much longer than a few days herself.

Not that there wasn't plenty of work for the both of them. Lots of cleaning and cooking to do at an inn, there was. But Holly didn't mind. Cleaning had to be done whether at a little place of her own, like she'd planned, or working for someone else. And she liked to cook.

"Miss Holly?"

That Frenchie. It sounded like he was just outside the outhouse door. What did he want now? At least he wasn't calling her *Anglaise* now. He pronounced "miss" like *mees.* Though she'd never admit it to him, his accent was cute. Him, too, in any ugly sort of way. But he'd told her straight off how he hated the English, and she was just off the boat from London, if you didn't count them five years of bond service. "Yes, *Monsieur* René?" If he was being formal, so would she.

"Are you all right?"

He sounded worried, bless him. She smiled to herself. He must have thought she was spending all this time in the little building because she wasn't up to snuff. She shoved open the door. "I'm just finishing up in here."

She looked out to find his back turned away, like he was respecting her modesty, and she laughed. "You can peek now," she said. Slowly, he pivoted, keeping his eyes down. Sweet man, despite his silly dislike of the English. His gaze rose slowly, up the pink dress she'd borrowed from Mariah, she had, though Mariah hadn't been around to ask. The top was much too snug in all the wrong places. Or maybe the right places, for they sure made Frenchie's big eyes grow even bigger. She had left the top button undone but had tied, in a strategic location, a large kerchief she'd found in the stable and washed.

"You are not unwell?" he asked.

"No, just busy." She held out the rags and lye soap. "This place sure needed a scrubbing."

He looked surprised, then that great, heavy mouth of his

flopped in a big scowl. "You should not work so hard, *mademoiselle.* You must recover from your ordeal, grow strong."

"Oh, I'm very strong," she said. She stepped out the door, wishing she had shoes other than the moccasins them Indians had insisted that she wear. The Indians, and what they'd done . . . she would not think of them now. Besides, at least she was shod, which was better than she'd been back in the home country. She walked up to René, made a fist and flexed her arm right in front of that funny face of his. "Feel my muscle?"

He blushed. She couldn't remember if she'd ever seen a man do such a thing, and it made her feel as warm and mushy as fresh buttered porridge inside. She'd an urge to hug him, to squeeze him like she would an orphan child—though not them nasty guttersnipes that roved the streets of London.

"Never mind," she said. "Now, don't you worry about me. I'll rest when I need to, but right now we've an inn to run. You have dinner cooking yet?"

He shook his head. She wanted more than anything to laugh aloud at the confusion in his eyes. Cute man. "I'll do it," she said. "You haven't lived till you've tasted my potato soup. It's a special English receipt; you Frenchies don't have anything like it, and that's why you aren't as long-lasting under the covers as a good Englishman."

"An Englishman as *puissant* as a Frenchman? Never!" He'd drawn himself up to his full height, but he wasn't much taller than she. A broad, hefty man he was, though—thick at the chest, muscled in the legs as could be seen by the straining of his leather pants. It strained in the front, too. . . .

Holly would have fun teasing this one, she would. But not a lot. He was a nice man who'd worried about her health. She liked this René, but she didn't dare like him over much. Once she'd thought things through, decided on a direction for her life now that Mack . . . well, she'd be on her way again soon to settle in the west.

There was no room in her life for a sweet, sassy Frenchman.

* * *

When Mariah and Thorn came back, Thorn acted like a bumblebee had gotten up his britches, grumbling and growling and stomping about as he unloaded the canoe. Holly admired the pretty fabrics Mariah had brought and nearly hugged her in happiness when she learned that Mariah planned to share them.

"For a price, of course," Mariah said. But it wasn't any too costly, far as Holly was concerned. All she had to do was help sew the dresses and skirts and blouses, to show Mariah how to do some for herself.

Nice lady she was. And as tolerant of Thorn and his grumbling ways as a too-fond mother with a sassy child.

No, not like a mother. Not with eyes that stared at him the way hers did, as though she could see right through his clothes. Lusty eyes, eyes that said come hither.

Maybe that was why Thorn was so out of sorts, even later, when he stomped to the smokehouse, saying he'd make sure the fire was still going, that there was food enough for a hundred, if they got so many guests. When he came out again, Mariah was dumping water from pails into a washbasin, she was. He stared at her as though every movement of hers needed to be watched, to make sure she did things right.

"Enjoying the view?" she snapped, like she didn't much take to being watched so closely, but still those eyes of hers kept undressing him.

Maybe he was resisting her . . . unlikely. Not when his look, too, was so sexy. But neither seemed to want the other to know, looking the way they did when each thought the other had turned away.

They didn't look like a pair who would resist each other much longer, Holly thought. Not much longer at all.

She'd have fun keeping track of them. She thought Frenchie saw it all, too, the way he made little frowns into his hands when he thought no one watched.

She'd ended up in a nice place to gather her thoughts, Holly thought. Till she left, people here would keep her busy just looking and speculating.

* * *

Mariah was surprised how quickly things fell into patterns over the next few days. Mornings, she awakened at dawn, most days without anyone rousing her. Holly rose then, too, and René.

Thorn would already be awake, prowling about the inn's compound with his long rifle cradled in his brawny arms. His stern vigilance always made Mariah feel secure. She wondered whether he ever slept, worried about the tired lines that showed about his shadowed eyes. Wanted to smooth those lines away, tell him despite himself that he wasn't to blame, no matter what the people at the fort seemed to think.

But of course she didn't touch him, not in the slightest, most meaningless gesture that he could misinterpret as caring, since he seemed to be avoiding her.

She kept her silence, too, except for inane pleasantries when they chanced to meet. "Looks like rain," she'd say when the skies were as gray as the pewter flatware and the trees dripped with the previous night's precipitation.

"Pretty day," she'd say when the heaven was as blue as the jays that squawked as they flew overhead.

He was always civil, but no more. The kisses they'd shared were no more than memories fading as fast as those of her life in her own time. Had she really used indoor plumbing and dishwashers and microwave ovens, flown in planes in a sky now devoid of all but birds?

Had she really been kissed so thoroughly, so erotically, by Thorn?

Would she give up the right to return to the former if given the chance to experience the latter again?

She laughed bitterly at herself more than once over the passing days. Her pain at his near ignoring of her was excruciating, but she refused to dwell on it. Her interest in Thorn was strictly physical, after all. She'd never allow herself to care for someone so unreliable.

His work on the palisade continued, and the spiked wooden fence about the inn's compound grew daily. When Mariah could, she watched him as he worked, usually shirtless, his taut muscles rippling beneath a sheen of sweat. He lifted heavy logs, usually with René's assistance but occasionally without, and used a hammer to nail in the wooden pegs that held the fence together. She wanted to offer to help, too, but since he avoided her, she was sure her overture would be unwelcome.

He still shot her glances now and then, sometimes fiery and sometimes sad, when he seemed to think she was too busy with a chore to notice. But he went out of his way to keep from speaking with her, let alone touching her.

So, she'd continue to admire Thorn from afar. Watch him, as though he were the Thorn in the script after it had been shot. On the movie screen. Equally unreal and remote. A gorgeous, sexy phantom on whom only fictional heroines dared to rely.

In the meantime, she was learning a lot about survival in this era. She now knew how to tend the fire, to light a new one when necessary. To cook a variety of dishes, and clean using the available tools and soap of the day.

Strangely, after all her questing for a home in her own bustling time, she found the peaceful, primitive life here appealing. A life she was becoming comfortable with—in a place she felt she actually could belong. One where she wouldn't always be picking herself up to go to a new location.

She was even learning to sew, by hand, using small, even stitches instead of the mechanically perfect ones from machines that had yet to be invented.

She was proud when she'd completed her first skirt, a long one of the plaid material she'd selected. The afternoon it was finished, she put it on, wearing it when she helped serve supper.

Thorn, sitting with their only guest of the day, said nothing. She put a glass of ale in front of him and whirled away, swinging the skirt so it billowed about her legs, showing her ankles. She hazarded a glance back toward him. His stare rose from her feet up toward her face, and she felt herself flushing, particularly when he glanced at their guest, who also watched her legs.

No reason for her to feel uncomfortable. She'd worn skirts way above her knees in her own time.

But she wasn't in her own time, she reminded herself. Still, she kept her gaze defiant. "Notice anything different about me, Mr. Thorn?" she asked.

"Saucy, is she not?" asked their guest in a cultured bass voice that contrasted amazingly with his appearance, for he was a short, skinny trapper with a beard like a goat's.

Mariah saw Thorn stiffen. "That may be, Ambrose," he replied, glaring at her.

She shuffled her feet in indignation; he should be irritated with their rude visitor, not her. But then one corner of his mouth turned up in a smile that worried her. It was the first she'd seen in days, and she didn't know where it had come from.

She found out with his next words. "Perhaps, Miss Walker, you are cleaner than usual."

She drew in her breath, ready to throw something at him in her sudden embarrassment. Until that day, she'd taken only sponge baths, using water in the basin in her room. But hours earlier, she'd bathed, for the first time, in the cool, sparkling stream—in the nude.

Holly had stood guard. No one could have come by without her warning Mariah.

But though Mariah had cautioned Holly, maybe she hadn't noticed Thorn creeping silently in his moccasins through the forest he knew so well. Had he seen Mariah there, with no clothes on, reveling in the cold, clean water of the stream?

A blush heated her from her toes up to her hairline. And he'd been staring at her ankles as though she were wanton just for showing them. Hypocrite!

Unless . . . maybe he'd only heard about her bath. With a sidelong smile of her own, she said, "I can't guess why I should be cleaner now than all the other times I've . . . well, you know." She lowered her eyes, then looked up at Thorn tauntingly from beneath her lashes. "Times when even Holly was busy with other things. Don't tell me you haven't known."

He stared at her, his thick chest rising and falling raggedly and his gaze growing heated. She guessed he was imagining her there, unprotected and nude countless times in the mountain stream.

An answering molten feeling surged through her; she had to be careful, for in teasing him, she was affecting herself. The idea of his seeing her naked was enticing. What if . . . ?

Forget that. She couldn't let things go farther than teasing. Not here. Not now.

Not with Thorn.

As she turned, she noticed their unkempt guest's eyes staring at her in confusion Fortunately, their references had probably gone right over his head. "Care for some more ale, Mr. Ambrose?" she asked sweetly.

"As Thorn knows, I never turn down an offer of a sweet libation." The old goat leered at her, and she frowned.

"And you, Mr. Thorn," she continued. "I suppose you could do with another drink."

"Yes, Mariah." His voice reeked with British civility, but there was a huskiness to it as well. "I would like . . . a drink."

Thorn wished for more than just a drink. That was the problem. "I will get more ale," he said, rising. Needing to move away.

He had seen Mariah at her bath, had suffered the sweet torment of glimpsing her lovely, slender body bared beneath the waterfall.

He had seen Holly, too, keeping watch. But she was no match for someone who had studied the skills of the Indians.

Thorn had left quickly, quietly. But the sight had burned itself into his mind. Had burned other places as well.

That had been the first, the only time Mariah had bathed at the falls. He kept watch on her. He would know. Still, his heartbeat quickened at the idea of more.

How could he bear Mariah to be so close, so untouchable? But to wish otherwise was foolhardy. She would never be his.

Yet he thought often of the kisses that had seared themselves into his senses. . . .

Being alone with her on the trip to Fort Pitt and the trading post had nearly undone him. In the pirogue, he had been taunted every moment by her nearness. He had felt her behind him as surely as if she stroked him with those poor, overworked hands.

Then, in the town, to have seen her flirting again with that Francis Kerr had been nearly more that he could bear.

His peace of mind had been damaged further upon entering the bastion of the fort, although Ainsley had been right; Thorn had needed to do so to cast from his shoulders some of the weight of the years and events of the past. He appreciated his friend's open support. He wished, however, that Ainsley had not flaunted his presence so before the men.

But his guilt would never be purged. Maitland had reminded him all too clearly that no one else would forgive him his sins, so why should he? He had spurned Mariah's kindness to him as they had headed back, for he could not do otherwise.

Now, he stood at the bar, quietly pouring ale into a glass pitcher. Mariah remained seated beside Ambrose.

"So my friend Thorn finally has a woman." Ambrose's voice was low enough that he could have thought Thorn unable to hear. He was wrong.

"Hardly." She glanced toward Thorn, looking embarrassed. Uncomfortable.

Obviously, she did not have the same disquieting thoughts about him that he did about her. An unwanted sorrow washed through him.

Yet she had made that strange comment at the pirogue about two people caring about one another. Might she have meant that she could, after all, have feelings for him?

And what if she did? It made no matter. It was impossible.

"Do not let my speculations bother you, kind maiden," Ambrose continued in a whisper. His voice grew louder. "I am the one who caused this inn to be here. Did Thorn tell you so?"

"Really?" she asked.

Thorn rejoined them as Ambrose drew conspiratorially close to Mariah. He saw her wrinkle her nose. Ambrose, his hairy, unkempt friend, smelled as bad as he looked.

"You see," Ambrose began, his head hunched toward her, "there was a time when my trapping business was new and not very successful. I found myself seeking shelter in my travels from any kind soul who would grant it."

"And Thorn was a 'kind soul'?"

Thorn felt himself stiffen at her words, but the smile she gave him was not mocking. In fact, she seemed amused.

"Not exactly," said Ambrose, turning his back as though to speak without Thorn's participation. "That was how I helped. I begged his indulgence each time I came. At first he refused, though he had already built his delightful stone cabin. Eventually, he allowed me to stay, and I repaid him in pelts. And later, money. He told me soon that he was accepting payment for lodging from other travelers—and the result, young lady, is this inn." He patted her arm with a filthy hand. To her credit she did not wince. Ambrose turned once more to face Thorn. "Is this not true? Are we not the best of friends now?"

Pretending to be stern, Thorn said, "We are indeed friends, even though you have taken much credit for my efforts and decisions." The story was not far from the truth, although Ambrose was but one of many who had come asking for lodging. At first, Thorn had refused all who came from the direction of Fort Pitt. He did not wish to host any who knew of his shame there. Eventually, it no longer mattered. He had been determined to survive, and there was money to earn by taking in guests. He clapped Ambrose on the back. "I do owe you much, my friend."

The sound of voices erupted outside. Thorn rose. "Since you turned me into an innkeeper, I must see if I have new guests." He left the room.

Mariah, eager to get away from Ambrose and his aroma, excused herself and quickly followed Thorn from the kitchen.

A pretty roan horse was tethered outside, and a pile of animal hides lay on the ground beside it. Farther in the courtyard, Thorn greeted new arrivals. Familiar arrivals. Francis

Kerr and his group of would-be settlers had returned.

For a moment, Mariah felt delighted to see them—but then she swallowed hard as she recalled the screenplay and its graphic, brutal dramatization of what happened to the settlers. When they hadn't been attacked by the soldiers before, she'd chalked it up to another error in the script. But did their renewed journey west mean that it might still happen?

Impulsively, she ran toward them, her plaid skirt swishing about her legs. "Francis!" she cried. Holly was already there, standing among the pack-laden horses and talking excitedly with the settlers as René stood off to the side, watching.

Francis shone a tooth-filled grin as she approached. His clothing and red hair were damp; some rain had fallen a while earlier. He took her hands in his short, boyish fingers before she could retract them. "Mariah, my dear, I counted the days before I saw you again, but with my tallying of coins at the trading post, I feared losing track. So, instead, here I am!"

She grinned. "You're full of blarney, Francis." She looked sidelong at Thorn as he hovered over the homesteaders: Francis's sister Ann, their pockmarked friend Edgar, his red-faced wife whose name Mariah could not remember, and the rest. His glower spurred her to touch Francis's arm. Though she knew the answer, she asked, "Why are you here?"

Laughing, he said, "We seized an opportunity. There was word of Indian unrest northeast of here, and most of the soldiers from the fort were sent that way. The remaining ones were too few to worry about a handful of sneaky settlers, so here we are! But I did not wish to go on without stopping here to ask you again to join us. Holly, too, of course."

He turned his smile on the other woman, who grinned impishly. "Of course," she echoed. "You men could always do with another woman willing to follow you to the edges of nowhere and cook you a hot meal without complaint, isn't that right?"

"You have us pegged, Miss Holly," Francis replied. "Are you coming?"

Mariah watched Holly glance from her to Thorn to René, whose face was nearly as impassive as Thorn's at his most frustrating. "Not this time," Holly said. Mariah almost laughed at the big grin that washed over René's face and disappeared as quickly as a camera flash. Not that she'd seen one for ages.

The settlers stayed long enough only to wolf down the hurriedly prepared meal. Ambrose was still there, and his deep voice boomed jocularly as he traded tales with the others. Then they all were finished and in the courtyard again.

"So long, Mariah," Francis called. "Tell the soldiers, if they come, that we've gone by water, would you? That will give us more time if they do arrive." Soon they all were gone, though Ambrose had headed in a different direction on his pelt-laden roan horse.

Mariah wondered if that was the last she'd hear of the settlers. She wished them the best. Imagine, heading somewhere to start a new life without having any idea where, having to start from scratch to build a place out of what nature provided.

Amazing. Courageous.

Just what the screenplay had portrayed. And then its fictional soldiers had routed the settlers.

But here the soldiers had dealt with the settlers more than a week earlier. That incident had played out differently, as usual, from the script.

The matter was closed.

But Mariah remembered, several days later, that she could be sure of nothing here, even if something seemed covered by the script. Events had been plotted, however erroneously, by Pierce.

A troop of soldiers arrived from Fort Pitt led by Ainsley, Maitland among them.

Were they after the settlers? And this time, could Mariah prevent the homesteaders from being hurt?

When the soldiers arrived, Mariah stood just outside the palisade wall, which now extended three quarters of the way around the compound, working with Holly on plans to expand the garden. Some soldiers were in red-coated splendor, others in uniforms of other colors or buckskin. Though dressed differently, they marched nearly in unison considering the forested terrain. Carrying rifles, they came from the direction of the river.

Ainsley was first, his small, dark eyes all but hidden beneath his tricornered hat. He swept the hat from his head, bowing as though to royalty. "Good evening to you, ladies. Have you food and lodging for some weary soldiers?"

Mariah wanted to send them on their way, but not if they'd catch the settlers sooner. She was about to respond when Holly curtseyed, holding out the skirt of the green dress she'd made from fabric Mariah had bought at Pittsburgh. "Welcome, good sirs." Holly's voice was sweeter than wild cherries. "If you come and rest yourselves in the tavern, we will prepare a meal worthy of you." Her usual, common-British accent had been replaced by a mocking version of aristocracy that mimicked the soldier's, and Mariah put her hand up to hide her smile.

"That sounds wonderful indeed," Ainsley said. He looked quizzically at Holly, and his eyes beneath their overprominent brows seemed to sweep her. "You must be the other new serving girl my friend Thorn told me about."

"That I am, sir." Holly led Ainsley around the partial palisade wall. The other soldiers followed. Maitland, with his sharp, pointed features, touched his hat politely as he passed Mariah, but his eyes were cold. That boy was along, too—the one with the small beard who looked incongruously familiar to Mariah.

There were more soldiers this time than the last, perhaps twenty in all. Mariah couldn't help the sickly sense of fear that seemed to compress her insides so she could hardly breathe.

Thank heavens Francis and the rest had a head start of several days. Maybe they'd be far enough away . . .

"Ainsley!" Thorn had been working on the palisade fence. His shirt was off, and Mariah couldn't help staring at his muscled torso glistening with perspiration. He hurried to his friend and grasped his upper arm with his left hand as he shook his right one vigorously. "Glad to see you, man."

"And I you," Ainsley said. "I have not visited here at your inn for far too long."

"Why are you here?" Mariah asked, joining them. As if she didn't know. They were after the settlers.

Ainsley looked at her grimly over his broad, upturned nose. "There is another Indian uprising. We have come to warn you and others, and to see if we can save some of the foolhardy who have determined to settle in the west."

Mariah drew in her breath. Francis had mentioned, unconcernedly, that the soldiers had been off fighting Indians. That had been his group's chance to escape.

Had it also become their chance to be killed?

"We would like to stay the night," Ainsley said. His smile revealed his uneven, prominent teeth and did not reach his lusterless eyes. He looked exhausted, as did the other men.

They had been fighting Indians, he said, and the problem had not been resolved.

Poor Indians, Mariah thought. Poor soldiers. If only she, with her knowledge of the future, could somehow help them all.

She nearly laughed aloud. Sure, she could just tell these men, "Don't worry. In less than fifty years this area will be empty of Indians. They'll have been driven west. And less than a hundred years after that, they'll have been forced to live on reservations or be assimilated into the rest of the country." Or she could tell the Indians to stop fighting, that they could save their lives, though not their homes, by being passive.

Right.

She realized that Thorn, Ainsley and Holly were all watching her. Had she said anything aloud? She didn't think so, but she must have been staring into the distance in her reverie. She forced a smile. "May I serve you gentlemen some refreshments?" she asked. She basked in Thorn's pleased expression, focusing determinedly on his gorgeous face rather than his gleaming, bare torso. At least, for once, she was doing what he wanted her to do.

"I will put away my tools, wash up and then rejoin you,"

he told his friend, clapping him on the shoulder as he headed for his stone house in the middle of the compound.

Mariah motioned the soldiers into the common room, and they headed inside. Mariah hung back, touching Holly's sleeve. "I'll start entertaining the soldiers, but we'll need some help. Will you find René? I think he said he was going after fish."

Mariah went inside. Soldiers were scattered around the room, seated on the benches at the puncheon tables. A couple, including Maitland and Ainsley, stood at the bar.

"Here you are." She poured ale and rum into tankards. She served herself some ale, too—she needed a bit of bracing. She raised her own mug, and the two men looked at her in surprise. "May I propose a toast, gentlemen?"

"Certainly, Miss Mariah." Ainsley's smile was wide and friendly, though tired. He seemed like a nice enough man. He was Thorn's friend.

Maybe Mariah could convince him to leave the settlers alone.

Not much chance she could get this soldier to lay off the Indians, though.

"To people of the past," she said. "May they live together in peace."

Ainsley and Maitland glanced at each other in apparent puzzlement, then took swigs from their tankards as Mariah did the same. The ale was cool and bitter but tasted good. She took another long sip and asked one of the many questions on her mind. "Are we safe from Indians here?"

"No one is safe anywhere, Miss Mariah," Maitland said. "But the Iroquois seem to be massing north and west of here. This is not one of the worst places to be."

"How far west?" Mariah asked.

"How far west did your settler friends go?" countered Ainsley. "They did pass through here, did they not?"

Mariah didn't want to answer, nor did she want to lie. "Are there enough soldiers to help the settlers?"

Ainsley shook his head, his prominent top lip tucked into the bottom one in a sorrowful grimace. "We try. That is why we wish to enforce the Proclamation Line, to keep more people from settling and getting killed. This warfare with the Indians is inevitable as long as they believe their land is being stolen.''

The man appeared to bear no animosity toward the settlers. He was in charge of this troop. Surely the screenplay's soldier attack on homesteaders had been satisfied by the earlier meeting.

As soon as she had a few minutes, Mariah would escape to her room in the stable. She wanted to refresh her memory about what the script indicated might happen next. To the best of her recollection, she realized with dismay, the next event after the settlers' attack consisted of Matilda's capture by Indians when she was away from the inn.

And Mariah was cast in Matilda's role. Did her attempted kidnapping by Nahtana satisfy that scripted prediction?

But she'd thought that had occurred instead of a visit to Thorn by a friendly Indian.

Regardless, to make sure the kidnapping incident couldn't come true, she would stick tight here. No matter what.

In the meantime, she didn't want to hear any more about warfare and fighting. Or, for that matter, events that might be predicted by the screenplay.

There were other things she wanted to hear about, though, and this might be the perfect opportunity.

She wanted to know more about Thorn.

First, she did her rounds as barmaid, quickly refilling cups and laughing with the soldiers, most of whom seemed to be having a good time. That one, though—the bearded young man—mostly drank and watched and only smiled now and then.

As soon as she could, Mariah ended up behind the bar again. Thorn could return at any moment, and she'd questions to ask first. But she had to approach them subtly. ''So,'' she said to the two officers, ''where are you both from originally?''

''England,'' Ainsley replied. She'd kept his cup filled, and he'd have drunk a lot in a short time. ''Thorn and I grew up together. Hasn't he told you?''

"He's pretty closed mouthed about his background," she replied. "Tell me more."

Maitland gave her a dirty look, and she was glad when he joined some men at a table. Apparently he wasn't interested in Thorn except to harass him.

"We were from Essex, east of London." Ainsley's voice was slurred. "Thorn was the third son in a wealthy family from an estate near the town of Rayleigh." He hesitated. "Second son, after a time. There was an unfortunate incident with his older brother. . . . Well, never mind. I was the eldest son in a not-so-wealthy trades household from the town. Thorn and I got into mischief together from the time we were tiny lads, and when it came time to seek our fortunes, we decided we'd join the army and venture to the colonies together."

"That's wonderful!" She wanted to ask Thorn's old friend about how they'd arrived at Fort Pitt. More, she wanted to know how Ainsley had perceived the incident with the kidnapped child and suicidal woman that had led to Thorn's disgrace, but she kept those questions to herself. Maitland's table wasn't far away, and he could be eavesdropping. The room was filled with other soldiers who might also listen in. Instead, she asked, "What kind of mischief did you get into?"

Thorn, fortunately, was taking his time. Between her duties as barmaid, she laughed at the escapades described by Ainsley, who grew more and more drunk: stories of two rowdy young men who'd taken advantage of their good looks and important families. "Thorn had a tutor and his father allowed me to study with him. We went through . . . oh, I can count five offhand. Not one appreciated the snakes we stuck in their beds, the wenches we paid to show up at inopportune times, crying for the fathers of their brats. Good thing old Thorn had gone through his own list of tutors when he was a boy, or he'd have kicked me out and made Thorn buckle down alone." The stories graduated from practical jokes to wenching of their own, and Mariah couldn't help smiling sadly for the carefree youth Thorn had once been.

But then Thorn himself came into the room. "We've just

been talking about you, old fellow,'' Ainsley cried.

Thorn looked taken aback for a moment, training his usual glare on Mariah, but Ainsley slurred, ''The good old days back in the homeland. Do you remember Phelps, that doddering old tutor your father thought was so spry?''

Thorn laughed. ''Spry because we set his shoes afire. He couldn't stand in one spot then.''

The two were soon involved in reminiscences, and Mariah listened raptly, enjoying how happy Thorn sounded, for a wonderful, welcome change. Holly came in, and Mariah was able to stay at the bar while the other woman served the men at the tables. ''Frenchie is cooking supper,'' Holly told Mariah. ''He'll need us to help in a while.'' She hurried off as a soldier held his tankard in the air.

''So, Miss Mariah,'' said Maitland, who'd come up beside her, ''have you an idea when supper will be ready? We must eat soon, bed down early to get a start first thing in the morning. Perhaps we will yet be in time to help those damned fool settlers.''

Mariah felt a lump rise in her chest. The settlers she'd met—Francis, his shy sister Ann and the rest—could have been slaughtered by now. ''I'll go check on supper,'' she managed.

For the next hour, Holly and she were kept busy finishing the cooking and serving drinks.

She almost enjoyed herself as she forced herself again to banter with Ainsley and Maitland and some of the soldiers.

Soldiers, too, who might not survive their next encounter with Indians. An encounter that could come the very next day.

Most of them seemed cheerful, carefree. As though they'd no concerns at all about the dangers they would soon face—dangers that ought not exist at all, if only Mariah, with all her knowledge, weren't so powerless.

And then there was that young man with the beard who still laughed only rarely with the rest. When he wasn't staring at Thorn with narrowed eyes, he was belting down rum.

Why did he look so familiar?

Going behind Maitland at the table he now shared with

Ainsley and Thorn, she leaned over the fox-faced man. "That soldier there." Conspiratorially, she pointed toward the young man. "I think I've met him before, but I can't remember his name. What is it?"

"Shepherd," Maitland said. "Will Shepherd."

For a moment, Mariah didn't react.

And then it struck her. She swallowed her gasp of dismay. Her concerns about this young man who scowled so angrily at Thorn were not misplaced.

His name was Will. Short for William.

She had asked Ainsley if there was a Billy at the fort, but she hadn't asked the question correctly.

Billy was also short for William.

If the screenplay held any truth, that young man could be the one who'd challenge Thorn to a duel.

The one who would kill Thorn.

Chapter Fourteen

Thorn had watched over Ainsley's shoulder, forcing himself to listen to his friend, to laugh with him, as Mariah Walker flirted with that weasel-faced corporal, Maitland. She'd tossed her head more than once in a movement he had come to recognize as natural to her, so that her lovely golden hair, still unrestrained by a cap, swayed at her shoulders.

The sensual motion was not lost on Maitland, judging by the stiff set of his shoulders and the boisterous sound of his voice.

Thorn did not care what the woman did, or upon whom she bestowed her considerable favors. They did not belong to him. They never would. She was simply his employee, and that would soon end, he had no doubt.

But observing her lighthearted exchange with the corporal had pierced his gut as acutely as many other wounds that had plagued him over the last years. Wounds that did not tear his skin but his soul.

Except—why did she pale so suddenly? Her mouth was agape with no sound coming out of it, and her lovely green eyes compressed in seeming agony.

"Excuse me." He slipped around Ainsley and grabbed Maitland's thin shoulder. "What have you said, man?" he demanded, ready to thrash him for any insult to the woman.

Mariah placed her small hand upon his sleeve. "It's no big deal. Really. I asked about the man over there, and Corporal Maitland told me his name: Will Shepherd. I knew of someone with a similar name who . . . who did something unpleasant, and I found the recollection upsetting. That's all."

Thorn glanced at the one designated as Shepherd. The impertinent young fellow stared back, his jaw jutting beneath his beard. There was something familiar about him, but no more so than any other of the current crop of soldiers at the fort; Thorn had seen nearly all at some time. He turned back to Mariah.

She had not told him everything. He was certain of it. She still looked ashen, and her story seemed poorly fabricated. Her stricken gaze remained on him as though there were more she wished to say. He'd a sudden urge to hold her. To comfort her. Yet she'd made it clear she did not want his assistance.

"Perhaps you can see what is holding up supper." Thorn knew he sounded ill-tempered, but her demeanor had startled him. And why the devil did she not explain what was on her mind?

That was not fair, he realized. Perhaps her problem was best revealed to someone she trusted. In private.

He felt his fists clench. Of course she would not trust him. And the idea of being alone with her might sound pleasant, but it was fraught with perils he did not wish to consider. Had not the few times they had been alone turned disastrous? She had tempted him over and over to forget his resolve to touch no woman ever again.

Mariah's eyes were downcast. She spoke quietly. "Holly said supper would be ready at any moment, but I'll check." She turned to go.

A pang of something he could not identify plucked at his gut. This meek obedience was not like his feisty serving wench. He leaned toward her, saying low in her ear, "Mariah . . . will you explain to me what is wrong?"

"Yes," she said hurriedly. And then, "No." Her voice was low, and it broke, as though something vile choked her. "I'm sorry." She took a step away from him.

He grabbed her arm. "We will speak of this later."

There was unspeakable sorrow in her green eyes. "I'm not sure how to tell you. Or whether anything will help." She hurried from the room, her brown skirt swishing about her ankles.

"Such an odd young woman," Ainsley said, "but most attractive." There was a speculative gleam in his eye that Thorn wished to wipe away, with force if necessary. But he controlled his anger. He was pleased, after all, to have the opportunity for discourse with his old friend once more.

Yet as he conversed amiably with Ainsley, his mind remained on Mariah. His mind now seemed ever on the woman, no matter how he wished otherwise.

Now, with his former comrades from Fort Pitt about, he was reminded more clearly of his own failings. Why was it he felt he could share his problems with Mariah Walker, that to do so might help cleanse him of his cowardice?

He would not, of course. It would be one more link between the two of them, and he already had to brace himself far too often to keep from pulling her into his arms, from touching her, from burying himself so deep within her that not even he could find himself.

No, he dared share nothing with her.

If only she would share what troubled her with him. . . .

Somehow, Mariah made it through supper. She couldn't be sure, after all, that Will was Billy. And if he was, she could be prepared. Could prepare Thorn. Knowledge could be useful.

Then why was it affecting her this way?

Maybe because something inside, some terrible intuition, told her she'd guessed right. Will *was* Billy.

Though she felt in a daze, she forced herself to smile and banter with the soldiers as she served loaves of bread, steaming plates of fish and fresh peas from the small garden. She had a role to perform, after all. She was a servant. There had never been such characters in the modern comedies on which she'd worked, but all serving wenches she'd seen in old movies were lighthearted and merry.

But who knew what the actresses hid inside?

She made it a point to speak with Will Shepherd. "How do you like our fare this evening?" she managed with a flirtatious smile, though she felt distant, as if she were watching someone else on a movie screen.

"I prefer a young, plump hen," he said with a leer at her breasts, causing a round of guffaws from the other soldiers at his table.

"And I prefer an older, more seasoned rooster myself," Mariah retorted, never losing her grin. Whoever wrote her lines was doing a good job.

Her comment caused even more laughter, and Will grew pink as one of his friends cried, "You need to do a bit more strutting, Will, so this pullet will pull your—"

"Now, mind your tongue," Holly interrupted, breezing over to refill the tankards of ale.

Mariah heard the renewed laughter, the increasingly boisterous chatter, the suggestive comments as though in a fog. This Will Shepherd—he seemed like all the rest of the soldiers. Though there'd been a glumness about him before, now he was acting as animatedly ribald as the rest. He looked young, not out of his teens, despite his dark beard and mustache. His eyes were a pale shade between green and hazel, but the only unusual thing about him was the frequency with which he glanced at Thorn.

But was that really so unusual? Mariah did the same thing.

Her employer seemed to be enjoying himself with Ainsley. He seemed happier now than at any other time since she'd come here. Still, he looked in her direction often with a question in his gaze. A hint of sorrow, now and then, too.

Several times, she sashayed in his direction, watching herself play her role to the hilt. "More fish, Sergeant Ainsley?" she asked.

His overbite became more prominent as he grinned, revealing uneven teeth. "I'll take anything you'll serve, Miss Walker." He lifted his tankard of ale and said, "To good times and good servants." He took a long swig, smacked his lips and winked.

Mariah almost grinned at the decisively blank expression on Thorn's face that did not quite camouflage the annoyance in his glistening brown eyes. But that would have been a genuine grin, not an actress's smile. It would have required that she push her way out of the fog that surrounded her.

Better that she stay there, desensitized, not caring that she believed she knew who would take Thorn's life.

Unless she were able to right that particular wrong.

She had to. She could not let Thorn die. Not that horrible, preventable way. There was no need for him to fight a duel, no matter what the provocation from the irritating young Will.

Maybe she could start right now to stop what the screenplay had foretold. She shrugged aside the haze that had paralyzed her inside and joined her boss at the food-laden puncheon table. "Mr. Thorn, do you know all the soldiers here?"

He didn't look at her as he said, "No." The starkness of the barked word told her that he didn't want to know them. But his wants did not, at that moment, matter.

"Sergeant Ainsley, would you please introduce everyone?"

Ainsley blinked eyes fringed with sparse lashes. "Well . . . certainly, Miss Walker." His enthusiasm, thought Mariah, was underwhelming. But he dutifully began, table by table, making each man stand as his name was called.

"Good," Mariah said when he was finished. "An innkeeper should know all his guests by name, right, Mr. Thorn?"

Trapped, he gave a brusque nod, but his eloquent stare shouted at her to forget this nonsense and become invisible, like a good servant.

She didn't. "Let's get our guests to help with the dishes. What do you think, Mr. Thorn?" She knew what he thought after their episode with sweet, shy Mrs. Rafferty more than a week earlier, so she didn't give him a chance to answer. "How about carrying some stuff to the kitchen for me?" She smiled sweetly at Will Shepherd, who blushed as he rose among the guffaws and jeers of his fellows. Their voices soon stilled as she recruited more of them.

Soldiers bussed dishes. Others dried pots and baking dishes or washed the tops of the tables. They were directed by a muttering René and teased into doing more by a playful Holly. Even Maitland, his sharp features more pinched than usual, pitched in amid the catcalls of his troops when Mariah shamed him into it.

When they were done, Mariah led them all back into the common room, where Thorn stood with Ainsley at the bar.

Holly followed. "What're you up to?" she demanded softly. "You've got Frenchie fit to be tied that all those men stormed his kitchen in such a manner. And now you've got 'em all lined up like for a Christmas wassail line, you do."

"I . . . I'll explain later." But Mariah doubted she could do that. Though she'd found Holly a dear, patient friend, how could she burden her with the secret that would make Mariah seem like a crackpot? "Now," she said, "it's time to thank our guests." She insisted that Thorn shake each man's hand. Though there were a couple of scornful glances and an occasional grip that looked as limp as wilted lettuce, each man complied.

Except Will Shepherd.

He hung back, and then, when he was almost the last man left, he said, "Pardon me, Miss Walker, but my stomach is churning something fierce. Nothing against your supper, of course, but the smell in here has made me ill. I need to use the necessary."

Maitland's narrow lips curved into an evil grin. The flaring of Ainsley's nostrils was all the more evident because of the way his thick nose turned up at the end, but the fire in his eyes seemed directed more at Mariah than toward the defiant soldier.

Mariah felt as though someone had rammed her in the gut with one of the logs Thorn was using to build the palisade. Instead of helping, of causing the two men to shake hands and behave amicably, she'd only made things worse.

"Had you met Will Shepherd before?" she managed to ask Thorn.

He shook his head curtly, causing a lock of burnished dark hair to fall across his broad forehead. "Not that I recall. And I most certainly have no wish to make his acquaintance now."

Eventually Will returned to the room and stayed to one side with some cohorts, far from where Thorn conversed with Ainsley. The summer evening turned into night, and Thorn, René, Holly and Mariah lit lamps about the room, bathing it in dim, flickering light. The lingering scent of supper receded into the smell of stale ale and liquor as the men toasted everything from the king to their horses.

The time until the soldiers retired dragged, but eventually Ainsley called out, "Men, we will rise early tomorrow. It is time we were abed."

They were well trained. The men drained their tankards with no grumbling and headed off to rest.

Soon, the common room was cleared. Not even Thorn remained, for he and René followed to make sure the men had everything they needed.

Mariah tried to go to her room, but Holly stopped her. Despite the soothing tone of her voice, her question was what Mariah had feared. "What did you wish to accomplish when you tried to get that young Shepherd to shake Thorn's hand?"

Mariah sighed, sinking onto one of the hard wooden chairs. "Was my intention that obvious?"

"Perhaps not to all, but I could see in your eyes your dismay when the young scoundrel failed to partake in that symbol of friendship."

Elbows on the table, Mariah buried her face in her rough hands. She ached to confide in someone, to unburden herself of the impossible secret she carried deep inside. Of the people she'd met here, she sensed Holly might be the most sympathetic. Feeling moisture fill her eyes, she said, "If I told you what's going on, you'd think me completely bonkers."

"Bonk—"

"Crazy," Mariah amended hastily. She'd have to learn to watch her use of her time's slang.

Holly sat and held Mariah's wrist. "There were times when I was indentured," she said softly, "that I believed I would go . . . bonkers. Without freedom, a soul has nothing, you see. And five years seemed so very long, it did. But then I would seek out Mack, and he would tell me, 'Do you know, Sister, that we have only one thousand ninety-five days—' or whatever it was—until we are our own people, here, in this new land of opportunity?' Dear Mack was always so cheerful. He was my strength."

It was Mariah's turn to touch Holly sympathetically.

Holly's hazel eyes had filled, but she patted Mariah's hand and smiled. "I did not tell you this to make either of us sad, but to show you how it helps, at times, to talk with someone else. Should you ever wish to tell your 'bonkers' story to me, I would be most—"

She was interrupted by footsteps on the stairway at the end of the room. Thorn and René descended. Thorn stopped beside Mariah. "Do you wish to explain your behavior this evening?"

She shrugged at Holly. "I believe Mr. Thorn is out of sorts. What do you think?"

"I think," said René, "that Miss Holly and I have chores elsewhere. Do you not agree, Miss Holly?"

"Most certainly, Mr. Frenchie." Holly rose and curtseyed to the men, winking at Mariah, who scowled at her friend's defection.

"Coward," Mariah muttered under her breath, not sure whether she referred to Holly or herself.

"I beg your pardon, Mariah?"

She knew Thorn was asking her to repeat her words, but instead she smiled sweetly. "How kind of you to beg my pardon for your atrocious behavior."

"*My* atrocious behavior?" There was a fierce look in his brown eyes that would have made her cringe if she hadn't been expecting it.

"I don't know of anyone else who—" She stopped suddenly, sighing. Why get into a fight with him? It wouldn't stop him from getting into another deadly . . .

She refused to think about that. She allowed her attention to be captured by the table before her. She hadn't noticed the wood's grain before, the attractive sworls that formed an uneven pattern in gold, sepia and cinnamon.

"What is wrong, Mariah?" Though the gritty, British-accented voice sounded impatient, there was a touch of concern in it, too. He sat beside her and touched her arm. "If Maitland insulted you, I wish to know it."

She turned to face him, unsure how to respond. The small, comforting contact of his hand was almost more than she could bear. "It wasn't an insult but information. I told you—" She had to stop as moisture flooded her eyes.

"What information could upset you so? Was it about your beau, Pierce?"

She choked off a laugh. "Pierce isn't—" She had to stop as she gathered her thoughts. "If you really want to know," she said, "I'll tell you. It's about you. But you need to—"

Boots clumped on the stairs as a soldier hurried down. It was one of the younger boys, clad in a baggy undershirt and his uniform trousers. As he neared the two of them, his grin revealed a rotting tooth. "Someone ought to brew an ale that does not pass right through a body." He hurried outside, followed by another soldier with the same apparent goal.

"Come." Thorn took Mariah's hand, and she reveled in his gentle strength when she felt so weak. "We will go somewhere quiet to talk."

The air was warm and so damp that Mariah immediately felt a sheen on her skin. There was a full moon that night that swept a shining swathe across the compound, but Thorn skirted the light. He led her far from the outhouse and its line of sodden soldiers.

But in the first place he tried, the stable, they heard voices. Holly's and René's. Very low.

"Not here." Mariah suspected they needed to be alone.

Thorn obviously thought so, too, for he pulled her away with the hand he still held.

They went inside the smokehouse, but Mariah immediately began coughing. The heat there, too, was overwhelming.

"By the stream?" she asked.

She saw him shake his head negatively in the moonlight, a glint reflecting from his eyes. "Not at night, with the danger of Indians about. No, there is a safe place where we can be alone."

To her surprise, he led her to his own house.

At the door, Mariah hung back. Safe? She recalled the last time she had been inside. The squirrel that had invited her in, her uneasiness at being there without Thorn. Her dismay at seeing his uniform hanging on the wall.

His reaction to seeing her there. To her hands. To her.

She really didn't want to talk to him anyway. How could she explain?

And surely she couldn't do it here.

She grasped for an excuse to get away. "I thought," she said softly, "that it was inappropriate in this time for a man and woman to be alone together like that."

" 'This time'? That is the kind of comment I hear from you for which I wish an explanation. That, and why you knew before it happened that the settlers would be followed by the soldiers, and why you are upset this evening."

She couldn't, of course, explain any of it to Thorn. His house was as good a place as any other to dissemble. If he wasn't offended, she certainly wouldn't be. Besides, before Holly arrived, Mariah had been working at the inn alone with two men. She'd probably already ruined her reputation in this era.

At least, she noted, the house's shutters were closed. Maybe no one would even know she was here.

She was pleasantly surprised to find Thorn's house even cooler inside than the inn. Its stonework walls and the open windows probably had a lot to do with it.

She watched Thorn's muscles work beneath his clothes as he knelt to stir up ashes in the fireplace and ignite a straw from the resulting lazy fire. He used it to light an oil lantern.

"Sit," he commanded, pointing to the bench beside his worktable. She obeyed, though her eyes strayed toward the bed. Fortunately, it was at the far side of the room. But with the two of them in it, the house suddenly seemed quite small.

"Now," he said, "I wish to know what is troubling you. Is it merely that your flirtation with the soldiers will soon be ended? Perhaps you should return to Pittsborough, where men from the fort can play your games any time." He ended with soft fury in his tone.

That made her cringe. She'd wanted him to show some emotion; now he had—anger. With her. And she wasn't sure why.

All she wanted was . . . what? She didn't know now. To be able to prevent the incidents yet to come in the screenplay? If the script were to come true, she would wander away from here like Matilda. Then she'd be kidnapped by Indians.

She'd had a taste of that already, with that Nahtana. She wanted no more.

Later, Thorn would die at the hands of a young man named Billy. Will. The soldier who had just enjoyed Thorn's hospitality.

Anguish rounding her shoulders, she stared as he sat beside her. The lantern hung on the wall behind him, so he was backlighted, and the crevasses below his cheekbones were dark shadows. His uneven chestnut hair formed a regal mane about his head and thick neck. She wanted to see his mouth, to see if it smiled at her or was in its usual grim, straight line. She wanted to see his eyes, too, to try to read behind them to his thoughts.

"I understand," she said in a monotone, "that people in the wilderness are allowed to keep their own secrets."

"Strangers may," he agreed. "But you are my employee. You make an impression on all of my guests. I am entitled to know about you."

She smiled bitterly. "Maybe you are, at that. But you'd think me crazy if I told you."

"Do you think I believe you to be totally rational now?"

Shaking her head, she stood and paced the room, listening to her boots echo along the wood floor. Her arms were crossed, as though she hugged herself. "All right, I'll tell you. But you have to promise you'll let me stay here."

"Should that not depend on what you have to say?" She thought she heard a tinge of amusement in his tone.

"No," she said, crumpling inside. He wanted to send her away, but she wouldn't let him. She faced him squarely. "Regardless of what I tell you, I want your guarantee that it won't make a difference."

"All right. I promise you can stay, no matter what."

Fine, she thought, relief shimmering through her. But what could she tell him?

The truth, she supposed. But an abbreviated version.

She stopped pacing near his chair, then groped for an approach. She settled on, "I knew about you, Thorn, before I came here."

In the dim light, she saw his back grow stiff. "How is that?"

"I read about you."

His hand reached out in a gesture that appeared pained, and she hurried on. "Not in newspapers here or in the east. Someone has written a story about you. One in which you are a kind, brave, sympathetic figure." She hesitated, then plunged ahead, unable to keep her voice from breaking. "A hero's story, in which you die at the end."

He stood so close that his chest nearly touched hers. "And who wrote such a valiant but sad tale?" His voice was mocking, but she could hear his interest.

"The man named Pierce, the one I wanted to find at Harrigan's trading post."

Thorn was silent for a moment. "I do not recall meeting any Pierce. How did this man know enough to write a story about me?"

"I'm not sure. I think he sent me here to change things. He told me to 'right a grievous wrong.' " She stammered a little over the phrase that had haunted her all her life.

"And what wrong is that?"

Taking a deep breath, she moved away from him. She stopped near the wall that was decorated with his discarded uniform. "In the story, you die in a duel. A soldier named Billy calls you out. I think . . . I'm afraid he's that Will Shepherd."

Silence once more. And then Thorn laughed. It was a genuine laugh, the most merry sound she'd heard from him since she'd arrived there.

"It's not funny." Warm tears ran down her cheeks. "I couldn't bear . . . I can't stand even thinking about . . ." She'd had enough. She ran toward the door, only to find her way blocked. "Let me go!"

She felt his strong hands grip her shoulders. "Tell me," he said quietly, "why you act this way. Why does it matter to you whether I am killed in a duel by this callow soldier?"

She knew the answer, of course. She'd done exactly what she'd had no intention of doing.

She was no smarter than her mother.

She'd fallen in love with an unreliable man. With Thorn.

But unlike her mother, she didn't have to tell him. Or act on it.

But *was* he unreliable? He had told her so from their first meeting, but he'd always come through for her. Maybe the man she loved was, like the fictional Thorn, utterly dependable. Still, she didn't dare reveal her feelings. He wouldn't want her love. And if he continued to maintain his unreliability, he might not, in fact, come through for her sometime when it counted.

"Your demise wouldn't matter to me," she lied, trembling with emotion. He had to feel it, too. He still held her shoulders.

"I do not believe you." There was a thickness in his deep voice, and he pulled her close.

She struggled, but he was too strong. He held her tightly against him. "What do you want from me?" she cried.

"I do not know." He sounded as bewildered as a lost child. But he reminded her of a child no longer when she felt the soft touch of his lips on one eyebrow. "Only this, I suppose," he whispered, then touched the tears on her cheek with his tongue. "And this." His voice was barely audible, and then his mouth fastened on hers.

Her mind told her to fight him, just as it told her to fight the idea of loving him.

But her mutinous body betrayed her. Her lips participated

in that heated kiss, reveling in the strength of his against them, opening to allow his tongue to slide inside her mouth to tangle with hers.

"No," she tried to say, but it came out as a groan filled with so much passion that it startled her. She heard a moan in response as Thorn drew closer still.

Every nerve ending that he touched thrilled at the contact. Her back arched as he stroked it, causing her breasts to thrust against him. Her nipples hardened at the impact, and she felt herself growing weak, losing rationality to sensation. He grasped her buttocks, and she pressed forward until stopped by the strength of his body. She felt a hardness that left no doubt that he was as aroused as she.

"Here," he whispered. She found herself floating across the floor. No, she wasn't moving any longer. She was lying on a hard mattress. On a bed. Thorn's bed.

This was getting beyond control. She should leave.

But she felt his hands at the buttons on the back of her dress. He pulled the material from her shoulders, revealing the chemise beneath. And then it was gone, too. Soon, so was the rest.

She was there, naked, with Thorn. This wasn't right. She wasn't to get involved. He was undependable. He was . . . "Oooh," she heard herself gasp against his mouth as his hands closed over her bare breasts, cupping them, kneading them gently. His rough palms stroked her nipples until they ached, and then he drew his mouth from hers. She began to protest until she felt his lips on one sensitive nub, then the other, tugging them gently till she nearly sobbed at the sweet torture. The soft cleansing by his tongue left her breasts moist and yearning for more. "Please," she whimpered. Her hands had not been at rest, but she could not feel all of him. He was still clothed, and she protested the unfairness by tugging at the hem of his shirt.

He pulled away, but only for as long as it took to strip off his clothing. She opened her eyes to look at him in the faint, flickering light of the cabin and nearly cried aloud at the beauty of his body. She had already seen, as he'd worked, the breadth of his shoulders, the thick muscles of his arms and chest, sculpted not by the gym workouts of her day but by the hard, necessary labor here. His waist was thin, his hips narrow. He had a small thatch of dark hair between his pectoral muscles that swept into a thin line down to his navel and beyond, where it grew into a larger expanse.

There was no mistaking the intensity of his passion. The sight of his thick, jutting organ sent a surge of something warm and fervent through Mariah. She felt suddenly weak yet charged with an energy she had no words to describe.

She could not help herself. She reached out her hand and grasped him.

He groaned and throbbed in her hand, igniting her yet further.

He sent his fingers exploring down her body, tracing the lines of her back, her buttocks, and then forward to the center of her, where she felt her own moistened throbbing.

"I did not intend—" he began, and she could tell from the tautness of his tone that his teeth were clenched. She stopped his words with her mouth, loosening his teeth with her tongue.

"Mariah." His words were a moan, and she did not stop touching him, stroking him, arching her back so she could more easily meet his fingers where he delved into her secret core. She nearly screamed aloud as he teased her with his clever hand.

Again, he dipped his head, seeking her breasts with his mouth. He did not stop his sweet nether massage, and she felt herself writhing, sure she would break apart in ecstasy.

"Thorn," she heard herself whimper.

"Do you want this, Mariah?" His husky voice came from low in his throat. "I do not know if I can stop, but I will try if you wish it."

"Don't stop," she murmured. "Please."

She felt her legs drawn apart, and then the most wonderful, heated sensation of being filled and surrounded all at once as he entered her and his weight bore down on her from above.

"Am I hurting you?" he whispered.

"No," she assured him. "It's—"

She gasped and stopped speaking as he pulled back, then thrust his loins against her once more.

"Do you still wish more?"

She pushed her own hips upward and found his mouth with her own. "Shut up, Thorn," she whispered against him.

He obeyed her, setting a rhythm below. She answered and followed, meeting him, responding to his ever-quickening lunges. Gasping, she tried to keep her mouth against his, until the very end, when in a whirlwind of ecstasy, she spiraled over the top, even as she heard an answering groan from him.

For a long moment, she didn't move, feeling his throbbing inside her, reveling in the closeness of his moist, hot body against hers. His breathing was ragged and loud, and she felt the rapid pace of his pulse where her ear rested against his chest—or was it hers?

For a long and wonderful time, she lay there, first beneath him, then beside him, trying to catch her breath. Daring to wonder how this had changed things. What would happen between them next, when they spoke once more?

But then she felt him draw away, and she had her answer. Oh, he didn't move much, but there was a rigidity of his spine that had nothing to do with sensuality as his respiration became more controlled. Though his hands remained at her back, they were still, frozen, remote.

She knew she'd made a mistake. She'd had sex with her employer, who just happened to be a very attractive, very unreliable man.

It had felt good. No, wonderful. Better than she'd ever imagined—and she'd imagined a lot.

But now she was going to pay for it. And the idea of Thorn's belittling what had just happened between them made her very, very sad.

"Well," she said, deciding the best defense was an offense, "that was very pleasant, but I have work to do." She pulled away.

"This should not have happened, Mariah." His voice was weary. "I apologize. But I will not marry you."

She stood, grabbing her clothes and holding up her dress

in front of her. She made herself laugh aloud. "Marriage? Who said anything about marriage? In my day . . . I mean, where I come from, there's no talk of marriage just because a couple of consenting adults have a little fun in the sack together."

He pulled the bedclothes over himself so only his chest remained exposed. If he only knew, Mariah thought, how much of a turn-on it was just to see this aspect of his gorgeous, masculine anatomy, or, for that matter, any other part of him, he'd pull the covers over his head.

Not that she wanted to touch him any more. Not now.

"Where is it," he asked, "that you come from? That is one of the many questions I wanted to ask of you. And have you had 'fun in the sack' with many men?"

He sounded so conversational that she wanted to hit him. Instead, she scurried around to the side of the bed to which he wasn't looking and began dressing. At least he had the decency not to look, but it took her forever, for her hands were trembling.

As she put on her clothes, she talked. "I'll answer your last question first. No, I'm very particular about whom I sleep with. Or I was, anyway. The only other man was one I trusted. We were engaged to be married until I learned he was no more reliable than any other man."

"I see." Thorn's voice was soft now, and sympathetic. "I am sorry, Mariah. You do not have to tell me anything more."

"Of course I do. Let's see. Your other question: Where do I come from? Well, all over, actually. You see, I told you once about my parents. My father believed in following his dreams, but they never, of course, came to fruition. I tried so hard to love him but—well, you don't want to hear that."

"Mariah, please do not misunderstand. I did not wish to hurt you. I never intended this to happen, but this was—"

"Interesting, wasn't it? And rather fun. Though a one-time experience, I'm sure. No need for any more, not when that was so . . . well, pleasant. And final."

She didn't let him talk. She didn't want to hear any more of his apologies.

In fact, she wanted to anger him. That way, this would never happen again. She couldn't let it, after all. She had to burn these bridges before she was hurt even more.

It hurt too much, this rejection after all that wonderful, unforgettable lovemaking, with the man whom she, oh, so regrettably, loved.

And what about . . . oh, geez! She'd been so caught up in sensation that she hadn't even considered protection. Though it probably didn't matter here; there was none. What if she were pregnant? If she had to stay here, she might have to raise a baby alone in an era when the stigma could be overwhelming. She had to get home. Now.

Pierce, you bastard! she thought. Get me out of here.

She was completely dressed now, though she couldn't vouch for how accurately she was buttoned. Her whole body shook, and she glared at Thorn, wanting to slap him suddenly, to throw herself into his arms. "You know what?" she said through gritted teeth. "I think I will confide in you after all. Do you really want to know where I'm from, Thorn?"

She hurried to the foot of the bed and sat on a chair facing him. She made herself smile pleasantly.

"Yes," he said softly. "I do wish to know where you are from, Mariah."

"You're just curious, of course," she said. "I know it doesn't make the slightest bit of difference to you, but here it is anyway. I have lived all over the place, just like I said. But I got from place to place by flying on jet planes. Up there, in the air." She pointed to the roof of the stone house.

"You do not need to act crazy, Mariah."

"Crazy? I'll tell you about crazy. I was sent here from the future, Thorn. Just imagine how it felt to be drawn from a time of all the comforts you could imagine to this primitive existence. You couldn't even begin to consider how it would be to take full meals bought at supermarkets from electric freezers, to be cooked in minutes in microwave ovens. To travel with hundreds of horsepower without horses."

She watched as the expression on his strong features changed from coolly interested to utterly incredulous. "Mariah, I do understand why you feel upset, but to make up so many—''

''The reason I know so much about you is because Pierce wrote a screenplay in which you are the hero. Do you know what a screenplay is?'' She didn't wait for him to respond. ''It's like a script for a play, except the play is performed by actors who act in front of a camera that records all the action. Then the whole play can be run at screens all over the world before millions of people at once. In my day, there are lots of special effects, too. Weapons are much better than your silly, one-shot Pennsylvania rifle.''

He stood and walked toward her. ''Stop this, Mariah.''

She backed away, placing the table between him and her. ''Sure, I'll stop. But I'll tell you first the reason I was so upset before. You see, at the end of the screenplay about you, you're challenged to a duel by a young soldier named Billy. I think I know who he is now—that Will. I don't know what he has against you; that's for you to find out. But I think the 'grievous wrong' I'm supposed to right here is that I need to stop this duel. And do you know what? I'm not sure I can.''

She hurried to the door of the house and pulled it open. ''I only wish,'' she said, ''that I didn't give a damn.''

She slammed the door behind her.

Chapter Fifteen

Mariah didn't sleep that night.

It had nothing to do with the hardness of the straw-filled mattress or the rustling of hay as she tossed and turned, for her body seemed to float with delicious memories of touches and caresses, kisses and thrusts. It was happy, sated, relaxed.

But her mind . . . Oh, her mind! It was grounded in terrible, irrefutable reality. Her head ached unbearably, her thoughts swirling in a grief-laden tornado.

At the vortex of everything was Thorn.

The image of him, his muscles hardened by physical labor, his pervasive masculinity, was etched forever in her mind.

She was glad, for it was a sight she would surely never drink in again.

How sweet and tender and giving his lovemaking had been. And utterly, erotically unforgettable.

Then, when he was no longer consumed by the heat of passion, he'd become himself again: formal. Remote. Unreliable.

Hurtful.

She hadn't been kind, either. Or wise. She'd bombarded

him with the truth in a way sure to convince him of her insanity.

The saddest part was that she'd ruined any possibility of his remembering their lovemaking with anything but disdain: for her, for her quick and easy response, and, afterwards, for her lies.

Except, of course, they were the truth.

Each new thought of how he would now regard her sent tears flooding her eyes. How could any rational man believe she was from the future? She could hardly believe it herself.

And as far as preventing the duel—well, she'd fixed things all right. She'd thrown the idea in with jet planes and movies and microwave ovens, made it sound just as credible in this time of low, or no, technology.

That was one grievous wrong that she'd somehow have to right on her own; Thorn wouldn't believe her enough to try to keep out of trouble. And he didn't seem to know Will Shepherd.

Was the duel Pierce's grievous wrong? That no longer mattered. It was the one she planned to tackle.

At long last, morning arrived. Her room passed from coal blackness to fuzzy gray, and she sat on the edge of the bed. Despite all that had happened, she reveled in the soreness of her muscles, skin and other areas that had been integral to their lovemaking.

At least she had a wonderful memory.

Sometime today, she would have to face Thorn. She'd do so coolly. Bravely.

She'd keep her misery to herself.

What would happen next? From beneath her mattress, she drew out the page on which she had written her recollections of the screenplay. She'd jotted down all the details she could remember but knew now what a waste of time that had been. Nothing happened exactly as depicted. Yet there was a hint of portent in each major episode.

Only three had not yet occurred, any one of which was enough to scare her.

The first would be Matilda's—her—capture by Indians. But she'd be wary. She wouldn't leave the inn, no matter what. This was one part of the screenplay that wouldn't follow real life.

Next, her notes reflected a raid at the inn by vandals. She'd no sense of why or when that might happen.

Finally, there was the duel. Very finally. And that, too, she had to modify from the script. But how? She needed a workable plan.

A knock sounded on the door. ''Mariah? Are you awake?'' Without waiting for an answer, Holly pushed open the door and walked in. She stopped, shoving her hands onto her ample, apron-covered hips. ''What happened to you?''

''What do you mean?'' Mariah felt herself redden. Did it somehow show, her delicious, ill-fated lovemaking with Thorn? She touched her own warm cheek.

''You look like something I saw drowned in the water at the London docks.'' Holly shook her head so the cap over her pale hair bobbed. ''Some big, sad-eyed fish, it was, that had grown too tired to swim.''

Mariah threw off her covers and swung her feet over the side of the rustling bed. ''You're right. I'm too tired to swim or to do much of anything else. But we've got a lot of people to feed breakfast, so I guess I'd better start my gills humming.''

''And your tail swishing,'' Holly agreed. They both laughed, though Mariah knew that the sound from her mouth was more hollow than mirthful.

Mariah dressed quickly, with Holly's help, in her brown dress and apron. She still couldn't bring herself to wear a cap, though she'd been admonished time and again by Holly that the custom wasn't just based on fashion; it was to keep a woman's hair from being ignited by fire as she worked over the hearth. She had thought of braiding it up. On the other hand, Mariah's hair, though it hung beneath her shoulders, was shorter than most women's in this time.

This time. There it was again, the thread that wove through all of Mariah's thoughts. She didn't belong here. She'd made that clear to Thorn the night before.

She'd a mission to accomplish, though, thanks to that

damned Pierce. But even though she'd knowledge of what might come, she'd no way to stop it.

She was going to let Thorn down. He was going to die.

She would be the unreliable one.

They were just outside René's open door. Fortunately, he wasn't there, for in a fit of pique at herself and her impossible situation, Mariah kicked her toe hard into the hard earth floor. She was glad as pain shot through her.

"What, deary, is the matter?" Holly hurried after her as Mariah limped into the stable. Taking her arm, Holly swung Mariah around so they faced one another. In the nearest occupied stall, a sorrel horse snorted and stamped. "If you slept at all last night, your eyes didn't get the message, for they painted great dark circles beneath themselves. And now you're stubbing your toe on purpose. I want to know what's ailing you." A sly glint appeared in her close-set hazel eyes. "Of course I know what it is."

"You couldn't possibly," Mariah said coolly.

"Thorn."

Mariah closed her eyes for a pained instant.

"I was right!" Holly sounded pleased with herself.

Mariah pulled away and slowly walked through the stable. Misery filled her insides like air in a balloon, its pressure expanding as though she were going to explode.

Were there such things as balloons now?

She turned suddenly at the door. "All right, Holly. I'll tell you the truth. You won't believe me any more than Thorn does, but when things happen the way I predict, at least I'll have another witness."

Holly's eyes widened even further, and her lips rounded in surprise. "Predict? Then you're a seeress?"

"In a way, I guess."

They exited the stable. The compound was filled with soldiers on their way to the outhouse or standing around talking.

Thorn was nowhere in sight. That didn't surprise Mariah; he was seldom in the compound early in the morning.

She wasn't looking forward to their next encounter.

"Why don't we go after some water?" Holly suggested.

They went into the kitchen first. René had already stoked

the fire and was readying salt pork for frying. "*Bonjour, mes demoiselles,*" he called. "We shall have a busy morning, *n'est ce pas?*"

"It's certainly *pas,*" Holly agreed, baiting the man so his toadlike features scrunched into a frown.

Mariah would have laughed again if she hadn't felt so miserable. And concerned. She'd made up her mind to tell Holly the truth but was worried whether it was the right thing to do.

"Would you like company to the stream this morning?" René asked.

Mariah hesitated. She wanted to speak to Holly alone, but she knew what the next incident was supposed to be and didn't want it to come true because of her imprudence. "Sure." She ignored Holly's irritated scowl.

They didn't have an opportunity to speak until they'd brought back water and René had left them tending food while he entertained the guests. Mariah still hadn't seen Thorn, though on most mornings he would have appeared by this time.

He was avoiding her. The thought increased her anguish.

After stirring the bubbling porridge and setting a kettle of water over the fire for tea, Mariah turned to Holly. "Okay," she said. "If you're sure you want to hear my whole sad story—"

"I'm sure."

The two sat on stools at the worktable, measuring flour and water for bread. "This is going to sound crazy," Mariah said.

"I've a big tolerance for craziness, I have."

Mariah took a few seconds to gather her thoughts, then began speaking. She decided to work her way into the incredible part of her story, describing her childhood first. "It was terrible! My father was a dreamer of the highest sort, a liar who kept promising my mother the world and instead abandoned her—and me—over and over. I couldn't help loving him, charmer that he was, but I hated him, too. My mother, though—he finally killed her with the broken promises, all the waiting.'' She pounded her fist into the soft lump of dough she'd just made.

Holly, kneading dough, clucked sympathetically.

''When she died, I left home, such as it was, for good. But all through my childhood, no matter where we were, I had strange dreams. I heard a voice tell me, 'You must right a grievous wrong.' ''

''An omen!'' breathed Holly.

''I suppose. But there's something else you should know.'' She took a deep breath, bracing herself for denials, accusations of craziness, whatever. ''My home—I was born in the year 1968.'' She heard Holly's gasp but kept her eyes trained on her flour-covered hands.

''You . . . you aren't . . . I mean . . .''

She stopped Holly's stammering by continuing. ''I'm not from this time, Holly. I'm—''

René walked in. ''Ah, ladies, you are busy, I see. *Bon!*'' He puttered around for a while, checking on the food, grabbing clean tankards from a table. The room remained silent. ''Did I interrupt something, *mademoiselles?*''

Mariah hazarded a glance at Holly, who regarded her with a wide-eyed stare. ''Girl talk,'' Mariah confirmed.

''Then I shall leave.''

''Ah, these conspiring young ladies,'' René said morosely. ''One moment friendly. The next . . .''

Glancing away from the horse he curried, Thorn looked at his friend curiously. Was conspiracy the explanation for Mariah's strange claims? Somehow, she was working with Holly for . . . what? To take over the inn? Unlikely.

What else could they possibly want from him?

Thorn knew what he wanted from Mariah . . . didn't he? He wanted her to leave. To stay. To stop confusing him.

Their lovemaking the previous day had been like nothing he had ever experienced. She gave of herself completely. There was nothing subservient about her in bed, any more than otherwise. Her wonderfully lithe body had spurred him on, had encouraged him to heights he had never thought attainable.

He had not intended to touch her when they first went to his home. He had wished only for a quiet place for them to talk. But all the frustrations of their previous heated kisses, of seeing her bathe, of wanting something from her that he could not himself identify, had robbed him of his hard-won self-control.

It would not happen again. He did not dare let it.

Especially after she had made such a mockery of it by her wild tale. A traveler from the future, indeed!

And yet . . . it would explain much. If he could accept such nonsense. Which he could not.

"All right," he said to René as he turned back toward the restlessly stamping horse and again applied the brush. "Tell me about this ladies' conspiracy."

René sighed. "I think there is nothing really to tell. I merely wish I could understand what a woman thinks, my friend."

"So do I," Thorn said. "So do I."

After René had gone, Mariah told Holly, "Please don't tell anyone that I come from the future."

The girl nodded. "But, Mariah, are you certain—"

"I know how crazy it sounds. But that's the reason I know what's going to happen next—more or less. I don't have perfect knowledge. I'm not a seer. I'm a normal human being who's gone through a totally incredible experience."

A soldier walked in. Holly gave him a drink of water, never taking her eyes from Mariah. Mariah realized that there would be more interruptions the longer they stayed in the kitchen without serving the guests. "Look," she said, "try not to judge me. If you want to hear the rest of the story, let me tell it quickly."

While kneading soft, pasty dough in her hands, she raced through her tale, trying to explain her career in an industry created to show plays as moving pictures. "What's important about this," she said, "is that last thing, before I left my time, I read a script for a play that seems to follow real life here. The characters in it . . . Well, they included Thorn. And a woman named Matilda, who came to his inn as a servant, and others I've met, too. It was written by a man named Pierce, and I've good reason to believe he's the one who sent me here. The last thing I heard him say was, 'You must right a grievous wrong,' and the same words were written into his play, too.'' She left out the part about his calling her ''my daughter.'' That was an added complication she'd yet to figure out.

''Then this Pierce, was he haunting you through your whole life? Was he a messenger from God or the devil? Who is he?''

Mariah shrugged. Holly was clearly enthralled by the story. Her close-set hazel eyes had never been wider, and her mouth was open wide enough that she seemed to inhale Mariah's very words.

''Anyway, I've reason to think that Pierce is here, in this time, somewhere. I've apparently taken on the life of the play's Matilda character, more or less.''

''Then where is she?'' Holly sounded confused.

Mariah shook her head. ''I've no idea. Maybe Pierce did something to her so I could take her place. Or maybe she's a figment of his imagination. There's more in the play that's different from reality here.''

''What?'' Holly leaned further toward Mariah.

''Well, for one thing, Thorn's personality is different from the man in the play.'' Mariah didn't explain how, or how disappointed she'd been. ''Some episodes I read about have come true, though not exactly as written.'' She described the incident with the river rats, the wolves, the Indian who was supposed to be friendly. ''You already know about my prediction that the soldiers would follow hot on the trail of the settlers; that was in the play, too, though it indicated that the homesteaders would be attacked by the soldiers.''

''You may have stopped that from happening.'' Holly sounded awestruck.

Mariah shrugged. ''Maybe. But right now . . . well, I'm scared. The next episode in the play is the capture by Indians of the Matilda character. And that seems to be me.''

Hearing a choking sound from beside her, Mariah turned

to Holly to see her suddenly begin to cry. "You must stop that no matter what." The young woman swiped the back of her hand over her eyes.

Mariah recalled that Holly had been captured by Indians but had never really spoken of her experience. "Holly," she said gently, "it sometimes helps to speak of bad times."

The outside door opened and Thorn strode in. It was the first time Mariah had seen him since the night before, when ecstasy had turned so swiftly sour.

Even the sight of him now made her want to cry out in pain for what had been gained, then lost.

But the last thing she wanted was for him to know how affected she'd been.

Keeping her gaze determinedly on the dough in her hands, she asked, "Would you care for some tea, Mr. Thorn? We already have water on to boil." Her tone was steady, thank heavens.

"Not right now, thank you." He spoke in his normal, deep, gravelly voice with its appealing British accent. Not a trace of feeling in it. She watched him from the corner of her eye. Though he glanced at her, he quickly looked away. His strong, blunt chin remained raised, his face impassive.

Damn the man and his emotionless hide!

He walked through the kitchen and out the door to the common room. Only then did Mariah let out her breath in a loud whoosh. She hadn't even realized she'd been holding it.

She turned back to Holly, who was shaping her dough into a rectangular loaf. Tears still filled her eyes, but aside from her sniffling she'd stopped crying.

"Are you all right?" Mariah slipped an arm around Holly's shoulder. She felt like crying herself but was glad she had Holly to worry about. "I'm sorry Thorn came in. I thought it better that I not call attention to you."

"You're right," Holly agreed, her voice choked. "I oughtn't have acted in such a way, but—"

"Don't apologize." Mariah took Holly's loaf of bread and put it on one of the long-handled paddles propped beside the hearth. She slid it into the oven like a pro, then went to get her own loaf while Holly mixed more dough. "Won't you tell me what happened? I'd like to hear."

Holly wiped her eyes with the back of her hand, leaving a small streak of flour that Mariah dabbed off with the edge of her own apron. "It weren't much of a story. Mack and me, we left our bondage soon as we could and tried traveling west with a bunch of other settlers. We didn't know the first thing about protecting ourselves, and we was found right away by Indians. Mack, he tried to save me, but—" Her voice broke.

"You don't need to go into any detail," Mariah said sympathetically.

"There was this Indian, a Delaware, who took me," Holly continued. "His name was Ouiagat, and he made me a sort of wife." She blushed. "I didn't have a choice, you see. But he was kind, and so I stayed with him, though I was always alert for a chance to escape. But before I could, the Delawares I was with met up with some renegade Iroquois. I didn't understand what was happening, whether they were at war or just trading, but then, there I was, with the Iroquois. And this bunch was awful."

The cloud of terror descended over Holly's face and tears reappeared in her eyes. Mariah reached toward her, touching her dough-blotted hand with her own. "Don't think about it any more," she said.

"But I have to," Holly contradicted. "You said you might be taken by Indians, and you need to know. The one who got me, I think his name was Nahtana, was the worst! I was made his servant, and he hit me all the time, even when I couldn't understand what he wanted. He acted like my husband, too, so cruel he was. But I found my chance. I escaped. Then he found me and tied me and beat me and . . . well, he left me for dead. And I would have been, too, if not for you."

Nahtana! He must have been looking for another servant when he'd tried to drag her off. Mariah shuddered. "I'm glad I found you when I did."

While they finished the other loaves of bread, Holly described more of her experiences with the Indians. Although they had killed her brother, Holly had little bad to say about any of them—except Nahtana.

"I've met him," Mariah admitted.

"You have?"

As the kitchen filled with the appetizing aroma of baking bread, Mariah described her brief encounter with the Indian who'd tried to drag her into the forest by the hair. Her forehead had moistened in the hot room, but her story still made her shiver. "I thought from the screenplay that the guy was Thorn's friend, so I wasn't particularly scared at first."

Holly snorted. "That animal is the friend of no one. He has a stone for a heart, he has."

Stone . . . yes! "You just reminded me of a line from the script," Mariah said excitedly. "That's what Matilda said to the Indian who abducted her: 'Your heart is as hardened as the rocks to which you have bound me.' The scene was described as a cliff near a river where the water had weathered huge boulders into odd, smooth shapes. I wonder if there is such a place." And whether she'd be captured and taken there, though she kept that thought to herself.

As she placed the last loaf of bread in the slot in the fireplace used as an oven, René burst into the room. "We must serve breakfast *vite*! Quickly! The soldiers, they wish to leave soon."

A short while later, as she laid food on the tables, Mariah eavesdropped on conversations in the common room.

"I'll say one thing for Thorn." Maitland, his heavy red coat buttoned to his pointed chin, dipped a spoon into the trencher he shared with Ainsley and the other officers at his table. "The chap can track. And we need to find those settlers right away."

To arrest them, Mariah thought.

As though reading her mind, Maitland continued, "If they've started asserting tomahawk rights to claim land, we'll have to arrest them, but better that we be the ones to catch them if they continue to disobey. They'd get a fair trial before being sentenced to death. If it's up to the Indians . . . well, there'd be no trial, just a string of scalps." He laughed, and Mariah shuddered at the shrill, ugly sound.

Will, the young man Mariah now thought of as Billy, sat at the next table. He wiped his scrawny beard with the back of his sleeve. "You aren't going to invite that coward to join us, are you, sir?"

"Why not?" Maitland asked. "If the Indians attack, we can always use Thorn as a shield—if he isn't already off somewhere making eyes at a squaw."

Mariah cringed as everyone laughed except Ainsley. And Thorn. He stood at the bar, wiping clean tankards that had been in use already that morning. Only the narrowing of his eyes betrayed the fact that he'd heard. What did he feel? Hurt? Rage? Why didn't he say anything?

This was the group of guests to whom Mariah had hoped he'd never need to play host again, she reminded herself. No wonder he tended to avoid his customers when René didn't nag him.

"Seriously, Thorn," Ainsley rose and joined his friend, "we would like you to help us find these settlers. For their own good, so we can get to them before the Indians." Ainsley gave a cultivated shudder and crinkled his turned-up nose. "We saw what other renegades have done over the last weeks with homesteaders who crossed their paths."

Would Thorn actually go with them? The idea made Mariah quake inside—for him, and for herself. Though Matilda had left the safety of the screenplay's inn when she was captured and Mariah had no intention of going anywhere, anything could happen with Thorn away.

And Mariah knew full well that real life here didn't always follow the script.

"I regret to say I cannot come." Thorn sounded not at all regretful, and Mariah smiled with relief at the stack of trenchers she carried. "If the Indians are on as much of a rampage as you say, I must stay to defend my inn."

"Tell you what," Ainsley said. "You have little to finish on your palisade, and we need your tracking abilities. If you promise to come, we will first complete your fortress, and then I will leave a small cadre of troops here to protect your home."

To Mariah's dismay, Thorn did not immediately decline. Eventually, he agreed.

In a flurry of activity, Ainsley's men finished setting up the remaining spiked logs around the compound. Thorn had already made the gate, and they helped him hang it.

Mariah's fear grew as quickly as the palisade. She prayed the gate's bolt was sturdy enough to keep anyone out.

Except Thorn.

She wasn't pleased to find that few troops would be left behind, the most senior a corporal junior to Maitland named Whisby.

Will—Billy—would remain, too. That didn't provide Mariah with any more confidence.

Standing beside Holly and René behind the gate, clasping her poor, sore hands behind her back, Mariah watched with trepidation as Thorn left on horseback with the British soldiers.

He glanced back over his shoulder as he rode out, meeting her eye with his usual impassive look that didn't ease her fragile frame of mind.

"Good-bye," she whispered.

Did his lips move in his own good-bye to her? Or was she imagining it?

She went through her afternoon chores in a daze, starting at every noise she heard, forcing herself to laugh at her folly. She was here at the inn, after all. Matilda was kidnapped when she left its shelter.

She didn't even leave the palisade's confines for water at supper time. She sent soldiers instead, including Will.

She wasn't at all surprised when he and the others came tearing back through the wooden fence, terror in their eyes, as animal-like whoops followed them. With René and Holly, she tried to get the gate closed after them. Unsuccessfully.

In moments, the compound was filled with Indians.

Among them was Nahtana.

Chapter Sixteen

Mariah stumbled. As she pitched forward, her boots caught on her long brown skirt. She put out her hands as she fell—only to be drawn up short as a hand grabbed her hair.

"Ouch!" She raised her hands to her head at the excruciating pain. She caught at the wrists of the man who'd hurt her, but he batted them away.

"No," he said. It was, perhaps, his only English word. The same word he had used with her before.

She had been taken by Nahtana.

"Leave her alone," a faint voice piped up indignantly behind her.

She turned slowly, since the horrible fingers that smelled like animal grease were still wound in her hair. Even this slight a movement caused pain, but she had to look. "I'm all right," she managed to say to Will, one of two other captives from the inn. Both were soldiers. Both were ashen, filthy with livid spots on their cheeks where they'd been struck.

But both were alive.

She had seen the young corporal, Whisby, lose his scalp

within the inn's compound, so she supposed she should be grateful that Nahtana seemed to like her hair right where she grew it. And that he'd left two others alive—for now.

She didn't know what had happened to Holly or René. She was afraid to wonder about them.

One of the other Indians gave Will a rough push, as though to punish him for sticking up for her. He, too, stumbled but righted himself and continued forward.

Mariah felt as if she'd been walking for weeks, although it could only have been hours. The shadows in the thick forest grew darker, the sun-speckled clearings fewer, but night had not yet fallen. She wasn't certain how she had kept going. She simply kept putting one foot in front of the other.

Sometimes, though, the carpet of dead leaves and moss gave way to fallen logs or vines. She was too tired, too frightened, to pay much attention to them. That was why she had stumbled. Why the Indian still had his fingers wrapped in her hair.

"Where are we going?" she asked Nahtana conversationally. Perhaps if she acted friendly, he'd be kinder.

He responded vocally, though she couldn't interpret what he said. She couldn't tell whether he even understood her question. He did, at least, let go of her hair. But he still walked beside her. She glanced at him. He wore the same outfit she'd seen him in before: buckskin shirt, breechcloth, leggings and a pair of moccasins. The braid hanging from the middle of his head looked rattier than before; making war on settlers must give little time for personal hygiene.

His features weren't very discernible in the darkness of the forest, but she sensed his scowl. What did he want from her?

She remembered Holly's story. Some Indians took white women as slaves or wives yet treated them nicely. But Holly had been beaten by Nahtana.

Swallowing hard, Mariah didn't let her steps falter again. Her heart pounded hard in her terror, but she began to talk soothingly, hoping the man beside her would respond to her tone. "I wish I could explain the future to you. I've nothing against you and your people." She glanced at him. His dark eyes were focused on her, but he said nothing. "In fact," she continued, "in my time, we recognize the injustices done to Native Americans. This was your land. Your culture depends on not allowing it to be stolen. But no one can stop the flow of soldiers and settlers. I'm really sorry, but your culture is doomed. Maybe you can make it easier on yourself if you—"

"No!" he said again. He gave her back a strong shove that nearly toppled her. With a cry of fear, she continued walking.

Night had fallen. No light penetrated the canopy of trees, and Mariah hadn't any idea where she was. She tripped more often now, unable to see obstacles and functioning only mechanically, half asleep.

And then—they broke through the shelter of the forest. Before her, illuminated by the barest sliver of moon and a universe of stars, she saw, in shades of blacks and grays, a cliff at the water's edge. One where odd-shaped boulders abounded. The air smelled damp, and she heard the grumbling of a waterfall.

"The rocks as hard as your heart," she whispered to Nahtana, who held her arm.

He grunted, clearly unable to understand, for he did not retaliate for her words.

But the sight gave Mariah hope, however slight. Something in the screenplay had come true.

Did that mean she dared to hope that her Thorn would rescue her, as Matilda's had?

She nearly laughed aloud. Even if the real Thorn were dependable, he was off hunting settlers. He'd never find her.

Not that he'd look.

Nahtana pushed her into a cave. He brought her a gourd of water and a piece of jerked meat. She fell asleep before she had finished eating.

"Miss Mariah!"

The soft, feminine voice in her ear startled Mariah awake. She'd been having the most terrible dream, in which the script's prediction of an Indian capture had come true, and—

She opened her eyes. She was sitting inside a dim cave, leaning against a wall, her wrinkled, filthy dress tucked beneath her. She could hardly breathe in the mustiness. Will and the other soldier, whose name, she'd learned last night, was Paul, sat across from her. Their hands and legs were trussed together.

"Miss Mariah."

She turned to look for the source of the words—and there was Mrs. Rafferty. Little Elk, who had been a guest at the inn . . . had it been only a little more than a week earlier? "What are you doing here?" Mariah whispered.

"My husband trades with the Iroquois. This is a spot where they often camp in this area."

"I'm so glad to see you!" Maybe her salvation would come from another source than Thorn. She glanced around to make certain none of their captors was near. Only one of the Indians was in the cave, at the entrance, looking out. Mariah whispered, "Please, take us with you when you leave."

Little Elk shook her head vehemently so that her plaited dark hair flew in ropelike strands. "I am so sorry." Her dark eyes looked infinitely sad. "My husband and son will not interfere, for that would mean no more trade, and danger for them. But when we are next at Thorn's inn, I will make certain he knows who has you. He may be able to track you."

Fat chance, Mariah thought, tears of hopelessness flooding her eyes. "Where are we? Is this where these Indians live?"

"No, this is but a resting spot. The Iroquois live in long houses some distance away. They have moved recently, though, so I know not exactly where." Her pretty, youthful face was filled with sympathy, but then it brightened. "I nearly forgot. I saw the man Pierce. He was at Harrigan's trading post. He sent a message, should I see you again: He will join you soon."

"Pierce?" Where was the slimy worm who'd gotten her into this predicament? Did he know that the real Thorn was different from his fictionalized version, that Mariah couldn't depend on his rescuing her?

Did he care?

He must. He wanted her, after all, to right his grievous wrong. But what if *she* were wrong, that his intentions had nothing to do with Thorn's duel?

Still, his presence in the past, his message, gave her hope.

"Now, come," Little Elk said. "I can help you while I am here." She drew Mariah to her feet—a difficult task since her muscles had cramped from her exertion the day before and from sleeping on the ground. Little Elk took Mariah outside the cave to relieve herself and wash her face.

The river they'd camped beside was wide here. Mariah wondered which it was, in this area where rivers were plentiful. The Ohio, she suspected, for it was wide, forested on both sides except for this boulder-strewn clearing beneath the cliff.

The sky was overcast, and humidity hung in the air—suitably morose weather for Mariah's feeling of despair. What could she do now?

Escape, she decided. As soon as she could, without Little Elk's help, without Thorn's. Without Pierce's.

On her own.

And if she had to leave Will here—well, maybe she could prevent him from dueling with Thorn that way.

But how would she feel if he died here?

Little Elk took her to a fire, where her husband and son sat with Nahtana and some other Indians.

"Hello," Mariah said, greeting Rafferty and Zeb. How could they live with themselves if they left her at the mercy of these Indians?

Rafferty, his gray beard even more scruffy than Mariah remembered, scratched under his arm and said, "Miss Walker, ain't it? From Thorn's inn?"

She nodded. "I was taken from there yesterday and would like to go back."

He shrugged.

Zeb just looked at her with a speculative gleam in his beady eyes. "I hear tell these braves know how to handle a woman right well.'' He obviously recalled Mariah's rejection of him and seemed pleased that she was going to receive her comeuppance.

''I can translate for you with Nahtana,'' Little Elk said. ''Is there anything you wish to know?''

Everything, Mariah thought. ''Ask him why he took me and when I can go back to the inn.''

Little Elk translated. Mariah was dismayed when Nahtana's narrow, dark-complected face screwed up into a nasty smile. This was the first time she'd been able to see his features clearly: a large, straight nose; dark, small eyes with no brows; a thin-lipped mouth with oversized teeth. He said something in return.

Little Elk said sadly, ''You are to be his slave. You will not return to the inn. Once he and his braves have gathered more pelts for trading, their original mission on this journey, you will be taken to their home. I am sorry, Mariah.''

A million objections sprang to her lips. She was an American citizen, not a slave. She didn't belong here; she wanted to go home, to the twentieth century.

She wanted Thorn.

She had to find her own way out of this. She asked, ''Why? I'm not a very good worker. He can ask Thorn or René.''

Little Elk translated, then waited as Nahtana gave a guttural laugh, then spoke. The woman continued, ''He says you will learn. You and the others will be brought into their tribe in recompense for their land being stolen.''

Mariah's heart contracted. ''But I had nothing to do with that.''

''You live at Thorn's inn, which is on land that was among the Iroquois' hunting grounds.'' Little Elk shrugged. ''My people and others who live here did not understand this need to own land until your people began claiming what once had belonged to all and to none.''

For a moment, Mariah stood silently, considering her options. Nahtana, still grinning, stared as though waiting for her response. Mariah looked down, hiding her disgust and defiance. No sense in antagonizing him. Instead, maybe she could lull him into thinking she accepted the situation. ''All right,'' she said stoically to Little Elk, then waited for the translation.

Nahtana's snide smile hadn't wavered once. Why should it? He had her right where he wanted her.

Right where the rocks were as hard as his heart.

''What are you doing?'' Mariah, her pulse racing in fear, was being dragged to the edge of the boulders by an Indian with an unusually large potbelly hanging over his breech-cloth. He smelled of rancid animal grease.

Will was there, and so was Paul. They'd been removed from the cave earlier, and they were each tied to a tree. In moments, so was Mariah. The large Indian walked away.

Her first day in captivity was nearly over. The Raffertys had left the camp earlier. Mariah had felt depressed to see Little Elk go, and the Indian woman, too, had seemed sad to leave her. Now the captives were the only non-Indians in the camp.

''Do you know what's going on?'' Mariah asked Will.

He shook his head groggily. He was slumped over, though conscious, and his hands, like hers, were tied behind a thin tree. He was beside her, and Paul was tied to another tree on Will's far side.

She noticed what looked like fresh bruises on Will's cheeks. ''Have they been beating you?'' she asked in horror, remembering Holly's tale. At least she hadn't been mistreated . . . yet.

''We'll be all right, Miss Walker,'' Will said, though his words were garbled, as though it hurt him to speak. ''Paul and me both.''

Mariah was seated on the hard ground, and a drizzle of rain began to fall. With her hands bound behind the tree, she couldn't even dry her face. She wished she could do something to comfort Will and Paul—even though she still considered Will partly an enemy.

Would she, too, be beaten? If her limited knowledge of Indian culture was correct, women were not treated with the European sense of gallantry.

That hadn't happened to Matilda in the screenplay, but Mariah knew she couldn't depend on its prediction.

Tears joined the raindrops, but only for a minute. She gathered her courage, even as she decided to collect information that might help her out of this mess—and maybe even out of the past. "Will, did you see what happened to Holly or René, the other people from the inn?" He shook his head. "Paul, did you see them?"

"No, ma'am," said the other soldier. "I didn't see them killed, either, so maybe they escaped."

Mariah prayed that was so. She turned toward Will as best she could in her awkward position bound to the tree and asked, "Did you know Thorn before you came to the inn last week?"

He sat up straight. "Why are you asking?"

"Just wondering."

"He knew him, all right," Paul piped up behind them. "He's talked of no one else from the time he joined the cadre at the fort."

"Really? Why is that?"

"Let it suffice to say, Miss Walker, that the man is a damned coward, begging your pardon again, and I wish to teach him a lesson." The topic of conversation had perked up the young soldier, but Mariah didn't like what he had to say.

"You're wrong about Thorn—" she began.

"No, miss, I'm not," he interrupted. Then he sighed. "But it makes no difference. These savages will not let me live long enough to do what I must."

Would she? Mariah wondered. Had she come all the way across the centuries to die here at the hands of an angry Indian for nothing? If Will died here, she'd not have to do anything to right Pierce's "grievous wrong."

She wiggled her hands. The ropes cut into her skin. She needed an escape plan—one that included finding a knife.

If only Thorn were around, skinning rabbits. She nearly laughed out loud in bitterness as she recalled his very first words to her: "No one should rely on me."

* * *

Night was falling. The air grew cooler but remained damp. The nearby weathered rocks were forming deep, forbidding shadows. Mariah couldn't see the river beyond them, but she heard its swift, rushing noise.

She smelled meat cooking over a fire somewhere. Her stomach growled. Were they going to starve her to death instead of beating her?

She wondered which would be worse.

Meantime, she was afraid she was going to embarrass herself. They had only loosed her once during the day, and even though they'd given her nothing to drink, she felt as though her bladder was going to burst. If they'd intended her to die of dehydration, they'd forgotten the rain that had changed from a drizzle to a downpour some time earlier, then stopped.

Or maybe they just assumed she wouldn't be smart enough to keep her mouth open to collect the moisture.

Now, she sat in mud. Her hair was starting to dry but still hung in damp waves about her face. She tossed her head in a futile attempt to get the hair out of her eyes.

"Will?" she whispered, looking toward the young man tied to the tree beside her. He was asleep—or was he unconscious? Beyond him, Paul, too, was slumped over, only his bindings keeping him erect.

Her arms ached. So did her legs, her back—every muscle she'd become aware of since starting manual labor in this time. Were the Indians going to make them sleep here, tied to trees?

What a fascinating scene for a movie, she told herself, trying to keep from screaming, from crying. Even Pierce's stunning script had missed much detail—the sound of owls hooting in the forest behind her. The buzzing of the insects that landed persistently on her bare cheeks, even when she moved her head to scare them away. A scratch on her nose stung from perspiration.

"Will!" she tried again, but he didn't stir.

She heard a sound from the woods, and a group of Indians emerged, carrying stacks of animal pelts. The others who'd remained with the captives came to greet them, their voices all raised in apparent glee. The mission Little Elk had described might have ended successfully.

Did that mean they'd head tomorrow for the Iroquois's long houses, wherever they might be?

Thorn's face intruded into her thoughts, his strong features, his hooded brown eyes as unfathomable as a river, his broad neck—and the wonderful, muscular body that had loved hers so well, so briefly.

Would he blame himself for what had happened to her? No; he didn't need more guilt to heap upon all that already burdened him. Her misfortune had nothing to do with him.

If only she could tell him so.

If only she could tell him that, no matter what, she loved him.

A small sound of despair escaped her lips. One of the bare-chested Indians who held an animal skin looked toward her. She opened her mouth as though she were stifling a yawn.

"You guys going to cut me down so I can get some food and sleep?" she asked.

The Indian just looked at her blankly, but Nahtana emerged from the crowd. He smiled his cruel smile at her again, then showed her the knife he was carrying. She tried not to flinch as he brandished it in her face. Then he cut her bonds and drew her painfully to her feet.

This was it! His opportunity.

Thorn watched as Mariah stumbled, obviously stiff from being tied to the damned tree. He gritted his teeth as that bastard Nahtana grabbed her, not gently at all, and dragged her back to her feet. She cried out, but softly.

Mariah Walker was a brave thing. Her courage shot an arrow of remorse deep into his soul.

He should not have left the inn.

Knowing the Indians were attacking settlements, he should not have left her alone.

No matter that the soldiers were there. Little good they'd done.

Or that René and Holly were there. They had barely been able to take care of themselves.

He watched as Mariah wrested her arm from Nahtana's grasp and pointed toward the edge of the trees. She pantomimed turning his head away. She wanted privacy.

Good girl! he thought.

He glanced at the men still tied to the trees. The soldiers, including the one who'd spurned his handshake.

He would leave them there.

With a pang of agony deep inside, he remembered other lives that had been lost due to him. A young boy, stolen away while picking berries.

The boy's mother, who'd killed herself in despair.

Damn! No matter how unworthy they were, he had to take these men along.

First, he needed a diversion.

He had already circled the encampment, slowly, stealthily. Picking his way about the rounded rocks.

The rocks that had led him here. To Mariah.

He still tasted the bitter anguish he had felt at hearing of her capture. It was tempered now, however, by the jubilation he had felt at finding her alive. He had not stopped to think why her well-being mattered to him. He'd had to act.

Many of the Indians were inside the cave. Their campfire was just inside it, sheltered from the earlier rain that had left the forest dripping.

The stack of pelts dried beside the fire.

Thorn studied the fire, then smiled. He had his answer.

Though he had not shorn his hair before he had left the small settlement where he had ventured with Ainsley and the rest, he had dressed similarly to an Iroquois, in a loose buckskin shirt, breechcloth and his usual moccasins. He had boiled walnuts and used the resulting dye to darken his skin.

He glanced around. Nahtana remained with Mariah at the edge of the woods. Two other Indians were outside the cave, but he'd seen neither before. Good. They might not recognize him.

He approached the first, who was small and thin and reeked of bear grease. Speaking in Shawnee, one of the Indian languages he'd learned, Thorn identified himself. "I am Elgas, of the Shawnee. I wish your hospitality for the night."

Many Indians prided themselves on hospitality. He only hoped that Nahtana wouldn't turn to see him before he had time to act. He approached the fire with his hands extended, as though he wished to warm them.

He knelt. Sticking from the edge of the fire was the end of a large, dry branch, nearly the size of his arm. He looked around. No one paid attention to him.

Swiftly, he pulled the branch from the fire and heaved it to the top of the pile of pelts. The skins, as yet uncured, were still damp, but the fur caught fire immediately, emitting a terrible stench.

The Indians inside the cave noticed it first; he heard their yells. With a force he felt to his toes, he kicked the campfire to further block their exit. From what he could tell, they were all trapped inside. He heard their angry screams.

The Indians outside the cave noticed the commotion and ran toward him. He tripped the first, fell with him onto the dust and bashed his head on the ground. As the second approached, Thorn knelt, balancing his weight on the balls of his feet, then sprang, clutching at the savage's throat with one hand. With the other, he pulled his knife from the sheath at his belt and plunged it into the Indian's chest.

He heard a frenzied growl from beside him and found Nahtana approaching. Where was Mariah?

There was movement behind the trees where the soldiers were tied. She was getting them loose, bless her.

"Here!" he called, tossing his knife in her direction, just as Nahtana leapt at him, brandishing a knife of his own. Thorn caught his thin wrist, but the Indian managed to keep the knife pointed at Thorn's eyes. He said something Thorn did not understand, but the meaning was clear.

He wanted to kill Thorn.

For long moments, they stood there. The sharp point of the knife drew slowly toward Thorn's face, but there was no time to be afraid. He had to act. He tried to reach around with a leg to trip Nahtana. The Indian anticipated and moved his thin, greasy body lithely back, not loosening his grip on the knife.

Suddenly he went slack, nearly drawing Thorn to the ground as he fell.

There stood Mariah, a large rock still clutched in both hands. She'd obviously used it to bash Nahtana. "We'd better get out of here," she said.

Thorn stooped to grab Nahtana's knife. "What about the others?"

"They're awake and loose, though if they're as stiff as I was, they're going to have a hard time."

Thorn glanced toward the cave, where the fire and pelts still blazed. A couple of Indians emerged from one side, coughing. "We'd better go."

The two soldiers did not look well, but they had apparently sized up the situation. "Thank you," said the older one as he limped into the dark shelter of the forest.

The other, the one who hadn't shaken Thorn's hand, sounded grudging as he repeated, "Thank you."

Thorn took Mariah's arm as they hurried into the woods. She was bedraggled, her hair loose around her face and her clothing torn. There were smudges on her face where either rain—or tears—had smeared dirt beneath her leaf-green eyes. There was a scratch along the side of her small, dainty nose, and her lips looked dry.

He'd never seen anyone more lovely in his life.

And brave. She'd knocked Nahtana over the head, perhaps even saved Thorn's life.

Now she kept up with him despite the growing darkness in the deep, shadowed forest.

"Thanks," she echoed after they'd gone some distance from the Indian encampment.

"You are welcome," he said gruffly. "But, Mariah, you must know—"

She stopped running beside him for just an instant and placed a small, callused finger on his mouth. "I know. You happened to be in the neighborhood hunting rabbits and just dropped in. But no one, Mr. Thorn, should depend on you."

She took her finger away, reached up to grab him behind the neck and planted a quick, groin-tightening kiss upon his mouth. Then she hurried into the forest.

Chapter Seventeen

"Slave driver," mumbled Mariah. She leaned against the rough bark of a pine tree. Her breath came in short spurts, and she felt so exhausted that she could have fallen asleep right there, standing up.

The forest was beginning to grow light. Though they'd stopped periodically to rest, the bedraggled group had been on the move since their rescue last night.

Thorn touched her shoulder. "Would you not prefer my slave driving to Nahtana's?"

"Point taken." She smoothed her torn brown dress and apron as best she could, then touched her crinkled, dirty hair. Oh, well. Thorn had seen her looking worse when she'd dragged herself from the river, the first time they'd met.

In moments, she found herself snuggled against Thorn's strong, hard body. One arm clutched her tightly to him. The other held his ever-present Pennsylvania rifle, though he'd left it in the woods while rescuing her from the Indians. "There would be no time to reload," he explained. "I had to rely on surprise."

"And strength," she'd said.

"And your assistance," he'd added with a smile that she shared.

Despite feeling so weary, she reveled in his closeness. Inhaled his leathery, masculine scent.

Wondered why he had come after her. Could he, perhaps, love her too?

"What did you do with your horse?" The idea of riding was infinitely appealing to her weary body.

"I sold it to the homesteaders as the soldiers hurried them back toward the east. Now I wish I hadn't; the Indians ran off the rest."

"Twenty-twenty hindsight." Mariah smiled wearily at his confused expression. "No matter."

"I know you are tired," he said, hustling her along once more to match his relentless pace. "But we must hurry. I killed only one Indian, unless some perished in the cave. The others, if smart, will catch more animals to trade and go home. Nahtana, however, never thinks of peace but of revenge. And he is their leader."

Mariah nodded, her head feeling leaden on her neck. "How long will it take till we get back to the inn?"

He peered at the soldiers who lagged behind. "If they keep up, only a few more hours."

"Hours!" Mariah couldn't hide her dismay.

He gave her a comforting squeeze. "You can withstand it, little one. You have already borne so much."

Little one. At five foot five, she wasn't very tall, but she wasn't particularly little, either. She was smaller than he, of course, at close to six feet.

But his words had sounded more of a term of endearment than a description. Mariah smiled to herself and plodded on. "Isn't it time to tell me how you found us?" It wasn't the first time she'd asked, but he'd insisted that they not speak for a while, to conserve their energy.

"Hey, Thorn."

Mariah looked back.

It was Paul. "Will has nearly passed out, and I'm exhausted, too. Can we stop for a while?"

"I am all right," came a thin voice behind him. "Do not stop on my account."

"Do we dare rest now?" Mariah asked, looking toward Thorn in the increasing light.

He shook his head, causing his nut-brown hair to catch on the shoulders of his Indian-style buckskin shirt. She'd noted the darkened tone of his skin before, but she'd known him too well to mistake him for an Indian. Maybe his disguise had bought him a few precious seconds with her kidnappers, though.

"I know of an area near the river not far from here," he said. Though there were wrinkles at the corners of his brown eyes and a grim set to his mouth, he seemed to bear up best of all of them under the strain of their difficult trek. Of course, he hadn't been captured by Indians first. But to catch up with them as quickly as he had, he mustn't have slept for two days. "We can rest there, but only for a while. I need to return to the inn."

Mariah was afraid to ask the question that had been on her mind since their rescue, but she blurted it now. "Holly and René—are they all right?"

Thorn nodded. "They led me to you. Holly, anyway. René knew of a recess beneath my house, and he was able to secrete Holly there when the Indians came. Unfortunately, he was unable to get to you. When you had gone, they came after me."

"Had you reached the settlement? Were Francis and the others all right?"

Thorn's even pace stopped, then started again, but he no longer guided her with his touch. Mariah looked up to find him glaring at her. "Francis is fine. I will take you to him, if you wish, instead of to the inn." He pulled up his broad chin and stared straight ahead.

She ran her hand up the soft, warm material at his solid back. "I don't wish, Thorn. I want to be with you."

Again, he missed a step, but he did not look down at her as he hurried onward. "There are things I do not understand." He seemed to search for words, and Mariah, struggling to keep up, waited for him to continue. "Holly said you told her the same story you had related to me, about coming from the future and being the participant in a play. She said you had predicted the Indian attack, though you thought you would be taken only if you left the inn."

"That's right." Mariah was unsure from his careful tone whether he was accepting or denying. "The script I read was only partly accurate."

"It did, I understand, say that you would be taken to a cliff near the river where the water had shaped large rocks into smooth ones." There was still no inflection in his voice. "The nearest place to fit that description was where I found you."

"Thank you for trying there," she said simply. Maybe she should have learned by now that she could not rely on Thorn. He had told her so often enough.

Instead, she had learned that she could.

"What is the next occurrence your . . . script predicts?" he asked slowly.

"Then you believe me?" She couldn't keep the joyful note from her voice.

"I do not believe such an incredible tale," he contradicted. "However, you did know the soldiers would follow the homesteaders visiting my inn, and you seemed to have predicted your own capture—and rescue."

She searched for a way to explain in a manner he might, somehow, accept. "As I told you, Pierce wrote a story about a man named Thorn who was a lot like you. Not all the story follows real life here, but some does."

"The Thorn in the story—he was dependable?"

Mariah drew in a quick breath. How astute this man was! She considered his question for only a moment before saying, "Yes. As I said, he was a lot like you."

He pulled her in front of him, grasping her arm so tightly that she winced. "Just because there have been times when I have acted as your make-believe hero did does not mean that I am he. I do as I wish. When it suits me, I help people, but sometimes even then it turns out wrong. Mostly, I do not even try." He stalked off, leaving her standing there.

"What's wrong with him?" Will, who had caught up with

them, stared after Thorn. His boyish face seemed to have aged years beneath his ragged, dirty beard.

"He's—he's just tired, like all of us," Mariah dissembled. As they started to follow Thorn, Will tripped, and she reached over to steady him. "Are you hanging in there?"

"Hanging—"

Oops. Exhaustion made her careless with her language. "I mean, are you able to keep up?"

"I'm still here, am I not?"

Mariah smiled, then turned serious again. "Thorn rescued us. Doesn't that make you feel better toward him?"

"If you mean, do I forgive him for what he did to—" He stopped. "No, I will not explain my opinions. But if you are asking whether I will forgive him before he answers for his sins, I must reply no."

Miserable, Mariah forced herself to speed up to get away from Will. Maybe she shouldn't have cut him loose. He could still be with the Indians, unable to pursue his unexplained vendetta against Thorn.

Unable to challenge Thorn to a duel.

Impulsively, she caught up with Thorn. "You asked what else the script had in it. One thing is that damned duel, and I still think it will be against Will." She nodded her head back toward the young man.

"Perhaps I should have left him there." Thorn's words echoed her thoughts, but his tone was mild.

"Maybe." She set her pace to match his again. "Look, if I can predict something else that actually occurs, will you take me seriously?"

He reached over and gently tweaked her chin. She closed her eyes briefly at the tender touch. "It will then, of course, be easy for a rational man to accept that a woman with no skills came here not as the pampered child of a rich man in the east, but from the future."

She felt her eyes blaze at his gentle sarcasm. "I told you about my damned father," she stormed. "At least you can believe that."

He said nothing for a long moment. "Your vehemence about that does, I must admit, sound convincing."

He veered toward the left, touching her arm so she followed. She glanced behind to make sure Will and Paul saw their turn, then asked, ''What about my vehemence about the rest?''

''I do not know what to think. You do not seem crazy. In fact, you appear to be incredibly, courageously sane. And yet—''

''And yet, you can't believe I'm from the future. I don't believe it either—or, rather, that I somehow wound up in the past.'' She knew she sounded defeated. She looked down at her poor, work-damaged hands, which symbolized to her all she'd gone through. When would she wake up and find out she'd somehow been cast as an actress in a film gone awry?

When would she find Pierce and make him fix things? What if she couldn't right his damned grievous wrong? She couldn't do much to control a fanatical young man bent on avenging something too terrible even to reveal—or a stubborn woodsman who wouldn't run from any fight, even if he believed in her.

Which he didn't.

And he certainly didn't care for her the way she did him.

''Okay, Thorn.'' She made herself sound forceful. ''Here's the scoop. Though I don't remember details, the screenplay said that, before the duel, your inn would be taken over by raiders. I don't know who or why, but the Thorn in the script prevailed.''

''Raiders? Taking over my inn? Are they Indians, Miss Walker?''

She pondered for a moment. ''No. From what I can recall, they were traders of some kind.''

She winced as Thorn laughed. The fact that he laughed at, instead of with, her hurt. ''Indians, I can understand. Maybe even settlers being stalked by Indians or soldiers. But . . . traders?'' He calmed down, but there was still a merriness in his tone. ''All right, Mariah. I will watch out for . . . traders who take over my inn!''

''What's wrong?'' Mariah's sweet voice came from beside Thorn, at the edge of the forest.

He put out a hand to shush her and to stop the soldiers who stumbled behind them.

The gate to the palisade was open, but just slightly.

He had sent René and Holly back to the inn with a volunteer cadre of Ainsley's forces. Mariah's friend Francis and the other settlers had agreed to return with the remaining soldiers to Fort Pitt until the current barrage of Indian attacks had ended. There were rumors that a treaty was being negotiated with the Iroquois chiefs to buy a considerable amount of land to be made available for settling. The homesteaders had agreed to wait and see.

René might leave the gate totally open, to entice travelers to enter. More likely, in these times, he would keep it closed and bolted.

But he would never leave it slightly ajar.

"Stay here," he ordered them in a whisper. He looked doubtfully at the soldiers. They were in no condition to help. "All of you must go back into the forest."

"What's wrong?" The words were repeated. He glanced down at Mariah. Her green eyes were troubled, and her sweet mouth had compressed into a worried frown that he suddenly had an urge to kiss away.

But he didn't. There was no time for such foolishness.

"I do not know what is wrong," he said. "I only know *something* is." He managed a quick, ill-humored smile. "Perhaps your raiders have invaded my inn."

He heard her sudden intake of breath. "How do you know?"

"A feeling. Plus, the position of the gate is not as René would leave it if all were well." He quickly checked his rifle to make sure it was ready, if need be, to fire.

Perhaps he was being foolish. Perhaps René had not yet returned to the inn. The young, sprightly Holly, with whom his friend seemed so amazingly taken, might have convinced him to go off somewhere, to neglect his duties.

Unlikely, though. Not René.

And even Holly had seemed to take the job, into which she had insinuated herself with Mariah's help, quite seriously.

"Let me come, too," Mariah demanded quietly. "Maybe I can help."

"You can help more if I know you are out of my way." He glanced again toward the soldiers. The two tattered young men listened to all that was being said, yet neither volunteered to assist him. Were they not shamed by the offer of a mere woman?

Not that Mariah Walker was a mere anything. She was unlike any other woman he had ever met.

The one named Will, whom Mariah said would be his doom, had a speculative gleam in his eye as he looked sidelong at Thorn. Maybe he was hoping that, if something were indeed wrong, someone else would end his troubles by slaying Thorn.

Not, however, if Thorn could help it.

Making certain the others were sheltered in the shadows of the forest and that his rifle was at the ready, Thorn dashed quietly into the clearing and toward the inn's gate, stopping with his back pressed against the palisade.

He listened carefully. From behind him came the usual sounds of the woods: leaves rustling in the slight breeze, the melodic chirping of robins interrupted by the strident caws of a crow, the chattering of a squirrel, perhaps his friend who visited him in his cabin.

From ahead, there were no noises at all.

That in itself was a warning.

Holding his rifle in his right hand, he used the left to push the gate open further.

Still no sounds.

He crept toward the edge of the gate and peered around it. The compound appeared normal.

Thorn entered and stopped, glancing this way and that, feeling strangely vulnerable yet foolish at his apparently unwarranted concern.

Still, he did not call out for René, as he would had he truly believed all was well. Instead, he ran toward the inn, passing his cabin and the smokehouse.

He was nearly at the kitchen door when he glanced back. Mariah followed, running, as he had.

Glaring, he motioned her to duck behind one of the closer buildings. She ignored him.

Until . . . "Thorn!" she cried. "Behind you. A gun!"

He turned, instinctively raising his rifle. He saw the gleam of a polished barrel stuck out the kitchen's window and fired beyond it, just as he heard another rifle's report.

The noises of a scuffle erupted from inside the inn as a third shot rang out. It sounded as though it came from the smokehouse, and he turned to look—just as Mariah, who'd nearly reached his side, fell.

"No!" His cry was an anguished moan. He hadn't time to reload; he was still in the open. He ran a jagged path toward the smokehouse to keep himself from being an easy target.

His throat closed as he passed the crumpled, still form of Mariah. He could only help her if he disposed of the danger.

He paused at the smokehouse door. He heard heavy, irregular breathing, a muffled curse. Pulling his knife from the sheath at his belt, he shoved open the door and leapt inside. The smell of his own anger and fear blended with the aroma of smoked meat.

"Hey!" shouted a startled voice. In the dimness, Thorn saw a familiar figure. The large man, dressed in formal clothing better suited for Philadelphia than the frontier, had apparently reloaded. As the man who had shot Mariah swung up his barrel to aim, Thorn took advantage of his suddenly unprotected middle.

He hurled the sharp, long-bladed knife.

It struck the man in the gut. The rifle fell.

Then the man.

Thorn grabbed a length of rope from a shelf on the wall. In case the man was still alive, he bound him tightly. Then he ran outside.

Mariah remained on the ground. Blood seeped through her tattered dress above her chest.

Holly, standing beside her, cried softly into her hands. René bent over the still figure, examining her.

* * *

Thorn barely spared a thought for whomever had first shot from the inn. If René and Holly were here, that danger must have passed.

Anguish swept through him. "Is she—" He could not go on.

She had relied on him, damn her!

Once more he had let someone down.

But this time it hadn't been a mere friend or relative.

This time, it was someone he loved.

He sank to his knees in the dirt, smoothing the waves of her honey-colored hair from her face. Her cheek was cool. Too cool.

Filled with terror, he looked at René.

It had been years since he had felt deeply enough to cry, but now his eyes filled.

"She is still alive," the Frenchman pronounced. His voice seemed to come from far away. "For now. The bullet, it went through her shoulder, but perhaps it grazed her heart, it was that close. We must get her inside."

Thorn carefully scooped Mariah into his arms and stood. Her limpness made her difficult to carry, but he treasured her slight weight. He inclined his head toward her face.

He felt the slightest of breaths from her mouth, but the metallic smell of blood hovered around her.

He took her to his own cabin. René pushed open the door.

"I'll boil water," said Holly, who had followed.

Thorn deposited his precious cargo upon his bed. Wincing as though he could feel the pain he'd cause if she were conscious, he peeled away the garments over her wound.

It was an ugly one, covered in seeping blood. Already it had begun to swell. He raised her slightly and pulled her dress from her shoulder. He saw the bullet's exit wound at her back.

Holly arrived with clean rags and a pail of water. "Some is on the fire for boiling, but I can begin cleaning her with this."

For a moment Thorn hesitated. He had done this to her. He should be the one to care for her.

"Be off!" Holly insisted. "Your sniveling will not help her. Cleaning the wound will."

Sniveling? Him?

Perhaps he was. In any event, he knew he was no good for Mariah. He should leave her to those who could help.

He stared at the lovely, still form for an agonized minute. She looked peaceful, her head haloed by waves of honey-rich hair. Her sweet lips were pale, parted as though she tried to tell him something—that he had failed her, no doubt.

Except for a small bruise, there was no color in her smooth cheeks. The scratch on her small nose stood out like a scar.

He reached his hand toward her as though in supplication, then snatched it back.

He would not ask forgiveness of her. She had no reason to forgive him.

He felt himself petrify inside, as though he were the rocks over which the rivers ran.

He did not deserve to be in the company of people.

He made himself turn to René. He had business to attend to. "Have we any invaders left to worry about?"

The Frenchman shook his head. "They were waiting to ambush you. They claimed at first they came for lodging, but I noticed that they had the horse and goods of Ambrose, poor fellow. I dared not attack for fear of their hurting Holly. But the diversion when you arrived . . . well, the one who was in the kitchen with us, he will trouble us no more."

"What happened to the soldiers who came back here with you?"

"They seemed eager, and so I released them to return to the fort. Had I but known . . ." René shook his head sorrowfully.

"I left the two soldiers who'd been taken with Mariah in the forest." Thorn waited for René's censure for not having made Mariah stay there, too, but none came. "Find them, if you will, and have them check on the other marauder in the smokehouse. He's trussed like the animal he is, and I can but hope that my knife gave him his just reward. The soldiers may make themselves of use by taking charge of both of these animals, alive or dead."

* * *

Night had fallen. Thorn stood at the bar in the common room, nursing a large tankard of ale. He had eaten no supper. He had wanted none. He hoped for the oblivion of drinking overmuch brew, but oblivion was not to be.

The marauder whose gut his knife had pierced was dead. He had not wished the scoundrel buried near the inn, so he had insisted that the soldiers, with René's supervision, drag his large carcass for burial toward the river. That was where he had first seen the wretch who had tried to harm Mariah, who had, perhaps, killed her now.

For Thorn had finally recognized these well-dressed villains. They were the men who had been terrorizing Mariah when she had first appeared in the woods, begging his help.

He'd warned her then not to rely on him.

He took another long draught of ale, wanting to remember no more.

"I've spoken with our captive," said a voice beside him. René planted his large behind upon a chair near Thorn. The second rogue, the one René and Holly had subdued, was bound within the smokehouse. He was the younger one, the one called John Brant. The soldiers would take him when they returned the next day to Fort Pitt.

"Did he explain how they had happened to have Ambrose's horse and goods?" Thorn was only half interested despite considering Ambrose his friend.

He looked at his hand where it lay on the bar beside his tankard, at the veins on the back of it and his own blunt fingers.

That hand had killed a man that day, the one named Samuel. It had hurled a knife with perfect aim.

But it had not been able to save Mariah from being shot.

"He claims Ambrose is alive, though perhaps he has a severe headache," said René. "They came upon him downriver and decided that owning all the goods of the three of them was better than trading some of theirs for some of his. *Les bâtards!*"

Thorn nodded. "If they were downriver, we must check at Harrigan's to see if they know of Ambrose's fate." He paused. "Did your friend Brant explain why they wished to ambush me?"

"He is not my friend!" René exploded. He walked around the bar and poured himself some rum. The swig he took was long, and he thumped the glass down upon the wood. "They wished revenge for your taking Mariah from them. They heard she was still here, and they had seen the man Pierce near Harrigan's. He had hired them to bring her to him. Because they'd failed, Pierce had given them no money."

Pierce. That name again. Thorn watched his fingers curl into a fist and pound against the bar.

Pierce wanted Mariah. Who was the man? Had he actually written the story of which she spoke? Or had he conspired with her for reasons unknown to get her to concoct that ridiculous story about being from the future?

Was he her husband? Her lover?

And why, despite his purposeful freezing of his emotions, did it hurt Thorn so much to think of it?

"So," he said, "they failed to kill me, but instead took their revenge by harming Mariah." A pain stabbed at his gut, as though he had taken the knife he'd hurled at Samuel instead of that rogue.

"How is she?" René asked softly.

"How would I know? Holly is with her, not I."

"I would wager," said René, "that she would heal faster by knowing of your presence at her side rather than Holly's or mine."

"Then she is a fool!" shouted Thorn. He cast his hand over the smooth surface of the bar, sweeping the metal tankard from it. The flagon fell on the floor with a clatter, tossing ale all about.

"She is not the only one," René grumbled. He took his own glass and headed toward the kitchen.

Thorn stared after him. Had René dared to imply that Thorn was a fool? He would fire him. He would fire that Holly about whom René seemed to care so much.

He would fire Mariah. If she lived . . . no, he would not think of that.

He would run the inn himself. Better yet, he would close the inn, remain in solitude.

He needed no one.

He found himself, a short while later, standing outside his house in the darkness. He carried no candle.

About him, the compound that he had wrested from the wilderness by his own hands, his refuge against the outside world, now looked shadowed and unfamiliar.

Even his home seemed foreign. He found his fist raised, as though to knock on the door. He stared at the offending appendage, then lowered it deliberately. He turned the knob and walked inside.

Holly, sitting on the side of the bed, rose with a gasp. "Oh, Thorn, you startled me, you did."

He strode across the room and looked down.

"Thorn," came a faint whisper from the bed.

Mariah was awake!

He sat gently upon the mattress and took her cool, fragile hand into his own. He was barely aware of Holly's speaking into his ear. "I will get myself drink and food but will come back to sit with her whenever you wish." In moments she was gone.

"Mariah." Thorn heard his voice croak.

"The raiders," she managed, through dry and cracked lips. Holly had dressed her in a shirt of his, and she looked as lost as a small child dressed in adult garb. Her skin was nearly as pale as the white shirt.

"Would you like some water?" he asked.

Her head moved in a weak shake. Her eyes seemed to focus beyond his shoulder. "The raiders," she said again. "They came. You believe me now."

What was she talking about? Was she delirious?

And then he understood. She thought the scoundrels who had lain in wait were the raiders she'd claimed to predict from her play. From the future.

Mariah had lived her entire life here in delirium. Or she was part of some nefarious scheme he'd yet to comprehend. With that Pierce, perhaps.

But how could she maintain it while so injured? No, he

knew in his heart that she plotted nothing against him. But her sanity . . . ? He surely could not accept that she told the truth.

Could he?

"You believe me?" she insisted in her weak voice. She tried to rise, and he pushed her gently back to the bed. Through the sleeves of his shirt, she felt hot. Had she a fever already? He touched her brow. It was warm but not unduly so. She wriggled under his touch as though struggling to rise once more.

"I believe you," he lied.

She grew calmed immediately, closing her eyes. Her long lashes, the shade of honey, rested on the soft rise of her cheeks. Despite his myriad conflicting emotions, he could not resist; he stroked his thumb gently across her cheek.

Her eyes fluttered open once more. "You will be careful," she said. "Of Will. He would not speak—" Her words faded.

"Don't try to talk," Thorn said.

But she did not obey now any more than she ever had. "He *is* the one. He hates you. He did not say why." She drew in a deep breath, and her lips pursed as though she were in pain.

"Enough, Mariah." He was becoming alarmed. She was using all her energy to talk to him rather than saving it to allow her body to heal—if it would.

"Promise." He could barely hear the word.

"Hush."

"Promise," she insisted.

"What, Mariah?" He had, perhaps, to humor her before she would remain quiet.

"Promise you will not . . ." Again her voice faded, but then she began again, "You will not duel with him."

He wanted to promise, if it would calm her, but it would be a lie. He could not know if he would fight Will. If the foolish boy challenged him, he might have no choice. "Mariah, I—I'll talk to him. Calm him. Try to convince him not to fight with me."

Her soft green eyes seemed to focus on him for the first

time since he had come into the room. "Thank you," she said.

And then she was no longer conscious.

"Mariah!" he said in alarm. He touched the side of her throat. A pulse beat there, perhaps too slowly but at least, he realized, she was alive.

For now.

He stood abruptly and hurried from his cabin.

Chapter Eighteen

Thorn threw open the door to his cabin. He gasped, as though he could not breathe.

He barely noticed as Holly came running from the inn's kitchen. "Is she all right?"

"I—I think so." He shoved his fingers through his hair. "She tried to talk to me, and now she's asleep."

"I will check on her." The tow-haired woman edged past Thorn into his house.

He leaned against the cool stone wall, attempting to compose himself. Mariah's wounds were bad. She had lost much blood, and she was very weak.

He slammed the heel of his hand against the stones, allowing the pain to wash over him. That was pain he could understand, not this gnawing at his heart.

It was guilt again, of course. He had once more allowed a woman to suffer for his ineptitude.

He did not care for her. He did not dare.

But he still wished for her to live.

Holly, René and he had cleaned her wounds and bandaged them. Now it was up to Mariah to heal.

She had to rest, yet she had insisted on talking to him. On assuring herself that her prediction of raiders had made him believe in her incredible tale of coming from the future.

Foolish woman! Brave, yes. And beautiful, and strong, and unique. Lovable.

He snorted aloud. *He* was the one who was foolish.

For despite all his self-admonishments, he did love her.

Worse, his brain must be addled, for he wished he could give credence to her strange claims. Perhaps he could comfort her with his conviction.

But how could he accept that she had come from the future? If anything, he would find it easier to believe she had read a play that—

That was it! The play! If there were such a thing, would she not have it among her belongings? He strode toward her room, intent on doing something to keep him from dwelling on his fear for Mariah.

His fear that she would die.

Inside the stable, the sole horse was the roan that belonged to Ambrose. He would need to replace the others, which the Indians had loosed. Was his friend Ambrose truly alive somewhere?

After passing the horse stalls, he entered Mariah's small chamber. Inside, he closed his eyes in pain. The clothes tree held garments he recognized from her wearing of them. The aroma Mariah had assumed since arriving there hung in the air: the sweetness of baking bread mixed with a touch of candle wax and the tang of burning wood. He inhaled it, drinking it in. "Mariah," he whispered into her empty room. "You must get well."

He gave his head a mighty shake. No time for such sentimentality. He had undertaken a mission.

Where might she have hidden the play?

The room was small and sparsely furnished. It contained few places for concealment.

He looked beneath the chipped washbasin upon the small table. Not there. He knelt on the hard wooden floor. It was spotless. He smiled wistfully, imagining Mariah here, scrubbing her own habitat with the same vigor she used in the inn. The play was not beneath the bed. Among the bed clothes?

He found something under the mattress. Not the play, but the piece of paper he had torn from his ledger. On it was tiny writing, as though Mariah had tried to conserve its every inch, in the untidy hand he had seen before.

And several ink blots. He closed his eyes, forcing himself not to recollect the night he had tried to teach Mariah to avoid blotting.

He brought the paper beneath the window, into the waning light of day, to read what was upon it.

"My screenplay recollections," it said. "First were the river rats, though they were grungy—" Thorn wondered at that word's meaning. "—in the script and dressed like proper Revolutionary gentlemen in Pgh." Revolutionary? What did she mean? And "Pgh"—was that Pittsborough? "Matilda was a fool for going with such slime balls." That was a descriptive word, thought Thorn. "And I was tricked by their clothes and their mention of Pierce, the son of a—"

She had not finished the phrase—perhaps to save paper, for Mariah was not one to avoid cursing. Thorn again found his lips twisting in a bittersweet smile.

The page went on to mention him. "Matilda's Thorn appeared from nowhere and helped her; the real thing had to have his arm twisted—or at least his rifle grabbed."

"Damn!" Thorn breathed aloud, forcing himself not to crush the fragile paper in his hand. Even here, he could not escape his own unreliability. It had followed him from England all the way to Fort Pitt, and to his own inn. He made himself swallow his pain and continue to read.

Mariah described Matilda's attack by wolves: "Again both Thorns came through, despite their differences in attitude." Next, an Indian at the inn: "Conflicts with the script; the real guy was definitely no ally of Thorn's."

At that point, Mariah had written: "Above happened already; following are to come." From that he could tell when she had written her notes. She next listed the incident in which the homesteaders were set upon by soldiers after their arrival at the inn.

Had her knowing intervention prevented Francis and the rest from being injured by the soldiers?

Then, the Matilda character, on an outing away from the inn, was stolen by Indians. The fictional Thorn had stalwartly rescued her.

And he, when Mariah was taken? He had been far from stalwart. But he had gone to her assistance.

Look where that had gotten her. She had warned him of raiders invading his inn, and he had scoffed. Those very raiders had shot her. The knot in his gut twisted even further as he thought of it.

Her notes did not reflect Matilda's injury. Perhaps it had not happened in her play.

Perhaps it had happened instead to Mariah because of his own stupidity. His unreliability. He cursed aloud. "I am sorry, Mariah."

There was only one more item on the page. The duel. At the rivers' confluence. "This must be the 'grievous wrong' Pierce dragged me here to right," Mariah had written.

Pierce. Thorn had been jealous that Mariah sought this strange man, yet she had explained who he was and that she was to right Pierce's "grievous wrong." That he had brought her to this time to do so.

And if she lived, if she succeeded, would Pierce send her back to her own time?

He laughed aloud, an utterly unpleasant sound in the stillness. He was beginning to think her tale might be true.

More likely, she was delusional.

More likely, if she survived, when she left him it would be to return east, where she had come from in the first place. But no matter where she went, she would go.

The devastation to him would be excruciating.

But most likely of all was that she would die.

A spasm shot through him, so sharp he nearly cried out. "No!" he whispered. He loved her. Despite all his warnings to himself, that, at least, was true.

And because of it, he needed to believe in her. But to convince himself of so bizarre a tale . . . ?

He forced his eyes back to the page. "In the script, a young man named Billy calls Thorn out in a duel right at the Point at Pittsburgh. Who is Billy? Why does he want to hurt Thorn? Can I stop it?"

Thoughtfully, his hand shaking, Thorn returned the paper to its spot beneath the mattress. So what, now, was the answer?

Was the lad named Will, one of the soldiers he had rescued with her, equivalent to the "Billy" in her play? The one who wished to kill that Thorn?

If the Will here wished to kill *this* Thorn, did that not prove Mariah's tale?

Part of it, perhaps. And only if Will had not known her previously, had not schemed an elaborate plan with her for reasons Thorn could not imagine.

He had to know.

Thorn put away Mariah's paper, then hurriedly left her room and the stable.

There he was. The bearded young soldier named Will stood in the cleared area in the midst of the compound.

Perhaps Thorn could learn his answers, right here and now. "What have you done with the raiders?" he called.

"René and Paul dragged the huge, dead one toward the river to bury him," the young man answered sullenly. He was a thin fellow, and he had lost his hat. The hair on his head and face were unkempt, spotted with dirt and leaves. "I've got the other trussed like a turkey in the smokehouse. Paul and I will take him with us to the fort tomorrow."

"Thanks," Thorn said. "I owe you. Come inside, and I will give you a drink."

He saw confusion play on the lad's face. "All right," he said with obvious reluctance.

Thorn showed the boy, in his tattered red British uniform, to a seat at a table. He gave him a tall glass of rum. Thorn got his own glass and took a seat beside the soldier. "So," he said, "your name is Will?"

The boy nodded.

"I understand you hate me. That you wish to kill me?"

The boy made a choking sound that neither confirmed nor denied. The mottled flush on his face, his inability to meet Thorn's eye, told Thorn nevertheless that he was correct. That Mariah was correct—about this, at least.

"Will you tell me why?"

Will slammed his glass down hard on the table. He stood so quickly that his chair fell to the floor with a clatter. "You killed my mother!" he shouted.

Thorn felt the blood drain from his face. His limbs went rubbery. He had helped to kill his own brother and sister-in-law, but this young man had nothing to do with that. No, there was only one other woman to whose death he had contributed.

He had paid little attention to this soldier previously, but now he noted the familiarity of his gray-green eyes, the downturning at their edges. The straightness of his upper lip beneath his mustache. The beard hid whether his chin was sharply pointed, but there was a pinchedness about his nose. His hair was darker now, no longer the youthful shining brown that Thorn recalled but a dark and silty brown, and there was no childish pudginess in his flesh. But Thorn recognized him. "You!" he breathed.

"Yes," Will said. He kept his fists clenched upon the table, and his knuckles were chalk white. "I was the one kidnapped on your watch. Stolen away, not by Indians but by . . . well, never mind about that. It ought not to have happened. Ainsley—he is your friend, do you realize that?"

"Yes." Thorn clutched his glass as he stared at the boy who had grown to manhood in six years.

"He has taken your side in many a conversation with me over the past weeks. He maintains your innocence. He claims you did not intend to fail at your duty to ensure the settlers' safety. He says the woman distracting you flirted with you, not the other way around." His voice had grown as cold as a winter gale. "In my view, it makes no difference."

"You are correct," Thorn agreed. His heart was thudding within him, not from fear but from wretchedness. "Whatever the distraction, it should not have kept me from my duty. I am responsible.'' He had grieved long for this boy who'd now returned, and for his mother.

He dared not ask for absolution. It would not come from this boy, and it would certainly not come from himself.

''And then . . . then, my mother . . .'' continued Will.

''She went looking for you.'' Thorn kept his voice carefully neutral to hide the emotional turmoil seething within him. ''We all tried to help.''

''She trusted you. She even cared for you, I am told. But you failed her. And then, Ainsley said, she killed herself.''

''Yes,'' Thorn said simply. ''She did. She walked into the water at the Pittsborough Point when no one was about.'' He paused. ''So why are you here, Will? Were you so called by the lure of soldiering that you had to come to the frontier, or was it something else?''

The lad was on his feet in an instant, his hands at his sides, as though he reached for pistols holstered there, but there were none. ''I came to kill the man who made my mother die.''

Thorn felt spent. In his cabin lay a beautiful, plucky woman who might die because of him. There were those in England for whose death he was responsible. This young man's mother had taken her life because of him.

He wished no more blood on his hands.

He stood, spreading his arms out beside him. ''Then kill me, Will,'' he said simply.

The young man stared, his mouth agape. Then he knit his dirt-brown brows together in a furious scowl. ''No, I wish for you to know it is coming, to anticipate and to fear. But the fight must be fair, to both of us. I have practiced long with pistols. Ask Ainsley; I am the most skilled at the fort.''

''Despite your age?'' asked Thorn.

Will nodded. ''After all that has occurred, I am not feeling well enough for the fight to be enjoyable. And this would be too quick, for I wish you to think about it. Consider yourself challenged to a duel, but this is not the time.''

''Or the place,'' Thorn said. ''I believe it must happen at the confluence of the rivers that form the Ohio.''

Will's expression darkened. "Where my mother died? If that is what you wish."

"It is ordained." Thorn felt himself smile wryly. "But let me ask one thing, and I wish a truthful answer. A condemned man deserves that at least, does he not?"

"What is it?" Will sounded suspicious.

"Miss Walker. Mariah. Is she a friend of yours?"

"No." The young man spoke with no hesitation, and his tone indicated puzzlement. "How would I know her? I first saw her here at the inn, working for you." He hesitated. "She is a brave woman. In the face of Nahtana and the rest, she showed little fear. Even threatened them with the doomed fate of Indians, though they did not seem to understand. She kept our spirits from faltering . . . much. But, no, I did not know her before. Is that important to you?"

His voice took on a hard tone, as though he would change his mind if Thorn indicated his knowledge of Mariah was important. His hatred would require that.

But Thorn shrugged. "I was merely curious. She seemed to know how you felt about me."

"I made that clear while we were in captivity. I think she hoped . . . well, your helping to save us did not change my mind about what I planned. You should have saved my mother instead."

"I understand." Thorn poured Will more rum. "Get your strength back. Someday soon we will see about our duel." He left the common room.

Outside, night had started to fall. From beyond the palisade, Thorn heard the sound of an owl, and he stopped to listen.

It came again. It sounded real. Thorn doubted the Indians would return for a while, and it was not their calls that he heard.

He peered into the smokehouse. The fire smoldered as it should.

He closed the door behind him and sat down in the heat, inhaling the aroma of curing meat.

Mariah had been right about Will. She had not met him before. The lad wished to kill Thorn.

She had predicted so many things on her blotted sheet of paper, all from the play she said she had read.

He actually had begun to believe her. She had come to him from the future, perhaps to save him from his own folly.

What was he doing here, on the smokehouse floor? She could be dying, without him there.

He sprang to his feet and ran to his house. René was just leaving it.

"Is she . . . how is she?" asked Thorn, grabbing his old friend by the shoulder.

René shook his head. "There is high fever, and the wound, it seems infected. And those two, those silly women, they send me for bread."

When Thorn burst into the room, Holly was resting her behind on the side of the bed, fretting and holding Mariah's poor, hot hand.

Startled, she half stood, then lowered herself again. " 'Bout time you came to see her." She put all the scorn she felt into her words. Didn't he know that he could give Mariah the will to live, to heal if she could, by admitting he loved her?

But this bloke wouldn't do that easily. Holly knew that.

At least she had the satisfaction of seeing how shattered he looked. Those brown eyes of his drooped at the edges, they did, and she'd have guessed he'd grown a whole fan of wrinkles there in the last hour. He'd not have looked half bad with the dark beard that had started to grow, but the hair on his face only showed up the hollows that had begun to dig out his cheeks.

Well, let him suffer, Holly thought. Mariah was suffering, and Thorn hadn't helped enough.

"Is she hungry?" Thorn towered over the bed. "René said you sent him for bread. Should she not have broth instead?"

"The bread's not for eating." Holly stood to face him. "It was Mariah's idea."

"Give her whatever she asks for," he commanded.

As if Holly wouldn't.

He looked down at Mariah. Her eyes flitted open, they

did. Seeing him, didn't the poor lamb's ashy face just light up like the rising sun? She murmured something, but Holly couldn't hear it. Neither could Thorn, she figured, for he sat down on the bed so carefully he looked almost dainty for one so big.

"What was that?" he said, his voice gentle like a feather. He leaned down, put his ear close to her mouth.

"Medicine." Holly heard the word this time as it puffed from between Mariah's dry lips.

Thorn looked at Holly like he still didn't understand. "Medicine," she repeated irritably. "She said that in her time—" Holly stopped, her hand rushing toward her mouth, as though to push what she'd said back inside. "I mean, where she's from—"

"I know she says she's from another time, Holly." Surprisingly, Thorn didn't sound scornful. Holly glanced at Mariah. Her eyes had closed again. She'd told Holly Thorn didn't believe her, but the man just might be accepting now.

And that could help Mariah more than near any medicine. If she knew it.

But there was no indication that she'd understood. She seemed to be weakening. Slipping away.

Thorn bent over Mariah, his hand cupping the side of her face. Holly knew how hot those cheeks were, how feverish.

Not a good sign. Not at all.

"Mariah," Thorn whispered. "I spoke with Will. Everything you said about him . . . you were right."

Mariah's eyelids fluttered. Those eyes of hers, though—this time, when they appeared ever so briefly, they looked like they couldn't focus, not even on Thorn. She murmured something that sounded like, "He's Billy."

"That's right." Thorn's deep voice was rough about the edges, but he kept it soft, he did. Good fellow. "Do you know who he is? He's the boy who was lost picking berries. He said it wasn't Indians who stole him away, but he hasn't told me who did. But—" Holly saw Thorn's Adam's apple dip up and down along his throat; poor fellow was choking with emotion, he was. "But he's here to avenge his mother's death. That's why he wants to kill me. In a fair duel, he says, when both of us are rested and ready."

That damned duel, thought Holly. Sounded like it was another of Mariah's predictions that could come true.

"You were right, Mariah," he continued. "About that and so much more. You must get well now to see." His voice was near to breaking. His heart, too, by the sound of him.

That was good for him, Holly decided. And for Mariah, too.

Mariah muttered something, but Holly could not hear. "What was that?" she asked.

Thorn shook his head slowly. "I didn't catch it." He turned his head toward Holly, and she could see the sadness in his eyes and his solemn mouth. He turned back toward the still figure on the bed. "Please repeat that, Mariah."

Her eyes, opened now, stared blankly past his shoulder. Her words came slowly, one at a time. "I—must—right—a—grievous—wrong."

"That's from your play, is it not?" Thorn asked. "Pierce told you that?"

She glanced toward him then and seemed to see him. A small smile lit her flushed face, and she nodded. "No duel," she whispered.

Thorn lifted her hand in his, pressing it against her cheek. Holly could see the effort it cost him to speak. "If I can avoid it," he said, "no duel."

As Thorn watched, Mariah closed her eyes and went slack. A wave of terror passed through him. "Mariah? Mariah—" He was vaguely aware of Holly running toward them as he swept Mariah into his arms. He pressed his face against hers. "She's breathing," he told Holly—and himself, feeling relief as wide as the night sky wash through him. "She's just sleeping. But she feels so hot."

He heard the door open and turned as René entered. "Frenchie!" Holly hurried toward the Frenchman.

His hands were full, but he threw an arm around her and pulled her close. "Mademoiselle Mariah—how is she?" he asked.

"Not good." Holly's voice cracked, and Thorn saw her bury her face against René's strong shoulder. They, at least, had each other for comfort.

Without Mariah, Thorn had nothing.

"Did you find the moldy bread, like Mariah wanted?"

René thrust out the towels he held. "*Absolument,* but—"

"Good!" She took the towels from him, unwrapping their contents as she carried the bundle to the bed. Thorn looked at the bread covered in a layer of green and white. "Good thing the Indians scared us away just after baking bread, it was," Holly said. "There was plenty left, and it grew this horrible stuff while we went for help." She took Mariah's hands and patted them till she stirred. "Dearie, we've the moldy bread now. What're we to do with it?"

At first, Mariah didn't waken. "Wait," Thorn said, not wanting to disturb her. But Holly rubbed her hands more briskly, till Mariah tossed her head from side to side, then opened her eyes. "Ohhh," she moaned.

The sound was welcome, for it showed she was alive. But it pierced Thorn's heart, for it reflected her pain.

Holly repeated her question. Muzziness faded a bit from Mariah's face. "Yes," she whispered. "Mold. I never paid attention. So common. No big deal."

"What does she mean?" Thorn asked.

"I don't know for certain," Holly said. Then, to Mariah, she insisted softly, "You have to tell us how to use this stuff."

"Not sure." Mariah's voice was weaker again. Her next word sounded something like "penny-shilling," but that couldn't be right. Pen-a-sill-in? Then she rambled for a minute. "Drink it, maybe. Put it on wound, too. No pills or needles here. Don't know. No time. Try anything. May not work."

"I don't understand," said Thorn.

"The *mademoiselle,* is she, how you say, out of her head?" René broke in.

"No," Thorn stated. "Do whatever she says. She'll have the answer." Maybe she'd learned something in the future that could help her.

He laughed grimly inside. He would accept anything now, even such a wild story, if it would heal her. Hadn't he already begun to accept it, after reading her notes, speaking with Will?

"Let's mix some of this stuff in water," Holly said.

Thorn pitched in, making a paste. Holly unwrapped the bandages, glancing at Thorn and René. Thorn realized that she was trying to preserve what modesty of Mariah's she could with the two men in the room. No matter. As lovely as her body might be to Thorn, he wanted only for it to heal.

He drew in his breath sorrowfully as Holly bared the bullet wounds. They looked ugly, red and sore, with ridges of pus under the skin at the edges. There was a bad odor about them.

Mariah's moan of pain as Holly bathed her injuries made Thorn rise and begin pacing. He had done this to her. He had not protected her. And now she suffered.

Holly put the ill-smelling paste upon the wounds, covering them again with bandages. "Are you sure that will help her?" René sounded doubtful as Thorn helped him gently lower Mariah back to the bed. She was as limp as a rag doll.

"It'll work." Thorn made his voice ring with conviction. It was what Mariah had said to do. It had to work.

Holly added more water to the paste so it was runny. She put it in some broth. "Here, dearie. Medicine." She took a little in a spoon and guided it to Mariah's closed mouth. She was asleep again, or maybe passed out from the pain.

"I'll do it." Thorn sat on the bed, propping Mariah in his arms as though she were a weaning babe, then took the spoon. Mariah groaned and moved, but he was gently forceful, making her open her mouth so he could pour in the mixture. He rubbed her poor, smooth throat till she swallowed.

He got several bites down her. He felt some satisfaction, at least, for that. "You two get some rest," he said to the others. "I'll stay with her."

He paid no attention to their leaving. He cradled Mariah against him, resting his face on her damp, uncombed waves of hair, and closed his eyes.

"Get well, Mariah," he whispered. "Please." He murmured it over and over. To her. To whomever was listening in the near empty room.

If he hadn't known himself better, he'd have thought he was praying.

Chapter Nineteen

That night, Thorn insisted on staying in the room where Mariah lay. It was, after all, *his* room.

He sat in a wooden chair he had made by hand, at Mariah's bedside. She slept fitfully, tossing from side to side in her fever.

At least he could tell she still lived. But for how long?

Moldy bread, indeed.

Still, each time she awakened just a little, he ran to the hearth for a bowl of the loathsome concoction of broth and fungus that he simmered over the low fire all night. Cooling it, he propped Mariah in his arms and fed her all she would take—usually no more than a couple of spoonsful.

He watched Mariah's poor, flushed face with its closed eyes, their lashes curling over her cheeks, her waves of hair, damp from perspiration, unkempt upon her pillow.

Despite it all, she was beautiful.

And fragile. For the first time since she had appeared in his life, she could not stand up to him, defy him. Anger him.

Stimulate him.

He spoke to her quietly, now and then, knowing it was

safe, for she could not hear. "Do not die, Mariah, I beg you. If only I had taken the bullet . . . but you were protecting me when I ought to have been saving you." He heard the catch in his throat and stopped until his voice was steady once more. "If you wish anything else to help you heal—more moldy bread, or ointment from worms from the bowels of the earth, or the scrapings from the sole of a hostile Indian's moccasins . . . anything—I will get it for you." He laughed bitterly. He had named ingredients of home remedies of which he had heard—though he held little faith in them. And such conceit he had shown in promising her the impossible!

But she believed in the impossible.

She had come from the future. He now accepted that. Though incredible, it explained much about her, and about her predictions.

Near dawn, she stirred for perhaps the sixth time, and he again gave her some of the miserable broth.

When she'd finished taking but a spoonful, he rested the bowl on the floor and took Mariah's small, hot hand. Her eyes were closed. Her chest rose and fell unevenly beneath the blanket.

"Please, Mariah," he pleaded. And then the words he had been hiding within himself surged out as though torn from him by a force he'd no power to resist. "I love you."

There was no reaction from her. Just as well. He'd no business telling her such a thing.

No business even thinking it.

He bent over to rest his head on the bed beside her. The sheet smelled of the rumpled straw mattress beneath, lye soap, Mariah's salty perspiration—and her sweet fragrance.

He closed his eyes for just a moment. He was tired, so tired. But he could not sleep. . . .

A touch on his head startled him, and he sat up.

Mariah was looking at him. Though her head still rested on the pillow, her color was better, less flushed. Her lovely green eyes were again the color of new forest leaves, and they were bright and clear, seeming to focus directly on him.

"Thorn, were you here all night?" Her voice was soft yet strong.

"Someone had to be here." He tried to make his tone gruff, but there was a lightness to it he could not disguise; she was awake and lucid.

"Holly could have stayed, or René."

He shrugged, then reached toward her, smoothing back the tangled, damp waves of golden hair from her forehead and placing his hand upon it. It was cool! He dared to ask, "How do you feel?"

"Like I was run over by a Mack truck, but . . . oops. Let's see . . . like I was hit by a runaway carriage."

Strange talk again that he could not understand. But now he knew why. "Is a 'Mack truck' something from the future?"

Those green eyes of hers opened wide, and her pretty mouth rounded in surprise. "Do you believe me now?"

He hesitated for only a moment. "Yes, Mariah, I believe you. Especially your story about moldy bread." He leaned forward and gathered her into his arms.

Mariah hated feeling helpless, but her body wasn't cooperating with her urge to get out of bed and do something. At least not quickly enough to suit her.

But her wounds were healing. When Holly removed the dressings, Mariah dared to glance down at the ugly, torn area that was scabbing over. Reddish, but not infected, thank heavens. She wished she had some aspirin, but the pain was a dull ache that she could tolerate.

She'd had no idea whether moldy bread could help at all, but she knew mold was the basis for penicillin. Her improvement might have had nothing to do with the "medicine" she'd prescribed for herself. Or it might have cured her.

She slept a lot. She wasn't sure how long she'd actually lain there in Thorn's bed till one morning, when she asked René.

"Not long, Mademoiselle Mariah, for such serious wounds to heal."

"How long?" she repeated grumpily, tired of being coddled.

"About six days," he said, and then he left the room.

Mariah settled back on the bed. That meant she had been there six nights, too. Nights during which Thorn had insisted on staying at her side, sleeping in an uncomfortable chair.

It was, after all, his house. But there were other beds in which he could have slept.

He'd wanted to be with her; the idea made her insides sing.

That first morning, when she'd regained consciousness, she had been amazed to see his dark hair spread across the sheet beside her waist. She'd studied it for a long moment, more closely than ever before. It was richly brown, mostly dark as the richest teak yet sun-bleached at the top to a lighter redwood. It was straight and uneven, and the most adorable head of hair she had ever seen.

She had needed to touch it, and so she had, awakening Thorn.

He'd pretended to be crabby, but she could sense his relief that she was awake. He seemed glad to see her.

She'd been amazed and delighted when he'd admitted he finally believed she'd come from the future.

And when he'd left later, after Holly returned, Mariah had closed her eyes and remembered a dream she'd had while unconscious. A dream in which Thorn had promised her mold and earthworms and shoe scrapings . . . and had said he'd loved her.

Delirium certainly made one's imagination run wild, she thought.

"I heard you were awake." The rich, British-tinged voice made her smile, especially when she looked up to see the large, beloved body of Thorn filling the doorway.

"René's such a tattler." She crossed her arms behind her head. She wished she had a mirror—but better that she didn't. She knew she'd hate what she saw. "I thought I'd just laze around here for the rest of my life. It's pleasant for a servant to have the tables turned, after all, and have the master of the inn serve *her*."

"A maid as sassy as you will not long have anyone at her beck and call." He crossed the room and towered above her.

There was a smile in his voice, and his soft brown eyes twinkled.

"Is that so? Well, what if I plan a relapse?"

His mouth curved down, and his brows furrowed. "Do not do that." He sat on the bed beside her and took both of her hands in his. "I do not think I could bear that, Mariah."

His kiss was gentle, reverent, as though she had become a distant and respected relative.

But she felt better. Much better. She pulled her hands away and threw her arms around him, ignoring the resultant pain at her right shoulder. Her lips opened against his, and she boldly thrust her tongue inside the sweet, waiting cavern of his mouth. His tongue was waiting, and for a long, wonderful moment they played teasing games with one another that made Mariah's body ache in places that had nothing to do with her wounds.

But then he drew back. "I am sorry, Mariah. This cannot be good for your healing."

"It's wonderful for my healing. The best medicine I could get."

"Except for bread mold."

"Except for bread mold," she agreed, pulling him toward her once more.

But their kiss was interrupted by the clearing of someone's throat. Thorn pulled away and glared at René, who stood in the doorway.

"*Pardonez-moi.*" Though the light was behind his head, Mariah could see that his large eyes studied the floor, and his squat, compact body swayed, as though he were ill at ease.

"Oh, Frenchie, no need to be embarrassed," came a female voice from behind him. He stumbled slightly, as though he'd been shoved into the room, and Holly appeared. She was dressed in Mariah's pink dress with the scarf tucked about the neck. "We're all friends here, we are." She came closer, then leered up at Thorn. "Making sure our patient has no more fever, are we? Or are we causing a new one?" She laughed.

Mariah glanced at Thorn. Once, he might have frowned

or stormed from the room. Now, he smiled and said, "Not yet, but maybe as soon as I'm sure she needs no more bread mold."

"That's what we came here for, isn't it, René?" Mariah noticed that Holly no longer mispronounced the Frenchman's name on purpose. In fact, she seemed to say it as a caress, and René shot her a tender grin.

"We need more flour," he agreed, looking at Thorn. "Our bread supply must be replenished since we turned it all into mold."

"We think Mariah's well enough that you can look after her for a few days," Holly said.

"Where will you be?" asked Thorn.

"We will go tomorrow to a trading post," René said.

"Harrigan's?" The word slipped from Mariah's mouth. Thorn's back was toward her, and she saw his shoulders freeze. But he knew now that Pierce was no one for him to be jealous of.

But he also knew, she reminded herself, that if Pierce was who she said he was, he had something to do with her being here.

And something to do with when she'd leave.

A frisson of delight fluttered through her. Maybe Thorn cared whether she stayed or left.

She wasn't sure now what she wanted herself. But she was certain that she had to see Pierce again. Make sure she understood why he'd sent her here.

Get his help in preventing the duel, though maybe Thorn's having rescued Will Shepherd with her was enough. Maybe Will would have determined that he really didn't want to kill the man who'd saved his life.

"Perhaps Harrigan's," René agreed. "Or perhaps we will go to Pittsborough." He was looking at Thorn as though for a cue. As the inn's owner seemed to relax, so did René. "I believe Pittsborough more likely."

That was all right, Mariah thought. What she needed from Pierce could not be sent as a message with a couple of friends.

Although it would help if someone would tell the ugly old son of a gun that she demanded to see him.

But who could say if he was still at Harrigan's after all this time?

Besides, whether or not the duel was the "grievous wrong" Pierce had sent her to right, she was going to right it anyway.

She looked at the wall where Thorn's old uniform still hung and sighed.

"What are you doing?"

The raised voice from the doorway startled Mariah, and she grabbed for the bed to keep from falling. "I'm getting up on my own for a change, that's what."

"Here, I'll help."

"Not with this, you won't." She glanced significantly toward the chamber pot that stood in all its ugly pottery glory beside the foot of the bed. She was still mortified that, during her fever, people she cared about had had to change the bed clothes beneath her, but since she'd begun to heal Holly had helped her in and out of bed to take care of necessities. Even that was embarrassing for someone accustomed to using flush toilets without assistance.

But now Holly and René were gone, left early that morning for the trading post. They'd insisted on waiting to make sure Mariah was healing, not leaving until two days after they'd begun talking of their trip.

"All right," Thorn agreed, his deep voice meek from his own discomfort. "I will leave you alone."

But before he left, Mariah said, "There's one thing I would like you to help me with."

"What's that?"

"I need a bath. Will you accompany me to the stream later? I'm nervous about going there alone."

He appeared shocked. "Washing is not good for a convalescing person."

"In my time, we know that bathing is essential in the healing process. People have learned the importance of sanitation."

"You must miss your time very much." Thorn's voice sounded sad as he left the room.

She could have called after him to deny it, but she couldn't . . . not entirely.

In her own time, if she'd been shot, she'd have been popped right into the hospital and treated with antibiotics and painkillers.

She probably wouldn't have been shot at all.

But in her own time, she would not have met Thorn.

Although she felt light-headed and sore, she'd no trouble taking care of herself. When she got back into bed, she sat upright, utterly bored. She looked around. Now and then, Thorn's squirrel had appeared in the house, looking for a handout. It had provided a diversion during her recuperation. But it wasn't there now.

She dressed and left the room.

Thorn was in the kitchen, which was full of delightful cooking aromas. Another good sign of her recovery, Mariah thought. She must be hungry.

Thorn's eyes lit up when he saw her, and she smiled—until he frowned once more. "Mariah, what are you doing? You must stay in bed, get your energy back."

"Well, I can't dance the lambada yet, but—"

"Another invention of your time?"

"Close enough." She sank onto a bench at one of the worktables. "I'm feeling much better. But I'll just watch for a while, okay?"

"All right." He ladled a bowl of broth from a kettle on the trammel and put it in front of her. It smelled wonderful, and she devoured it quickly. "Mmmm—no mold. Is there any more?"

His grin crinkled the corners of his eyes. "You must be feeling better. If you're ready to skin a rabbit, I'll go hunt some fresh meat."

Mariah placed the back of her hand dramatically on her forehead. "Oh," she moaned, "I'm feeling so faint." She let herself fall forward just a little, then grinned up at him.

He gently tweaked her nose. "All right, Miss Walker. I

believe that if I'm ever to get you well, I must skin animals myself."

"You got it, buster," Mariah agreed. At his puzzled expression, she rephrased, "Absolutely, Mr. Thorn," and they laughed together.

He served them stew from another pot hanging above the fire and sat down beside her. "I am ready to hear about your time. Tell me of its wonders."

A lock of dark hair hung over his forehead, and his soft brown eyes regarded her keenly.

"Well . . . where to begin?" She told first of the Declaration of Independence, the Revolutionary War and the young country's struggle to establish a democratic government. Recalling his early military career, she continued with the War of 1812. "We're not a particularly peaceable country," she admitted, "but we're still the best in the world." Then she went through the western migration, the Indian wars and Civil War. Counting on her fingers, she enumerated the wars of the twentieth century, from World War I to the Gulf War. "The way fighting methods changed is amazing." She described airplanes and jets and Stealth bombers, automatic weapons and atomic bombs.

His eyes stayed wide. "It is a wonder," he said, "that anyone is alive in your time to tell about such awesome weapons."

She sighed. "There's more nasty stuff, too, like pollution, and tears in the ozone layer and global warming." He placed his hand over hers on the table, as though sharing her distress as she explained. "Lots of endangered animal and plant species, too. That's one great thing about being here; it's so untouched. But there are good parts of my time, too. Movies, for example, like the one whose screenplay brought me here."

"Ah, yes. Tell me of that."

She did, plus electricity, television, telephones and computers, automatic washing machines and dryers and microwave ovens.

He shook his head as though to clear it. "If I had not vowed to believe what you said, I would think you the most imaginative person to ever walk the earth.'' He paused. ''You are not simply joking with me, are you?''

She shook her head, then watched in dismay as Thorn's mouth tightened and a stony expression returned to his eyes. ''What's wrong?'' she asked.

''With all you have left behind, you must hate it here and yearn for your return.'' He stood, turning his back to her. Beneath his ecru shirt, his broad shoulders were stiff.

''There are things I have here that I don't there.'' She kept her voice soft as she touched his back.

''What?''

''Well, the sense of accomplishment I feel each time I learn a new skill essential to living. In my time, people would perish if their conveniences disappeared.''

''As yours did when you came here.''

She nodded. ''Also, in the future, people are so busy with their lives that they've little time for one another. Friendship is hard to find. People here . . . well, you care about one another. And that's something not all the technological wonders in the world can replace.''

The look he turned on her was so tender that her eyes teared. ''You were lonely.'' She nodded. ''People in this time can be lonely, too.''

''I know.'' Lost in the depths of his eyes, she wanted to throw herself into his arms. She ached to smooth away the furrow between his dark brows, to stroke the hollows of his cheeks where the shadow of his beard appeared beneath his tanned skin, to outline the edges of his parted lips with her fingertips.

Oh, yes. There were things here she could not replace in her own time.

But he turned away quickly. ''You wished for me to guard you while you bathed. Perhaps this would be a good time.''

''Sure.'' But Mariah felt hurt. She'd thought he'd been about to kiss her, but instead he'd withdrawn.

He kept silent watch behind her as they ventured to the stream. He carried his long rifle, Mariah her towel and some of the soap Holly had made, pink and scented with raspberries.

Mariah remained alert to every sound: the summer breeze rustling the leaves of the oaks and hickories; the distinctive calls of robins, blue jays and crows; a squirrel's scolding; the rushing sounds as they neared the stream.

Thorn followed her along the water till she reached the noisy falls. "Here," she said. He nodded.

She hesitated, her heart beginning to hammer in her chest. What if the Indians returned? What if—

"I will keep watch, Mariah," Thorn said, as though reading her mind. He reddened, apparently realizing that what he'd said could have more than one meaning. "Not upon you, of course. You shall have your privacy. But I will permit nothing to intrude on your bathing. Nothing."

His vehemence reassured her. She watched as he walked to the rim of the sheltering trees and kept his back turned. She still found a bush behind which to remove her clothing, her eyes never leaving the comforting steadiness of his set shoulders, the long rifle barrel gripped in his sturdy fingers.

She left on her plain white chemise, just in case of trouble. She still felt nervous out here, half expecting, after her terrifying experiences, that Indians or marauders lurked behind every tree. If she had to run, she wanted to have on some piece of apparel.

She didn't doubt for an instant, though, that Thorn would protect her. Not any longer. No matter how much he protested, she knew better now. She could—and did—rely on him.

She waded into the water at the shoreline. It was cold! To get used to it, she knelt and plunged into the shallow water, gasping as the chilly wetness closed over her body.

Standing again, she picked her way carefully over the rocks and oozing mud of the bottom, and ducked beneath the waterfall to finish wetting her hair. She lathered it as best she could with the hard, fruity soap, then rinsed. When she had finished with her hair, she moved away from the flow and ran the hard, fruity soap along her arms.

She glanced at Thorn. He hadn't moved, except to lift his head, as though he was listening. She smiled, continuing to wash but keeping her eyes on him.

She realized that the light chemise wouldn't provide much covering if she had to flee—not when wet. It fit rather like a second skin, leaving nothing much to the imagination.

What would Thorn think if he turned and saw her like this? The idea felt deliciously enticing, and a lazy warmth eddied up through her body.

But he wouldn't, she knew. He was too honorable.

She untied her chemise at the neck and pulled it away so she could strip away the bandages and examine her wounds.

Though still red, they seemed to be healing well. She bathed them carefully, as she did the rest of her body.

Again, she looked toward the spot where Thorn stood.

He was gone!

The iciness Mariah felt had nothing to do with the temperature of the water. Where was Thorn?

He wouldn't have left her. Not voluntarily. Had someone sneaked up, attacked him?

Was he lying somewhere on the bank, hurt? Dead?

A terrified sound welled up in her throat. Without thinking, she dashed toward the shore. She hardly felt the hardness of the stones she stepped upon, stubbing her toes. She felt as though she moved in slow motion, the water about her legs impeding her progress.

"Thorn," she whispered, barely able to hear herself above the noise of the disturbed water. "Thorn!" Her voice rang out.

He tore from the forest, his rifle readied and his head bent as he sighted along it. He aimed it first at one side of her, then the other. "What is it?" His shout was muffled as he kept his head down. "Mariah, what is wrong?"

She reached the shore and ran to him, half crying in her terror. "You!" she cried. "I couldn't find you, and I was afraid something had happened."

"I was patrolling to ensure your solitude." His eyes flicked alertly from one side to the other, but he lowered his rifle. "You saw nothing that frightened you? Heard nothing?"

"No," she admitted. She was out of breath, and adrenaline coursed through her, syncopating her wild pulse rate. Studying his face, she saw his own fear written there. "Is everything all right?" She needed to touch him for reassurance but didn't dare; the last thing he'd need to protect them both was a clinging woman.

He held up his hand for quiet, seeming to concentrate on their surroundings. Then he looked down at her. "Everything is fine," he said, "as long as you are unharmed."

His eyes moved over her, from head to foot, and the alarm written in them appeared to segue to another stormy emotion that Mariah did not, at first, understand. Not until she looked down at herself. She had forgotten, for a moment, the way her chemise clung, leaving her no secrets. Her breasts were boldly outlined, the nipples erect and straining.

"Oh," she said quietly. She felt a pulsation way below that made her sway on her feet, and the heat that flooded her had little to do with the sun that beat upon the water.

He grabbed her beneath the arm as though to steady her, and the supportive touch made her even more wobbly instead. She wanted to throw herself into his arms, to make him chase away her terrors, to kiss him until kissing was no longer enough. . . .

"Mariah, have you finished bathing?" His voice was hoarse, his British accent even more pronounced.

"Y-yes," she stammered.

"Good," he said. "Then it is time to return to the inn."

She grabbed her clothes from where she'd left them, neatly folded, upon the ground. She threw on her blouse and skirt, heedlessly bunching her petticoats under her arm. She stepped into her boots without bothering to don stockings first.

She stared into Thorn's face, finding his smoldering glance locked upon her eyes, as though he knew better than to look below, as though the blouse provided no barrier to his ability to see what was under it.

"Come," he said.

His arm was around her as they hurried, side by side, along the uneven dirt trail through the woods. Mariah's unsteadiness was balanced by the unerring pace of Thorn beside her, and she looked more at him than at where she was going.

His eyes, too, did not stay on the forest path. Mariah caught his gaze over and over. She'd have to use the smoldering in the depths of his brown eyes next time she needed to resuscitate the inn's banked hearth fire; it sure did the job of stoking her own inner blaze.

He led her through the gate in the palisade wall and bolted it behind them. He guided her within the compound to the door of his sturdy stone home. "Will you come inside, Mariah?" he whispered, his chest rising and falling beneath his pale shirt as his breathing betrayed how much he cared about her answer.

Her smile was unsteady. "Just try to keep me out," she replied.

Chapter Twenty

He kicked the wooden door closed behind them. Mariah stood uncertainly. What did he want her to do?

What did *she* want to do? Oh, that was easy. She glanced toward the bed in which she'd spent so much time over the past weeks—alone. She had been so eager to leave it. Now . . .

She started as he buried his hand beneath her hair and gently squeezed her neck. She looked up and found him also staring at the bed, an anguished expression deepening the lines around his eyes. Then he turned that same tortured look on her. "Are you feeling well, Mariah? Is there still any pain? If only I could have taken the bullet instead—"

"Nonsense," she interrupted softly, smoothing the furrow between his brows with her fingertip. "You were busy saving all our lives. I don't know how to use your blasted gun; that was your job. If I had to distract those crooks by getting shot, well—"

"Shut up, Mariah." But he didn't need to say it; his lips on hers did the job.

His kiss was tentative at first. So was the way he held her, as though she had turned into a fragile thing. But gentleness wasn't what she wanted. She deepened the kiss, drawing him closer with her own eager fingers wound in the soft nest of his hair.

He cupped her jaw in his hands. His mouth did not stay still and pliable upon hers but roved over her face, her eyelids, her chin, and along the sensitive softness at her throat. She moaned, and he sucked the sound into his own mouth as his hands tugged at the buttons of her blouse. She helped him undo them, then felt the material and the thin chemise below disappear. Somehow, the mattress was beneath her, and she lay back onto the bed.

Her breasts were bared to him, and she slitted her eyes open sufficiently to see how his gaze devoured her. His hands cupped her, squeezing just enough to cause her nipples to spring up to meet his lips. She gasped at the sensation that shot flames through her, causing her hips to writhe.

"I'm so sorry, Mariah," he said, and she felt him touch the healing wound at her shoulder. The minor pain that remained there was nothing like the yearning ache that spread throughout her, and she gently removed his hand, kissing its heel and placing it back on her chest.

"I'm fine, Thorn. Or I will be, if . . ."

She didn't finish, but he got the message. His hands stroked where she had placed them, then forged a path downward, over her belly and beneath her skirt, till she felt him urge her legs farther apart, exploring her. "Oh, Thorn," she murmured, rising enough to allow him to remove her skirt and to grant him freer access.

But his touches were not enough. She opened her eyes to find that he was still fully clothed. "Hey," she protested, pushing him gently away.

And then it was her turn to fumble with clothing, to pull it away and touch and taunt and investigate. To inhale his masculine aroma, to taste the saltiness where his skin was smooth and where it was covered with hair. The territory had been explored before, but that made it no less exciting. His enjoyment was obvious in the rasping of his breath, the swell of his arousal. She held him in her hand, rubbing his length and establishing a rhythm that made him groan.

He pulled away then, but only long enough to draw himself on top of her. He remained still at first, as though afraid he was hurting her. "Please," she whispered, her hands at his hips.

That was all the encouragement he needed. He entered her, taking up the rhythm that she had started and adding to it a more powerful one of his own until her gasps became small moans and, quite suddenly, she exploded into a galaxy of sensation. She heard his cry as he gripped her sides, and he, too, climaxed.

He lay on top of her as his breathing quieted. Though she became aware of the slight throbbing of the wounds at her shoulder, his weight was wonderful on her, and she held him tightly against her.

But soon he rolled off her. They lay on their sides. Her chest nearly touched his, and she ran her fingertips up the crisp line of hair between his pectorals.

He caught her hand and brought it to his mouth. She felt his lips kiss it ever so gently, and then he held her hand against his cheek. She gazed into his brown eyes and found them looking at her with sweet, caring intensity.

She couldn't help it. She had to tell him how she felt. "I love you, Thorn." She braced herself for him to pull away, to give her excuses and disclaimers. To tell her how foolish she was.

But he didn't. Instead, he squeezed her hand all the more tightly to him. "I love *you*, Mariah."

Thorn could hardly believe the bliss he felt with Mariah. They spent the next days together, learning more of each other's minds and bodies, making love with an abandon he had never imagined. His happiness grew to such a magnitude that he felt as though he had taken wing on one of her machines of the future and soared to paradise.

They left his home to eat now and then. The fire in the inn went out, but they dined on meat from the smokehouse and fresh beans and carrots from the garden Mariah had tended with Holly.

But not moldy bread. "I've had enough of that for a lifetime," Mariah insisted.

He kept the palisade gate bolted; the last thing he wanted was the imposition of guests.

Not even guilt intruded on his euphoria. He had mentioned it one of the first times they had lain in bed, sated and catching their breaths, but Mariah had become angry, sitting up stark naked with her hands on her hips. If that was the way women of the future were, lovely and uninhibited by false modesty, he nearly wished he had been born then.

Except he needed no other woman from the future. He had Mariah.

"Don't you ever, ever tell me again that I can't rely on you," she'd raged at him. "Don't you realize that each time you've told me that, you've saved my life?"

"But—" he'd tried to say.

"That very first time we met, you turned your back, but when I hadn't the foggiest what to do with your rifle, you used it and scared off those bums."

"I should have killed them then," he fumed.

"Maybe. But you killed one when it really mattered."

"But you were shot."

"And I'd have been dead if you hadn't gotten them first. Thorn, don't you dare contradict me." She'd put her hand across his mouth, and he'd watched her with amusement as she tugged the sheet over herself, her lovely green eyes scowling at him. "You saved me from Nahtana, not once but twice. And those wolves. All the time you said you weren't dependable, all those times I tried to save myself, *you* came through. Do you understand?"

"Yes," he'd said meekly, trying to keep the laughter out of his voice. "I understand."

And he believed her—almost. Maybe he had learned something in his exile to the wilderness. For this woman, perhaps, he had learned reliability.

But there was still that other woman he had failed. Who had died. As had those he had failed in England, his own kin.

And would Mariah be reliable for him? He wondered

about that often. She had come from the future. Would she stay?

On the third day on which they had been alone together, Thorn showed Mariah how to make bullets from molten lead. He never let his ammunition get too low, and he would soon need an additional supply. Mariah's eagerness to learn the skills of this day seemed boundless.

Her concentration on the task caused her to bend her head forward so he had to smooth her soft waves from her face for fear she would get lead in her hair.

Her sweet lips pouted until she looked up at him. The smile she gave him made him throb beneath his breeches, and it was all he could do not to reach for her and pull her toward the bed.

Bed. They had spent much time there, and as glorious as their experiences were, they caused him concern, too.

He leaned forward across his worktable and said, "You realize, Mariah, that I have accepted that you come from the future."

"I know." Her voice was delighted. "Isn't it amazing?" She looked back down in concentration to the molds she was filling.

"Do women from the future . . ." He sought for a way to phrase the matter delicately. "Here, when a man and a woman are together the way we are, the woman may get with child."

"In my time, too, unless they're using protection." Mariah looked up. "Things sometimes fail even then. But don't worry. You don't have to feel responsible if I get pregnant. I thought about it after the first time we made love, too, though nothing happened then. In any event, I chose to go to bed with you, and I'll handle the situation, if it occurs."

"I do not wish for you to 'handle the situation,' " Thorn found himself saying. "Mariah, are you staying here, in this time? I wish . . . I wish to marry you."

Her small jaw dropped. "Oh, Thorn," she whispered. He saw tears puddle in her wide green eyes. "You don't know how much I want to say yes. But I don't know whether I'll be able to stay. The screenplay—well, you know it's different from reality. Matilda and her Thorn didn't have a happy ending, but that was because he . . . he died. Even though you won't fight in that dratted duel and that damned grievous wrong will finally be righted, I don't know whether I'll have a choice about staying."

The idea of losing her caused a wall of pain to slam him in the gut. He said slowly, "But you would stay if you had a choice?" He did not give her the opportunity to answer, for his mind focused on the rest of what she had said. "The duel. You believe I will not fight against Will Shepherd."

"You told me he was the boy who was stolen all those years ago, and that he blames you for his mother's death. You saved his life. You're even now. And besides, even if he still calls you out for a duel, you told me you wouldn't fight."

She looked at him sidelong beneath her lovely, long lashes. Her smile was bright. Perhaps too bright, for she seemed to know his reply before he spoke it.

"I only said I would fight no duel if I could avoid it." He kept his voice soft, and he watched his hands as he worked the cooling bullets within his fingers. "If he challenges me still, Mariah, I will fight."

"But you *can* avoid it! You shouldn't—you can't—"

"I let that boy be stolen. His mother's death resulted from that. If he wishes to fight with me, I will fight. But I will not hurt him."

He felt the stillness beside him. Mariah had stopped working. She even seemed to be holding her breath. "You'd let him kill you?" she finally asked, her voice barely audible.

"If that were what he wanted. But first, you and I will marry, so that if you should be with child, the babe will have a name."

She pushed off from the table so quickly that two of the molds fell off and top and bottom separated. The nearly set lead balls rolled along the floor.

"You damned primitive woodsman!" she shouted. "Go ahead and kill yourself, if that's what you want. That'll follow the screenplay. It won't right the cursed 'grievous wrong,' but I'll let Pierce worry about that. If I'm pregnant, the baby will have a name: mine. And, if you think I'd stay in this wilderness without even a decent bathtub, you're even more foolish than I thought. I could only be interested in a man who's reliable to *me,* not just to some antique, self-destructive sense of what's right. I want to go home. To *my* time, when chivalry, thank heavens, is dead!"

She stalked from his house, slamming the door behind her.

Mariah sat on her bed in her room in the stable. It was the first time she had been there in a couple of weeks—since she'd been wounded.

Why, she wondered, had she ever admitted she loved Thorn?

Oh, the fact she'd told *him*—well, that didn't matter. Much.

What really hurt, though, was that, all those weeks ago, she'd admitted it to herself. And now he'd said he loved her, too. But he would do nothing to stop this foolishness.

One way or another, she was going to lose him.

Most likely, he was going to die.

If she were only able to return to her time before then, she could always delude herself into thinking that his life wasn't really cut short in his prime. That Will Shepherd came to his senses, even if Thorn never did, and never called him out in a duel. That Thorn died a crotchety old man, here at his inn.

She threw back her head, closed her eyes and called out, "Pierce, I've had enough. Come and get me. Send me home."

She opened her eyes and looked around. Nothing, of course. She was still alone.

She listened. No sounds other than the restless stamping of the single horse in the stable next door.

Pulling her piece of paper from beneath the mattress, she stared at it. Maybe there was a clue in her recollections.

But nothing jumped out at her. Except her memorialization of that hideous duel.

To think that she was beginning to like it here, in this time. To feel, almost, that she had finally found a home.

People who cared about her. A place she really enjoyed being.

Never mind that it hadn't all the luxuries she'd come to expect.

It had Thorn.

But it wouldn't have him forever. And so she had to leave. Now. Before she saw him die.

She had a hard time falling asleep that night. She kept visualizing the duel scene in the screenplay. Trying to recall the dialogue.

Seeing how Matilda wept when it was over.

"Where are you, Matilda?" she whispered aloud. "I'm ready to give you your life back." Though she didn't really wish that heartache on anyone. Least of all herself.

Of course Matilda didn't answer. And Mariah finally slept.

Mariah was cooking supper late the next afternoon when she heard voices outside in the compound. Frightened at first, she pulled up a corner of the paper at the kitchen window.

There, standing beside the roan horse that had been in the stable, was the skinny trapper with the goat's beard, Thorn's friend Ambrose. He *was* alive. Mariah smiled. Thorn was undoubtedly thrilled.

Not that she cared about his feelings. Not any more than he cared about hers.

She hurried out to greet them—and to get more food from the smokehouse. She was, after all, still a servant here. She had work to do.

Ambrose had brought others with him. For the next few hours, Mariah had no time to dwell on her anger with Thorn or her fear for him. She was too busy catering to their guests.

She cooked the hearty meal herself. Though it consisted of the usual smoked meats, hominy and vegetables from Holly's garden, she was thrilled that everything came out just right. She was learning how to get along well in this time—right when she wanted to leave it the most.

Ambrose insisted that she sit at the table with him to eat. "I want to hear your tale of woe caused by those miserable ruffians who attacked me," he said.

Mariah smiled cordially. "I'd much rather hear your story," she said, not looking at Thorn, who sat with them.

Between huge bites of food washed down by hearty swigs of ale, Ambrose orated. His version of the saga made him sound like a conquering hero rather than the loser in a fight in which he'd been conked on the head.

Soon Thorn was the center of attention, describing how he had saved Mariah and the others from the Indians, only to be caught up immediately in the fight to save his inn. He responded with no reticence, laughing heartily along with the others.

Mariah compared him with the man she'd first met, who joined his guests for meals only on the insistence of his friend and employee, René. Who'd listened more than talked, and seldom, if ever, laughed.

He seemed to be changing—like the Thorn in the screenplay, who'd shunned other people but gradually became reacclimated to his society.

Just in time to die in the duel.

She'd had something to do with the change in Thorn, she thought. She hadn't let him get away with his moody avoidance of people any more than René had. She'd insisted that he hire her, and Holly, too. She'd been friendly to their guests, and some of it had probably rubbed off on him.

Alone in the kitchen later, washing the dishes, she wondered if she should just have left him alone.

Mariah was delighted when Holly and René returned late the next morning, though she'd already spent the time since dawn feeding their guests, seeing them off, then cleaning up the inn.

She was glad, at least, until she saw their grim faces.

"We were at Pittsborough," Holly told Mariah as they stood in the kitchen, putting away goods the two had brought.

Thorn walked in just then with René, the two carrying a barrel of flour. Mariah looked away as Thorn tried to catch her eye.

"Now is not the time to speak of this, Holly." René cast

a glance toward Mariah that made it clear she was not to hear.

"She needs to know," argued Holly. She sashayed her buxom body toward Thorn and planted herself before him. "Thorn, we were told to deliver a message to you, though I don't—"

René cut in. "It is a message you must not heed. But it is from that young man Will, the one you saved from the savages."

"It was a strange message, it was," cut in Holly. "He said he is ready."

Thorn's eyes were directed straight toward Mariah. He had no expression on his face and spoke calmly. "So am I."

A light rain splattered into countless concentric circles on the surface of the swiftly flowing Ohio. Mariah sat on the same crosswise slat of the pirogue that she had used for the last trip upriver, ignoring the beautifully forested hillsides beyond the banks they passed. She recalled how pampered she had felt on the earlier trip, the lady of leisure being rowed up the river.

Now, she felt numb.

Once more she watched Thorn's back as he knelt in the prow, wielding the oars. His strength had to be even greater than she had imagined, for he managed to move the boat swiftly ahead, despite going against the rapid current fed by the storms of the last few days.

If only he were weaker. Though she couldn't yet see it, she knew they were not far from Pittsburgh. Water dripped from the wide brim of Thorn's hat and onto the leather coat he wore against the weather. Mariah had finally resorted to wearing a cap, but it offered little protection from the drizzle. She pushed it back from her forehead, exposing some of her damp waves, and looked up into the sullen gray sky. No break in the clouds at all. The sky was doing its best to reflect her dismal mood.

She straightened the damp skirt of her pink dress. She'd worn it to try to cheer her, but it wasn't succeeding. Not at all.

Thorn's shoulders were squared, the way they had been all morning. Since their latest argument, before breakfast, he hadn't said more than two words to her.

But she'd insisted, despite everything, on coming along.

"I have to be there," she'd argued as she set the trencher of porridge on the puncheon table in the common room for the four of them: Thorn, Holly, René and her. "If that damned duel is the 'grievous wrong' I'm supposed to right and I fail, I may never get home. Though I can't reason with you, maybe there's a chance I can succeed with Will."

"If he has come back to this area solely to extract his revenge, nothing you can say will convince him otherwise," Thorn said calmly.

"I have to try!"

In the end, he'd given in. And now she regretted it. She could have stayed at the inn with Holly and René. They could have waited till word came from the fort about the outcome of the duel, and . . .

No! She sat up straight so vehemently that the boat rocked, and Thorn shot an irritated glance over his shoulder.

"Sorry," she called. But she wasn't sorry. Not at all.

She would convince Will Shepherd he was wrong. She would stop the duel.

Somehow.

They turned a bend in the river, and her heart stopped for an instant. She couldn't see the town or the fort in the distant mist, but she knew they were there. Thorn and she would be there much too soon.

"Thorn," she called impulsively over the sound of the rushing water.

He looked over his shoulder. There was a sheen on his face from the dampness, a hollow resignation in his eyes.

She swallowed hard, wanting to scurry toward him in the pirogue and rest her head against his back, beg him to turn around.

Instead, she said, "How much longer?"

"Are you growing eager?" His attempt at a smile was futile, succeeding only in moving one corner of his otherwise set lips.

She scowled. "Forget it."

She looked ahead of them again and saw an outline in the mist: the rising embankment sheltering the sparse buildings of the town and, beyond, the earthen ramparts of Fort Pitt.

"Oh, no," she whispered to herself, running her chilled fingers along her throat.

In what seemed like moments, they rounded the edge of the Point and pulled up to the bank where they'd landed before. It was a muddy mess now. The water was much higher, and Thorn had to drag the pirogue a distance to protect it from floating away.

What did that matter now? He wouldn't need it to return to the inn. Neither would Mariah. No matter what happened here, she would remain in this town—or, if she could find that blasted Pierce, go home.

While Thorn was distracted with the boat, Mariah used the opportunity to hurry up the sodden path. This time, she didn't head for town but directly for the fort.

She passed the closest bastion, then climbed into the small raised island she'd been told was the West Ravelin. She crossed the wooden drawbridge, noting that the rain had elevated the river and that the moat called the "Isthmus" was, for the first time that she'd seen, filled. The guard at the far end was the same man she'd seen when she'd arrived in this time: young and homely, with pockmarked skin. His tricornered hat held a small puddle of water. He held a rifle at his side, one less cherished than Thorn's, judging by its lack of polish on the wooden barrel and the dullness of the metal firing mechanism.

"State your business, miss," came his voice in its coarse British accent.

"I . . . I'm here to see a soldier named Will Shepherd. Please hurry. It's important." She glanced down the path she'd taken. Fortunately, she didn't see Thorn, but she knew it would not take him long to catch up.

The guard looked dubious. "If you tell me what you want with Shepherd, I can find out if he—"

"Sergeant Ainsley, then. He's a friend of mine." He was a friend of Thorn's. He surely would want to know about the travesty about to occur—and to stop it. "Tell him it's about Thorn. I need to talk to him right away."

"All right, miss."

The guard hurried across the bridge and in moments was replaced by an older soldier who said, "Private Root went to find the sergeant, miss. I'm here filling in."

Mariah looked around nervously. Thorn was striding up the mud path, nearly at the base of the ravelin. "See the man behind me? I need to get inside the fort without his following. Can you help?"

"Is he bothering you, miss?"

"Yes," she said firmly.

"Miss Walker! Welcome." Ainsley came to the bridge to greet her, a broad smile revealing his uneven teeth and crinkling his small, deep-set eyes. His uniform looked perfect, as though he'd just donned it for a special occasion: red coat, beige breeches, high black boots and a tricornered hat. "Thorn!" Ainsley cried, spotting his friend at the far end of the bridge. Thorn hurried toward them, and Ainsley grasped Thorn's shoulder as they shook hands.

Will Shepherd, also in full uniform, joined them at the end of the bridge. He did not meet her eye, or Thorn's, either. The young, bearded man stared straight ahead or at the ground, and he had apparently whipped himself into a fury, judging by the feral glint in his pale green eyes as he cast furious sidelong glances at Thorn.

Ainsley glanced behind him at Will. "My impulsive young subordinate, here, tells me—"

"I told him it was time!" Will broke in. "I am recuperated from the Indian attack and fully prepared to do what is necessary."

"What's necessary is—" Mariah began,

"Perhaps we should discuss things first," Ainsley interrupted, putting an arm around Thorn. He steered him through the gap in the fort's earthen walls and into the protected area.

"Good idea," Mariah called after them. "Maybe you can talk some sense into him." She planted herself in front of Will, who'd begun to follow. "Will, you can't go through with this. Thorn saved your life."

"But he took my mother's." He frowned, and Mariah noted again the fury in his eyes. "Now, if you will excuse me." He sidestepped around her and hurried after the other men.

Mariah did not intend to be left behind. She followed, holding her pink skirt off the ground so she didn't trip in the mud. But Ainsley and Thorn ducked inside a door into the dirt ramparts that surrounded the fort. Mariah was stopped from pursuing them by Maitland, who had apparently been waiting for them. The sharpness of his features seemed underlined by his broad, nasty grin. "So our brave Thorn is finally about to meet his comeuppance."

Swallowing her dislike for the man, Mariah asked as calmly as she could, "Aren't there laws against dueling?"

"Army regulations forbid such fights, of course, but who here is going to arrest young Shepherd? He just happens to have chosen a time when our commander, Captain Edmonstone, has gone east to confer about the Indian situation."

"What a coincidence." Mariah didn't attempt to hide her sarcasm. She glanced toward the door through which Thorn and Ainsley had disappeared. Shepherd paced outside. "What are they doing in there?"

"That is the way into the casemates, where we store weapons and ammunition. Thorn is choosing a weapon. It is the prerogative of the person challenged to a duel."

"He'd better select marshmallows at thirty paces," Mariah muttered.

Maitland looked puzzled, then asked, "May I see you to town, Miss Walker? Perhaps you can wait at Allen's trading post."

"Wait? Why?"

"Surely you do not wish to be present at the duel. Your friend Mr. Thorn's demise will not be a suitable sight for a lady to observe."

"What makes you think he'll lose?" Not that she wanted to see him kill Will Shepherd, but surely the more seasoned Thorn would be a better shot. If Thorn forgot his stupid sense of gallantry and defended himself.

"I have seen young Will practice for this event. He will

not lose. Besides . . .'' Maitland's tone turned snide. ''Under the circumstances, after Thorn's shirking of his duty caused the lad's mother to die, do you really believe he will defend himself fully? He has shown little sense of honor, but in this, he might redeem himself.''

The others expected him to be killed, too! Without defending himself! Mariah rounded on Maitland, her fists clenched. ''Don't you ever say such a thing. Thorn has more honor in his left eyebrow than the rest of you have in your whole darned fort. If you had any honor, you'd stop this travesty.''

Anger drove deep lines into Maitland's narrow face, but he turned away, his voice cold. ''Pardon me, Miss Walker.'' He clapped a hand on Will's shoulder as he passed. ''Good luck,'' he said. He shot a satisfied glance back at Mariah, then disappeared into the magazine.

Mariah's insides felt like chilled spaghetti. She had to stop this.

But how?

Back home, she'd worked her way up in the film industry from gofer to unit production manager. She'd learned to troubleshoot, to nogotiate the small production company's way into any size towns where they wanted to film, to negotiate out of costly, bothersome situations. One of her greatest skills was convincing people, creating win-win situations.

That was something she could do now.

She approached Will. His forehead shone beneath his tricorner hat, and his brow was knit sternly, as though he were worried. Good. ''So tell me,'' she said conversationally, ''supposing you kill Thorn, what are you planning for the rest of your life?''

The young man rubbed his mustache as he inhaled sharply. He glared at her. ''I plan to remain here as a soldier, of course.''

''But from what I gather, your whole focus for years has been on avenging your mother's death. Do you have any other goals?''

He looked puzzled.

She touched his uniform sleeve. "Come on. Can we go somewhere to talk?"

"To the confluence," he said. "I shall await Thorn there—if he dares to come."

The confluence. The Point. In her day, this whole area, Point State Park, had drawn her like a magnet. She'd sensed emotion here, and destiny.

If only she'd just gotten back on the plane, left Pittsburgh. Never finished reading the screenplay.

Never learned about Thorn.

But she had read about him. Met him, thanks to Pierce, that absent, interfering son-of-a-gun.

Fallen in love with him.

She'd yet to confront Pierce, to ask him what he meant by sending her here. By calling her his daughter.

But first, she'd a grievous wrong to right.

Chapter Twenty-one

"How do you get to the Point—the confluence—the fastest way?" Mariah asked Will Shepherd. Not that she wanted to arrive there quickly to hurry things along; just the opposite. Somehow, she had to get to Will, convince him to call off this tragedy in the making.

She inhaled deeply, not knowing what to do. She'd always been good at winging it in difficult negotiations as a unit production manager.

But she'd never been faced with a situation in which the outcome would be so critical—literally life or death.

Thorn's.

"The nearest way to the Point is over the Isthmus toward the West Ravelin," Will replied. "The same way you entered. But the duel will not be suitable for a woman to—"

"Show me, please. I just want to see where it will be." She glanced toward the casemate door. She heard nothing, saw nothing. Good. If she moved quickly, Thorn wouldn't see her talking to the young man.

And so what if he did? It was a free country. Or would be.

Will was already heading between the rows of barracks, and Mariah joined him, trying to ignore the squishiness of the mud beneath her boots, the slow raindrops that dampened her face. She held up the edges of her long pink skirt, for whatever good that did. "So, Will," she said, "I've been curious. Where did you spend all that time after you were kidnapped till you returned here? Were you brought up by Indians?"

His laugh was anything but humorous. "Even after our experience together, I nearly wish that were true. No, thanks to Thorn I was stolen away by my beloved grandfather." His tone oozed sarcasm. "He brought me up in Philadelphia."

"Your grandfather?" Astonishment slowed Mariah's steps, but only for an instant. She was careful not to lose her footing as she caught up.

"My father's father. He came after me, you see, after my father died and my mother ran away with me." Without slackening his pace, he looked at her with irritation scrunching his eyes. "I do not need to bore you with this unpleasant tale."

"I'm interested. Really. So why did your mother leave?"

This time his laugh sounded more like a bull's frenzied snort. "My father's family had money. My mother's—well, her father was the blacksmith who'd worked for my grandfather. The match was not one blessed by heaven—or my grandfather. He hated my mother, made her life hell. Even I recalled that. So when my father caught a fever and died, there was nothing for her there."

"How old were you?"

"I was eleven. The man of the family. I agreed with her decision to leave. I applauded it, for my grandfather was a stern and nasty old man, and I was delighted for the opportunity to get away. But neither of us counted on his determination. I was his only remaining heir, you see." His tone was bitter. He was walking faster now, as though he couldn't wait to get to their destination.

The place he'd kill Thorn.

Mariah's voice was shrill. "So he followed you here?"

They'd reached the drawbridge, and Mariah climbed onto

it behind Will. "Yes," said the young, bearded soldier. "But the evil old bastard—excuse me, miss—didn't want to confront my mother. She'd already gotten a job at the tavern, you see, and begun making friends. Instead, he sneaked around, waited for his chance." He paused and looked back at her, a sneer on his face. "Thorn made it easy for him. Grandfather probably waited till Thorn was the one in charge of guard duty; Ainsley told me Thorn already had a reputation for dereliction of duty."

Ainsley? Thorn's good friend? "What do you mean?"

But Will had already greeted the sentinel and headed over the flat bridge, his boots clumping on the wooden boards. The noisily flowing water in the ditch below was dirty brown.

On the other side, Mariah walked at Will's side on the mud-covered path along the Monongahela and past the buildings that made up the Low Town. Toward the Point.

A feeling of dread constricted Mariah's insides. The time approached much too quickly. She'd done nothing to stop the duel.

"Will," she said in desperation, "if your grandfather stole you away, don't you think he bears a little responsibility for what happened to your mother?"

"Of course." He turned a cold gaze on her. "Once he had me all to himself, he tried hard to raise me as a 'gentleman' patterned after him, though he was anything but a gentle man. He made quite an effort to eliminate what he called the taint of my mother's low blood. But I wanted nothing I had left of my mother eliminated. When I was old enough and escaped, I told Grandfather Porter just what I thought of him for all he'd done. I told him I was taking my mother's maiden name: Shepherd. And I told him I would never return."

Porter. Why did that name sound familiar . . . ? Of course! That was the name of the Pierce character in the screenplay, the one who had told Matilda she had to right the grievous wrong.

A pounding began in Mariah's temples. The past was intersecting with her present in a manner she didn't understand.

Pierce was Porter. This young man had been named Porter. Pierce had called her his daughter. Was she somehow related to Will?

Never mind that now. She had to think. "Will, did your mother ever call you Billy?"

Stopping in his tracks, he appeared startled. "How did you know that?"

"Never mind. But have you ever considered how she might feel if she knew you planned to kill Thorn?"

The drizzle had stopped again. Will removed his hat and shook it. Beads of water flew everywhere, some showering Mariah. But he looked agitated, as though trying to distract himself. "I've thought about it." He sounded defensive. "I remember Thorn from when we were here. My mother seemed to like him. Ainsley told me Thorn and my mother were . . . very close." He hesitated. "That might have been another reason my mother killed herself, Ainsley said: not only losing me, but finding out, too, that Thorn was nothing but a rake who'd let me be stolen while he flirted with another woman."

"I see. And Ainsley told you this?"

"Yes." Will restored his hat upon his head and walked again in the direction of the Point. It was close now. Much too close. "But Ainsley was reluctant, you understand. He did not wish to discuss anything from that time with me. Thorn is his friend."

Thorn's friend. Mariah's mind was racing. Thorn had told her that Ainsley had been his friend from childhood. But he fed Thorn's feelings of undependability. And he'd revealed to this young man things that encouraged him to hate Thorn.

What was going on?

She hadn't time to figure that out now. They had reached the confluence, the muddy triangle where the two swift-flowing, swollen rivers merged into the third.

The place where the duel was to occur. Thorn would die.

Mariah's heart beat a tempestuous, frightened rhythm inside her chest. He'd told her he loved her, but that hadn't been enough to keep him from coming here. Nor had her admitting her love for him.

She was furious with him for not listening to reason.

But she couldn't let him die.

Mariah looked up, praying for a miracle, but she didn't find it in the weather. Though clouds still scudded across the sky, a brilliant blue shone between them. Dampness hung in the air in the mud-lined spot where the rivers met at the Point, but the heavens no longer wept.

And Mariah—how could she keep herself from needing to cry, much too soon?

She tried to recall something, anything, from the screenplay to use to keep Will from proceeding with this travesty. "Will, what if I told you that, if you kill Thorn now, your soldiering career will be over?"

That hadn't been clear from the script, for the story ended right after the duel. It had been implied, however.

"It won't. Ainsley said he would protect me, if necessary. And others will understand, too, that I have to avenge my mother."

Ainsley again.

As if he'd heard her, he appeared in the distance with Thorn, on the path along the Monongahela. He carried a rectangular wooden box.

It had to contain Thorn's weapons of choice.

Why hadn't Will been there to observe the selection? He couldn't trust Thorn to pick something satisfactory.

Did he trust Ainsley?

But Ainsley was Thorn's friend.

She watched silently for minutes that passed in an instant as the two men hurried forward, proceeding much more quickly than she had done with Will.

Coming here, toward the Point. Toward the inevitable duel.

Mariah grasped for something to stop it, finally recalling what Will had last said. "How, Billy? How can Ainsley protect you?" She knew she sounded desperate now.

"He will make certain the captain understands. He has influence, you see."

"If he has so much influence," Mariah asked, "why is it he is only a sergeant?"

For the first time, Will appeared confused. Tilting his large hat, he bowed his head as though he were thinking, and he stroked the edges of his beard.

Thorn and Ainsley had nearly reached them. Had they heard her comment? Ainsley, as usual, was smiling, but the pulling of his narrow upper lip over his uneven teeth appeared almost like the unholy grimace of a death's head. There was no humor in his small serpent's eyes, either.

Too brightly, Mariah said to Thorn, "Did you know it was Billy's grandfather who stole him away? He's been living in Philadelphia all this time."

It was Thorn's turn to look confused. He turned toward Ainsley. Against the peacock garishness of the British uniform, Thorn looked tall and broad shouldered and stunningly handsome in the plainness of his white shirt and dark breeches. The leather coat he had worn for protection on their rainy trip upriver now hung from one shoulder, braced there by a strong hand.

How could Mariah bear to lose him?

He said to Ainsley, "I thought you told me the poor lad had led an unbearable existence all this time in the custody of savages."

The soldier shrugged. "That was what we had speculated all those years ago, was it not?"

"Yes, but—" Thorn stopped and gestured toward the solidly crafted box in Ainsley's hands. "What does it matter?"

"Indeed," agreed Will, who now stood by them. A breeze swirled, whipping up a soft mist at the surface of the rivers. Mariah looked around, feeling her breathing speed up and her toes grow icy. Thorn and Ainsley, Will and herself, stood near each other on the muddy triangle that formed the confluence, with the embankments of Fort Pitt looming beyond.

Mariah gnawed at her lower lip as Thorn lifted the lid of the box Ainsley held. Two long-barreled dueling pistols, with intricate silver swirls decorating the barrels, sat inside.

She tasted blood as she bit down too hard. This wasn't happening. She groped for something to stop it. Where was Pierce?

And Ainsley—why wasn't Thorn's friend stopping it?

Maybe she could find some common ground between the two warring men. "Thorn, Will tells me that his mother was a dear friend of yours. It must have hurt terribly when she died."

Thorn turned and said woodenly, "She was a fine woman." He reached a hand out to clasp Will's shoulder. "I never meant what happened then. If I could have taken your place—" He stopped and inhaled visibly. "I am more sorry, Will, than you will ever know. All these years, I envisioned you undergoing the torture of the damned by the Indians who had captured you. That image, along with finding your mother the way she was . . ." Agony constricted his features, and Will surprisingly, wonderfully, appeared sympathetic.

But only for an instant. "If you cared for her at all, why did you flaunt your interest in other women before her?"

Thorn's strong chin lifted as though he'd been struck. "Our relationship was not such that my courting other women, even if I had, should have mattered. But I did not. And I flaunted nothing." He hesitated, a look of sorrow darkening his features. "Did your mother tell you we were . . . close?"

Mariah could just see a new blanket of guilt hovering about his broad, though drooping shoulders. "No, she didn't," Mariah interjected brightly. "Will just told me he learned about his mother's interest in Thorn from Ainsley."

"Ainsley?" Thorn looked at the uniformed soldier beside him. "What did you know of Mary Porter's feelings?" His voice had a catch, as though he waited for a new blow. "Why did you not tell me?"

Porter again, Mariah thought. Mother of Billy, daughter-in-law of the Porter/Pierce character. Her head swam.

"No matter." Ainsley's voice was gruff, and Mariah stiffened her spine so as not to shudder under his irritated glower.

"Oh, I think it matters a lot." Mariah felt as though she'd stepped onto a slippery bank of mud at the edge of the rushing Ohio. "What else has Ainsley told you, Will, since you came back to the fort?"

Will rubbed his beard in obvious irritation. "As I mentioned to you, he confirmed Thorn's frequent shirking of his duty back then. His womanizing. The way he treated my mother. That was all I needed to know.''

''Sounds like he tried hard to convince you to forget about this duel.'' Mariah's sarcasm was lost on Thorn, whose confusion was evident in the narrowing of his eyes. ''I suppose, too, that Ainsley tried to prevent you from perfecting your ability to shoot with dueling pistols.''

''Not at all,'' Will said. ''He was most helpful.''

''Well,'' said Ainsley briskly, lifting a pistol from the box he still held. He handed the box to Thorn. ''This interlude has been fascinating, but best that we get this over with.''

''Best that we stop it right now,'' contradicted Mariah. ''Don't you think so, Will? For now, at least. Maybe there's more to this story about your mother that Thorn can fill in instead of Ainsley. Thorn, if you weren't off 'courting,' what were you doing when you were supposed to be guarding the people picking blackberries?'' Mariah recalled that René, too, had suggested that Thorn was off flirting, shirking his duty, when the boy had been kidnapped. But he'd also said that Thorn remained quiet about the entire affair.

René had learned what had happened from Ainsley.

Thorn hesitated. His back toward Mariah as he stooped, he placed the box on the ground, its lid closed, then stood again. A strange, troubled expression turned his brown eyes dark, and he tensed his jaw as he spoke. ''I was indeed distracted by another woman,'' he said softly. ''I have long admitted so, although I chose not to discuss the affair, for it made no difference why. Or so I thought.''

''But—'' Mariah began.

''I believe I may have been wrong,'' Thorn interrupted, looking off into the distance. ''The woman's name, I recall, was Sally. She was weeping on my shoulder that afternoon, for she had a broken heart. She said she had been seduced by a soldier, and then mere minutes earlier, discarded. She said she had been told to seek me out, that perhaps I could help. I realized I was to be elsewhere, but there were other, subordinate soldiers I relied upon to tend the settlers. What happened was, of course, ultimately my responsibility. Yet I did not feel right abandoning Sally when she acted so grief-stricken as she told her tale."

"Who told her to seek you out?" Mariah asked. "And did she say who'd seduced her?"

"Well, yes," Thorn said. "She—"

"Lies, of course," Ainsley said. "I never touched the wench. If she told you it was me, she was simply—"

"What I was about to say, Ainsley, was that she never revealed the soldier's name." Thorn's voice grew as frigid as mountain snow as he pivoted to stare at the man he'd considered his friend. "But I believe you now have. All she named was the man's rank and that he came from England. That would have fit you and several others." He hesitated. "After all that happened, I did not think about her difficulties again until long after she had left Pittsborough, and then it did not matter."

"None of this matters." Ainsley turned from Thorn. "Whatever else happened, Will, your mother, sweet Mary Porter, relied upon this man. He let her down, caused her to kill herself. Right here, did you know? He found her body after she had drowned herself here, at the confluence of the rivers."

But Mariah could not let the momentum she'd started stop like that. "Aren't you convinced yet, Thorn?" she said softly. "Ainsley is the one who really wants this duel."

"I? I wish nothing." The soldier's face turned nearly as red as his uniform. "Would you believe the lies of this woman above our friendship, which has lasted so long?"

Thorn did not hesitate. He did not look at Mariah. He simply said, "Yes."

"Enough!" Ainsley cried. "Will, now is the time to avenge your mother's death. Do you, after all this time, wish to lose the opportunity?"

Will, standing closest to the promontory, observed the others with incredulity narrowing his pale green eyes. Fog swirled around his feet. Still, the sky remained a brilliant blue. "I . . . I'm confused, Ainsley," Will admitted.

"Do it! Now!" Ainsley rushed forward, thrusting the gun he held into Will's hand. The young man stared at it dumbly, lowering it so it pointed toward the mist at his feet.

"Now, damn it!" Ainsley pulled Will's limp arm up, steadying it till the pistol was aimed at Thorn. "Shoot him!"

Will shook his head beneath its tricornered hat. "I can't until I understand . . ."

"Well, I can." Ainsley grabbed the gun from Will and aimed it at Mariah. "All right, my dear friend," he sneered at Thorn. "Will you duel with me this day, or will I spill this one's blood?" He paused. "Perhaps I will anyway, once I have disposed of you. She made my plans change, and I am angered."

"Do not do this!" Will lunged toward Ainsley, but before the young man could wrest the pistol from him, Ainsley used its butt to strike him on the temple just below the brim of his hat. The young man crumpled.

Mariah tried to use the opportunity to run away, but Ainsley rushed forward and grabbed her. He pressed the end of the dueling pistol's barrel so tightly against her forehead that pain shot through her head. "Not so fast," he said. "In fact, I believe I shall kill you right now. Then Thorn will have reason to duel with me, will you not, Thorn?"

They were near the edge of the point. Thorn was not far inland, but too distant to reach her in time if Ainsley chose to pull the trigger. "Please, Thorn," she whispered. She was about to tell him to go away so at least one of them would survive, but she felt a frisson of dismay catapult through her as he shrugged indifferently.

"Don't bother begging me for help, Mariah." His voice was as icy as she'd ever heard it. "She means nothing to me, Ainsley. And I have told her more than once that she shouldn't rely upon me. I find myself bored with all of this drama." He turned on his heel and began walking away.

Mariah cringed, waiting for the shot that would end her life. She'd thought, after all this time, that Thorn had learned that he was dependable. But now, when it mattered most, he wasn't.

Or was he?

Ainsley thrust her aside, and she fell to her knees in the mud. She looked up to find Ainsley pointing the pistol of Thorn's retreating back. "Thorn!" she cried out—just as the pistol fired.

Chapter Twenty-two

Thorn whirled, assured himself that Mariah was out of his way, then fired. Ainsley had missed, but Thorn's bullet hit its mark. Ainsley fell to the ground, clutching his chest below his left shoulder.

Thorn sagged, the pistol he had taken from the box and hidden beneath his jacket now barely dangling from his fingers. Relief turned his bones as formless as the mud beneath his boots. Mariah was unharmed.

But he had shot Ainsley, the friend of his youth. The one who had stood by him through all his adversity. Had encouraged him. Had tried to convince him that what had happened each time had not been his fault.

The one who had turned on him so completely, so incomprehensibly.

He hurried to Ainsley's side as swiftly as possible on such insubstantial limbs and knelt before his bloodied compatriot. He touched his chest. It rose and fell, but irregularly. Thorn began removing the uniform that hid the wound he had made. "Ainsley." His voice was little more than an emotional rasp. "Do not die, my friend."

Ainsley had stood by him in their village in England, had told him many a time that Thorn was not responsible for the death of his oldest brother and his bride. It had not been his fault that the wheel of the carriage in which they rode was loose, even if he had been the one to grease it last. While Ainsley watched.

Nor was it truly his fault that the lad Billy—Will now—had been stolen, Ainsley had maintained staunchly. There had been others on patrol that day, Ainsley among them. But Thorn had been the one assigned to the berry pickers.

Where had Ainsley been that day? Thorn could not recall.

Thorn had not caused Billy's mother, Mary Porter, to kill herself, Ainsley had reassured him. But she had died.

And Ainsley certainly had wished for this duel.

Thorn had trusted Ainsley more than anyone else in his life—until Mariah. But he had been a fool in many things.

In this, too?

Thorn's groan must have sounded aloud, for Mariah knelt beside him and grasped his shoulder.

"How is he?" she asked. Her beautiful green eyes were turned anxiously on him, and anguish was written on her face. For him. For his pain.

But he did not wish her pity.

"I do not yet know." His tone was abrupt, and he saw hurt where before he had seen compassion. "See to Will."

The young man sat erect in the mud nearby, rubbing his head where it had been struck, but he was clearly all right. Mariah did not move. "He could have killed you," she said.

"Or you." He paused. "I trust you did not rely on my saving you."

"You pigheaded—never mind. This isn't the time to tell you again what I think of your darned claims of unreliability. I did have a moment, though, when you walked away . . ."

"As well you should have. He could have shot you then." Thorn didn't believe Ainsley would have. But he had thought he knew Ainsley. If Thorn's judgment had been errant and Mariah had been killed . . . He winced at the very thought, just as Ainsley moaned. "You must leave here, Mariah. Leave this town."

''And you, I suppose. Are you going to blame yourself for this, too?'' She sounded angry now.

''Should I not have seen this in him years ago?'' He dipped his head forward and closed his eyes, letting the despair, so familiar to him now after so many incidents, take hold of his insides and compress his very entrails. ''I do not understand why this happened. Does he hate me?''

''Yes,'' came the faint reply from below. Dry lips were drawn back over Ainsley's irregular teeth, and his eyes remained tightly closed, as though to hold in his pain. He was nearly as pale as the bloodstained white shirt once had been.

''Why?'' Thorn braced himself to hear, should Ainsley continue.

A brittle sound came from his old friend that Thorn interpreted as a laugh of irony. ''You were the son of the lord of the manor,'' he rasped. ''I was the son of the village storekeeper.''

Astonishment flooded Thorn. ''With two brothers above me, I could never inherit. And you and I were compatriots.'' He needed to know more, much more. But he had to stop the bleeding. He returned to the job of slowly stripping away clothing that had already begun to stick to the wound.

Ainsley winced, and Thorn eased off. ''One brother died.'' Ainsley's rasping voice sounded snide to Thorn—or was it pain making him smile?

''Had you something to do with his death?'' The words erupted involuntarily, but he'd no time to rue them. There was the wound. Thorn sucked in his lips. It appeared ragged and deep and close to the heart. And, if he was any judge, fatal.

Ainsley turned his head.

''Here.'' Mariah was again beside Thorn. She had stripped off the bottom of her skirt, torn it into rags and soaked it in river water. ''We'll try something cleaner later, and maybe some bread mold, too. But this is the best I can do for now.''

As always, she was resourceful. Dependable.

Lovable.

Unlike him.

She helped bathe the wound while he avoided looking at her.

What must she truly think of him now? He had purported to run away when she was in mortal danger. But he had relied on his knowledge of Ainsley before making that decision. Despite all, Ainsley had always been a man of determination. His goal had been to injure Thorn, not Mariah.

Thorn sighed raggedly, swabbing the ugly wound that he had caused. "Please, Ainsley," he said. "I need to know why."

"Am I dying?" came a soft voice. "Probably, and that is good. I've no wish to live now. All has failed."

"But—"

"Hear me." His voice sounded surprisingly strong, though it remained low. "You wish to know why, so I will tell you before I cannot. I thought I helped you by what happened with your brother, and had we stayed the middle one would have met a like fate. My ambition then, you see, was to become the assistant to the squire of the area. Perhaps even to succeed him should he, too, meet an untimely death." He gasped as Thorn prodded for the bullet, which was still inside.

Thorn had not intended to hurt him further, but his anger rose despite his sorrow for the man he had injured. "I see," he said with deceptive softness. "Go on."

He continued trying to find the bullet. Mariah, as squeamish a woman as he had ever met, earned his further admiration as she silently helped. Will looked on.

"You were so aggrieved by your brother's demise—and your supposed role in it—that we had to leave. We came here, where there was to be opportunity for all. I thought that at the frontier I would rise above my background, even above yours. But you were soon captain. And I, even after all this time, remain a sergeant." He turned his head and spat to the side.

"Jealousy," murmured Mariah, blotting a rag against the still-bleeding wound.

"Needless," Thorn replied. "I was no better than him or anyone else. Worse than most, perhaps."

"Then you believed in your failings." Thorn winced at the glee in Ainsley's frail voice. "I achieved what I wished. I worked with the old man, Billy's grandfather, to allow him to take the lad, and did all I could to see it would reflect on you."

"You seduced poor Sally, too," Thorn said.

Ainsley's smile was an ugly grimace. "Yes, and there was more I did and blamed on you. You see, Mary Porter learned of my conspiracy with her father-in-law after the boy was gone. I told her myself, since I wanted her. I said I would help her get the lad back." He moved slightly and winced. He took a deep breath, and when he spoke again, his words came more slowly and painfully. "She grew hysterical, threatened to tell you. I could not let her do that. I helped her lose her footing at the source waters of the Ohio, held her under for a bit, then made certain her suicide was blamed on you."

Thorn saw a movement from the corner of his eye. Will had rushed toward them and stood looking down at them, tears in his eyes.

"We have avenged your mother's death together," Thorn said to him softly. "I believe it is nearly over." He turned back to the friend of his youth. "Was that all, Ainsley?

"No." The voice was surprisingly loud. "It could never be all. Even when you retreated to the wilderness to be alone, even there you became successful, starting an inn and becoming quite the man of commerce." He began to cough then, a great, hacking sound that made Thorn despair for his life.

"I am sorry, Ainsley, for whatever pain I caused you. It was always unintentional. I considered you my friend."

He heard a sharp intake of breath from Mariah beside him and looked up to see her staring toward the Point. He followed her gaze—to find a stooped old man standing in a boat beached upon the muddy shore, surrounded by a mist so thick that it nearly obscured him.

"Grandfather Porter!" exclaimed Will, who stood.

"Pierce," Mariah whispered. "You bastard."

* * *

He was the same small, stooped old man Mariah remembered oh, so well, his facial features sharp and bony, his hairline receding. She knew him as Josiah Pierce. Now, though, she knew his name was Porter.

Wasn't it?

The grin he wore, as he shambled toward her through the coiling mist, was as huge and misshapen as a jack o'lantern's. It made her shiver inside as though she'd stepped into a spider's web. "You did it, my dear," he said in the hoarse voice she recalled from all the horrible nightmares. "You stopped the duel." He paused, as though for dramatic effect. "You, my daughter, have righted the grievous wrong."

She dared a glance at Thorn. Still kneeling beside Ainsley, he stared up at the old man as though the area had just been invaded by slimy three-headed aliens. Will stood there stroking his beard, appearing half poised to run. Clearly he was less than thrilled to see his grandfather.

"All right," she said to the old man. "Why don't you tell me what this was all about?"

"Certainly, Mariah. Come." He was so short that when he draped a hand on her shoulder, he almost seemed to hang there. Fortunately, he didn't put much weight on her.

She looked once more toward Thorn. He was tending to Ainsley, the man he had considered his friend. Mariah longed to stay, to comfort him for his losses caused *by* this man—and the loss *of* this man.

But she had knowledge of her own to gain. And so, ignoring her pain, she went with Porter. Pierce. Whoever.

The mist near the Point seemed to dissipate as they passed, moving upriver along the Allegheny in the direction in which they walked. Their path took them along the shore that had been graded in an upward slope, then hollowed geometrically to protect the growing Lower Town. "What would you like to know, my dear?" asked the man she'd known as Pierce in a voice she could only interpret as triumphant.

"Everything!" she blurted. "What was this all about?"

His hand still hung on her shoulder, and its bony fingers

tightened their grip. "My life. My children's lives. *Your* life, for I am your ancestor."

She stopped walking and swung around to face him. She thought she got a whiff of cigar smoke. "I gathered you thought we were related; you called me your daughter." She couldn't keep the disgust from her voice. "But how?"

"In this time, young Billy is my only heir. But he will marry and have children. They will have children, and so forth. Many generations from now, you will be the result." He maneuvered around her and began to walk again on the path along the river. The mud seemed to be drying up wherever they walked, though the mist still swirled beside them on the flowing water, and Mariah could feel its warm humidity.

"I see." But she didn't, not really. "Then Billy is my great, great-something grandfather."

He nodded. "And I'm two greats beyond that." He smiled up at her, revealing his ugly yellow teeth. "And you, my dear, have managed to make all our lives wonderful!"

"Just how did I do that?"

They'd reached an area where the embankment rose abruptly before them, and the old man chose a path to their right. It led upward to the town.

Mariah saw no one there. No one anywhere around. But mist still swirled about them.

Pierce—she believed she'd always think of this man by that name—continued as they walked, "Though you couldn't stop me from making the mistake I did those several years back, you prevented it from turning into the utter disaster it was before your intervention. And you kept my descendants from having to pay forevermore."

She tried to keep the impatience from her voice. "Okay, Grandpa." She drew out the title ironically. "How about being a bit more specific?"

"All right," he said. "You know by now how I stole Billy from his mother when he was eleven years old."

She nodded. "Your son died and you didn't like his wife."

Pierce shook his head slowly, as though at his own folly,

and his white hair was caught up in the breeze as though it were the mist on the water. "In my younger days, I was a snob."

That was only seven years earlier, Mariah thought. Or was it? In this time, that was true, but he'd also hung around in her era. Did he dart from time to time, or had he somehow survived that long?

She hoped he'd explain.

The path on which they walked ended at the major dirt road within the town. Pierce led her to the right. He continued in his hoarse voice, "I was angered when young Mary, my son's widow, ran off with my grandson, and decided to come after them. I wanted him to be raised a gentleman, you see. When I got here, I sneaked around for a few days. I was caught by a man named Ainsley."

At Mariah's start, he smiled again. "Ah, yes. The man your friend Thorn shot. He was most useful, for he himself had a grudge he wished avenged. He helped me set up Billy's rescue and made it appear as though Indians had stolen my grandson. My payment to him was to make certain all evidence of the dastardly deed pointed to the fault of Thorn."

"I see." She itched to tell Thorn this additional bit of nefarious behavior by Ainsley. Or should she?

They arrived at a fork in the road, and Pierce directed her to the left. She noticed that they'd begun a circle of the fort, outside the Isthmus. Mariah glanced back behind them. The road seemed to have disappeared into the curling mist, and she shuddered. All this was enough to make her believe in the supernatural.

As if traveling in time hadn't already.

Plus this strange story of generations. She half believed it, on top of everything else that had happened. What reason would Pierce have now to lie?

"There is more to know about Thorn's friend Ainsley," Pierce said. "I did some checking, after I had Billy and learned his mother was dead. Ah, in my younger, more foolish days, I was ever so glad. She could never trouble us again. But she did, in a most unexpected way. What I first heard was that she had killed herself in despondency over losing her son. Not a twinge of guilt did I feel then, for he was *my* grandson. Only later did I learn that the story was quite different."

"Ainsley killed her," said Mariah.

"He told you, then," Pierce said. "And I had conspired with him." Pierce was silent for a few minutes as they continued their stroll around the perimeter of the Isthmus. The Point was now to their right, but Mariah saw only the mist obscuring the buildings of the town.

She was beginning to feel tired. It had been an exhausting day. "Please finish the story," she said. "I want to go find Thorn and get back to the inn." If, of course, he wanted her to go. He'd been less than inviting before.

Had she imagined, those days earlier, that he'd said he loved her?

Now wasn't the time to think about that.

"All right, I will finish. As you now know, the grievous wrong you were to right was Thorn's death at the hands of my grandson, Billy. Billy thought Thorn guilty of causing his mother's death. I, I'm sorry to say, never disabused him of that notion." He paused. "In fact, there is a lot I am sorry about when it comes to the way I dealt with my grandson."

For the first time, when Mariah looked at him, she felt a little sorry for him; he looked quite old and time-ravaged. Guilty, perhaps.

Good. Of everyone in this story, he and Ainsley shared all the guilt. Yet Thorn had been the one to shoulder it all this time.

"Before your intervention," Pierce continued in his hoarse monotone, "the duel occurred in that time. It shouldn't have. Thorn had no culpability in the death of Mary. But I let the duel happen. I let Billy kill the man shamelessly. And Billy suffered for it later. He took to drink, was unkind to his wife and children. And those children grew up hurting their children, and so forth, for generations to come."

The idea slapped Mariah just as they reached the second bridge she'd already crossed that day. "Then that was why my father was such a terrible person, so cruel to my mother, so unreliable. And why my mother took it."

"Exactly." Pierce did not sound proud. He looked at his booted feet and shrugged. "You were named for poor Mary, did you guess? There has been a Mary or a Maria or Mariah in each generation. As a reminder, though none knew the tale save me."

How incredible! thought Mariah. This entire tale amazed her.

Though no more than the fact that she'd traveled in time.

As they walked slowly now, Mariah looked toward the shrouded Point, still unable to see anyone. She wondered if Ainsley still lived. For Thorn's sake, she hoped so. But somehow he would need to pay for his sins.

As, apparently, Pierce had done.

They arrived at the pentagonal stone blockhouse, the very spot where Mariah had reached this time.

"I have a question," she said. "Whatever happened to Matilda, from the screenplay? Everyone else had a real counterpart here, but I took her place."

Pierce's grin this time appeared genuinely happy. "She was partly my fabrication for the screenplay," he said, "and partly you." Pierce paused, then continued, "Through the centuries, I was forced to wander this earth as a spirit, observing one pitiful generation of my descendants after another. But the forces who punished me thus also gave me the chance to find someone among my descendants courageous enough to come here and change everything so that all who followed could find happiness despite what I had begun. But there was no one . . . till you. I was permitted to speak in your dreams and then to acquire a corporeal form once more to meet and recruit you. You were the first descendant in all those years sensitive and brave enough to hear me, to change the course of history."

Such an honor, Mariah thought sarcastically. And then she considered for a moment. Perhaps it was.

"I had to find a way to intrigue you," Pierce continued, "and so I wrote the screenplay."

"Well, you did get my attention," Mariah acknowledged.

"I had to guess how you might interact with all the real people, you see. That was part of the reason why real life did not completely follow the script I wrote. Also, I was not here during most events; I had to interview people to find out what had occurred and who said what, and often there were different stories to choose from concerning the same matter."

"Typical," said Mariah.

"It was a wonderful screenplay, was it not?" He looked at the ground with false modesty.

"It was," agreed Mariah with a reluctant smile. "But what about the things that happened as written that no one besides Matilda—or me—could have known about?"

Pierce shrugged his bony shoulders. "Poetic license? Or perhaps just part of the chance to correct the past that I was given. In any event, some of what I wrote with no foreknowledge was permitted to come true." Pierce's voice grew stronger. "And now I thank you, my daughter, for righting the grievous wrong. It is time to send you back home."

"Home?" Mariah's heart started pounding. What did he mean?

"To your own time, of course."

Where—and when—was home to her now? She'd been attracted to Pittsburgh in her time. But the inn? And Thorn? She protested, "But—"

He did not stop speaking. "You have changed the course of history for your forefathers. When you return, you will find that your own family is large and loving. Your mother is alive and happily living with your very kind and stable papa. You'll recall everything, but it is unlikely that you will tell your tale, for who would believe it?"

Who indeed? she wondered. The idea held boundless appeal. Imagine Mariah Walker growing up in a caring environment, surrounded by reliable, loving people. In a real home.

Heaven!

But that wasn't all she had to consider. She'd come to like it here. She had friends. And . . . "What about Thorn?" she asked.

Pierce looked at her blankly. "Oh, yes. You weren't really as foolish as the Matilda character I created to fall in love with him, were you? That was never truly in my plan."

Nor in mine, Mariah thought.

But she had.

"Now," Pierce said, "it's time. Just put your hand here against the blockhouse wall."

She stepped back, but her head began to ache. A familiar lethargy surrounded her.

She felt Pierce pull her forward, take her hand and place it against the stonework.

She began to fall asleep.

Chapter Twenty-three

Thorn let the pirogue float downstream along the Ohio. The storms had ended yesterday, but the river had not yet calmed; it plunged forward at an unusual speed for this time of summer, still overflowing its banks.

Its swift volatility matched his mood.

Ainsley had died. Not immediately, though. Thorn had continued to kneel beside him, cradling him in his final agony. Anguished that their friendship had come to this.

Thorn had not wished to stay for the funeral, but he had remained at Pittsborough for an extra day anyway, trading for goods for the inn at the trading post.

And, mostly, to search for Mariah. He'd walked through the town, about the fort, even to its far side and through the fertile orchards and fields of the King's Garden, which fed the soldiers. The storms had poured rain down upon him, and still he had looked for her.

No Mariah.

The last time anyone had seen her, she had been walking off with that man Porter, Will Shepherd's grandfather.

Or was he Pierce, the man Mariah had been speaking of since the time she had come to his inn?

If her story were to be believed—and he had, amazingly, come to believe it—the man had brought her here from the past. "To right a grievous wrong," she'd said. She thought it was the duel she had foretold between Will and himself. The one that had nearly come to pass.

The episode that had resulted in Ainsley's death.

"Damn it, man," he spoke aloud, wondering if the person he'd believed his friend could somehow hear him. "Why did you never tell me? Maybe I could have . . ." What? He didn't know.

But he'd have done all he could to prevent the horror that had occurred.

Now Ainsley was gone.

And so was Mariah. With that Pierce. Thorn had known, even as he had done it, that his search would be fruitless. Pierce had probably sent her back to her own time. Her purpose here had been accomplished.

Had she given any thought to remaining?

But why should she? She had told him of the wondrous conveniences of her time. Seeing a shadow on the muddy brown water, he looked into the sky as a golden eagle soared and dipped overhead. In Mariah's time, there would also be mechanical things she had called "airplanes" that carried people more swiftly than he could even imagine. There was indoor plumbing and instant cookery of packaged and purchased food—all that he could not ever hope to offer her here.

Not that he had tried. He had taken her to bed, foolishly declared his love—then argued with her, when all she wished was to save his worthless hide.

He hadn't deserved her. And now she was gone.

Where was the stony barrier against pain he had built around himself? It had disappeared just when he needed it most—to help him live with the agony of losing Mariah.

Eventually, the current took him across from the pier he had built into the river. He rowed to it and tied up the pirogue.

This was where he had met Mariah, when she had been chased by those rogues weeks earlier.

The rogues were dead now, but not before they'd hurt her. *He'd* hurt her, too, though not physically.

Carrying his rifle and as many supplies as he could, he dragged himself through the woods toward the compound and his inn. It was late afternoon, and a muggy heat hung in the air, even in the shade of the tall oak and hickory trees. A hanging grape vine touched the top of his head, brushing hair into his eyes, and, with his hands full, he tossed his head impatiently to tame the errant lock.

He reached the clearing. Before him was the tall palisade wall, with its pointed logs appearing, he hoped, formidable to raiders.

He wondered idly how Mariah's friends, the settlers, were faring in their new homes. Perhaps he would see them someday. Trade, with that Francis Kerr, fond recollections of Mariah.

At the gate, he called out, "René!" Putting down the goods in his arms, he swung a metal cylinder that hung on a rope and beat out a tattoo against the gate that they had arranged to show who stood outside. Guests would not know the signal, but they would understand to rap with the metal bar until they got a response.

Now, though, nothing happened for long minutes, and he tried again.

"Thorn!" came the call of a familiar male voice from inside. "Is it you?"

"Of course, René. Were you expecting someone else?"

"We always expect guests at the finest inn in west Pennsylvania." The gate swung open, and there was his squat friend, beaming a huge smile that faded as soon as he saw Thorn's face. "*Mon ami,* you look terrible. Come, and we will fix you."

We. He used the word continuously, and Thorn guessed why.

His supposition was confirmed when Holly skipped out of the kitchen door toward them, wearing a blue dress that Mariah and she had sewn from the material bought weeks ago in Pittsborough. Her close-set hazel eyes sparkled as she looked Thorn up and down, then said, "It's a mess you are, Thorn. A fine mess."

"Now, Holly." René put his arm about her, and his large eyes narrowed fondly as she gazed up into them. He turned back toward Thorn. "There is *quelque chose*—"

"Something!" Holly interrupted. She leaned toward Thorn conspiratorially. "Did he always forget his English when he was nervous?"

Thorn nodded. "As long as I've known him." He walked wearily toward the inn.

"Let us tell you," Holly said, placing herself in front of him. "Frenchie, dear, will you do the honors?"

For a brief, hopeful moment, Thorn dared to imagine they would tell him that Mariah was here waiting for him.

But, no. Their news was about them.

"We will be married," René said. "I have asked Holly to be my wife." His round face looked worried. "You do not mind another worker here permanently, do you? If so, we will go—"

"No," Thorn interrupted with a wave of his hand. "Of course I don't mind." He made himself smile, took René's hand and pumped it with what vigor he could muster. "Congratulations to both of you." He took Holly's hand when she offered it, too. Like Mariah's, it was rough, a busy woman's hand.

Now Mariah would be able to take care of her hands, let them grow soft and smooth once again.

He sighed but hid his sorrow by pulling Holly into his arms and giving her a hug. "My sincere good wishes." He kissed her on the forehead. She smelled slightly of yeast and baking bread—like Mariah.

He felt his throat constrict. He had gone through much over the past years—the guilt in the death of his brother and sister-in-law, the disappearance of Billy, the death of the boy's mother. And now Ainsley. But nothing, ever, had been as painful as the loss of Mariah.

He wheeled on the others, realizing what they had left

unsaid to spare his grief. "You haven't asked me about the duel, or about Mariah."

"No," said René solemnly.

"We figured you would tell us when you were ready," Holly said.

We again. The word hurt him, now that he knew he would never be a *we* with Mariah.

"I'll tell you over supper," Thorn agreed. "But first, I wish some ale. There are two barrels still on the boat. We'll go for them in a while, René."

The Frenchman nodded, then helped Thorn carry flour and beans and molasses and salt pork into the kitchen.

Thorn went into the common room to pour himself some ale—and stopped.

There, behind the bar, was a vision: Mariah Walker in a brown dress with an apron over it, appearing like a bar maid.

Here, in Thorn's inn.

He took a moment to find his voice. "Mariah." He sounded to himself like a wounded crow. "What are you doing here?" he said more strongly. The pounding of his heart was so intense he wondered that it did not vibrate the bottles behind the bar. Mariah stood before him!

"I work here," she replied.

"You left Pittsborough without a word." His tone was more gruff than he had intended, but all the pain of the past days would not allow otherwise.

She bent her head to look at the glass she polished with a rag. The waves of her honey-colored hair spilled about her face. "Yes, I did. Would you prefer I go back?"

He hesitated for only a moment. He hurried to her, practically vaulting over the bar until he held her warm and solid form in his arms. She was real!

"No, Mariah. You are exactly where I wish you to be." His fingers were in her hair, tipping her head back so he could look into her face. What did she wish?

There was a luminousness in her leaf-green eyes that told him she was near to crying. He kissed her cheeks, her forehead, her eyelids—and tasted salt as the tears began to spill.

"I was afraid—" she said.

"You must never be afraid," he said fiercely. "I will take care of you."

She pulled back, her eyes flashing despite their moistness. "I'm not the sort of woman who needs to be taken care of," she said with sweet belligerence. "But—"

"Yes?" He waited, half afraid to hear what sort of woman she was. Did she need to be near a city, where there were at least more amenities than he could ever hope to offer here?

Or was she about to tell him that she was returning, after all, to her own time?

"I am the sort of woman who needs a man who's reliable. Who recognizes he's dependable. It helps that he always comes through, of course, and I know I can rely on him even when things look impossible. But I want him to acknowledge it."

"If that's what it will take to keep you here," he said, reaching out to rub the softness of her hair between his fingers.

She closed her eyes, as though savoring the moment. But then she said, "That's not all." She leaned her side against the bar.

"What else?" She was torturing him.

"I need a man who will promise never to duel, no matter what the provocation."

"But—" What if he had to defend his honor? *Her* honor?

"Promise!"

"All right," he said reluctantly. "But Mariah—what happened when I could not find you?"

"Pierce tried to send me back home. It was tempting, in fact." She told him an incredible tale of what she had done by stopping his duel—helping Pierce's descendants over generations. Including herself. "And he swore I'd go home to a big, loving family."

"That sounds wonderful, Mariah." He grew quiet, then said, "I cannot offer you that, or much else."

"I have a loving family here, with Holly and René. And you."

The last sounded questioning, and he pulled her tightly

against him once more. "Oh, yes, Mariah. And me. I love you. I will always love you."

Mariah pulled back just a little to study his face. There was an earnestness in the depths of his brown eyes, and she reached up to smooth the furrow that dimpled between his dark, knitted brows and to smooth away the lock of chestnut hair that had fallen upon his forehead.

He'd said it again. He loved her.

"I love you too, Thorn," she whispered. And she'd earned the right to stay here.

Even Pierce had agreed.

She'd fought so hard against falling unconscious again that Pierce had finally quit. "Do you actually want to stay in this primitive time?" he'd asked her. "Not even meet this brand-new, wonderful family of yours?"

"Yes," she'd said with no hesitation.

"Fascinating!" he'd said with unabashed glee. "I'd no idea that a modern woman like you could fall in love with an outcast woodsman when I wrote that into Matilda's role. I just thought it might intrigue you more with the story."

She'd been intrigued. She still was.

Pierce had insisted that he bring her here to the inn rather than leaving her in Pittsburgh in the middle of the chaos of Ainsley's shooting. He had even promised to go back to her time to tie up whatever loose ends would be caused by her disappearance. She'd no idea how, but she had no doubt that, with everything else he had done, he could accomplish this as well.

She'd been waiting here for Thorn since the previous day. Hoping he, too, remained intrigued with her.

And he did. Thank heavens, he did!

"Mariah? Are you all right?" He peered questioningly into her eyes. "You have grown so quiet."

"Just thinking about Pierce and the favor he did by bringing me to this time, even though it was for his own selfish purpose."

"He did me even more of a favor, you realize. He cleared my name—and, most important, brought you to me." He stroked her cheek gently with his thumb, and she closed her eyes, leaning toward him.

When she was tucked up close against him once more, she heard him whisper gently into her ear, "Mariah, will you do me the great honor of becoming my wife?"

Once more, she pulled back to study him. No more did his expression reflect the stony distance that had been so familiar. He had bared his emotions to her, and now she reveled in the loving warmth in his eyes, the hopeful smile on his solid, narrow lips.

"I would be proud to," she replied, her voice quivering with emotions of her own.

As though to seal the promise, he placed his lips upon hers, gently at first. His taste was intoxicating, like the ale from the barrels nearby. She wove her fingers into his hair.

For an instant, she let herself think of how chafed and work-hardened her hands had become. She was proud of them once more. Their dryness and calluses showed her adjustment to this time in which she'd chosen to remain.

She used her hands to draw his head tighter toward hers, and felt him deepen the kiss.

"Mariah," he whispered harshly against her mouth. His tongue forged a path between her teeth, and she met it eagerly with her own, letting him set a darting, familiar rhythm that left her weak.

His hands roved the length of her back, and she let her own venture along the smoothness of his shirt, then pulled it from the waistband of his trousers. She sleeked her hand along his heated bare skin. He pulled her closer yet, and as he squeezed her buttocks she strained forward, feeling him harden. As she ground herself against him, she heard a whimper and realized it was her own.

"Ah, *mes amis!*"

"Damn!" Thorn whispered, pulling away to glare at René. Mariah didn't feel in the least embarrassed. She'd walked in on a similar scene between Holly and René when she'd first returned to the inn.

Now, the other couple stood with their hands linked, equally huge smiles lighting their faces. "You look a lot better now, Thorn,'' Holly said with a big wink.

He still held Mariah close by his side, and she leaned against his solid body, knowing he would always be there for her.

''I feel better, too,'' he agreed. ''You didn't tell me we had a guest.''

''I'm not a guest,'' Mariah protested. ''I'm family.''

''Yes,'' he said. ''You're family. Close family.'' He bent down and, right in front of the others, gave her another long, torrid kiss on the mouth. Obviously he wasn't embarrassed, either.

She matched his ardor, eager to experience all the kiss promised. But when it was over, she looked at him and smiled. ''I'm family,'' she repeated. ''And I'm finally home.''